ONE
WAY
TO BOOT
HILL

Westerns by Max O'Hara

WOLF STOCKBURN, RAILROAD DETECTIVE

HELL'S JAW PASS

KILL RED

ONE WAY TO BOOT HILL

ONE WAY TO BOOT HILL

A WOLF STOCKBURN, RAILROAD DETECTIVE WESTERN

MAX O'HARA

PINNACLE BOOKS
Kensington Publishing Corp.
www.kensingtonbooks.com

CHAPTER 1

On a hillside above the railroad tracks where a small outcropping of rocks jutted from desert scrub and cedars, Wells Fargo detective Wolf Stockburn scraped a lucifer to life on his cartridge belt. He touched the flame to the quirley he'd rolled while waiting for the bank robbers to show their ugly faces.

Of course, not having seen this particular bunch of train thieves before, he didn't know what they looked like. Also, the previous times they'd robbed the West Texas & Cerro Alto Railroad, they'd worn flour sack masks. So no one knew what they looked like.

Having been a railroad detective for Wells Fargo for longer than he cared to ruminate on at length, Stockburn saw all train robbers as green-horned, yellow-toothed, fork-tailed devils. He'd run a few train-robbing women to ground, even the comeliest among them. In his experience, that would be Alta Hall. She had been pretty to look at, but you didn't want to turn your back on her and risk getting a rusty Arkansas toothpick slid between your ribs for your foolishness.

Stockburn let the hot Texas wind blow out his match

and drew the peppery Mexican tobacco deep into his lungs. He wasn't worried the owlhoots would smell the smoke, for he was downwind of their position roughly a hundred yards west along the rails. He'd spotted them through his spyglass an hour ago, where they'd holed up to wait for the train.

Hunkered down, he was also waiting for the next West Texas and Cerro Alto flier out of Bottleneck, Texas, thirty miles back up the line, near the west flank of the Cerro Alto Mountains and twenty miles south of the New Mexico border.

Stockburn had smoked half his cigarette and was about to take another drag when a train whistle cut through the hot dry afternoon silence interrupted occasionally by a wind gust or the screech of a hunting hawk. The engineer cut loose with the horn as he started his climb up the gentle grade to the crest of the pass just west of where the detective waited. The engineer blew the horn again. One long, mournful wail followed by two shorter, lighter-toned toots likely alerted the passengers and crew of the slow-down and the mile-long climb.

Stockburn heard the locomotive's dragon-like panting and the thunder of the wheels on the glistening iron rails. Soon he could feel the reverberation of the big beast through the ground beneath him. A few minutes later, the black Baldwin locomotive pushed its snub nose around a bend in the ridge wall, turning toward Wolf as it continued climbing the grade, blowing steam, panting like an old dinosaur, pulling the tender car and the rest of the combination along behind it.

A thick black guidon of coal smoke ribboned up from the giant diamond-shaped smoke stack to billow back over the yellow tender car before streaming southward as the north breeze caught and tore it. The coaches trundling behind the tender car groaned and swayed and screeched and clicked their wheels over the rail seams.

"Here we go," Stockburn said, keeping his head behind a thumb of rock. He quickly fieldstripped his quirley and let the wind take the shredded paper and tobacco. "Here . . . we . . . go . . ."

He'd just said *go* when, as if on cue, the silhouettes of three men rose from the top of the curving ridge east of Stockburn's position, on the same side of the tracks, and roughly the same distance above the tracks.

As the three shadowy stick figures scuttled to the very edge of the cliff, two more rose behind them. All five, Wolf saw, were holding rifles. The long guns looked like very small sticks, but they were rifles. Train robbers didn't carry sticks and those five were outlaws, all right.

Stock thieves, most likely, for the train was hauling one hundred and fifty head of prime west Texas beef to Las Cruces farther up the line and then beyond to the several relatively recently established Indian reservations in Arizona Territory and in northwestern New Mexico Territory. Like wolves on the blood scent, stock thieves had been preying on this stretch of rails between Bottleneck and Las Cruces for the past eight months. So far, they'd absconded with nearly two thousand head of beef on the hoof.

That was making the half-dozen ranchers, mostly small, fragile outfits up in the Cerro Alto Mountains around Bottleneck, madder than old wet hens. Other detectives and lawmen had been brought in over the past eight months, including two stock detectives and three deputy U.S. marshals out of Albuquerque. One of the stock detectives had taken a bushwhacker's bullet to the neck. He'd live, but he and his partner had been sent back to Albuquerque.

The three federals had flat-out disappeared somewhere south of Bottleneck, when they'd ridden out to track the stolen beef.

Fresh off another investigation in New Mexico Territory, Stockburn had been brought in to run the wolves to ground as he'd proven so good at over his fifteen years with Wells Fargo and even before that, as a lawman of some renown.

Wolf watched as the big black Baldwin engine roared and panted, climbing the gentle inclination and spitting steam from its pressure release valves. A little over a hundred yards distant, roughly the size of a caterpillar from his vantage, and hugging the wall of the same ridge, it stretched out as the rest of the train came around the bend to fall into line behind the engine. As the big, shrieking and chugging beast trundled on up the rise, its wheels clacking loudly over the rail seams, one of the men on the ridge stepped off the cliff.

He was maybe ten, fifteen feet above the engine. He held out his left arm and the rifle in his left hand for balance— a skinny bird spreading its wings.

He dropped straight down to land on the Baldwin's roof, falling to his knees as soon as his feet made contact. The wind tore his hat off his head and he flung a hand out to grab it but missed, and the hat blew away on the wind. The sudden movement made him lose his balance for a second, and he almost tumbled off the roof before lowering his free hand to the roof beneath his boots, settling himself.

As the man looked around, Wolf thought he saw the momentary shock and fear on the man's pale features.

Stockburn smiled.

The engine continued straining up the grade, pulling the tender car, two passenger coaches, a Pullman sleeper, a dining car, a freight car, and several stock cars along behind it. A little red caboose trailed at the end. Two more men leaped off the cliff and onto the passenger coach behind the tender car. The last two men dropped a moment later onto the second passenger coach.

As the first man leaped down off the Baldwin's roof and into the engine's pilot house, the other four desperadoes slithered like snakes down out of Wolf's sight, as well.

"All right," Wolf said, watching the train growing larger and larger as it closed the gap between them. "So that's how you're gonna play it, eh? You're gonna go after the passengers first, then the stock. Well, we'll see about that."

Closer and closer the engine crawled. Stockburn could see two men in the engine's pilot house moving around quickly, violently, maybe throwing punches. The engineer or possibly the fireman wasn't going to give up control without a fight. As one man threw a fist at the other, the nose of the big, roaring black dragon slid farther up the grade until it was directly beneath Wolf's position. No longer able to see inside, all he could see was the top of the engine's large, barrel-shaped body . . . and the flat, black steel roof of the pilot house.

The roar of the straining beast was nearly deafening.

Wolf spread his arms, holding his 1866 Winchester Yellowboy repeater in his black-gloved right hand. He held his black felt, silk-banded sombrero on his prematurely gray head with his other hand, not intending to make the same mistake the first desperado had.

A man was little without his hat. His father had told him that a long time ago, before the Cheyenne raiders had killed his parents and kidnapped his sister, and he still believed it. He tended to cling to the tidbits of fatherly and motherly advice he'd received since he'd stopped receiving it so young—only fifteen years old when the Cheyenne had burned his family's farm in Kansas.

The engine's black steel roof came up fast, hammering against the soles of the rail detective's low-heeled, square-toed cavalry boots. He dropped to his knees so the wind was less likely to hurl him off his perch, then, leaning forward, one hand flat against the floor, the other holding the Yellowboy, he tipped his head to listen to the goings-on in the pilot house directly beneath him.

". . . told you to stop the damn train, you fat stubborn mule!" a man yelled shrilly.

A strained voice responded with, "I'm tryin'! Gimme a minute, you blue-tongued little firebrand!"

"How 'bout I give ya this?" The firebrand's rhetorical question was followed by a resolute smacking sound.

The other man grunted.

Wolf dropped his legs over the backside of the roof, then quickly lowered himself straight down to the pilot house floor, directly in front of the tender car. As he crouched low and wheeled around, he saw a man lying slumped backward against a pile of coal in a large scuttle along the engine's rear wall. He wore pinstriped overalls and a pin-striped watch cap, dented where a rifle barrel had been slashed against it and the head of the man wearing it.

The man—the locomotive's fireman—was groaning and stretching his thickly mustached lips back from tobacco-rhymed teeth as he held his hand over the dent in his hat.

Straight ahead of Wolf a big man—nearly as tall and broad as the detective himself—was about to smack the engineer with the barrel of a Winchester '78. The big man's back and thick shoulders faced Wolf as the train robber confronted the engineer slumped back against the locomotive's control panel at the front of the pilot house. The engineer glowered up at his big assailant with a mix of fear and cold disdain.

Wolf tapped the big train robber's left shoulder. "Hey, sonny?"

"Huh?" The big man turned, a puzzled expression on his face. He brought the .45-70 around, as well. "I thought I told you—" His eyes widened when he saw that it was not the fireman who'd tapped his shoulder.

Wolf grinned, then slammed the butt of his Yellowboy against the dead center of the big, dull-eyed man's forehead. The big man grunted, then, lights out, fell back against the control panel. The engineer sidestepped the big man, looking down at him and grimacing in revulsion. He turned to Stockburn just then lowering his rifle, and smiled.

"Wolf! What the hell brings you way out here to this canker on the devil's butt?"

"Hi ya, Arnie. How's things?"

"Well . . ." Arnie Langenbottom glanced at the big man who skidded down the control panel to lay unmoving on the locomotive's iron floor.

"There's more peckerwoods where that one came from." Stockburn crouched to pull a pistol out of the train robber's holster. He tossed it over the side of the rolling locomotive, picked up the man's rifle, and turned to the brakeman. "How're you doin', Jasper? You gonna make it?"

Jasper Wiggins kept rubbing his head and scowling at Stockburn. "Oh, I'll be fine, Wolf. Just fine. Alma says my head's harder than her favorite iron skillet, and that skillet's got a big dent in it for proof, so I reckon I'll live to shovel coal another day."

"Good for you." Stockburn handed the robber's .45-70 to the fireman. "Hold this firestick on your friend there. If he comes around, give him another love tap to put him to sleep again. Or . . . shoot him. It's your call." He glanced at Langenbottom again. "Keep this heap movin'—will you, Arnie? I don't want the other robbers to get too comfortable."

Langenbottom nodded. "You got it, Wolf! I'll keep it movin' if you can call this movin'!"

Stockburn turned, climbed up over the locomotive's rear panel and onto the narrow iron shelf running along the side of the tender car heaped with coal. He cat-stepped along the shelf, keeping one eye on the gravelly, rocky terrain sliding past on his right, the other eye on the two passenger coaches rattling along behind the tender car. He held his Yellowboy straight up in his left hand.

A man's angry shout rose from inside the coach directly behind the tender car. A woman screamed. The scream was followed by a gun blast. A man yelped.

Stockburn's heart lurched. He increased his pace along the narrow iron shelf, hearing another man shout, "Why in the hell isn't this train stoppin'? What the hell is Scrim up to, anyways?"

Straight ahead of Stockburn, a man poked his bearded head out of a window of the first passenger coach. The man's mouth and eyes widened when his gaze landed on the big man in the black frock coat, black sombrero, and black ribbon tie hanging one-handed off the side of the tender car.

The man pulled his head back into the coach and bellowed, "We got trouble, Danny!"

The bearded face was thrust out the window again. This time it was accompanied by the man's shoulders and arms as well as a Spencer carbine—one of those .56 caliber long guns that can punch a hole in a man half the size of Texas!

CHAPTER 2

The bearded train robber brought the Spencer up to his shoulder—he'd already cocked the thing—and narrowed one eye as he aimed down the barrel at Wolf. Stockburn winced and ducked as flames lapped from the barrel. The rifle roared. The big-caliber slug skimmed Wolf's right cheek before caroming beyond the train to spang wildly off a rock.

"Damn!" the bearded man said, bunching his lips in frustration.

He'd just started to cock the big Spencer again when Stockburn jacked a round into his Yellowboy one-handed, snapped it to his shoulder, took hasty aim, and squeezed the trigger.

A quarter-sized hole appeared in the bearded man's forehead, just above his bushy right brow. As his head slammed back, the man dropped his rifle then slumped down the side of the train, half in and half out of the coach until his head and shoulders pulled the rest of him out of the window to smack the ground beside the tracks. He rolled wildly, quickly falling back out of sight among the rocks and twisted cedars.

People were already shouting and yelling inside the

coach car, but after the bearded robber fell out of the window the shouts grew louder, the yelling and screaming shriller.

"What in God's name is happening?" a man bellowed angrily inside the coach, above the din of the frightened passengers. "*Who the hell is out there?*"

Stockburn hurried forward along the iron ledge then leaped down onto the front vestibule of the first coach in the combination. He pressed his back up against the coach's front wall to the right of the door and edged a look through the door's upper pane.

Inside were a dozen or so passengers, a few women and children among them. The women and children were crying while the men looked nervous, some holding the women in their arms, shielding them from bullets with their own bodies.

Two men stood in the car's center aisle. That they were part of the train-robbing gang, there was no doubt. They each held a burlap bag and a rifle. They were grubby, raggedy-heeled men in dusty, badly worn trail garb and appeared as nervous as the passengers. Crouching, they whipped their heads around, looking for the hombre who'd blasted their partner out the window.

One turned his head toward the front of the car just as Wolf started to pull his head back. Spying Wolf, he jerked with a start and said, "*There!*"

Wolf edged his left eye across the door again to peer through the window. He drew his head back sharply as the rifle of the robber nearest the door lapped flames, thundering. The bullet ripped through the glass. Another shot came close on the first shot's heels, tearing through the side of the door about three inches left of Stockburn's right shoulder.

Wolf turned, jerked the door open and threw himself

forward, hitting the center aisle on his chest and belly as the train robber's rifle belched once more. The bullet screeched over Wolf's head to bang loudly into the tender car. Wolf raised the Yellowboy and sent two .44 rounds ripping into the rifleman's chest, sending him pirouetting backward like a drunken dancer, tossing his rifle into the passengers, all of whom gave a collective, wailing cry of holy terror.

The second owlhoot, who'd been standing eight feet behind the now-dead one, also gave a desperate yell. As Stockburn pumped another round into the Winchester's breech and raised the rifle, the second man ran out onto the coach's rear platform then turned sharply to the left of the door, out of sight.

"Dammit!" Stockburn lowered the rifle and strode down the aisle toward the coach's open rear door.

He stopped when the drumming of running feet sounded atop the coach. The drumming stopped, replaced with a wild, Indian-like whoop and a rifle barked. The bullet punched a hole through the coach's ceiling to hammer into the coach's wooden floor in the center aisle. There was another whoop and another rifle report. That bullet slammed into the leg of a man sitting close against the aisle. The man grabbed his leg and wailed.

Stockburn raised the Winchester and fired once, twice, three, four times in the general vicinity of the two holes the robber had placed there. A man's yelp sounded after the Yellowboy's fourth roar. A second later, a silhouetted body dropped down past the coach's left side windows. A grubby Stetson followed, nudged by a wind gust.

Near the back of the coach, a girl screamed.

Stockburn whipped his head that way. A tall, skinny lad in a bowler hat, pinstriped poplin shirt, suspenders, and batwing chaps had just bounded into the open doorway.

He'd come out of the second passenger coach, likely to investigate the shooting.

Only six feet from Stockburn, the skinny lad held an old-model saddle-ring Winchester. His long face with prominent front teeth and flat blue eyes was mottled red with apprehension.

He looked Stockburn up and down, anger and indignation growing in his eyes. Gritting his teeth, he bounded forward. He raised the Winchester, swung the butt toward Wolf, and screamed like a lunatic, spittle flecking from his lips.

The rifle's brass butt plate caromed in a blur toward Wolf's head.

Stockburn stepped back and to one side, thrusting the butt of his own rifle into the skinny lad's side. The lad yowled as he stumbled to the right, half falling over an old man and the old woman he had wrapped his arms around. The skinny lad regained his footing, swinging back toward Wolf, but as he began to raise his Winchester again, Wolf slammed the butt of his own rifle against the skinny gent's long, horsey mug—savage, smashing blows that sent the enraged younker to the floor, clamping his hands over his face and howling.

Stockburn picked up the kid's rifle and threw it out a window then continued forward, knowing there was one more robber who needed his horns filed. He'd taken only two steps, however, before the skinny kid screamed behind him, "Oh, you devil!"

Stockburn swung back around in time to see the bloody-faced young man raising a hogleg and clicking the hammer back.

Wolf's Yellowboy spoke.

"Damn fool!" he told the kid, who lay shivering as he died on the aisle floor between rows of howling passengers, including one screaming baby.

Stockburn didn't have to look far or long for the fifth robber, for just as he stepped out onto the second passenger coach's rear vestibule, a shrill curse sounded from the top of the freight car trundling along behind. Wolf looked up to see another skinny kid, this one shorter, dark-skinned, and with long black hair tumbling from a floppy brimmed hat— angrily gritting his teeth and aiming a rifle down at the railroad detective.

Stockburn threw himself back against the passenger coach as the kid's rifle spoke, drilling a round into the wooden vestibule floor two inches in front of Stockburn's left boot. Wolf bounded forward as the kid's rifle spoke again, hammering another round into the wooden floor, just off Wolf's right heel.

Before the kid could fire another round, Wolf stepped back out onto the vestibule and hurled a single round up where the kid was ramming another cartridge into his Winchester's breech. The kid howled, dropped his rifle, and stumbled backward, clutching his right shoulder.

Moving slowly as it continued climbing the long slope to the pass, the train pitched violently on uneven rails, sending the dark-skinned kid stumbling forward then falling with a scream over the side of the car, and landing with an agonized groan.

The kid lay two feet in front of Wolf, who crouched to grab the kid's shoulder clad in black-and-white checked calico. He missed the shoulder just as the kid rolled to the side, climbed to a knee, then, apparently without even thinking about it, leaped off the moving train.

Stockburn cursed as he watched the kid strike the ground beside the rails and roll, losing his hat, long black hair flying wildly. As the kid rolled to the bottom of the railbed, Stockburn dropped to a knee, cocked the Yellowboy, and raised it to his shoulder. He angled the rifle from his right to his left, tracking the black-haired kid as he fell farther and farther behind Wolf's moving position.

No point in wasting a round. The kid was a hard target. Spry as a puma, he was once again on his feet, running through the rocks and desert scrub south of the tracks.

"Damn!" Wolf wasn't going to let even one of these killers free to continue his depredations elsewhere. Even a scrawny, long-haired kid.

Wolf rose as another figure slid into the periphery of his vision, and he turned sharply toward the roof of the rear car, snapping the Yellowboy to his shoulder once more.

"Hold on, Wolf! Hold on!"

Wolf blinked up at a tall man wearing a Boss of the Plains Stetson. The man held a double-barreled shotgun down low along his right leg. He held up his gloved left hand in supplication. The long, spruce green duster he wore was billowing back in the wind behind him. To his cotton shirt was pinned a Wells Fargo copper shield. He grinned, flashing a silver eyetooth. "It's your old pal, Sandy McGee! Don't shoot!"

Stockburn dropped the Yellowboy's barrel. "Sandy, what the hell?"

"I was about to ask you the same thing. What the hell you doin' way out here in this parched perdition, Wolf?"

"What's it look like, you old reprobate?"

"Me an' Rascal Studemyer is back guarding the stock!" the tall, gray-haired, gray-bearded express guard bellowed into the wind. He hooked a thumb to indicate the three slatted stock cars rattling along behind him. "I came out to see what all the fuss was about!"

"Stay with the stock, Sandy," Wolf said, turning his head to ponder the fawn-colored ground sliding past him. "I should be done here in a minute!"

Stockburn stepped up to the edge of the vestibule.

"Wolf, don't you dare!" McGee objected. "You ain't as young as you used to be, fool!"

Stockburn barely heard the old express guard's admonition, for he'd just stepped off the vestibule and into the wind blowing past the train. Holding his rifle out high and wide to one side, he hit the sloping side of the rail bed feet first and fell to his knees and rolled.

Sandy had been right. He was forty years old. He'd thought leaping on and off of trains was ten years behind him. Apparently, he'd been wrong.

As he came to rest in a billowing dust cloud at the bottom of the rail bed, he was mildly surprised and encouraged to note that he hadn't seemed to break anything. He'd held on to his rifle but he'd lost his hat. He gained his feet heavily, inwardly complaining against the ache in both knees and in his right shoulder, which had taken the brunt of the roll.

He looked to the south.

The skinny, long-haired kid was running through the scrub maybe fifty yards away, widening the gap between himself and Wolf. Wolf raised the rifle, aimed, and squeezed the trigger.

The hammer pinged on an empty chamber.

Again, Wolf cursed. He leaned the rifle against a sotol cactus jutting on his right, retrieved his hat, unholstered one of his two Colt Single-Action Army Peacemakers, and took off running. He winced against the pain in his knees and elsewhere but, swinging his free arm, he increased his speed. The kid was faster on his feet, but Wolf could see him wavering. Probably due to the pain in that right shoulder as well as to blood loss.

Wolf kept running, weaving around tufts of cactus and scattered rocks, clutching a silver-plated, ivory-gripped .45 in his right hand.

Ahead, slowing even more, head lowered and dragging his boot toes, the long-haired kid crossed a narrow wash. He dropped to a knee as he climbed the opposite bank.

"Stop or take one in the back, you privy snake!" Wolf raised the Colt and aimed, drawing a bead on the kid's back, between his shoulder blades. Wolf hesitated. Down on one knee atop the bank, the kid swung his head to peer over his right shoulder at Stockburn. The long, black hair partly hid his face, obscuring the dark-brown eyes gazing warily, painfully back at Wolf.

The kid turned his head forward, climbed to his feet, and continued running.

"Stop, dammit!" Wolf drew his finger back against the Peacemaker's trigger but did not fire. The kid was wounded. Also, he was a young—well under twenty. Those two notions conspired to make Wolf reluctant to backshoot him, despite the many people the kid's gang had killed—close to ten.

Wolf continued running.

He crossed the wash. As he dropped down the opposite bank, he swung hard left when he saw a deep gorge open on his right—an ancient, dry riverbed, most likely. Wolf took one more lunging stride to the south then stopped when he saw the kid climbing a low mound of rocks ahead of him, only fifty feet away.

"I'm gonna give you one more chance to stop!" Stockburn shouted, narrowing one eye as he aimed down the Peacemaker's barrel.

The kid gave a frightened cry then clambered up over the mound to drop down the other side.

Wolf strode forward. The gorge curved toward him on his right. Ahead, the chasm edged along the right side of the mound of desert rocks and prickly pear.

Wolf stopped suddenly. The boy had just shoved his

head up above the rock mound. He raised his rifle and
pressed his cheek against the stock. He planted the sights
on Stockburn's chest. Instinctively, Wolf raised the Yellowboy and fired.

The kid jerked back with a yelp, throwing his rifle wide.

Before Wolf could fully comprehend that he'd just
killed a young man not yet twenty, he spied movement on
the right side of the escarpment.

A man stepped out from behind the escarpment. He
wore a flour sack mask with the eyes and mouth cut out.
The eyes were a distinct pale-blue; they owned a decidedly
soul-chilling evil glint. A black hat shaded the upper half
of his masked face, and a hickory duster buffeted around
the tops of his black boots into which the cuffs of his
broadcloth trousers were stuffed.

He snapped a rifle to his shoulder and smiled behind
the mask, those cold eyes slitting and drawing up at the
corners. A demon's eyes. "Hello, Stockburn! Sleep tight in
hell, amigo!"

The rifle roared.

A hot fist of pain slammed into Stockburn's right
temple, throwing him backward, rolling . . . rolling . . . over
the lip of the gorge and down . . . down . . . down to
black nothingness.

CHAPTER 3

"Hold the torch up a little higher, Violet."

"I can't, Pa. My arm is tired."

"Just a little higher. I almost have it!"

"But I—"

"There!" Herman McDonald, or "Skinny," as he was known in the desert Southwest, smashed his hammer against the chisel once more. The thumb of appealingly colored rock broke free of the mine's stone wall. "I got it! The light, Violet! The light!"

"I'm holding it, Pa! I'm holding the damn light!"

"Don't curse and offend your mother, child."

"Mama's dead. How many times do I have to tell you?"

"Such a child, such a child. Here—give me the dad-gummed torch." Skinny took the torch out of his daughter's hands with his left hand and held it close to his face but far enough away that it didn't catch his weathered felt immigrant cap on fire.

As it gave off the cloying odor of coal oil, he waved the torch before him, sliding the mine's shadows this way and that among the rocks he'd recently dislodged from the cavern's walls and ceiling. His long, craggy face thatched with a thick salt-and-pepper beard broadened, his dark eyes twinkling with a delighted smile.

He reached down with his right hand and picked up the object of his long desire. He held up the yellow stone, and the torchlight danced and winked across the nugget, which was a little larger than a child's chunk of rock candy. One of those that sold for three cents as opposed to just one.

Violet whistled softly, impressed. "A nice match for the one you found yesterday, Pa." Frowning, she turned to glance back out the mine portal ten feet behind her. "Did you hear that?"

"Hear what?" Fairly panting from the exhilaration of his find, Skinny slipped the nugget into the breast pocket of his checked wool shirt then shoved the torch toward his daughter again. "Take the light again, girl!"

"I think I heard shooting, Pa."

"Shooting?"

"Yes."

Skinny tipped his ear toward the mine's entrance, frowning. After a few seconds, he bunched his lips and shook his head. "I didn't hear anything. Only a train. Those infernal tracks are nearby. Take the light, Violet. I'm going to work on the ceiling again. This little canyon is just itching to bestow upon us its lovely treasures! Rich, rich, rich! We'll soon be dining in Frisco with Jay Gould, Jim Hill, and Charles Francis Adams, dear child!" He laughed and pinched his daughter's cheek.

"There it was again, Pa," Violet said, having heard another thumping sound from somewhere beyond the little canyon in which her father had dug his mine. She could hear the low rumble of a train passing on the recently laid rails. She'd come to recognize the din after the two months she and the old man—old enough to be her grandfather—

had been working the little chasm they'd come across by accident as they'd prospected the desert east of Las Cruces.

The thumping sounds she'd heard could only be the sounds of distant gunfire.

What else could they be?

"It's your overactive imagination, Vy. Take the torch." Her father's voice was shrill with eager expectation. "There is more gold here. See the vein trailing along the ceiling there?"

"Here." Violet took the torch and set it down in the crumbled quartz, propping it between two stones. Its wavering orange light spread forward across her diminutive father and deeper into the mine. "I've set the torch right here. Mind it now and don't burn yourself. I'll be back in a minute!"

"Violet. No, no, no, child! Whatever is happening out there is no business of ours!"

Pretending she hadn't heard the old man's admonition, as was her way—he often scolded her for being as stubborn as her deceased, former saloon-girl mother—Violet scuttled out of the low-ceilinged cavern. She and her father, working together as they'd done for most of her years, had dug the mine into the canyon wall.

Violet walked past their two mules and pack burros and back along the chasm, following its narrow, meandering course to the east, peering up toward the crests of the ridges on either side of her. Both ridges rose roughly sixty feet above the canyon's floor, stippled with cedars, creosote shrubs, cacti, and mesquites.

Behind her, Violet heard her father muttering angrily but also resignedly. She could also hear the sharp, ringing blows of his hammer against the chisel, pummeling the rock as he continued to follow the vein deeper into the earth. He'd relented as he always did, knowing that when

Violet had her mind set on something, nothing save an act of nature could sway her from following through.

The truth? She wasn't just curious about the gunshots. She was bored. Deeply bored. She'd spent most of her life either wintering in a little one-room shack in Las Cruces or burrowing with the old man into the earth's bowels, holding torches for him when she wasn't tending a cook-fire or hauling out dirt and ore, sometimes working right alongside him with hammer and chisel or crowbar and shovel. Her hands were almost as callused as his were.

The gunshots did not frighten Violet. They were a welcome distraction.

She wanted to see what the shots were about to further that distraction. Anything to give her a few minutes away from the old man and his relentless pursuit of gold. Anything to see another human face!

She wasn't, however, prepared for the distraction of hearing a man's angry voice yell in Spanish from somewhere above. "Hello, Stockburn! Sleep tight in hell, amigo!"

Violet stopped with a gasp, pressing one hand to her chest and staring up toward the crest of the ridge on her right.

A gun roared.

Violet gasped again when a figure appeared at the crest of the ridge. It was a man. A man rolling and tumbling, limbs flying every which way, down the steep ridge. A broad-brimmed hat bounced along the ridge behind him.

Violet stood shocked and horrified, watching the man roll down the bulging belly of the ridge. He looked like a ragdoll—one with a thick thatch of gray hair—dust rising around him, rocks and gravel sliding along behind him. He rolled over his hat and it flew up behind him to again follow him down the ridge like a loyal dog.

"Oh!" he said as the slope pummeled him savagely. "Oh! Oh! *Oh!*"

He dropped almost straight down from the bulging sandstone belly to the canyon floor. He lay unmoving on his belly for several seconds, both arms thrown up above his hatless head. Dust wafted around him. A few more rocks and some sand dribbled down the ridge to land beside him.

He lifted his head, groaned, squeezed his eyes closed. Then his head flopped down to rest against the pillow of his arms.

"Where did he go?"

The voice jerked Violet out of her shocked stupor. She gasped then peered up the ridge as two men stepped into view at the edge of the canyon. She saw only the front of their hat brims and the rifles they each held out in front of them before she stepped quickly to her right and pressed her back against the ridge wall. Her heart thudded, racing.

Had they seen her?

The crunch of boots on gravel sounded from above. The crunching stopped. The two men must be looking down into the canyon.

"Do you see him?" one asked the other in Spanish.

Having been raised around the Rio Grande where there were more Spanish speakers than Anglos, Violet was fluent in the south of the border tongue.

The other man said, "Speak English, dammit. You know I don't savvy that bean-eater talk."

The Spanish man chuckled then said in English but with a heavy Spanish accent. "I asked you if you see him."

"No, I don't see him. But he's down there somewhere. We both seen him go over the ridge. You hit him, didn't you?"

"Oh, I hit him, all right. I rarely miss. A head shot."

"Likely dead, then. Probably down below that bulge."

"Maybe we'd better go down and make sure."

"No time."

Boots crunched as one man began walking away from the canyon as he said, "We have to catch up to the train before it starts down the other side of the pass. Come on!"

"I don't know," said the man with the Spanish accent. "I think we should make sure." He raised his voice to call to the other man. "What about the kid?"

"Leave him!"

"You sure. That was Sanchez's kid brother!"

The other man said something but his words drifted off beneath the crunching of his boots, and he was gone.

At least, Violet thought both were gone. She waited, pressing her back and the palms of her hands against the ridge wall, her heart still thudding, ears ringing from fear. If they saw her, they'd likely kill her, for she'd seen what they'd done to the man who'd rolled into the canyon.

Bad place, this desert. Especially in the border country. Maybe her father had been right. Maybe she should have minded her own business and remained in the mine. The fallen man was no business of hers. Likely an outlaw who'd gotten crossways with his gang and ended up down here for his treachery.

What had the man on the ridge called him? Stockton? Stockburn?

Violet drew a deep breath. What kid had they been referring to? If they'd meant *Rafael* Sanchez's kid brother, they'd been referring to Tomasito Sanchez. If they'd killed Tomasito, they'd made a very bad enemy in Rafael Sanchez.

Violet waited, heart still racing. Fear made her bones feel like heavy stone.

She slid her gaze up the ridge wall toward the crest. She looked down at the man lying on his belly roughly thirty feet away from her. The two men on the ridge hadn't been able to see him because he was lying beneath where the ridge wall bulged, concealing him from above

Violet could see him, however. He looked dead. She thought she could see red pooling on the sandy canyon bottom beneath his head.

Faintly, she could hear her father still pounding away with his hammer, desperate to find another nugget like the previous two he'd found. Violet wanted to return to him and to the safety of the mine. She wished she'd minded the old man for once and hadn't gone out there. She wanted no part of a killing.

No part of a dead man. If he was dead, that was.

Maybe he was still alive.

Violet wanted to return to the cave and pretend she'd never seen the man on the canyon floor nor the men on the ridge. But she couldn't leave an injured man. She had to walk over to him and see if he could be helped. Likely, he was dead. But if he needed help, she'd have to help him.

No. She shook her head, reconsidering. He was probably an outlaw. A killer. He'd probably killed innocent people. A man like that didn't deserve her help. She swung around and began to walk back toward the mine from which she could still hear her father's hammer banging away at the vein. She took three strides and stopped.

She couldn't do it.

She turned around, cursed under her breath. She'd learned a lot of curse words from her father and his crusty old prospector cronies, though she wasn't supposed to use such language herself. "It isn't fittin' for a young lady to talk that way. How's a blue-tongued girl gonna attract a man?" he always said.

Still, Violet cursed, almost in defiance of her father's and his friends' attitudes about how women should talk.

True, she might not attract a man, talking that way, but she wasn't likely to attract much of a man, anyway. She was too tall and raw-boned to be pretty, and it was only the pretty girls who got the men. At least, the good men. Besides, there were few good men in these parts. In fact, outside of her father, she didn't know a single one.

She stared at the man before her. Was he a good man? Likely not.

Still, she had to walk over and investigate.

She glanced warily up at the ridge again. She doubted the two killers would return. They were train robbers. They'd likely been after the train she'd heard pass earlier. They had more important things on their mind than making certain-sure one of their own men, who'd likely double-crossed them one way or another, the way outlaws were certain to do to each other, was dead.

Violet stole forward.

CHAPTER 4

Violet stopped near the man.

Her heart was beating quickly again. Her fear of the men on the ridge had been replaced by a fear of the man before her. Irrationally, she half expected him to suddenly lift his head and a gun, and shoot her. She knew that wouldn't happen. He was either dead or unconscious, but still the fear remained. The possibility that he was dead revolted her. She'd seen dead men before, and their images haunted her dreams at night.

"Hey," Violet said, lifting one of her boy-sized lace-up mining boots into the tops of which she'd tucked the cuffs of her faded denim trousers. She nudged the man's arm with the toe of the left boot. "Hey, mister . . ."

The man didn't respond.

It was definitely blood pooling on the sand and gravel beneath his head. Again, Violet prodded the man's shoulder, making his body jerk a little. "Hey, there . . . you . . . *mister*. You dead?"

Still, nothing.

She thought she could see his back rising and falling slightly, however, which meant he might be breathing. She dropped to a knee beside him and cursed. Steeling herself, she grabbed his left arm and shoulder with both of her hands. With a grunt, she pulled him over onto his back. It had taken some doing. He was a big, solid man. He had to weight well over two hundred pounds.

He lay belly up, facing her. It appeared he'd taken a bullet across his right temple. That's where the blood had come from. It dribbled slowly in two red streams down the right side of his head to the ground. It was already clotting, drying in the hot desert air. Violet found herself staring down at the man with keen interest.

He was a handsome man with chiseled, clean-shaven features save a well-trimmed mustache that matched his hair. His broad face with high, tapering cheekbones was deeply sun-bronzed. His hair was thick, and it was roached like a horse's mane. The hair didn't seem to match his age. He didn't seem old enough for gray hair, which stood out in striking contrast to the tan of his flesh. He was not a young man, but he wasn't old, either. At least, not as old as the hair would make him seem.

He was broad shouldered, muscular, and thick-chested, with a flat, hard belly and long legs, which also appeared thick and corded inside the dark twill of his trousers. He was also well-dressed. Not like a dandy, but close.

He wore a black frock coat of good cloth over a white silk shirt adorned with a black string tie, which also appeared silk. He wore a black leather waistcoat, as well, and black leather boots of the low-heeled, cavalry style.

Around the man's waist was a black, fancily tooled leather holster. The holster, positioned for the cross-draw on his left hip, was empty. The holster thonged on his right thigh contained a pretty, large-caliber revolver with ivory grips. She couldn't see much of the gun because of the holster, but it appeared to be silver- or nickel-plated.

The gold watch lying nearby must be his. It had probably

fallen out of his waist coat pocket. It was dented from the tumble down the ridge. Same with the hat—a stylish black sombrero with a black silk band. It had been badly abused in the fall.

The man didn't look like an outlaw. At least, not like any outlaw Violet had ever seen. Out in the godforsaken desert, she'd seen a few. This one was uncommonly handsome. Weren't outlaws usually lowly, ugly characters, or had she read too many of the dime novels of Deadeye Dick to pass the time back in Las Cruces?

Suddenly, the man's eyes were open, staring straight up at her. Such intensity in that brown-eyed gaze made Violet lurch with another start and step back haltingly. "Oh," she said. "Oh . . . you're . . ."

The man winced. He lifted his right hand to raise it to his head but got it only half raised before it flopped back down against his side. He grimaced, stretching his lips back from a full set of white teeth, groaned, then closed his eyes again.

He lay still. Unconscious.

"Violet?"

Again, Violet jumped. But it was her father's voice. She turned to gaze back in the direction of the mine. Her father walked toward her, his spindly shoulders customarily slumped forward. His big, work-gnarled hands hung down at his sides, like oversized claws. He lifted his watch cap and swabbed sweat from his dirty brow with a sleeve of his plaid wool work shirt, and continued moving slowly, heavily toward Violet and the injured man. He wore baggy canvas trousers held up on his skinny frame with snakeskin galluses and high-topped miner's boots so badly worn his faded red socks shone through in places.

"Violet, what're you doin' way out here? Didn't you hear me callin' you, girl? I need help with—" Skinny McDonald had come close enough now, having followed a gentle curve in the canyon, to see the man lying at Violet's knees.

Her father's eyes widened. His voice came in a shocked hush. "What in God's name . . . ?"

"Found him over here, Pa. He's been shot. By—" Violet glanced toward the top of the ridge above her—"two men on the ridge."

Skinny McDonald looked warily up at the ridge, stretching his lips back from tobacco-brown teeth. "Two men on the ridge, eh? They still up there?" An air of extreme anxiety had passed over him like a dark storm cloud. His craggy face had flushed behind his deep suntan, from the tip of his sharply pointed chin to the peak of his high, domelike forehead.

"They're gone, Pa. I think they were—"

"Claim jumpers!"

"No!" Violet hurried to reassure the old man. He was notoriously paranoid, always expecting that he and Violet were about to be set upon by men out to steal their claims or their pokes. "Look at him. Does he look like a claim jumper to you? He's no miner."

The old man fished the beat-up old conversion .38 revolver he always carried in a soft leather holster strapped around his skinny waist. He rarely took it off and when he did, it wasn't for long. He crept a little closer, hesitating. "Is he alive?"

"I think so. His eyes were just open. He's not a claim jumper, Pa."

"How do you know? He's too damn close to the mine, Violet. That's one thing I know for sure!"

"Put the gun down, Pa. You can't kill him!"

"Why can't I? He's too damn close to the mine! You don't know who he is or what he was up to. But he took a bullet, all right. If he ain't a claim jumper, he's trouble of some kind!"

Violet didn't want to tell her father that the injured man might be a train robber. In Skinny McDonald's book, the mere fact the man was close to the mine meant he deserved a bullet. She also didn't want to mention that the body of Rafael Sanchez's kid brother might be lying up on the ridge above the canyon.

For that would surely mean more trouble. The name *Sanchez* was synonymous with trouble in this neck of the desert.

Violet wasn't sure why she wanted to save the injured man from another bullet. Maybe it had been the expression in his coffee-brown eyes. She didn't think they were the eyes of an outlaw. She'd sensed an intelligence and right-eousness in the man's gaze, sequestered behind his obvious pain, even though their eyes had met only briefly.

"Let me check him over, Pa. Let me see if he's got anything on him that might identify him."

"Get away from there, Violet! I'm gonna shoot him and we'll bury him quick-like before somebody comes fer him!"

"No, Pa! Put the gun away! You're not gonna shoot him!" Violet rose and stepped up to the old man. She wrapped her hand around the old .38, and shoved it down against his hip, giving Skinny a hard, commanding look.

Sometimes Skinny was her father and she respected him.

Sometimes, however, the tables were turned. They each acknowledged the change at the same time. It was an un-written agreement between them.

Skinny acknowledged it and lowered his eyes in supplication, bunching his chapped lips inside his washed out gray beard.

Violet knelt beside the injured man again and raked her hands over his shirt and trousers, probing his pockets. "We have to check . . . see who he is. What if he's someone important? Maybe a passenger from the train."

"He's after our gold, I tell you," Skinny stubbornly pressed but only half-heartedly, keeping the gun low at his side.

"Hold on." Violet had found something in the injured man's back pocket. She pulled the soft leather wallet out from behind him and opened it. Her eyes widened when she found herself staring at a copper shield in which the words WELLS FARGO EXPRESS COMPANY had been etched beneath the insignia of an American eagle.

Beneath those words were two more words. SPECIAL AGENT.

Shocked, Violet held up the wallet to show her father the shield.

Skinny McDonald stared at the shield, frowning. He could see the shield but he couldn't read the words etched into it, so Violet said, "You wanna kill a Wells Fargo detective, Pa?"

"Pshaw!"

"Sure enough."

"Way out here?"

"You saw the shield."

Violet held the wallet in her hand and stared down at the injured agent. It would have been simpler if her father had been right and the man had been an outlaw. Then they could have more easily justified leaving him there.

But, now . . . Violet looked up at her father. "What should we do, Pa?"

Skinny grimaced and holstered the old revolver. He stared down incredulously at the injured detective. Slowly, he shook his head. "I don't got no time for Wells Fargo. He probably come on that infernal train. Don't ask me what made him get off. I got gold to dig!" He spat to one side, turned, and began limping back in the direction of the mine.

"Wells Fargo, Pa!"

"Wells Fargo ain't no business of ours!"

"You'd really just leave him here?"

The incrimination in his daughter's tone stopped Skinny in his tracks. He stood facing forward, then with a frustrated sigh, he turned back around to face Violet. "What you want we should do? He'll likely die, anyways. Looks like he lost a lotta blood. Besides, he could be trouble. We don't know what he got himself entangled with out here!"

Train robbers, Violet did not say.

She didn't want trouble any more than her father did, but she knew if she left the agent to die, she'd never be able to live with herself. As it was, she didn't think much of herself. She was the daughter of an old prospector and a saloon girl who'd died from drink one cold winter in a drafty shack on the outskirts of Las Cruces. Violet had been an accident, of course. No one had told her that, but that's what she was. A mistake. She'd been the unwanted result of a short-term business arrangement that had turned into a reluctant marriage stemming from some ill-conceived sense of obligation to the unwanted spawn of said arrangement.

Violet had little schooling, having taught herself to read by reading trash novels and wish books. She'd been following her father around this desert most of her life, slinging hash in a greasy café a couple of months during the winter to make enough money to finance their prospecting runs back into the desert in the spring—always chasing El Dorado with very little encouragement by way of treasure.

She was plain-faced.

She dressed like a boy.

She stole tobacco from her father and smoked cigarettes on the sly.

She drank beer when she could get her hands on it.

She had learned few manners. She cussed as much as her father did, and she was as wild as a jackrabbit. She couldn't add cold-blooded killer to that inelegant list of attributes. She wouldn't be able to sleep at night, and she'd have a devil of a time holding her chin up or looking anyone in the eye again. Not that she could now, being shy as a desert coyote, but—

No, she was going to do for the injured man whatever she could. Which wasn't much. But she had to try. He'd likely still die but then she'd be shed of him without feeling any worse about herself.

She gained her feet and walked past her father, heading back to the mine.

"Where you goin'?" Skinny called. "What're you gonna do?"

"Gonna fetch ole Angus, and then I'm gonna pack that fella home for tending."

Skinny wagged his head defeatedly. "You put that man on your mule, you're gonna bring trouble down on our heads, Violet. Mark my words!"

CHAPTER 5

Stockburn lived in an odd nether world of pain and fragmented dreams.

Vaguely aware of being moved, of being transported likely by a makeshift travois, he could smell the creosote smell of oiled canvas. He tried to wake, but long tendrils of unconsciousness clung to him stubbornly, held him fast to the dark soup of pain and a kaleidoscope of disorderly images assaulting him from his past.

Through it all, he kept seeing the brown face of a boy staring down a barrel at him, then a heart-shaped, sun-tanned face with soft hazel eyes. Large, round, satiny eyes, their corners were creased with concern. She wore a round-brimmed black felt hat from which long flaxen hair fell straight to her shoulders.

A big girl, a tough girl, pretty, maybe, if her nose had been a little smaller, her features a little more carefully molded.

He had a vague sense of being pulled on the canvas travois by a mule. From the deep well of unconsciousness he'd heard the beast bray a time or two. Occasionally, he heard the girl speak to someone other than himself. Her voice was far away, as though issuing from the bottom of a well. A man or maybe a couple of men accompanied the girl, for he thought he heard at least one man speak to her.

A few times, Wolf managed to open his eyes and saw the desert sliding past to each side. His head felt like a kettle drum with a tender nerve all but exposed beneath the thin, tautly drawn hide. A mad man or a savage was rapping away heartily on that drum.

Thank God a deeper consciousness opened and sucked him down into its relative sanctuary where he felt little sensation. Through the biting pain in his forehead, he imagined he was lying on a cabin floor and a rat was chewing on him. A rat with very sharp teeth. A burning sensation accompanied the painful gnawing, then both went away for a time.

Then the kaleidoscope went to work once more in his brain, turning . . . turning . . . and he saw his sister being taken by the whooping Cheyenne brave while their Kansas farm burned and their parents lay dead in the yard. He saw the horses he rode—and got to know better than almost any human being before or since—when, still wet-behind-the-ears, he rode for the Pony Express.

A time or two, Indians chased him—brief but terrifying images flashing through the kaleidoscope of his past. He saw his friend Mike, also a Pony Express rider . . . and he saw Mike's girl, Fannie . . . and then he saw Mike lying dead in a rumpled heap near the trolley tracks in San Francisco.

In that timeless swirl of tenuously connected dreams, he tried to call to Mike, to beg him to come back to the hotel room . . . that none of it mattered . . . that Fannie meant nothing to him, nor him to her . . . but Wolf couldn't get the words out. He felt as though his mouth were stuffed with marbles. He could save Mike if only he could get the words out, but try as he might, he couldn't do it.

He wept, his heart twisting painfully, still trying to call Mike's name.

He saw the face of the brown-skinned, long-haired boy just before the bullet blasted a hole through his head. Then back to his little sister, his dead parents, the rampaging Indians . . . a tornado he'd lived through in Dakota . . . and again Mike.

"Oh, Christ, Mike, come back! It meant nothing. Forgive me!"

The girl's face appeared before him again, briefly.

Firelight flashed in her hazel eyes as she leaned over him, frowning at him as she wrung a wet cloth out in a washbasin. "Easy," she said, her voice kind, gentle, sympathetic. "Lay back now. Rest easy. I think the fever's almost broke."

The word *broke* echoed around in his head, sounding like it had been spoken from behind a stout door.

Darkness again.

More images. Not so many and not such painful ones. A saloon girl he'd known in Wichita, when he was the town lawman. The Wolf of Wichita, the local paper had called him. Irene was her name. They'd had fun together though they were not in love. Or maybe that's why they'd had so much fun . . . and why there was so little pain when it ended and Irene married a shoe salesman named Mordecai Webber.

"Well, there you are. You're looking better." A girl's voice.

Vaguely familiar. He realized he was looking at her. She was standing at a small wooden eating table, rolling out dough with a rolling pin. The tails of her man's shirt hung down over her well-curved hips. Her flaxen blond hair hung in her eyes. She straightened from her work, held the pin in one hand, blew a lock of hair from her left eye, and said, "How do you feel?"

Her face was unlovely, a little crudely shaped, but she was pretty when she smiled. Her eyes reflected a rich and vibrant soul. That was where true beauty lay anyway. The pile of years and experience had taught the detective, no brighter or dumber than most men, such things.

A finger print of dough smudged her cheek.

Wolf cleared phlegm from his throat. Still, it was hard to speak. "Better," he heard himself croak. His right temple burned and ached, but not nearly as bad as it had pained him, even while he'd been asleep. The rat had gotten its teeth filed a little.

He looked around at the sparsely furnished stone cabin. There appeared only one room. A fire burned in the stone hearth to his left. He could hear the black range beyond the fireplace ticking, as well. The cabin was filled with the savory aroma of stew. Javelina, he guessed. Wild pig.

He turned to the girl again. She was silhouetted against the glassless window behind her, the shutters open to golden morning light. "Where . . . am . . . I?" he croaked again, his voice sounding to his own ears like the soft cawing of a sick crow.

"You're here, in our cabin—Pa's and mine. You're safe." The girl set down the rolling pin, walked over to a small, makeshift counter, and ladled water from a wooden bucket into a tin cup. She took it over to the cot on which Stockburn lay, covered with a blanket and a gamey-smelling wildcat hide.

She handed him the cup. Her hands were caked with dough and she had dirt under her fingernails. "You must be thirsty."

Stockburn took the cup and greedily drained it. She smiled, arched a brow. "That's a good sign my doctorin' skills were right adequate, after all." She sank into a straight-back chair angled beside his cot.

He raised a hand to his right temple, which had been the epicenter of his misery. He fingered a ragged line of thread stitching the bullet wound closed. "I'd say it was more than adequate, Miss . . ."

"Violet."

"Miss Violet. I don't know how to thank you."

"I'm just glad you made it, Mr. Stockburn." She smiled again, making her lustrous eyes dance prettily, set against the deep tan of her face. "Mister Wolf of the Rails," she added in a teasing tone.

Oddly, he thought he smelled beer on her breath. He glanced at the table again and saw a short brown bottle on it, near the pie crust she'd been working on.

Stockburn frowned. "How did you . . . ?"

"Saw the identification card in your wallet, behind your Wells Fargo shield. Oh, I've heard the stories. I taught myself to read by reading the newspapers and the *National Police Gazette,* when I can find it."

"You like a ribald tale, do you?"

"Like I said, when I can find 'em."

Stockburn chuckled. Then he frowned again, curious. "How long have I . . . ?"

"Since yesterday afternoon. It's still morning." She glanced at a clock ticktocking on the wall behind her. "A little after eleven. Pa went out to the mi—" She stopped, catching herself. Her rawboned face acquired a chagrined look.

"To the mine," Stockburn said with a knowing wink. "Don't worry. Your secret's safe with me, Violet. I don't usually go around blabbin' secrets of pretty gals . . . or their father's . . . especially when that pretty gal and her father saved my ragged behind."

She blushed and looked shyly down. "Thanks for sayin' I'm pretty."

"Why, you are pretty."

Her blush deepened, and she shook her head with the old knowing. "No. Anything but." Quickly, she changed the subject, looking at him again and saying, "I found your horse. If he's a smoky gray, that is."

"He is. In fact, Smoke is his name."

"I should say he found us when we climbed out of the canyon—Pa an' me—with you belly down across my mule. I apologize for that but we couldn't figure another way to get you out of there. You're a big, heavy man, Mr. Stockburn. After we got you out of the canyon, we fashioned a travois for the trip to the cabin."

"Nothin' to apologize for, Miss Violet."

"Anyway, as I was sayin', Smoke found us. He must've followed you to the canyon and was waiting on the rim. He followed us back here, trotting up every now and then to give you a sniff. To make sure you were still alive, I think. That's a loyal horse, Mr. Stockburn."

"Wolf."

Again, she blushed, glanced down at the work-calloused fingertips she was pressing together with nervous shyness. "Wolf."

"I've put that horse through a lot."

"Must be an interesting life, bein' a Wells Fargo detective." Violet picked up his cup from where he'd set it on his belly, and walked back into the kitchen area of the small cabin.

"That's one way to describe it."

"And dangerous . . . obviously."

"That's another way. Especially when you get careless." Stockburn remembered the masked man who'd appeared from behind the same mound of rocks the boy he'd killed had taken cover behind. He winced as he remembered drilling the bullet into the boy's head . . . and then the masked man with those cold devil's eyes rising from behind those rocks and hurling a blue whistler across Stockburn's temple.

Only vaguely did he remember the helpless feeling of rolling into the canyon.

As Violet ladled more water into the cup, she asked, "Are you hungry?"

Stockburn looked down at his belly covered by the blankets and bearskin, and frowned. "I'm not sure."

"Well, let me know. I have a stew on the range, and I'm about to make an apricot pie."

"That sounds heavenly, Violet. Say, I got a question."

"All right." She took the refilled water cup back to him then returned to the table where she'd been making the pie. She picked up the bottle, took a deep pull, and looked at Stockburn, flushing sheepishly, then ran the back of her hand across her mouth and gave a soft belch.

Stockburn looked at her incredulously. "You *are* drinking beer!" He glanced at the clock. "At ten in the morning?"

Violet shrugged, still flushing. "Pa's at the mine. You know what they say—when the cat's away. I brewed it myself. Pa's old partner, dead now—a shaft collapsed on him—was a brewmaster in Germany. He gave me his recipe. I don't get the ingredients that often, but when I do, I can brew up a gnarly batch of ale!" She winked and took another slug.

No wonder her eyes danced so prettily. Stockburn laughed.

"I'll fetch you one if you want."

"Maybe after the rat in my head goes back to where he came from." Wolf sipped his water and returned to the dead boy on the ridge. "There was a boy up above the canyon."

"Tomasito Sanchez?"

Stockburn frowned, curious. "I don't know his name. All I know is I shot him."

"You did?"

"Didn't have any choice. It was either him or—"

"Don't worry. I buried him." Violet shook her head. "Tomasito is no big loss though he could be trouble. No more than when he was alive, though."

"You found him?"

"I heard the two men on the ridge—the two who shot you—mention Rafael Sanchez's kid brother. When I got you back to the cabin, and after Pa went to bed, I rode back over there and found him. Tomasito, all right." The girl's tone had turned dark, ominous. "No one'll find him. He'll be our secret." She made a gesture of buttoning her lips and gave another soft belch, and blushed again.

Stockburn's curiosity grew. He sat up a little higher in bed, finished the water, and set the empty cup on the small table beside the bed. "Who's Rafael Sanchez?"

"One of Sheriff Paul Wagner's deputy sheriffs in Las Cruces. A tough man in town. Rafael, I mean. Not Wagner. He's old and washed up. Rafael is one of the toughest men around. Former outlaw. Comes from an old family in these parts. An old family of Mexican outlaws. His little brother, Tomasito, was following in his brother's footsteps. At least, in his earlier outlaw footsteps. I heard Rafael was trying his damnedest to rein in Tomasito, but Tomasito wasn't having any of it. Still, they were brothers. The last of their family. You know how the Mexicans are about family. Blood for blood."

"Blood for blood," Stockburn mused aloud. "I hope I didn't bring you and your father trouble, Violet."

"We won't say nothin' to Pa. He'd only worry."

"I bet your pa doesn't approve of me bein' here." Something in the man's words Stockburn had dimly overheard had given Wolf the impression.

Violet didn't answer that. She was busy arranging the flattened pie crust into a tin pie pan again, pinching down the edges. Her face colored a little. That was answer enough.

"I don't blame him. There were two bad men up there on that ridge. Three if you include the boy."

"Do you think they'll come looking for you? The ones who shot you."

Wolf shook his head. "Hard to say. I'm wondering why they didn't finish me off when they had the chance."

Violet looked up from her work, her eyes dark with gravity. "Maybe they had a train to rob."

Stockburn frowned again. "What makes you say that? I jumped off the only train out there at that time. Tomasito had been part of a gang holding it up.

It was too much of a coincidence for two different outlaw gangs to have been robbing the same train at nearly the same time. Way too coincidental.

Violet was pouring pie filling into the crust. When she'd spooned out the last of the filling from the bowl, she set the bowl down, took another sip of her beer, and looked across the room at Wolf once more. "All I can tell you is that as Pa and I were hauling you to the cabin, I heard gunfire from up near War Lance Pass. Pa's hard of hearing, and didn't hear it, but I did. I heard the squeal of iron wheels, too, men shouting . . . more shooting."

Violet shook her head slowly, fatefully. "Yessir, I think those fellas were part of a gang that robbed the train up near the saddle, just before the train would have started down the other side."

"That's impossible. Two gangs robbing the same train at nearly the same time?"

"I don't know what to tell you, Wolf. But, if so, that train would really be living up to its name—the Boot Hill Express!"

CHAPTER 6

"That tears it," Stockburn said, throwing the single wool blanket back. "I have to get up there and check it out!" With a grunt, he dropped his left foot to the floor.

"Wolf, that's a helluva nasty wound you got," Violet objected. "You'd best stay in bed until at least—"

"No, no." Wolf dropped his other foot to the floor and heaved himself to his feet. "I got two good friends aboard that train. Express guards. If I somehow got the wool pulled over my eyes, and fell for a dummy holdup—though there wasn't nothin' dummy about those bullets tearing through that passenger coach's roof—I gotta get up there and get after the second band of thieves! Gotta see how ol' Sandy an' Rascal made out—"He drew a breath to try and quell the pounding of the hammer in his temple. It didn't do much good. He'd just have to suck it up. He looked down at himself. All he seemed to be missing was his frock coat, his boots, and his hat.

He looked at Violet still sanding by the table, regarding him like a disapproving schoolmarm, one foot cocked forward, one fist on her hip, the other, flour-dappled hand on the table. She had one cheek sucked in.

"Where's my . . . ?"

"Over there."

Stockburn followed her glance to the front wall. Sure enough, his frock hung from a wall hook beside another hook from which his gun rig hung. His low-heeled, snub-nosed cavalry boots were lined up neatly beneath them. To his surprise, his Yellowboy was leaning against the same wall, to the right of his coat and his six-shooters.

"Is that yours?" Violet asked him. "I found it up near where I found Tomasito."

"It is indeed."

"I figured as much. A right snazzy firestick. I brought it out after Pa left so he wouldn't get suspicious about where I found it."

"Thank you, darlin'."

Wolf dragged his stocking feet over to the cabin's front wall. Grinding his teeth against the pain in his head, he pulled on the coat and strapped the Peacemakers around his waist, tying the right holster snug to his right thigh. He stepped into his boots then propped each one on a chair in turn, tucking the cuffs of his twill trousers into each boot top.

Finally, he picked up the Yellowboy, set it on his shoulder.

He drew another breath, gauged the pain level in his noggin. Not bad. Not bad at all. He'd been hurt far worse than this.

If the cabin would only stop pitching around him like a broomtail bronc, he might make it to the door without tumbling facedown like a drunk trying to cross First Street in Dodge City at 2 A.M.

He turned to Violet, who remained standing with that schoolmarm's disapproving scowl on her face made pretty by her gray, expressive eyes that danced a little from the beer.

He fashioned a smile. In his condition it wasn't an easy

task, but he got 'er done, by god. He pinched his hat brim to the girl. "Violet, I don't know how to thank you."

"You can thank me by crawling back into that bed before I have to scrape you up off the floor. You're a big man, you weigh a ton, and pickin' you up ain't gonna be an easy task since Pa's gone and I don't have anyone to help."

"You won't have to. I been hurt worse than this fallin' out of bed drunk." Wolf winked, turned to the door, drew another breath, and started walking.

He made it through the door and out under the brush arbor when the floor came up suddenly and slammed into his knees. That sledge hammer in his head smacked down hard on an especially large, exposed nerve.

He gritted his teeth as the little, covered stoop swirled around him and dark circles flashed in front of his eyes. The bright light of late morning dimmed. Not because of clouds but because he was on the verge of passing out.

Violet came up from behind him, dropped to a knee beside him. She arched a brow at him. "You gonna come back to bed now or you gonna wait till you go all the way down and I have to figure a way to haul you back up?"

Stockburn blinked his heavy-lidded eyes. "I reckon . . . I best . . . go back to . . . bed."

"Now, you're talkin'." Violet took his rifle and set it back inside the cabin then went back out and wrapped his left arm around her neck. "Lean into me."

Wolf did as she ordered. Together they got him back on his feet, back into the cabin, back into bed. She was a strong girl with sure feet and good hips. She removed his coat, hat, and gun rig, and hung them back on the hooks. She removed his boots then pulled the blanket up over him. She stared down at him and said commandingly. "Sleep."

The railroad detective gave a sheepish sigh and closed his eyes.

His worry about the train, its passengers, and his two old friends, Sandy and Rascal, managed to fend sleep off for maybe two minutes. But then the sandman flew in through a window and if not killed the pain in his head, at least tempered it with a warm, soothing blanket of deep slumber.

He woke a time or two throughout the afternoon.

Once, he opened his eyes briefly to see Violet sitting in a chair by his bed, darning what he believed was one of his socks. She must have pulled it off his foot though he hadn't been aware of her doing so.

When he woke again, briefly, he saw her sitting on the other side of the cabin from him, in a beat-up old rocking chair with deer antler arms against the far wall. She had her boots crossed on an overturned washtub before her. She was smoking a wheat paper cigarette and sipping from another bottle of beer. She stared at him with a vague smile quirking her mouth corners.

When she realized that his eyes were halfway open, a flush rose in her cheeks, and she turned away quickly, obviously embarrassed, and blew a smoke plume out toward the open door through which the smell of a late-afternoon rain emanated on a fresh, cool breeze.

Stockburn smiled and fell back asleep.

When he opened his eyes again, the cabin was considerably darker than it had been before. It was also filled with the rich aromas of the stew simmering on the little sheet-iron range in a corner of the small kitchen part of the cabin. The heat from the range was tempered by the cool air pushing through the door, and the glassless windows from which the shutters had been thrown back, the air itself spiced with fresh rain, wet sage, and cedar.

He saw Violet standing just outside the open door, on the stoop beneath the brush arbor, arms crossed low, her back taut. He couldn't see her face but the set of her arms and shoulders told him she was worried about something.

Wolf cleared his throat. "What is it?"

Violet turned her head to one side, glancing at him over her right shoulder. "Pa's not back yet." She turned her head back forward. "It's supper time. He's usually home by supper time. We always come back by suppertime."

Stockburn sat up. Concern for the old man raked him. He hoped his own would-be killers hadn't returned to the canyon to make sure he was dead and discovered Skinny McDonald instead. The old man's mine wasn't far from where Stockburn had landed at the bottom of the chasm.

Wolf swung his feet to the floor, noticing he was wearing both socks again and that the hole in the toe of the left one had been sewn closed. "I'll saddle Smoke and—"

"No," Violet said, turning and stepping back into the cabin. "He's probably still following that vein he discovered. When Skinny finds color, it's hard to pull him away from it. Can't blame him. We haven't found all that much color out in these rocks, despite all the years we've been looking for it. He'll come home when it gets too dark or wet to continue working."

"Are you sure?" Wolf asked. "I'm feeling a heckuva lot better."

It was true. That hammering in his head had tapered to a dull ache. The gash itself still hurt but it was nothing compared to the previous explosions inside his skull.

"Thanks to my doctoring." Violet strode over to him and leaned down, inspecting the wound she'd stitched closed. "Hmm. Looks pretty good. I sewed it up tight, all right. Put some salve on it, too, to keep infection out. It also helps kill the pain and makes it heal faster. Old Indian remedy I got from an Apache laundress in Mesila. Skinny uses it on his hands for arthritis. Swears it takes the pain right out."

Wolf took the girl's hand in his, smiled up at her. "Thank you, Violet. For what you've done for me. You could have left me on the bottom of that canyon where I likely would have bled out."

"Nah. That gash had clotted and was already starting to heal by the time I got you to the cabin. Besides," she added with a warm smile of her own, "I never could have left a man in your condition, Wolf."

He hoped to hell she wouldn't regret her actions, that he hadn't brought trouble to her and Skinny.

"I feel good enough to ride out and check on your father," he said.

"No need. I'm sure he'll be along soon, when he finally stops working and realizes he's hungry. Then food will suddenly become more important than El Dorado." She smiled again and glanced at the pot bubbling on the range. "You hungry? I make a mean javelina stew. That and rattle-snake is about all that Pa and I live on. It's about all I can cook, in fact, but that only means I've had lots of practice. It may not be as grand as what you're used to, but it's right edible."

"If you call beans and bacon cooked over remote camp-fires grand. That's what I'm used to. I may have a home base in Kansas City, but I'm out riding the long coulees, brush-popping owlhoots, far more often than I'm riding the cable cars."

In fact, Stockburn considered outlying places like this remote stone shack his home. Leastways, he felt far more at home here than he ever had in any city. Always a loner, he'd never liked being amidst large groups of people much. In fact, he preferred going it solo—just him and Smoke out on the windy wide-open—most of the time.

He liked being here with Violet, though. He'd felt an instant bond with this lonely, big-boned, rustic girl.

Stockburn sniffed the air. "That sure smells heavenly. And I do believe I'm hungry. Famished, in fact!"

Violet blushed. He saw her glance away and try to temper her smile so as not to look foolish though she inwardly rejoiced at having cooked a meal for a man not her father. "I got sour dough biscuits, too. Just took 'em out of the Dutch oven. They should be cool enough now to eat. I love biscuits with stew, don't you, Wolf? I have fresh pie for dessert. You want me to help you over to the table?"

"I think I can make it."

Violet extended her hand to him. "Better let me help. Just in case. You wouldn't want to fall and undo my handiwork, now, would you?"

"I reckon you're right."

He placed his hand in hers. Warm and inviting, she wrapped it around his own—as much as she could, anyway, hers being half the size of his. As she did, he saw a soft glow rise in her cheeks and a placid sparkle in her eyes.

Yes, she was lonely. In the full flower of young womanhood but living a lonely life out here with her old father. Wolf wondered if she'd ever had a boy call on her. If she'd ever been kissed.

While she wasn't traditionally pretty, there was something indeed beautiful about her, just the same. He could feel the young woman's hunger for fulfillment as he leaned against her and let her lead him over to the table though he did not really need the help. He felt a swell in her firm bosom, which she, maybe or maybe not inadvertently, brushed up against his ribs as they approached the table together. She left the swell there against his ribs for several seconds, and he could feel the heat rise in her hand clamped around his own, and radiate from her body.

"There you go," she said, breathless as she helped ease

the big man into a chair. She gave a nervous chuckle. "You did pretty well. You are feeling better."

"Couldn't have done it without you, darlin'. Boy, that does smell good!"

It tasted even better.

As they sat at the table together, Violet likely in her customary spot with her back to the door, Stockburn facing her from the opposite side with the range behind him, the only thing that kept him from more fully appreciating the savory vittles was his concern for the train and for Skinny McDonald. He felt well enough now to ride up and investigate the pass, but it was too late in the day, and the growing rumble of thunder told him the storm would bear down on them soon.

He'd have to wait until morning to investigate the rails at the top of War Lance Pass.

He could tell Violet's own worry about her father was growing. She didn't say much through the meal but every so often she turned her head to look quickly over her shoulder and through the open yard at the desert shrubs and cactus fronting the shack. She hoped to see her father out there with his mule and burros.

All that was out there, however, was the desert scrub, whose branches jounced more and more violently as the storm approached. The light dimmed. The air wafting through the door grew gradually cooler and heavier with the fresh smell of rain and brimstone.

Stockburn swabbed the last bit of stew from the bottom of his bowl with half of a baking powder biscuit, and stuck the biscuit into his mouth. As he chewed, Violet looked up from her own bowl again sharply, believing she'd heard something outside, and turned her head to peer expectantly into the yard. Seeing no one out there, she winced her disappointment, turned toward Stockburn, met his gaze, shrugged a shoulder, and drew her mouth corners down.

"Funny he's not back yet," she said, unable to conceal the worry in her voice. "It'll be rainin' soon. Skinny's always been able to judge a desert storm—how soon one will come, how long it will last, how much rain it will drop."

Wolf slid his bowl and bread plate away, finished the coffee Violet had served in a tin cup, and slid his chair back from the table. "I'm gonna head back to the canyon."

Violet looked up at him. "No, I'll go. You stay here and rest. I'm sure he's on the way. I'll likely run into him not ten min—"

Stockburn rose from his chair and held out his hand to her. "We'll both go."

CHAPTER 7

The wind blew and the plum-colored sky spit rain as Stockburn and Violet made their way back in the direction of the canyon—Stockburn astride his gray stallion, Violet riding one of her big, loose-jointed brindle mules.

He followed the girl through the wind-jostled chaparral, thunder rumbling more and more threateningly, distant witches' fingers of glinting blue lightning flashing above craggy ridges. Wind-blown dust swirled, pelting them along with the first drops of the cold rain.

"Gonna be a gully-washer!" Violet cried above the storm's growing din as she reined her mount up at the edge of the narrow chasm, which was like the slash of a giant knife gouging a jagged wound in the desert floor.

As she leaped out of her saddle, Stockburn swung down from Smoke's back to her right, near a rocky escarpment jutting up at the very edge of the canyon.

Violet led the mule onto a trail that dropped at a slant down the canyon wall behind the escarpment. Stockburn followed, leading Smoke. Neither the horse nor the mule was happy about being out in the storm. Smoke merely whinnied and shook his head. The mule brayed and occasionally stopped, stubbornly digging its front hooves into the ground. Violet angrily whipped the beast's withers with her rein ends, cursing and yelling, "I wouldn't be out here if I didn't *have* to be, Rowdy, you cussed fool!"

The mount gave a few more obstinate brays then, acquiescing to the girl's wishes, continued following her orders down into the canyon.

When they acquired the canyon floor a few minutes later, Violet led the mule along the floor to the east. After about two hundred feet they came to a tall wall of crenellated granite and limestone splitting the canyon in two. Violet led the mule down the right tine in the fork. Stockburn and Smoke followed close on Rowdy's heels.

Looking around the mule and the girl leading it, Stockburn saw the dark entrance of a mine shaft just ahead. At the base of the canyon's right wall the mine lay where the side canyon they were following curved sharply to the left. Violet must have found Stockburn beyond that left dogleg after his tumble down the ridge with that bullet-carved furrow in his temple.

Skinny McDonald's mule and his two burros stood where Skinny had tied them to picket pins on the near side of the shaft he'd dug into the ridge. All three animals were sort of hunched against the storm, the mule braying, the wind whipping the animals' manes and tails out to the right at sharp angles.

Cold tendrils of dread splayed themselves across Stockburn's back. Something wasn't right. He could feel the foreboding right down to his toes.

As Violet approached her father's mule and the pack burros, Stockburn dropped Smoke's reins. "Stay, boy!" He ran up around the mule and Violet and grabbed her arm.

"Wait here!" he yelled above the building storm.

She looked up at him, brows furrowed, worried eyes cast with an appalling understanding.

Stockburn turned away from her and strode quickly up to the mine entrance. Crouching, he peered inside. The light penetrated only a few feet. He removed his wind-battered sombrero then, crouching low because the shaft was several inches shorter than he was, sidestepped into the mine. He closed his right gloved hand around the ivory grips of the Peacemaker holstered on his right thigh.

He moved a few feet beyond where the light penetrated and stopped suddenly. Something moved on the floor, a shade less dark than the floor itself. The lighter shadow took the shape of a man. As Wolf's eyes adjusted to the dim light, he saw that the movement was at the fallen man's midsection. His belly was expanding and contracting wildly as he breathed.

"McDonald?" Wolf hurried forward and dropped to a knee.

Before him lay Skinny McDonald, all right. Wolf had only glimpsed the man from half consciousness, and heard his voice from the same, but the bearded desert rat who lay before him was old and skinny. He also had a gaping wound in his guts. He clamped his lumpy, arthritic hands over the wound but it wasn't doing enough to hold the blood and viscera inside him.

Stockburn smelled the stench of a torn bowel. He cursed. The man was a goner.

The crunch of gravel sounded behind Wolf. Violet's voice said haltingly, thinly, "Papa?"

She dropped to a knee on the other side of the old man. She sobbed and placed a hand on his spindly shoulder. "Oh, Papa—what happened?"

"Ah, hell," Skinny said in a pain-pinched, anguished voice. "I reckon . . . I reckon I'm a goner, honey. I'm so sorry." The old man sobbed. Tears shone in his eyes.

Violet crouched over him, sobbing. "Papa, what happened?"

Skinny looked from his daughter to Stockburn then back to Violet again. "There . . . was two of 'em. Nasty pair of curly wolves as I ever seen. Cold-eyed. Mean."

"Why'd they stab you?" Stockburn asked. He already knew the answer and it was tearing him up inside. But he had to hear it from Skinny.

"They wanted to know . . . where . . ."

"I was."

Skinny nodded, grimacing with pain. "D-don't worry. I didn't tell 'em." He hardened his jaws and his eyes though tears continued to run down his craggy, bearded face. "I wouldn't tell 'em. I'd never tell 'em and endanger you, honey." He looked at Violet, who lowered her head and wept. He placed one of his hands on hers, and squeezed. "But you . . . gotta leave, now . . . you hear? Sooner or later, they'll find the cabin. They figured we had one . . . near."

Skinny reached into his shirt pocket and pulled out a small gold nugget, a little larger than a sewing thimble. He pressed it into Violet's hand, closed her fingers around it. "Take that. I found another'n. The other two are in that sock in the cabin. You know where it is. A nice stake for you."

Violet lay her head down on her father's chest. "Oh, Papa!"

"Skinny, what did they look like?" Stockburn asked,

squeezing the old man's shoulder in desperation, fury burning inside him.

"Storm was on the way. It was too dark. C-couldn't see . . . much . . ."

"Big, small, short, tall—*anything!*"

Skinny winced and stared at the ceiling, pondering through the pain spasms. "One I think was blond. Had cold pale eyes. Blue eyes. Crazy eyes." He brushed his hand across his forehead. "Devil's eyes!"

Stockburn nodded, remembering the distinctive eyes of the man who'd shot him. "Anything else?"

Skinny gave his head a quick shake. He looked at Stockburn gravely. "Mister . . . ?"

Wolf looked at him.

"Take my daughter out of here, and end this for me, will you? The pain is somethin' awful. *Oh, lordy!* They stuck me just deep enough to grieve me for a good, long time. Not to kill me right off. I'll die for sure. I can smell my own guts. Oh, lordy, I just can't take it anymore!"

Skinny arched his back, kicked his skinny legs, and howled in bestial misery.

Wolf looked at Violet. She looked back at him. Her eyes hardened. The tears stopped running down her cheeks. She swabbed a shirtsleeve across her cheek, and nodded.

"I'll go." Turning to Skinny, she said, "Goodbye, Papa. I love you."

By now Skinny was so out of his head with agony all he could do was moan and wail and stare wide-eyed at the ceiling.

Violet rose to her feet, looked at Wolf and said, "Please . . . end this!"

Sobbing again, she swung around and hurried back out of the cave.

Stockburn placed his left hand consolingly on Skinny's left shoulder. With his right hand, he slid the right-hand Colt from its holster.

A minute later, he emerged from the cave with Skinny's body hanging slack in his arms. He lay the body down on the ground. The rain was coming hard. Already the canyon was flooding. Lightning flashed and thunder peeled, causing the ground to shake.

Violet dropped to her knees and flung herself atop the old man's body, bawling.

In the pouring rain, Stockburn tied Skinny's body belly down over the back of the old man's mule.

He and Violet would have waited out the storm in the cave, but the canyon was flooding. Water churned at their feet, rising to their ankles. They had to get out of there or risk drowning. Leading Smoke and the mules and burros up out of the canyon took some time. The mules and burros balked at the storm. The steep trail, paved with slide rock in places, slick clay mud in others, had been rendered treacherous by the rain. Even Smoke, usually the most surefooted of mounts, had trouble with it.

When they finally rode up to the small stone stable flanking the shack, Wolf and Violet were soaked clean through. Stockburn had given Violet his yellow oil slicker, but by the time she'd put it on, she was already as soaked as if she'd taken a swim.

Dismounting in front of the stable, Wolf turned to Violet. "You go into the cabin, honey. I'll tend your father and these animals. Get a fire goin' and get yourself—"

"No," Violet said, shaking her head. "I want to help." She paused and gave Wolf a direct look. "I have to help."

More tears oozed out of her eyes though the eyes themselves remained opaque with shock and anger. He could see the tears in the light of a near lightning flash. The flashing tears quickly merged with the rain.

Stockburn nodded. He knew how she felt. She wanted to see it through to the end with Skinny. He was dead but he was still very much alive in her heart.

Together, Wolf and Violet got Skinny safely stowed away in the stable, supported by a couple of saddle trees in a side room, and covered with a pair of wool saddle blankets. He'd keep there until they could bury him the next day. They tended the mounts, removing their tack and rubbing them each down carefully with scraps cut from burlap feed sacks. By the time they'd fed the mounts a bait of cracked corn apiece, fresh water from a rain barrel, and hay, all five animals were relatively content though they still started at the thunder claps.

Stockburn didn't blame them. It was a ferocious storm. But, then, that was the only kind the desert knew at the tail end of summer, which was monsoon season.

Hunched against the rain, Wolf and Violet closed the stable door, secured it, and then hurried around to the front of the cabin. Violet mounted the stoop and leaned forward to reach for the door handle.

Wolf grabbed her arm and pulled her back. "Hold it," he said above the pouring rain and the rush of the wind. "Let me go in first."

Violet looked at him curiously. The light of understanding flashed in her eyes. It was a grim, wary light. She nodded and stepped to one side.

Stockburn pulled his left-side Peacemaker, clicked the hammer back, and shoved open the door. He stepped quickly inside and to the left, extending the big Colt straight out in front of him, squinting into the cabin's thick shadows relieved only by the soft blue of lightning flares on the ridge behind him.

In those brief flashes, he inspected the cabin, half expecting to find guests. The deadly kind. He was only half relieved to find the cabin empty. He'd love to be able to relieve the fury burning inside him by punching the tickets of the two devils that had tortured Skinny and left Violet without a father.

It was just as well that they hadn't come, though. No point in putting Violet through anymore hell that cold, stormy desert night.

"All clear," Wolf said, lowering the Colt and closing a shutter against the storm.

Shivering, cold and in shock, Violet moved as though in a trance as she closed one shutter herself.

When Wolf had shuttered the last window, he pulled a blanket off of one of the cabin's two cots, wrapped it around the girl, and eased her into a chair at the table. "Sit down there," he said gently. "I'll get a fire going, put some coffee on." He, too, was shivering.

Shrugging out of his wet coat, he walked onto the stoop, shook the excess water out of the coat, and hung it and his hat on a hook, then removed his vest, as well, and hung it on another hook beside the coat and hat. He got to work coaxing a fire to life in the range, using the still-smoldering coals from earlier. He filled a coffee pot with water from the rain barrel, and set it to boil on the range.

He turned to Violet. She sat shivering in the chair, staring at the floor, her eyes wide with grief. Her lips moved but she wasn't saying anything. Her wet hair clung to her cheeks.

Again, Stockburn walked over to the girl, dropped to

one knee before her, and placed a hand on her knee. "Can you stand, honey? You'd best get undressed. Those clothes are wet and they're keeping you chilled."

She slid her gaze to him. He wasn't sure she'd heard what he'd said until she swallowed and gave a little nod.

Stockburn rose then gently pulled her up out of the chair. He lifted the blanket from her shoulders, held it up in front of him, and turned his head to one side.

"Get undressed. I'll set your clothes out in front of the range to dry. Don't worry. I won't look."

Slowly, facing him, staring at his chest though he didn't think she saw much of anything except her father lying dead in that cave, she started to unbutton her blouse. Her fingers were quivering, making the job next to impossible.

Finally, she squeezed her pale, quivering hands together, lifted her eyes to his, and said quietly, "Would you help me?"

Stockburn considered the plea for a few awkward seconds, then nodded. He dropped the blanket on the chair then stood before her, unbuttoning her man's wool work shirt that clung to her like a second skin. When he'd stripped the wet shirt from her shoulders, leaving only a revealing, wash-worn cambric chemise, he eased her back down in the chair, removed her boots and socks one at a time, and unbuttoned her denim trousers.

It took him some time to peel the soaked denims down her pale legs. She helped a little, but mostly she sat shivering and staring off into the cabin's deep shadows relieved only by the lightning flashes beyond the shuttered windows.

The rain rushed down on the shack. The violence of the rain and the thunder made the shack's hard-packed earthen floor quiver.

Stockburn was going to leave her pantalets on but just as he set the denims aside, Violet slid her fingers beneath the pantalets' waistband and began sliding the insubstantial garment down her thighs. She stopped at the knees, leaving the rest to Wolf, who slid them down to her ankles and then over each of her feet in turn. By the time he had the bloomers off, she was already lifting the chemise up over her head. She tossed the soaked undergarment across the table and onto the chair nearest the range.

Stockburn rose and reached for the blanket to cover her, but before he could grab it, she rose from the chair, facing him, and began unbuttoning his shirt. "Now you," she whispered.

He frowned down at her. Her hands were still quivering, but not as violently as before. He lifted his hands to unbutton his shirt then lowered them when he saw that Violet seemed intent on doing the job herself.

She stared at his chest again as she peeled the shirt down his broad shoulders, but he could see that her eyes were focused. She was no longer in that dark cave. She was here in the cabin. Her eyes owned a strange feverishness. Her chest rose and fell heavily as she breathed. In the intermittent lightning flashes, he saw the chicken flesh rising across her slender shoulders, down her long, pale arms.

A lump rose in Wolf's throat. A wild, animal heat touched his loins, hot blood surged in his veins.

He kicked out of his boots and helped Violet with his pants and his short summer underwear and undershirt until he stood naked before the shivering girl who was almost panting now with her own untethered heat raging inside her, fighting off the storm's chill, moving her closer to the tall man before her.

She looked up at him. She wrapped her arms around his

neck, and parted her lips. She pressed her chest and her legs up against him, set each bare foot in turn atop his. Suddenly he found his left hand on her shoulder, the other hand against the back of her neck, over her wet hair, tipping her head back, her face toward his.

He closed his mouth over hers.

CHAPTER 8

"Papa!"

The girl's scream plucked Stockburn out of a deep sleep. He turned to see Violet sitting upright in bed beside him, breathing hard. Slowly, as the dream dwindled and she realized she'd been dreaming, she closed her right hand over her mouth.

"Oh, darlin'," Wolf said, sitting up and wrapping his left arm around her shoulders. "I'm so sorry."

She sniffed and turned to him. "I dreamt Skinny was trapped in that mine. I always worried when he was working alone in there, that the damn thing would collapse on him. And I couldn't get to him in time. That's what happened to his friend, Hans Sweitzer. I always figured that's how Skinny would die. I never figured . . ."

Stockburn drew her against him, hugged her tightly, and rocked her gently. "I'm so sorry, darlin'. It's all my damn fault."

"No, it's not, Wolf," she said in a small voice against his chest.

"Oh, sure it is. If—"

Violet pulled her head away from his chest. "If you hadn't been shot by those two killers . . . and you hadn't fallen into the canyon? Is that what you mean, Wolf? Well, you had nothing to do with either one of those things. You were just trying to do your job. It was just bad luck, pure and simple. I miss Papa somethin' awful. I still can't wrap my mind around him bein' gone. It just doesn't seem possible." She shook her head slowly as tears streaked her cheeks. "But I don't blame you, Wolf. And you shouldn't blame yourself."

"How can I not? You're without a father now. You'd still have him if I hadn't tumbled into that canyon, even if I was shot into it." Violet opened her mouth to object; Wolf placed a finger over her lips, stopping her. "You're not safe here now. Those two killers might keep scouring the desert around the mine. Eventually, they'll find the cabin."

"I'm not afraid. Papa taught me how to shoot. I can take care of myself, Wolf. Besides . . . where would I go?"

"Why not Las Cruces? That's where I'll be headed after I dig up Tomasito."

Violet jerked her head back, making a face. "Dig him up? Why on earth . . . ?"

"Because I shot him. I'll take responsibility for him. I had to shoot him. I had no choice. Either his brother accepts that or he doesn't."

Violet shook her head slowly, darkly. "You don't know Rafael Sanchez, Wolf."

"I 'spect I'll get to know him."

"I think I'd be safer here than ridin' into Las Cruces with you. No offense, Wolf, but I'll manage right here just fine."

Stockburn sighed, drew his mouth corners down. He sandwiched her head in his hands and kissed her forehead. "Your pa wanted you to leave. He left you a stake."

"I'm home here."

"Lonely damn life for a girl. Even lonelier now without Skinny. You oughta go to town and find a man."

She shaped a sly smile. "Are you proposing, Wolf?"

He snorted a laugh. "I'm too old for you."

"After last night, I know that ain't true," she said with a coquettish air, reaching for him.

Wolf snorted again, threw his covers back, and dropped his feet to the floor. "That was a mistake. I hope you don't regret it. Going to bed with a man twice your age . . ."

"I enjoyed it. It was a nice distraction. Not that that was all it was. Hey, where you going? It's still dark. Come back to bed, you! I'm not through with you yet. I think I could get used to . . . last night." She smiled intimately and hiked a bare shoulder. She seemed to have no desire to cover her nakedness. But, then, after what they'd done together, why should she? "That was my first time, you know."

That had been obvious. In a good way, not a bad way. "It should have been a young man, Violet."

"I got no complaints. Where are you going? It's still dark outside."

He was stumbling around, retrieving his clothes from where he'd placed them with Violet's to dry in front of the fire. His head felt fine. At least, much better than it had only a few hours ago. He could thank Violet for that in more ways than one. He didn't usually sleep with young women. He usually preferred women with some years and maturity on them. Also, he thought young women deserved younger men. After last night, however, he thought his conviction on the matter might be faltering a little.

No. That was a one-time thing. Like she said, she'd needed the distraction from her agony, and he'd been happy to provide it for her. *Don't let her believe it was anything more than that, because it wasn't. She's young*

*and inexperienced. Lonely and vulnerable, besides. She
needs to look elsewhere for a man.*

"I have a long day ahead," Wolf said, pulling on his
pants. "I'd best get started on it."

"You're not going anywhere until you've had breakfast
first!" She hustled out of bed. Without wrapping herself in
a blanket or anything else, she started waltzing around
the kitchen, naked as the day she was born, jiggling beguil-
ingly as she set to work building a fire.

Wolf stopped unbuttoning his pants to watch her, smiling. She might not have been debutante-pretty, but at the
moment—naked and flushed from her first time—he believed she was the most beautiful woman he'd ever known.

He plopped himself into a chair. "All right." He had to
give her some time to get used to the notion of living
alone. "If you insist, Miss McDonald."

She smiled at him over her bare right shoulder, swinging
her long, flaxen hair. "I insist, Mr. Stockburn." She frowned.
"Hey, stop staring at my fat behind."

"Your behind is beautiful."

"Oh, go to hell!" she said, turning her face back forward, blushing.

Wolf and Violet had a slow, leisurely breakfast together.

They didn't say much. Wolf didn't try to get her to talk.
He knew the distraction of the previous night, him and her
together, was wearing off. The cold reality of the new day,
even dawning as bright and beautiful as it was, with the
rain seeping into the sand, was building in Violet's awareness. He could see the anxiousness grow in her eyes as
they sat sipping coffee at the table together, Wolf rolling a
quirley from his Durham sack and smoking it.

He was desperate to get moving, to find out what had

happened to the train. And to get after the men who'd killed Skinny.

He didn't let on to Violet, however. He wanted to stay with her for a brief time this morning, lending as much comfort as he could. He thought he'd help her dig a grave for Skinny and then help her with the burial, but when he mentioned it, she shook her head as she gazed over her steaming coffee cup toward the sunlit yard beyond the open window flanking Stockburn.

"You have your business to tend, Wolf," she said quietly, grimly. "I have mine."

"You're sure you don't need any help?"

She pursed her lips, shook her head. "I'll manage. I'll let the ground dry out a little then turn him under, say a few words over him. That will be that." He thought her fateful resignation was phony, but maybe it was a good start on the real thing.

Wolf leaned forward, closed his hand over her wrist. "In a few days, I'm going to come back out here to check on you."

She gave a wan half smile. "Thanks. I'll be fine."

"You sure you won't ride to town with me?"

"I'll stick out the summer here, maybe do a little more picking and digging, build that stake a little bigger. Then I'll leave. I don't know where I'll go. I'll figure it out."

Wolf glanced at an old Spencer carbine leaning in a corner of the cabin. "You know how to use that thing?"

Violet nodded.

"Keep your eyes and ears skinned—all right, honey?" Wolf squeezed her wrist a little harder. "If they come—a tall, sandy-haired man and a blond with the coldest blue eyes you've ever seen—either run and hide or blow 'em out of their boots. No questions asked. All right?"

She smiled shrewdly across the table at him, squinting

one eye. "I think you know me well enough by now to know which one I'll choose."

"I had a feeling you would, darlin'." Wolf winked at her and squeezed her hand. "I had a feeling you would."

An hour later, Stockburn took his time leading Smoke down into the canyon in which Skinny McDonald's mine lay. The trail was still wet and dangerous. Neither he nor the horse needed a broken leg.

The canyon itself was still damp but no longer a churning river or even a creek. After the hot sunlight had reached the canyon floor, dry patches of sand and gravel could already be seen. The water had run on down the arroyo or seeped into the ground, making way for yet another gully-washer later this afternoon.

Stockburn stopped at the mine and took a good look around, wondering if the two killers had left anything behind that might identify them. As he'd expected, if anything had been left, the storm had washed it away. Certainly, no prints remained.

Cursing his luck, he continued on up the canyon, passing the spot at which Violet's and her father's fates had become entwined with his, where Violet had found him lying belly down with that notch in his skull. He'd have given anything for it to have turned out differently—even if it meant that bullet had smashed his skull a little to the right, killing him outright. Maybe then Violet would have left him there, and the killers likely would have been content to have made water on his carcass and moved on, having no reason to investigate the canyon further and find Skinny at work in his mine.

Far better to die than to be the cause of someone else's demise, to leave a young woman without her beloved father.

But that's how it had happened. So, with a chip on his shoulder, and following the directions Violet had laid out for him, he continued on up the canyon until he found a trail up to the rim. He led Smoke away from the rim and back over to where he'd shot the young man, Tomacito, and where one of the masked shooters had shot Stockburn back into the canyon.

He felt as though he were going back in time—to a time long ago though it was less than forty-eight hours. Such a short time. But, then, it didn't take long for the Fates to clean the table in grand fashion according to a plan known only to them. They were cheaters, the Fates. They were not to be gambled with.

Wolf led the mount around behind the escarpment from which Tomacito had born down on Stockburn with his carbine. He saw the splash of blood in the rocks where the boy must have died. And then he found the low mound of rocks and gravel not far from where the boy had breathed his last and which marked the spot where Violet had buried him—near a gnarled cedar at the base of another scarp of weather-molded sandstone.

Soft thumping sounds sounded to Wolf's right. He stopped and turned to see the gray-brown blurs of two or three coyotes—or what must have been coyotes though he couldn't see them clearly—scampering off through the chaparral. Sure enough, coyote prints lay in the still-damp caliche around the makeshift grave. It appeared that Wolf had come in the nick of time. The coyotes had smelled the carrion and had started uncovering the remains.

A small patch of torn red cloth poked up between two rocks Violet had mounded over the grave. The boy's shirt.

Stockburn sighed.

He dropped Smoke's reins, took a few sips of water from his canteen, then dropped to his knees and went to work on the grim task of removing the sand, gravel and rocks until the open eyes of Tomacito Sanchez gazed up at him in death, a puckered blue hole marring the boy's otherwise unblemished forehead.

CHAPTER 9

Violet grunted, breathing hard, as she carried Skinny up the low hill just south of the cabin. She thought the hill, with a good view of the cabin and stable on one side and a pretty, red stone arroyo on the other, would be a good place to bury the old man—her father, though he often seemed more like a grandfather. He was so much older than her and even her deceased mother.

In the far distance to the northwest was the long, toothy line of the Organ Mountains, the light continuously playing across them throughout the day, sometimes changing them drastically in shape, color, and even size. Skinny often went up there in the early evening just before the sun went down, to sit and smoke his pipe while taking in the view and the quiet songs of the desert birds.

Violet liked the idea of him being close to her even in death. She liked the idea of being able to look up and see his grave. She also liked the idea that Skinny could keep a watchful eye on her, in return, even though she didn't really believe the dead could see anything. At least, she didn't think she did. She'd never had much time to play with such thoughts. She'd always been too busy with chores or helping Skinny dig for gold.

She was not the fanciful type. At least, she'd never considered herself to be. Maybe she'd been wrong.

When she reached the top of the knoll, she dropped to her knees and lay Skinny down beside a paloverde. She dropped him harder than she'd intended; the slack body wrapped in a saddle blanket struck the ground with a hard smacking sound.

"Sorry, Pa," Violet said, wincing. The climb had tired her more than she'd thought it would. Maybe part of the reason for that lay in the fact she hadn't gotten all that much sleep last night. The thought brought a sheepish warmth to her face. She probably would have felt guiltier about what she and Wolf had done, with Skinny growing cold out in the stable, if she hadn't known Skinny would not only have approved, he'd likely have clapped and whooped in celebration.

He'd been telling Violet for the past two years, ever since she'd turned eighteen, that she needed to take a break from burrowing around in the desert with her old man and to go to town and get "her ashes hauled." Well, she'd gotten them hauled, all right. The big railroad detective, as gentle as he was handsome, had been a great comfort as well as a distraction for her.

She shook her head to bring herself back to reality and reached forward to arrange the blanket over Skinny's face, for a flap of the blanket had fallen open to expose one half-open eye. When she'd rearranged the blanket to cover the eye, she walked over to where she'd leaned a shovel up against a juniper. She grabbed the shovel then stopped, remembering she'd intended to bring the old Spencer rifle up, as well.

She should have a gun within reach at all times. Wolf had been right—the two men who'd killed Skinny might keep looking for Stockburn and eventually end up at the cabin. If they did, there was little doubt Violet would end up just as her father had.

Or, men being men, raped first and then killed.

Violet glanced down at Skinny, then at the cabin that lay about a hundred feet from the base of the knoll to the north. She was reluctant to leave Skinny by himself. But then, at midmorning she doubted any predators were near. Besides, she'd be gone only a minute or two.

She set the shovel down against the tree then headed back down the knoll in the direction of the house. She gained the bottom of the knoll and, taking long strides, crossed to the house, mounted the stoop beneath the brush arbor, and shoved the door open. She went inside and emerged a few seconds later, stepping out onto the front stoop with the rifle in her hands.

She stopped to make sure the old .56 carbine, which Skinny had won from a buffalo hunter several years ago in a poker game in Mesila, and which he'd still used for hunting, was loaded. It was. Violet jacked a round into the action then depressed the heavy hammer. Holding the rifle in both hands across her waist, she stepped off the stoop and began retracing her steps up the side of the knoll.

It was getting hot, the cicadas were screeching, and the air was heavy from the previous night's storm.

Again, when she reached the knoll's crown, she was breathing hard and sweating. She should probably wait to dig the grave later in the day, when it was cooler, but she felt the need to get Skinny in the ground. Not weighing much over a hundred pounds, even in life he'd seemed vulnerable somehow—as insubstantial as a dry stick. Dead, he seemed even more exposed and at the mercy of the elements.

Violet's mind wouldn't rest until she had her father

safely interred with rocks mounded over his grave against carrion eaters.

She glanced down at the blanket-wrapped body, and frowned.

Again, a flap of the blanket had been pulled back, exposing that one, droopy-lidded eye. How had that happened? She was sure she'd tucked the flap down securely.

With no wind or even a breeze, it couldn't have come open by itself. Unless a bird had opened it. She looked around, curious. A little apprehensive.

Distantly, a couple of crows cawed. Were they the culprits? Had they or one of them dropped onto Skinny while Violet had gone to the cabin and then disappeared before she'd returned?

What other explanation could there be?

Violet looked around again slowly, carefully. A slight breeze sifted through the junipers and mesquites. Except for the cicadas, that was the only sound, the only movement. Violet nodded. Yeah, the crows must have opened the flap. Still, a strange apprehension touched her.

She was reluctant to set the rifle down. But the grave wasn't going to dig itself.

She set the rifle down against the tree, picked up the shovel, and stepped over to where she'd decided to dig the grave, about six feet north of Skinny's blanket-wrapped body. She looked around again carefully, an odd sensation of being watched gripping her.

She could see no one—only the desert scrub and clay-colored rocks and the cabin and stable to the north of the hill. Nothing moved around either building except the mules and the burros in the stable's corral. They stood sleepily in the shade of the brush arbor, heads and tails drooping. The only sound was the breeze.

Just her imagination. She'd never felt so alone. Skinny

was dead. Stockburn had been there only a couple of days. He'd shared her bed, gotten closer to her than any man ever had before, and then he too was gone. That was the problem. She'd never *been* so alone. Not so completely and utterly alone. Skinny was never coming back, and that was a hard idea to wrap her mind around.

Naturally, she was fearful. It made sense that she would make up threats in her head.

She dragged a breath deep into her lungs, shook her head as though to clear the clinging, uncomfortable thoughts, then used her right foot to stab the spade into the ground. She tossed the sand and gravel aside. Soon, working steadily in the hot sun, which she was accustomed to doing, having been raised in the desert, she had a good-sized pile of dirt beside a roughly foot-and-a-half deep hole.

She was about to plunge the spade into the ground again when something dropped with a thud onto the ground to her right. She turned her head quickly to see a small rock roll to a stop only a few feet away. She turned still farther to peer behind her, squeezing the shovel in her gloved hands, heart quickening again with fear.

Someone had thrown the rock. It hadn't thrown itself.

Unless she herself had flung it that far with the shovel. No. She'd already unloaded the last load of sand and gravel. The stone had landed beside her several seconds later. It couldn't have come from the shovel.

Fear built in her—a growing chill rising from the base of her spine.

"Who's there?" she called, hating the hollow, frightened sound of her voice.

She stared at a gently bobbing mesquite branch, trying to see behind it. She squeezed the shovel even harder, wishing it was the rifle. She should go over and retrieve the rifle. She knew she should, but she suddenly couldn't get her feet to move.

As she craned her neck to peer behind her, a thump sounded from in front of her.

With a gasp, she swung her head to stare back forward. Another small rock just then came to rest near the base of a paloverde about ten feet away from her.

"Who's there, dammit?" she called, louder and harder, anger beginning to mix with her fear. "Who's there? I know someone's here!"

It took some effort, but she got her right foot to move, and then her left one. Bunching her lips and hardening her jaws, she tossed the shovel aside and picked up the Spencer, ratcheted the hammer back, and aimed the carbine out from her right hip, swinging it slowly from right to left and back again, peering into the chaparral.

"I know you're here!" Rage was beginning to overpower her fear. "Show yourselves, you murderers!" Violet strode forward, nostrils flared, looking around carefully, wanting a target. "Show yourselves, you damn cowards!"

Suddenly, a face appeared between two mesquite branches fifteen feet away from her. "*Peek-a-boo!*" the man cried, bugging his pale blue eyes.

Violet stopped with a gasp, jerked up the Spencer, and squeezed the trigger. The rifle thundered. The bullet smashed into a branch where the man's mocking face had been a split second before. Half of the branch dropped to hang from the other half by a thin piece of green wood.

The man howled with mocking laughter.

"Damn you!" Violet cried, lowering the smoking rifle to work the Spencer's trigger guard cocking mechanism.

"Get her, Jess! Get her!" the man behind the mesquite bellowed.

As Violet raised the Spencer again, footsteps sounded

behind her as a long, slender shadow slid up over her right shoulder. Before she could turn, two big arms grabbed her around her waist from behind, and a man sour with the smell of wet wool and body odor picked her up off the ground. As he did, Violet kicked at him, cursing, trying to smash her elbows back against his head.

The first man—if there were only two—pushed through the mesquite branches, smiling coldly. He rushed toward Violet, ripped the Spencer from her hands, and flung it away. He grabbed Violet's face with one gloved hand, squeezing her lips together painfully, glaring at her. He had long, greasy blond hair and the cold, pale-blue eyes Stockburn had mentioned. Demonic eyes.

"Where's Stockburn, girl? You tell me or so help me!"

Violet jerked her face from his grip and glared at him, rage and fear a toxic mix inside her. "You . . . you killed my father. You murdered Skinny!"

The man behind her, keeping his ironlike grip around Violet's waist and holding her up off the ground, yelled, "Tell us where Stockburn is or you'll get the same, girl!"

"Only it's gonna be a lot slower for you!" shouted the blue-eyed devil facing Violet.

He took another step forward, thrust both hands at Violet, and ripped her wool shirt wide open. Buttons flew in all directions. He made a savage face as with another powerful thrust, he tore her chemise plum off her body and whipped it back behind him where the torn garment caught on a branch of the mesquite he'd been hiding behind.

He grabbed her breasts and squeezed painfully, shoving his ugly killer's face right up close to hers. His breath smelled like something dead. *"Where's Stockburn?"*

"Ow! You're hurting me!" Violet cried, sobbing now from fear, fury, and pain.

"You don't tell us what we wanna know, girl," the man

holding Violet warned, we're gonna rape you and stick a knife in your guts, just like we done the old man. An' then we're gonna leave you here to die *slow*!"

"You go to hell!" Violet cried.

She managed to swing her right boot up and plant it toe-first into the blue-eyed killer's crotch.

CHAPTER 10

The blue-eyed devil's face instantly turned pale except for the two forking blue veins bulging in his forehead. He gave a loud yelp then jackknifed over his unmentionables, covering the damaged extremities with his forearms. He lowered his head and nearly dropped to his knees, grimacing as pain overwhelmed him.

"Ow, *damn*!" said the man holding Violet. "You all right, Snake-Eye?"

Looking up, the brim of his black slouch hat rising and clearing his forehead, twin balls of steel fury shone with bayonet blades of bloody murder. "Give her to me," Snake-Eye said, quivering with quiet menace as he straightened slowly.

"Here you go," said the man holding Violet. Jess dropped her to her feet then gave her a powerful shove forward—right into Snake-Eye's arms.

"No!" Violet cried. "Let me go!"

Snake-Eye's unshaven face was a mask of savagery as he stuck one foot out and jerked her sideways, tripping her, thrusting her without mercy to the ground. She hit so hard stars danced in her eyes. Before she could push up on to her elbows, the man was on top of her, kissing her, biting her lips, grunting and cursing and thrusting his hips painfully against hers.

He lifted his head then grabbed the waistband of her pants in both hands, trying to pull her denims down off her hips. "Help me here, Jess!" he grunted, fumbling with Violet's belt buckle. "Help me get her pants off!"

"No!" Violet cried.

"Oh, yes!" The man called Snake-Eye laughed without an ounce of mirth, two inches from Violet's face. "Honey, you're about to be given the ride of your—"

Something smashed into the ground maybe six feet to Violet's left. She heard the thump and saw dust plume in the corner of her eye. A half second later, the crack of a rifle reached her ears.

Both men froze and looked at each other.

Another bullet plumed dirt to Violet's right, ringing shrilly off a rock. The crackling report followed a moment later.

Snake-Eye and Jess jerked their heads around then stared down the knoll in the direction of the cabin. As they did, Violet heard the growing thumps of a galloping horse as well as the metallic rasp of a rifle being cocked.

"Damn—it's him an' he's got the drop!" shouted Snake-Eye.

Quickly, gazing anxiously down the slope, he buttoned his pants then grabbed his hat and ran across the crown of the knoll, following Jess, who'd already bolted. Dazed, Violet sat up and shook her tangled, dust-streaked hair from her face. She stared down the slope up which a big man in a black coat, black sombrero, and black ribbon tie fluttering out from the collar of a white shirt was just then galloping a smoky-gray horse.

"Wolf," Violet heard herself whisper. "Wolf!" she sobbed.

Bounding up the knoll, Stockburn rammed another round into the Yellowboy's action, raised the rifle to his shoulder, and squeezed the trigger. He was firing blindly up toward the crown of the knoll. He pumped two more rounds at where the two men who'd been attacking Violet had disappeared, scrambling away as fast as two mules with tin cans tied to their tails.

Cowards.

They'd attack a girl but they didn't have the stomach for standing and facing the man they were after. They'd wait for better odds. On the other hand, Wolf was glad they hadn't stayed and fought but had fled. It's what he'd hoped they'd do. He hadn't wanted to risk Violet taking a bullet. That was why he'd fired wide, hoping to spook them off the girl, which he had.

Still, they were chicken-livered devils—that was for sure. At least, he knew the kind of men he was dealing with now. They'd kill and kill brutally—just like they'd killed poor Skinny Macdonald—but only when they had the odds.

Wolf wanted to continue after them, but he had to see to Violet.

He checked Smoke down in front of the girl, who lay on her side, closing her torn shirt over her bare breasts. She drew her knees toward her chest, eyes squeezed closed, sobbing.

Wolf leaped down from the saddle, hurried over to her, and dropped to both knees beside her. He set his rifle down and placed his hand on her arm. "Are you all right, honey?"

She sat up and flung herself into his arms, wailing. "Oh, Wolf—they were . . . they were . . ."

"I know, honey. I know. I saw."

As he'd approached the yard from the direction of the cabin, he'd heard her screams. He'd cut the blanket-wrapped body of Tomacito Sanchez free of Smoke's hindquarters then shucked his Yellowboy and flung lead up the knoll, wanting to get the men off of Violet first and foremost. He'd worry about running them to ground or killing them later.

"It's over now, honey," he said, holding her taut against his chest while she bawled. "They're gone."

"They killed Skinny, Wolf! They were the two who—"

"I know."

"Butchers!"

"I know, honey. Let it all out."

Violet looked up at him, tears flooding her eyes, rolling down her dirty cheeks. "They were going to . . . each one . . ."

"I know, but they didn't. They didn't hurt you too bad, did they? You'd tell me if they did, wouldn't you?"

Violet shook her head. "They didn't. Not too bad." A new rush of tears oozed out of her eyes. "Wolf, I was sooo scared!"

"I know you were, honey." He drew her against him again, squeezing her tightly, running his hands soothingly across her back, wanting to caress all of the terror from her bones. "I heard your screams. I could tell you were horrified. I felt so bad for you . . . so damn angry. I knew then that they'd come here . . . looking for me." Stockburn hardened his jaws and fired a hateful glare up at the crown of the knoll. When he ran those two to ground, they were going to pay hard. They were going to die howling.

He returned his attention to Violet. "Can you stand, honey? Let's get you down to the cabin. I'm gonna try to track those vermin."

She looked up at him, renewed fear in her eyes. "Don't leave me, Wolf. Please, don't leave . . . ?"

Stockburn nodded. "All right, I won't."

"I just . . . need a little time."

"I know you do, honey. That's fine. Let's get you back to the cabin. I can track them later."

"I hate to be such a baby. It's just . . . nothing like that's ever happened to me before."

"You're not a baby, Violet. You're frightened for a damn good reason." Nothing like that had ever happened to her before, and she didn't even have Skinny here to comfort her.

Stockburn helped her to her feet. She held her shirt closed with one hand as she walked over and crouched to retrieve her torn chemise. She looked sadly down at the blanket-wrapped body of her father, then at Wolf. "I have to bury Skinny."

"Let's get you down to the cabin and into a hot bath." Stockburn wrapped his arm around her shoulders and led her gently down the knoll toward the cabin. "I'll finish digging the grave. Then we'll bury him together."

Stockburn poured Violet a couple fingers of whiskey, and opened one of her favored beers. While the girl sat at the kitchen table gathering herself, sipping the beer and the whiskey, he heated water for her at the range, and filled a corrugated tin washtub.

When she was comfortably ensconced in the steaming water, he washed her back while she leaned forward,

hugging her knees. Leaving the whiskey and the beer on
a chair beside the tub, he rolled down his shirtsleeves and
buttoned the cuffs. He set his hat on his head, grabbed his
rifle, and headed for the door.

"You won't go far, will you, Wolf?" Violet sat with her
knees raised above the soapy water, resting her chin on
them, the frightened plea showing in her eyes.

Stockburn turned to her and gave her a reassuring
smile. "Not far at all. I'm just gonna dig that grave. I'll let
you know when I'm finished. Then we'll bury Skinny together."

"Those men. Those killers"—she flared a nostril, and
her eyes turned cold—"will . . . they . . . come back?"

"If so, I'll be ready for them." Wolf winked, then opened
the door and went out.

Smoke stood ground-tied at the hitch rack fronting the
cabin. Stockburn swung up into the saddle. As he turned
the horse around and put it up the knoll toward where
Skinny lay near the hole Violet had started digging for
him, he cast his gaze beyond the knoll toward the southwest where the two killers had headed. They'd probably
picketed their horses somewhere on the knoll's far side.
No telling where they'd lit out for when they'd mounted
up. Stockburn wanted to track them, but he wouldn't leave
Violet alone. Not after what had happened to her. If he
didn't get after them soon, their tracks would probably
be wiped out by the next monsoon rain, which would
likely hit in a few hours.

He'd have to let them go for now. He'd hunt them later,
after he'd figured out what to do with Violet. He didn't
want to leave her alone. He hoped he could convince her
to ride into Las Cruces with him. She'd be safer there than
at the cabin by herself.

Unless those two killers returned while he was still there, that was. Like he'd promised Violet, if they came, he'd be ready for them. They'd die hard. And then Violet's worries would be over.

About those two, at least.

She'd given Stockburn a fair description of each. She'd also said that they'd called each other Snake-Eye and Jess. The one with those devil's blue eyes was Snake-Eye, of course. The sandy-haired man with the Texas-creased brown Stetson was Jess. Stockburn couldn't remember any train robbers going by either name. Apparently, they'd heard of him, however, because the one who'd shot him, just before Stockburn had shot him, had called the detective by name.

It was almost as though they'd been waiting for him. As though they'd known he'd be on that train . . . which meant they must have someone feeding them information.

There was still much about the Boot Hill Express . . . and the fates of his two old express guard friends who'd been riding it . . . he had yet to investigate. He would do that as soon as he'd helped Violet lay Skinny to rest.

Near the top of the knoll, he stopped Smoke, ground reined the mount, hung his coat and hat on a cedar branch, picked up the shovel, and went to work. As he dug steadily, ignoring the slight remaining pain in his bullet-burned temple, he kept a close eye on the cabin as well as on his immediate surroundings.

Nothing moved around him. At least, nothing threatening. He had a feeling the two killers had, finding him in relatively good health, decided not to tangle with him anymore. They'd probably expected to find him laid up and defenseless.

They'd had a change of heart when they'd found out he was anything but.

They—or the leader of their stock-thieving gang—certainly wanted the Wells Fargo detective scoured from their trail. That must mean the cattle weren't that far away. At least, not in Mexico yet. They must be holding them somewhere nearby, and didn't want Stockburn running them down.

The ground was sandy with only a few rocks, so in a half hour he'd dug a rectangle roughly five feet deep. Standing in the grave, he was prying up one of the last rocks from the bottom when he heard a door latch click in the dry desert air. He turned to see Violet step out of the cabin in fresh denims and a red calico blouse.

Her damp hair, freshly brushed, shone in the sun as it flowed back behind her shoulders. She stepped off the stoop and climbed the knoll. Raising a half-smoked cigarette to her lips, she approached the grave with a pensive air.

She glanced at Wolf standing in the grave, his shirtsleeves rolled up his tanned, corded forearms, and smiled. "Thanks, Wolf. I should have dug the grave myself. I don't know what's gotten into me. I've never been a silly, simpering girl before. I've never much admired the type." She crossed her arms on her chest.

Stockburn hoisted himself up out of the grave. "You've been through a lot."

"You have a train robbery to investigate. Yet, you stayed here . . . with me." She frowned up at him, curious.

Stockburn walked up to her, planted a tender kiss on her forehead. "I couldn't leave you, Violet."

The girl had a hold on him. She was young enough to be his daughter, and he didn't easily tumble, but he'd tumbled for Violet McDonald. He felt an urgency to get after the train robbers, but that urgency was tempered by a reluctance to leave this singular young woman. He liked her tough but gentle spirit, and the way her eyes danced unexpectedly. Memories of last night—her first night with a man—haunted him, drawing him even closer to her.

He couldn't get too close, though. His time here was short. His time everywhere was short. He was a drifter. He might have a fancy badge tucked away in a leather wallet, and a steady if modest paycheck, but he was essentially a drifter. Always had been, always would be.

He smiled down at Violet, canted his head toward the blanket-wrapped body of her father. "Ready to say goodbye?"

Violet looked at Skinny, drew her mouth corners down, and nodded.

Stockburn used his lariat and two large slipknots to gentle Skinny into the grave. When the body lay where it would remain through the ages, he loosened the knot with a flick of his hands, and drew the rope up out of the grave.

He tossed the rope aside then reached for the shovel.

After he'd filled in the grave and he and Violet had mounded it with rocks to hold the predators at bay, both stood in silence on either side of it, Stockburn holding his sombrero down before him. Violet stood staring at the rocks with a searching expression.

"Any last words?" Wolf asked.

Violet raised her gaze to his. "I don't . . . know what to say, Wolf."

"Say what's in your heart."

Violet lowered her gaze to the grave again, and drew a deep breath, sliding her shoulders back. "Goodbye, Papa. I love you and I'm going to miss you. I hope we'll be

together again one day." She looked up at Wolf as though
for approval.

Stockburn smiled. "That wasn't so hard, now, was it?"

Violet gave him a wan half smile, dimpling her cheeks.

Stockburn glanced at the sky. Clouds were already
moving in.

"I'd best be pulling my picket pin." He walked around
the grave and placed his hands on the girl's shoulders,
tipped her chin toward his. "Won't you come to town with
me? I can protect you there. I can't protect you out here."

Violet placed her hand on his, caressed it gently, and
smiled up at him. "You won't have to. I'm as wily as a
jackrabbit now. I won't let my guard down. No one . . . and
I mean *no one* . . . will ever do anything like that to me
again." She hardened her jaws, shaking her head slowly.
"The fact is I'm alone now. I'd best start getting used to the
idea. I'm gonna stick it out here for the rest of the summer.
Follow Skinny's vein deeper into that shaft. When I have a
sizeable poke, I'll move on. Don't ask me where. I reckon
I'll know when I get there."

She broadened her smile. "Don't worry about me, Wolf.
I got gravel. Skinny always said so. You find out what
happened to the Boot Hill Express. You hunt the robbers.
Don't mind me. I can take care of myself."

She tucked her bottom lip under her upper front teeth,
blinked slowly, coyly. Those warm eyes danced again,
spectacularly. She rose up on the toes of her boots and
kissed his lips. "Thanks for last night. I will never forget
it . . . or the Wolf of the Rails."

Stockburn returned her kiss then mounted up and rode
back down to the cabin to tie the dead boy, Tomacito, to
Smoke's back, behind the saddle. He rode slowly away
from Violet still standing over her father's grave. A lonely
feeling dogged him.

He knew that loneliness. It was always there, haunting him since he'd been a boy, the way it does some people forever. Leaving Violet alone . . . partly due to him having brought bad luck to her and her father . . . made him keenly aware of the cold knife blade edge of it.

CHAPTER 11

Stockburn found little evidence of a train robbery on War Lance Pass. At least, no direct evidence.

He did find the overlaid tracks of many horses on both sides of the rails, possibly belonging to the men who'd robbed the train as well as to a posse that would likely have been sent out from Las Cruces to track the robbers.

The train itself as well any casualties, of course, had likely been trundled on into town.

Stockburn paused to give Smoke a breather, and both he and the horse a few sips of water, then made his way down from the craggy pass. He headed north and west toward the great stone sawblade of the Organ Mountains humping redly up out of the brown and lime-green desert before him. On the west side of those mountains, along the Rio Grande River, he'd find the little settlement of Las Cruces, which had grown up with the Atchison, Topeka & Santa Fe Railway.

By the time he reached town, the clouds had dispersed, reducing the threat of the monsoon rains at least for a time. The wind had kicked up, blowing the dust around the sprawling settlement's broad main street. Stockburn rode between the telegraph poles lined up along one side of the street and the transplanted mesquites along the other side, fronting the wood-frame or tile-roofed adobe business buildings as well as the large, Spanish-style Fountain Theater.

The wind appeared to be keeping most people indoors. A few dogs were on the prowl, and Stockburn passed a couple of ranch supply wagons driven by men crouched low in the drivers' boxes, holding their broad-brimmed hats on their heads, squinting against the grit. A few men lounged under the brush arbor fronting the El Paso Saloon on the corner of Main and Dona Ana Avenue—lean, sunburned men in cotton shirts, brightly colored neckerchiefs, and chaparajos—cow punchers likely taking some time off from one of the ranches dotting the verdant Mesilla Valley.

Stockburn stopped Smoke to gaze back over his shoulder, toward the town of Mesila that lay only a mile or so south of Las Cruces, where his pretty young friend, Sofia Vargas, worked with her mother in her mother's sewing and laundry shop. Wolf made a mental note to check in with the young woman before leaving the area. Together, they'd ventured into Mexico a few months back, along with Deputy U.S. Marshal "Lonesome" Charlie Murdoch. The unlikely trio had hunted a pack of vile killers led by the notorious Red Miller who'd murdered several good folks on the Texas side of the border, including Sofia's young husband, the express guard Billy Blythe.

Stockburn gave a little smile at the memory. It had been a rough and bloody trip, but a colorful one, as well. He hoped Sofia was doing all right. He had a feeling she was, for she'd taken up with the good-natured young drifter and sometime cow puncher, Hoot Gibson, who'd joined them in Mexico. Young Hoot had shadowed Miller's bunch after they'd murdered two of his cow-punching partners and stolen his horse.

When Stockburn had parted with Sofia, she and young Hoot had seemed awfully fond of each other. Hoot had been going to settle in Las Cruces and look for work on one of the area ranches. Wolf wondered how he'd fared. He'd find out later.

At the moment, he had the grim task of delivering the dead boy, Tomasito, to his brother, Rafael Sanchez, a deputy sheriff in Las Cruces and, according to Violet McDonald, a man to be reckoned with.

"Well, let's get the reckoning over with, pard," Stockburn said to himself. "Then you can get on with the main business of finding out what happened to the train." He nudged Smoke ahead with his boot heels, and continued forward, blinking against the blown dirt, goat heads, horse apples, and mesquite beans. He knew from previous visits that the court house was on Rio Grande Avenue, which was the next avenue ahead, to the north. He swung left down Rio Grande, paused briefly as a particularly nasty wind gust nearly blew him off his saddle, then reined Smoke up under the long brush arbor fronting the barracks-like, two-story adobe building with large painted letters running across its second story announcing DONA ANNA COUNTY COURTHOUSE.

A tall, dark man wearing a palm leaf sombrero stood beneath the arbor . He held a tin cup in one hand, a cane in the other hand. He had brown eyes and a mustache as well as a badly weathered and sun-seared look—the look of most Southwestern outdoor folk over the age of forty. With his dark gaze on the railroad detective, Sheriff Pete Rodriguez, winced noticeably and shook his head darkly. His thick, dark-brown, silver-stitched mustache rose to show the white line of his teeth, not with another wince but a curse.

Stockburn read the man's lips. He swung down from

Smoke's back and touched two fingers to his sombrero brim. "Hiya, Pete."

"Go to hell, Stockburn!" the man yelled beneath the wind. "You're trouble. You always *been* trouble. And now you're even packin' it across the back of your horse!" Like many Southwesterners, Rodriguez had been raised speaking Spanish and English, so he spoke both languages without a trace of an accent.

Stockburn tied Smoke to the hitch rack then faced the county sheriff again, drew a deep breath, and said, "Best come down here and take a look."

"Who is it?"

"Come down here and take a look."

"I can tell by the look on your face it ain't gonna be good."

"It's not." Stockburn glanced at the door and window flanking Rodriguez. He knew Rodriguez's office lay beyond that door and window, with the jail in the basement. "Your deputy here? Sanchez?"

Rodriguez canted his head to one side and narrowed an eye as he regarded Stockburn critically, pensively. The name *Sanchez* obviously hadn't landed well. Finally, he said, "Ah, hell."

He tipped back the last of his coffee, set the cup on the gallery rail, and limped down the three steps to the street. The last time Wolf had seen Rodriguez, the man had been limping from severe arthritis, the result of bones broken during his horse-breaking days. It appeared the sheriff's limp had gotten even worse. He moved more slowly, stiffly, leaning hard on the cane, and stretching his lips back from his teeth with every painful step.

He walked up to Stockburn, his gaze set confrontationally, and asked, "Why in hell are you asking about Sanchez?"

Wolf canted his head to indicate the dead boy hanging

over Smoke's back. Rodriguez followed his gaze, then shuttled his deep-set, dark-brown eyes back to Stockburn, and his expression grew even darker. "Don't tell me."

With another wince, he shuffled around Wolf and over to Smoke's left hip. He lifted the boy's head by its hair. He didn't have to look long at the slack face. He already knew who the dead kid was. He just had to confirm his suspicion. He released the hair and the kid's head slapped down against the horse's belly.

"Lordie!"

"It was him or me, Pete."

Rodriguez turned stiffly to Stockburn. "Don't doubt it a bit, but that don't matter. He's Rafael's younger brother. That kid was everything to Rafa. I mean, *everything*. Their parents are dead. Rafael was trying to get Tomacito on the straight an' narrow." He scowled suddenly, deep lines creasing his dark forehead beneath the brim of his sombrero, which the wind was threatening to rip from his head. "What are you doing here, anyway? You told me you was gonna scout the train. When you didn't show up when the train did . . . minus its load of cattle, I might add! . . . everyone thought you were dead."

"Close but no cigar." Stockburn pointed at his bandaged noggin, the bandage showing beneath his hat.

"Tomacito's?"

"No. One of the other train robbers."

"Tomacito was one of the train robbers?"

"One of the first batch, anyway."

Rodriguez's scowl deepened. "What the hell is that supposed to mean?"

"I wish I knew myself." Stockburn reached up to grab his sombrero brim to keep the wind from blowing it off his head. He narrowed an eye against a grit-laden wind gust. "I know the train was hit a second time. After I left it on the heels of Tomacito. What about the two guards in the express car?"

"Dead."

The word rocked Stockburn back on his heels. He'd anticipated the answer. Still, it was hard to lose friends. Especially those two old fellas so close to retirement. He and they had worked for Wells Fargo for a long time. He'd liked them both a lot.

Rodriguez continued. "Langenbottom trundled the train on into town once the robbers cleared out with all the cattle aboard. Damn near five hundred head of prime beef. The ranchers up in Bottleneck won't be amused. Some of them aren't going to be able to weather yet another loss." He paused, glanced at Tomacito again. The boy's dark-brown hair was blowing like a tumbleweed in the wind. "What's this about *batches* of train robbers?"

"The train was hit twice. Once when I was on it." Wolf glanced at the dead boy again. "The kid was one of those six. Then, after I leaped off the train on Tomacito's heels, I was shot by one of the men who intended to hit the train farther up the pass. I don't know what he and one other robber were doing out in the desert just then, when I happened to go after Tomacito. I'm thinking maybe they intended to board it. It was clipping along pretty slow as it neared the pass. They saw me and, recognizing me as a Wells Fargo agent, shot me to get me out of the way. That's the only way I can figure it."

"Tomacito's bunch *just happened* to hit the train before the second bunch hit it?"

"Sounds like it to me." A thought just then occurred to Wolf, and he scowled and looked off, teasing the notion like a fish on a line before he turned back to Rodriguez. "Unless the first bunch was sent in as a diversion."

Rodriguez drew a deep breath and released his hat, for

the wind seemed to be fading a little. "All I can tell you is that Rafael Rodriguez is going to be one piss-burned young deputy when he finds out that little broomtail brother of his is dead."

"Like I said, Pete, it was either him or me."

"Like *I* said, Wolf, it ain't gonna matter. Rafael is one hot-tempered ringtail. The town forced me to hire him because he is a good man—a good *gun*—to have on your side. Former outlaw himself, he got a wild hair to go straight after his old man, Juan Pablo, died. Though Rafael's way of going straight isn't exactly what most lawmen would call straight. But, he gets the job done. I sure as hell can't do it anymore." The sheriff tapped his foot with his cane. "My joints have all gone to hell. Can't even sit a horse anymore. Can barely hold a pistol. The whole county is waiting for the morning I can no longer crawl out of bed. Then they'll take my badge and pin it in it on Rafael's vest, and every rancher in Dona Ana County will rest a little easier. With the coming of the railroad, and the cattle boom up in the mountains, lawlessness has become a wildfire. I just can't keep up with it anymore. All I had was three deputies before Rafael came along, and now he does the work of all three of those scudders."

"Where are they?"

"They rode out to track the bunch that robbed the train!" Rodriguez said—again, as though he were talking to a moron. "Those five hundred cows they stole is as good as gold on the hoof. Do you know what the government is paying for beef these days? Hell, if I wasn't so stove up, I'd get back into ranching, though, just like gold, the boom is likely to bust. Sooner rather than later if we don't run these thieves to ground."

"I'm sorry about your troubles, Sheriff, but I got a few of my—"

"Shhh!"

Stockburn frowned at Rodriguez, who was scowling down the street to the south. "What is it?"

Rodriguez's joints might have been as lame as a toothless old horse headed to the glue factory, but he must have still had a good set of ears. Stockburn heard it a few seconds after the sheriff apparently had—the drumming of many galloping hooves.

The din grew louder and louder as Stockburn cast his gaze to the south. Gradually, a dozen or so men on horseback materialized like desert ghosts carried on the dusty wind.

Rodriguez flinched as he stared at the fast approaching riders led by a short, stocky young man in a red shirt and black hat riding a white-socked black stallion. "Well, I reckon you're about to meet the next sheriff of Dona Ana County whether you're ready to or not."

"I'm ready."

"Yeah?" Rodriguez said. "Well, I'm not."

CHAPTER 12

The posse thundered up to Stockburn and Sheriff Rodriguez, the ground reverberating beneath Wolf's boots until the dozen riders drew rein. The wind out of the northwest blew their dust against the buildings on the opposite side of the street from the courthouse.

Horses snorted, whickered, blew. A horse tied up the street whinnied; one of the posse mounts answered in kind. Several faces appeared in shop windows on both sides of the street. A few men stepped into open doorways, gazing toward where the posse milled in front of the courthouse, getting their sweat-silvered horses settled.

The posse leader, Rafael Sanchez, frowned curiously and with a customary arrogance and belligerence at Stockburn and Rodriguez, blinking against the wind beneath the brim of his low-crowned black sombrero. He booted his stallion up to within a few feet of the railroad detective and the sheriff, swept both with his incredulous, silently demanding gaze, then looked at the body sprawled belly down over Stockburn's horse.

With a dreadful knowledge touching him slowly and

against his will, he said, "What . . . what . . . ?" He looked at the body again.

The long, black hair and maybe the dead boy's denims and his red calico shirt and beaded necklace gave him away.

Terror touched Rafael's light-brown eyes. He looked at Stockburn again and said, "Who?"

Not waiting for an answer, he leaped out of his saddle—a medium tall, thick-shouldered, muscular man in his late-twenties and with longish hair curling down over his ears and the collar of his red cotton shirt with green piping and a green bandanna knotted around his neck. He wore a silver star proudly high on his left breast, chaparajos over black denims, and black boots with large silver spurs. He fairly lunged at the boy on Stockburn's horse, placing his hand on Tomacito's back then dropping to a squat to look up at the face hidden by the windblown hair.

He swept the hair away from the boy's face with one hand and gazed up in shock at the face of his dead brother. He made a strangling sound as he closed his eyes and pressed his forehead against his brother's left cheek. "No," he muttered, shaking his head. "No, no, no. Tomacito . . ." Placing both hands on the boy's head, Rafael swept the hair back from the wound in the boy's temple, touched the dried blood, then closed his eyes again. He pressed his forehead against the boy's dried wound, and shook his own head, sobbing. "No, no, no."

Stockburn and Rodriguez shared a fateful look.

The posse riders looked at each other, muttering, holding their sweat-lathered horses in check.

Stockburn felt a dull ache in his guts for the sobbing deputy.

Suddenly, Rafael stood and swung toward Stockburn

and Rodriguez, his eyes hard behind the sheen of tears, his jaws stiff. He was a handsome young man in an almost feminine way, with carefully sculpted features right down to the diamond-shaped cleft in his chin and the dimples in his cheeks. There was a granite hardness to his eyes, however. He placed a hand on one of the long-barreled Smith & Wessons holstered for the cross-draw high on each hip, in hand-tooled leather holsters, and, staring straight at Stockburn with no little accusing in his eyes, said, "Who did this?"

"I did."

Rafael drew the Smith & Wesson, aimed it straight out and slightly up at the taller man's head, and clicked the hammer back. "And who are you . . . *dead man*? We'll need a name for the marker."

Taking one quick step forward, Stockburn caught the firebrand deputy off guard. Before Rafael knew what was happening, Wolf had jerked the gun out of the deputy's hand, lowered it to his side, and stepped closer, his own raw anger glinting in his eyes.

"Pull your horns in and listen, you simple fool. I'm Wolf Stockburn. Railroad detective. Wells Fargo. If I'd shot your brother in cold blood, you think I would have brought him back to town?"

Rafael looked at the Smithy in Stockburn's hand. His eyes were as large as saucers. He couldn't believe the big man had been fast enough, and had gall enough, to take it away from him, nor that he'd allowed it to happen though he'd had little choice. Totally off guard, he flushed as a couple of the men behind him chuckled quietly, barely audibly, beneath the wind.

His eyes blazed again. "Never heard of you, Mister! Give me that damn pistol back, or—"

"Or you'll do what?" Stockburn tossed the gun away. It landed with a *plunk*. "Pull the other one? Go ahead. I'll take that one away from you, too, and shove it up your—"

"Hold on!" Sheriff Rodriguez interjected, limping up between the two men. "Stockburn is who he says he is, Rafael. Wells Fargo. I know him and will vouch for the man's integrity." He crooked a glowering stare up at the detective. "Though not always for his deportment."

Rafael swung his head and blazing eyes to the sheriff. "You saying my brother deserved to die, Rodriguez? You knew Tomacito! He was a good kid!"

"Rafael—now, listen. You know the boy was . . . was . . . well, having trouble settling down."

Rafael turned his enraged gaze back to Stockburn. "That doesn't mean he deserved a bullet!"

"He was robbing a train," Stockburn said, fists on his hips. "He laid a bead on me and was about to pull the trigger. I had no choice." He lowered his voice a little and added with genuine sympathy. "I'm sorry, Deputy. I wish it could have turned out different, but Tomacito gave me no choice."

"You say he was robbing a *train?*"

"He was with the first batch that robbed the train from Bottleneck."

"First *batch?*"

"Apparently, there were two sets of robbers," Rodriguez said. "Tomacito was with the first bunch. Stockburn took them all out. Including, unfortunately, Tomacito."

"That doesn't make any sense!" Rafael said. "Two batches of robbers?"

Stockburn looked at Rodriguez. "Did anyone talk to the passengers? They saw me take down the four aboard the passenger cars." What about the engineer or fireman?

Arnie and Jasper saw me knock out the man who'd entered the engine.

Rodriguez glanced at Rafael then switched his gaze back to Stockburn. He cleared his throat and looked down at his boots. "Well . . . they were pretty shaken up. And I reckon we just figured the robbers all wore masks, like usual."

"You didn't find any dead men aboard that train? Besides the express guards, I mean?"

"No!" Rodriguez said, suddenly defensive.

Rafael glared at Stockburn. "Even if there was a first batch of robbers, Tomacito would not have been one of them. He was a good boy. I got him straightened out. Sheriff, you know this. Tomacito worked up in Bottleneck swamping saloons and cutting firewood. Doing light carpentry. Tomacito was no train robber. He knows what would have happened if I'd caught him running with the wrong bunch."

Rafael looked at Stockburn again. He flared his nostrils as he took two quick steps back and snapped up his second Smith & Wesson. He smiled with menace as he clicked the hammer back and aimed at Stockburn's face, slowly moving his feet, staying just out of the bigger man's reach. "No, no. You murdered my brother in cold blood, amigo. I don't know how or where you ran into him. But you killed him in cold blood. Maybe by accident. I don't know. But you murdered my little brother, and I don't care if you are Wells Fargo, you won't—" He stopped as the metallic rasp of a cocking lever knifed through the wind, and a voice said, "Drop the hogleg, amigo! I have you dead to rights!"

Rafael looked around wildly. Stockburn looked around, as well. The voice was hard to pin down because of the wind, which muted it, muffled it, made it swirl around the street. Wolf thought it was a woman's voice.

"I said drop the pistol!" the voice came again. Sure enough—it belonged to a woman, all right.

Stockburn managed to follow it back to the opposite side of the street and up to a second-floor window of the Camino Real Hotel. A window was partway open. Through the gap poked a rifle barrel. Also through the gap, long, copper-red hair slithered, tossed to-and-fro in the wind, like red seaweed in swirling waters. Because of the sun glare on the window, Stockburn couldn't see the face behind the glass. Only the rifle, the hair, and the black-gloved hand wrapped around the Winchester's neck, the index finger hooked through the trigger guard.

Still holding the Smith & Wesson on Stockburn, Rafael stood frozen then let it sag. He stared toward the window, apparently as confused by the intrusion as Stockburn was. Sheriff Rodriguez and the posse riders were all staring toward that window and the beguiling red hair blowing out away from it, as well.

As though to jolt Rafael into action, the woman blew a round into the street, inches from the deputy's black, hand-tooled leather boots. The rifle's wail was swept up and away by the wind. Rafael cursed and leaped to one side, glaring up at the window. He tossed the Smithy away like a hot potato, to more chuckles of some of the posse riders.

He shot an angry glare at the posse men, who promptly sobered. Several reined their horses around and rode away. Several more followed, and then two and three more until only the other two men wearing five-pointed deputy sheriff's badges sat their horses in the street near Stockburn, Rafael, and Rodriguez.

The two deputies were trying not to smile as they shuttled

their gazes between Rafael and the red-hair billowing out the window around the protruding rifle barrel.

Furious, Rafael turned to Stockburn. "Who is that?"

"I have no idea." He was as befuddled as the stocky young deputy was.

Rafael looked at Rodriguez. The old sheriff shrugged.

Rafael walked over to Stockburn's horse and used a folding knife to cut his brother free of the horse's back. With a gentleness that touched Stockburn's heart, Rafael drew the small, stiffening body down from Smoke's back, shifted Tomasito in his arms and looked down at the face stretched taut across the broad cheekbones. The eyelids were partway open, the eyeballs glinting wanly in the washed-out afternoon light. The wind blew Tomacito's hair, obscuring his face.

Rafael looked at Stockburn, his mouth twisted with bitterness, his eyes bright with misery and fury. "This isn't over."

He glanced at the window. So did Stockburn. The rifle and red hair were gone.

Rafael spat in disgust then swung around and walked up the avenue toward the main street. Stockburn watched him go, feeling rotten.

When Rafael had reached the main drag then turned and disappeared behind the main street buildings, Rodriguez stepped up beside Stockburn. "I've never seen him get his horns filed like that. I doubt he ever did himself." He turned to stare up at the empty window then turned back to Stockburn. "Watch your back, Wells Fargo. He'll be more dangerous than ever now."

He turned to the other two deputies—a big man with a paunch and a fleshy round face studded with two-day-old sandy beard stubble, and a shorter, wiry man with a hangdog look but with a delighted smile remaining in his eyes. He'd enjoyed seeing Rafael get his hat handed to him but he regarded Stockburn with a fateful look, as though the railroad detective were a lamb marked for slaughter.

Rodriguez said, "What about the train robbers?"

"Lost 'em," said the bigger of the two deputies. "Just like last time. They use the monsoon storms to cover their tracks."

"Which way were they headed?" Wolf asked.

"South."

"Into Mexico?"

The big man compressed his lips and opened his hands. "Where else? Nothing else down there but the border."

Scowling, Rodriguez shook his head slowly. "Well, I suppose I'm the one who has to send a wire up to Bottleneck, lettin' the beef growers' association up there know they've lost another five hundred head. Hard to believe, though, that Tomacito was part of that bunch."

"Because he's so young?" Stockburn asked.

"Yeah, well . . . that and, well . . . when he got into trouble it was always small-time trouble. You know . . . stickin' up a bartender . . . stealin' a horse out of a livery barn . . . or robbin' a *puta*. That sort of thing. Penny-ante stuff."

"Did he run with a group? A group of four or five others, say?"

Rodriguez nodded. "All local boys. Bad seeds. Rafael told him to stay away from 'em."

Stockburn grimaced in frustration, looking around the windy street. "No dead robbers were on that train?"

Rodriguez bunched his lips, shook his head. "Rafael and I had us a look after the passengers were let off." Again, he shook his head. "The sawbones here in town took off a couple of wounded passengers and your two express guards, but no robbers. They was all gone by the time Langenbottom limped the train into town."

"Hmm. I wonder what they did with 'em."

"There was four, you say?"

"Six total, including Tomacito."

"Maybe the others was just wounded."

Stockburn shook his head and stared off, thoughtful. "They were dead, all right. As dead as Tomacito." Turning back to Rodriguez, he said, "Where's Langenbottom and the fireman, Wiggins?"

"Pulled out this morning, headed on up to Albuquerque and Las Vegas."

"Damn. I'd like to talk to 'em. They might know if those outlaws were one large bunch or two smaller ones who just happened to hit the train at nearly the same time."

"It'd make sense, them wantin' to bury their own. The outlaws, I mean."

"Especially if they didn't want anybody to know they'd been there."

Rodriguez studied the railroad detective, who was staring off again, thinking over what he knew about the robbery. "What's on your mind, Wells Fargo?"

Stockburn turned back to him. "You ever play much chess, Rodriguez?"

Rodriguez shrugged a shoulder. "A little."

"I'm starting to think Tomacito's gang were used as pawns." Stockburn unlooped Smoke's reins from the hitch rack and turned to stare across the street at the Camino Real Hotel. "I'll look into it further, probably ride down toward the border, see if I can kick up any sign . . . rumors . . . maybe a voice on the wind. You never know what you'll kick up down there."

"Just don't kick up any Apaches, Stockburn. There's still

a few wild ones haunting the border country. Banditos of all stripes, too. And Comanches native to the area, as well."

Stockburn started leading Smoke toward the hotel, smiling. "Oh, I know. This ain't my first rodeo, Sheriff."

"Hey, where you goin', Wells Fargo? Mexico's south."

"I need to rest my horse . . . and thank that red-headed, Winchester-wielding guardian angel of mine."

CHAPTER 13

Stockburn pushed open the hotel's heavy oak front door and stepped into the cool adobe-walled lobby, his boots clacking on the flagstone tiles. Good-sized with a high, arched ceiling from which an unlit coal oil chandelier hung, the lobby housed a big, scarred oak desk along the wall to the right and a couple dozen pigeon holes, most with keys residing inside them.

Beside the desk stood a potted lemon tree. A cream-colored cat lounged on a wicker basket on the desk's far end. On the wall opposite the desk, which wasn't currently being manned, ticked a grandfather clock.

Stockburn could smell cooking emanating from somewhere in the building, and a muffled din of pots, pans, and dishes as well as voices. "Hello?" he called, his voice sounding hollow in the high-ceilinged, adobe-lined room.

No response other than the din continuing from the kitchen somewhere down the hall that continued past the lobby as well as the stone stairway climbing the outside wall at the lobby's far end. The cat lying in the basket opened its eyes and stretched a front paw toward the newcomer, separating the pads and curling the claws. It purred and blinked slowly, stretching all four legs luxuriously.

"Hello, puss," Wolf said. "You the only one here?"

He walked up to the desk and turned the register book around to face him, looking down the short list of recently penned names. Three men and one woman had checked in the previous night. Two of the men had Spanish names; the third man was Bill Black. The woman's name, penned in ornate cursive in blue-black ink was Mrs. Barthelemy Dove. Since no man's name accompanied hers, Mrs. Dove seemed to be unattended.

Stockburn didn't know any Barthelemy Dove. But then, he didn't know Bill Black or the Mexicans, either. Since the redhead who'd assisted him out in the street had definitely been a woman, he slid his finger over Mrs. Barthelemy's name to the room number scratched in pencil to the right of it, tapped it, and started for the stairs.

Again, the languid cat stretched its paw toward him, purring. Stockburn paused to give the cat's belly an affectionate scratch, which kicked up its purring. He continued to the stairs and climbed slowly, taking two steps at a time, moving as quietly as he could on the balls of his boots. He'd been in the business long enough to know, despite what had happened on the street, he could be walking into a trap.

He might not have felt that way if it had been a man who'd helped file Rafael's horns, but women could be fickle. The redhead may have wanted to save his bacon only because she wanted to fry it herself. You just never knew about women. He proceeded with utmost caution around even the most magnanimous of bosomy matrons.

On the second floor, he continued to room 9 on the hall's right side. The door was unlatched and two inches of daylight shone between the door and the frame.

He was expected.

Stockburn slid the left side of his coat back with his left

hand and with his right, unsheathed the Colt holstered for the cross-draw. He raised the revolver and used it to nudge the door open slowly, wincing as the hinges squawked.

His heart thudded heavily. A gun could blast at any second, sending a bullet ripping through his guts.

He shoved the door two feet open, three feet, four feet . . .

Suddenly the door jerked open and the redhead stood before him, scowling, one fist on her hip. "Get in here, Wolf, you big galoot! I swear you fear women more than you would a whole nest of rattlesnakes!"

Stockburn lowered the Colt and dropped his jaw. "*Hank?*"

The girl threw herself against him, wrapping her arms around him, hugging him tightly. "Oh, Wolf—I thought you were dead!"

"Hank, what are you doing here?"

She looked up at him, fear and relief in her jade eyes. "I was in Tucson on assignment when the home office wired me that you might be dead. Mr. McCreedy said you were scouting the train headed here from Bottleneck, that five hundred head of cattle had been stolen, two express guards were dead, and you were missing. He sent me here to investigate and find you, 'living or dead'. His words."

"That sentimental cuss."

Samuel McCreedy was Hank Holloway's district supervisor stationed in Kansas City, two doors down from Stockburn's own boss, in the Wells Fargo office building on Missouri Avenue. Wolf never ran into the beautiful, red-headed, hot-blooded Henrietta Holloway in town, however. Like himself, she was usually riding the long coulees of the frontier west, tracking down the natural and not-so-natural predators of the iron horse, a still relatively new creature west of the Mississippi in the mid-1800s, and lucrative prey for owlhoots.

Stockburn and "Hank" Holloway had been thrown together by forces beyond their control roughly a year ago when a pack of nefarious human vultures was preying on the Union Pacific line in Dakota Territory, robbing and murdering all passengers and crew. Hank—an express agent then as opposed to an undercover detective, which she was now—had been the lone survivor of one such attack. When the robbers had blasted open the express car door, killing the guards, she had been thrown wide and buried under debris.

Knocked out, she'd been hidden from the killers.

Hank had survived the attack but awakened with one hell of a chip on her shoulder. Her determination to help Wolf track the thieving killers and put them down like the rabid dogs they were had been a force he had not been able to thwart any more than he'd been able to temper the Great Plains cyclone that had almost sent them, horses and all, hurling back to Kansas before the job was done.

Wolf and the fiery Hank had survived the storm a little worse for wear and tracked the killers to a quiet little settlement in east-central Dakota Territory, uncovering not only the owlhoots' hideout but a prairie town's perverse secret in the form of a deadly grudge against the Union Pacific rail line. The one good thing to have come out of the ordeal—well, two things if you count Wolf's and Hank's friendship, which had been forged by the fire of many shared travails—was Stockburn having at last found, albeit by accident, his long-lost sister, Emily, who had been taken by the rampaging Cheyenne who'd sacked the Stockburn family's western Kansas farm when Emily had been only eight years old. She now existed in the form of Melissa Ann Thornburg, a tough, beautiful rancher's widow raising her half-breed son, Pete, and wrangling a team of cowhands on a sprawling and lucrative stock operation near the Cheyenne River.

Looking up at Stockburn, Hank said, "I arrived in town only a half hour ago. I was about to go out and rent a horse and start looking for you. Of course, I was going to check in with the sheriff first, but I heard from the depot agent he wasn't worth much. A posse had been sent out, but—"

"They're back."

"I figured as much. You were quick to make friends with that deputy, Wolf."

"So were you." Stockburn grinned and nudged her chin. "Silly girl. He's a bad apple."

"I heard that from the depot agent, as well."

"Might have a target on your back for helping me out of that tight one."

Hank shook her lovely red tresses back behind her shoulders and fluttered her eyelids at the tall detective. "I'd do it all over again for you, Wolf."

"Don't you go thinkin' I can't take care of myself, little girl."

"How did you think you were going to get out of that tight one, since you left that bad apple with a second pistol?"

"I was going to pray for divine intervention."

"Well, you got it—didn't you?" The cameo-pretty young woman's flawless cheeks flushed and her smile turned saucy.

Stockburn snorted. "You're more of a caution than you were a year ago. I do believe that promotion has gone to your head."

"Oh, it has. It's made us colleagues, now. Almost equals." She flicked his ribbon tie with her thumb and index finger.

"I'm your senior by . . . well, by a few years." Stockburn pulled himself away from her and slacked into a chair in the room's corner, near the open window through which Hank had poked her rifle. As he dug into his shirt pocket for his makings pouch, he said, "As you can see, I'm alive and well."

"What happened to your head?"

Stockburn hiked his right foot onto his left knee and lifted a shoulder as he sprinkled rich black tobacco onto the rolling paper troughed between the first two fingers of his right hand. "A bullet crease. Nothing to worry about. I've cut —"

"—myself worse shaving." She stepped up to his chair, leaned forward, and placed both hands on the chair arms, crouching over him with an alluring smile on her face. The lace-edged, low-cut bodice of her metallic green traveling dress rose and swelled. "I've missed you, Wolf."

Stockburn twisted the quirley closed and returned her look with an all-business one of his own. If he were a few years younger or she a few years older, he might have taken her onto his lap and kissed those ripe cherry lips, which, against his will, was what he was imagining doing at the moment . . . but if wishes were wings, pigs would fly.

He had to keep it professional with Hank. She believed all the stories that had been printed about him and was enamored of his reputation. She thought she was in love with him, but she didn't yet realize how unlovable he was. He'd just as soon she never learn that priceless tidbit.

"You can go back to Tucson."

"Two express guards were killed. Five hundred cattle stolen. I want to help. That makes over two thousand total. Three deputy U.S. marshals missing, one stock detective wounded. And one Wells Fargo detective wounded." Again, she flicked his tie.

Stockburn scowled at her as he fired a match on a chair arm. "Not your expertise."

Wells Fargo usually assigned Henrietta Holloway to less brutish pursuits like counterfeiting, mail and insurance fraud, and confidence scams that put rail passengers in peril. A few months ago, she'd helped bust up a "Christian" acting troupe that had been using the rails to travel from town to town in western farm country performing skits from the Bible while on the side peddling blessing scams as well as phony money exchanges and pigeon drops. She performed her work incognito, or undercover, usually playing someone's young mail-order bride or an innocent albeit nosey daughter or sister.

"I'm finished in Tucson."

Stockburn took a puff off his quirley and blew the smoke out the open window. "Oh?"

"The counterfeiters who'd been using our express cars to transport their funny money absconded to the West Coast." Hank held her thumb and index finger a quarter-inch apart. "I was that close to closing them down. They were holed up on an abandoned rancho in Sabino Canyon. By the time I got there with two deputy U.S. marshals and a treasury man, they were gone. I found out from the ticket agent that three people matching their descriptions had boarded the train for San Diego. When I sent a telegram to Mr. McCreedy asking if I could follow them, he took me off the case. He said he'd put one of his West Coast agents on it."

"So, why the long face?"

"It was my first failure as a detective."

"Didn't you find out who they were?"

"Yes, I did. Two brothers and a wife of one of the brothers. But I didn't catch them. By the time another agent can get on their trail, they'll likely board a steamer for Baja or South America. Their little charade was quite lucrative and Wells Fargo has been left holding the proverbial empty bag."

"We all fail sooner or later, Hank. You got close."

"I let Mr. McCreedy down. I let the company down."

"Pshaw! You'll make up for it in spades."

"Yes, I will, Wolf." She smiled brightly. "I'm going to help you run those murdering stock thieves to ground."

"Hank, this is a rough one."

"Dakota Territory wasn't rough?"

"You shouldn't have been on that one, either. If you remember correct, you openly defied my orders to head back to Fargo, and followed me until we were both so far out in the tall and uncut I had no choice but to let you ride along. You hornswoggled me, you red-headed little polecat!"

"Well, then, I've hornswoggled you again."

"No, sir. Not this time. I'm sending a wire to McCreedy straightaway lettin' him know you did your job. You found me. He'll call you home."

"He might just do that."

"He will do it. I have seniority over McCreedy."

"All right— he will do it, you superior ass. But the next train headed north won't pull through Las Cruces for three days. What could I possibly find to entertain myself with in this sweltering little desert cow town for three days"— her cunning smile broadened—"except dog your heels?"

"Nope. Not this time." Stockburn flicked his butt out the window and rose. "You find yourself a nice stack of newspapers or wish books, and settle in, my dear." He planted a tender kiss on her forehead. "You have three boring days to kill in this sweltering little cow town." He gave her a hard, direct look. "If I see you on my trail, I'll write you up. You and I both know Sam McCreedy doesn't like his special agents written up. No, sir—that'd be a blight on your record. And I know how you hate blights on your record. Sorry, darlin'. It's for your own good."

Stockburn tapped two fingers to his hat brim then headed for the door.

"All right—have it your way, Wolf."

Stockburn reached the door and stopped, frowning. He swung around to face the pretty redhead again, regarding her quizzically. "You're gonna give up that easy?"

She crossed her arms on her chest and cocked a hip.

"Ah, hell."

Hank arched her brows at him. "What is it?"

"I know you well enough to know you have an ace in your corset. Or think you do."

She lifted her chin, smiling with great satisfaction.

"What is it?"

"Promise not to write me up?"

"Not sure yet."

She dimpled her cheeks. "Oh, you must promise, Wolf. I have some possibly valuable information."

"Regarding the stock thieves?"

"Possibly. I really have no way of knowing. So, technically, I wouldn't be withholding information from a colleague by not conveying said information. I have no idea what it means." She flashed a supercilious smile of girlish mock innocence.

Stockburn tightened his jaws in frustration. "Tell me what *said information* is and I'll let you know if it's valuable or not."

Cheerily, she said, "Promise not to write me up?"

Wolf drew a breath, let it out slowly. "Why do you always have to—"

"Have to what?"

"Never mind. All right. You can't hold back a cyclone and you can't talk sense to a redhead. I promise I won't write you up. Now, fork over the information. And if you have nothing, I'm not only gonna write you up, I'm gonna take you over my knee."

"Promises, promises." Hank stepped forward and slipped a small, folded piece of lined notepaper, like that from a very small notebook, from the gown's spectacularly filled bodice.

"I'll be damned," Wolf said with a droll chuckle. "I was right."

Hank held out the folded note. It was coffee-stained, and one corner was torn. It had likely come from a very old notepad probably residing in someone's sweaty shirt pocket. "You'll be the one to know if it's an ace or not."

Stockburn flared a nostril as he took the note from her. He opened it. Its aroma of cherry perfume had likely come after, as opposed to before, Hank had acquired it, he silently mused with a fleeting glance at her cleavage.

Scrawled in pencil diagonally across the small leaf were the words *The Buzzards dine well at Buzzard's Bench.* Wolf's heart quickened as he stared down at the note.

"Well?" Hank asked after a time. "Was it an ace?"

CHAPTER 14

"It was an ace, all right," Stockburn said, removing the note from his shirt pocket and setting it on the scarred wooden table in the rear corner of his favorite little café in Las Cruces.

He'd been starving after the ride in from the desert, so he'd led Hank over for a bite to eat. Well, more than a bite. As hungry as he was, he could have eaten a horse, tail and all. He'd settled for the carne asada with corn tortillas, a shot of tequila, and coffee.

Hank had chosen the same save the tequila. She prided herself on never imbibing on duty, though Stockburn had a feeling she never imbibed at all because she didn't like the stuff, which he did not fault her for.

He tended to like the stuff too much.

The stout, gray-headed Mexican waitress in a flowery print dress and wearing a crucifix around her neck had taken their orders, served their coffees and Wolf's tequila, and had retreated to the kitchen. The aromas of spicy Mexican cooking emanating from said kitchen made Wolf's stomach churn with anticipation and glee.

Returning his thoughts to the note laying on the table before him, he said, "I'm not sure what it means, but it doesn't sound good. Buzzard's Bench is a stage relay station east of here, between Las Cruces and Bottleneck. An old friend of mine and former Pony Express rider, Wooly Carson, runs the place with his Indian wife Gerta and their two old hostlers as well as three or four prostitutes. Wooly and the hostlers were once stagecoach drivers till they were put out to seed, tending the station.

"Buzzard's Bench is in the Buzzard Rock country, south of the sand dunes. Home to owlhoots on the run. Sooner or later, coming through the dunes up north or from Mexico to the south, the desperadoes usually show up at Wooly's place. He serves good food with all the trimmings up there in those parched rocks. Late at night and with his liquor flowing freely, Wooly gets served up a lot of information about the doings in this neck of the desert—most of it bad.

"It was from Wooly I learned where and when the train from Bottleneck was going to get hit. He overheard a man talking to one of his girls, and passed the information on to me when I came calling on him, which I usually do when I'm working in these parts. Eight times out of ten, Wooly turns out to be a gold mine of information."

"Could he describe the man he got the information from?"

Stockburn shook his head. "He didn't pay that close attention, and he gets so many men, they all run together. Most often, the bragging is all gas and nothing more. Wooly just told me the man said something about the next train getting hit an' hit hard, and the ranchers up in the Cerro Alto were gonna be cryin' in their morning coffee. Sounds like the rannie might've had a beef with one of 'em. Maybe he'd worked for one."

Stockburn drew a fateful breath and sipped his coffee. "I sure don't like the tone of that note."

"'The Buzzards dine well'," Hank said, gazing down at the scrap of lined paper.

"Nor the words," Stockburn added.

It was in the late afternoon, too late for lunch and too early for supper, with most of the Spanish folks still on siesta, only a few other diners here in the dark, smoky, earthen-floored, low-ceilinged adobe building. Those appeared to be gringo cowboys, either in town early to start stomping with their tails up or too late to head back to their respective ranchos after a supply run. Some of the ranches were a good day's ride, sometimes even a two- or three-day ride from town.

"Plenty ominous," Hank added.

"Where'd you get the note?" Stockburn asked her.

"At the livery barn. I boarded my horse at the Organ Mountain Federated Livery and Feed Stable, and asked if he'd heard anything about your fate. He was an elderly Mexican named—"

"Frisco Alvarez," Stockburn interjected. "An old friend."

"Mr. Alvarez said he hadn't seen you in town recently, but he did have a note for you." Hank glanced at the scrap of paper on the table. "When I told him I'd make sure you received it, he gave it to me."

"How'd Frisco get the note?"

"He woke this morning in the barn to find it tacked to his door. It was folded inside another small sheet with the words *Give to Stockburn* scribbled on the outer leaf."

Stockburn sipped his coffee. "I have to get out there. I'm gonna shove this meal down so I don't pass out from hunger on the way there." He took another sip of his coffee then reached into his pocket for his makings sack.

"*We* have to get out there," Hank said, pointedly.

"Hank, look—"

"We have an agreement, Wolf."

"I only agreed to not write you up. It doesn't mean—"

"It does so mean I'll be joining you."

"You don't have a dog in the fight, Hank. Why don't you just get yourself a hot bath and a stack of dime novels . . ." Wolf let the suggestion die on his lips. He could tell by the way the pretty redhead was looking at him, with those hard, jade eyes of hers, that she was having none of it.

She'd be riding along with him out to Buzzard's Bench, all right, whether he wanted her to or not. He reckoned he couldn't jail her or tie her to a hitch rack. That'd be downright unfriendly.

Oh, well. If danger was out there, she was putting her own pretty behind in it. Not Wolf. He'd rather she stayed out of it, but on the other hand, given the growing complexity of the situation, he'd be a fool to refuse her assistance. She had a sharp eye and a razor mind, to boot. She might catch something he'd overlook.

Of course, he wasn't about to admit the possibility to her.

He'd smoked only half his cigarette before his food came. He pinched out the coal, saving the quirley for later, then dined hungrily on the savory meal of tender, seasoned beef served with a pile of spicy frijoles, fried tomatoes, onions, and chili peppers, as well as plenty of salsa and corn tortillas. He sipped the tequila as he ate.

Before he knew it, his plate was clean. He smiled over at Hank.

She was swabbing the last of her own platter with a half-eaten tortilla. She sensed her eyes on him and looked up with a vaguely sheepish smile of her own. She popped the tortilla into her mouth and, chewing and smiling at the same time, said, "You were right." She brushed her hands together with aplomb. "Good grub!"

She was a pretty girl. All that red hair and smooth skin

tinted olive by the Southwestern sun, setting off those rich emerald eyes. She resembled a red-headed Mexican with Celtic hair. Staring over at her, he was touched with a familiar, nagging longing. A longing for what he wasn't sure.

Love?

Yeah, maybe that was it. Why not? Didn't he deserve it, too?

No, he didn't. Against his will, he remembered his old friend, Mike. More specifically, he remembered what he, Wolf, had done to Mike, his best friend and former Pony rider when they'd been deputy town marshals together in California. Mike had been his first true friend in all the world.

Wolf had repaid Mike for the honor by cheating on him with the girl Mike had intended to marry. Mike had walked in on them. It was as though he'd been knocked senseless by a sledge hammer. Mike had turned around and, in a daze, he'd walked out into the San Francisco street, and—

"Wolf, what is it?" Hank said, frowning across the table at him, those green eyes shot with concern.

"Nothing." Stockburn shook his head to clear the memory. He threw back the last of his tequila, scrubbed his napkin across his mouth and mustache, and slid his chair back from the table.

The memory always left him feeling a little sick and dizzy. Like he'd been slapped or punched in the gut. Why couldn't he scour the damn thing from his mind? he wondered. Penance, he supposed. Penance was one nasty, fork-tailed witch . And he deserved every bit of its wrath.

"Nothing at all, darlin'," Wolf said, rising from his chair. "Let's ride."

He'd just tossed his napkin onto the table when something flashed in the corner of his left eye. He only half saw it for a tenth of a second—sunlight glinting off the breech of a rifle and the silhouette of a man's hatted head at the lip of a third-story roof across the street. "Hank, down!" Stockburn hurled his big frame across the table and into her.

The young woman screamed as she crumpled beneath the big man's bulk. At the same time, a bullet pounded into a square-hewn ceiling support post behung with a chili ristra to Stockburn's right, making the dried peppers jerk and rustle. The crack of the rifle flatted out over the street.

"Stay down!" he told her as he gained a knee, palming both Colts.

Shattered by the bullet, only jagged-edged shards remained as he gazed out the damaged window, across the street, and up at the building upon which the shooter was on the run. At a crouch, rifle in his gloved hands, he ran to Stockburn's left, heading toward the rear.

Stockburn thrust both Colts through the window, knocking out the remaining glass, and triggered each one at where the bushwhacker's hatted head jerked as he ran. Cursing bitterly, Stockburn hurled one more round. The bullet buzzed off over the top of the building, skyward, for the silhouette of the hatted head had just then disappeared.

Behind Wolf, the stout Mexican woman who'd served his and Hank's food stood outside the kitchen door, rattling off spiteful Spanish too quickly for Stockburn to pick up more than a word or two at a time. She gestured wildly with her hands, a skinny Mexican kid with a soot-stained mustache peering skeptically into the dining room from over the stout woman's shoulders as she continued to berate the railroad detective.

Wolf looked down at Hank, who lay where she'd fallen

beneath him. She gazed up at him, eyes wide and round with fear.

"I told you this was no prayer meeting, honey! You stay here." He tossed some coins onto their table and tossed a sheepish smile and a nod at the stout Mexican gal who was still castigating him—apparently for the bullet that had nearly taken his head off. Glancing at Hank again, he said, "I'm gonna see if I can run that jasper down!"

"Did you get a look at him, Wolf?" Hank yelled as Stockburn hurried to the front door.

"No!" He wheeled left on the café's narrow front gallery and ran across the street and around the side of the bushwhacker's building—a mud-brick warehouse and the office building of a seed company—to the rear. He'd spied a man in a suit without a coat and with a pencil tucked behind his ear regarding him dubiously from the building's open front door, but he had no time to palaver. He poked his head around the building's rear corner, thrusting both pistols out before him.

He glimpsed the boot heels and flashing spurs of a man on the run away from him to the south, on Stockburn's right.

"Hold it, you chicken-livered . . ." Stockburn bellowed as he stepped out from behind the building and loosed two quick shots.

Again, he was a tad late. Both bullets merely plumed the dirt where the man's running feet had been four seconds before. As he disappeared around a bend in the alley, Wolf lurched into a run. As he rounded the bend, his quarry came into sight again.

But only briefly. Too briefly for Wolf to make out details other than the flashing silver spurs on the man's black boots. The man wheeled hard left and disappeared behind what appeared an ancient, crumbling adobe church, long abandoned.

Stockburn quickened his pace.

He followed the man's course behind the church and found himself facing a low, stone wall encircling an ancient cemetery. Stone markers and wooden crosses were interspersed with wild desert scrub. A moldering, faded red wooden door in the five-foot-high wall hung by one rusty hinge. The fresh scrape in the ground at the base of the door, and an obscured boot print in the sand and gravel, told Stockburn his quarry had fled into the cemetery.

Peering into the bone orchard, he aimed both pistols over the wall. Seeing nothing, he pushed through the gate, inadvertently tearing it off the insubstantial hinge. It thudded onto the ground. Wolf gritted his teeth at the sound that could make him a target as he continued striding forward amongst the stones, crosses, and garish stone and masonry monuments, some ringed with rusty wrought-iron fences. Cactus and greasewood choked the area; tumbleweeds were mounded high in places.

Stockburn reached the cemetery's far end, roughly fifty yards from where he'd entered. If there had been a door across the opening, it was long gone. Beyond was mesquite, barrel cactus, and a shallow arroyo littered with trash probably blown in from the main part of town. Beyond the arroyo was a small farmstead with an adobe shack flanked by a badly listing mud-brick barn with connecting stable and a woven ocotillo corral in which two jackasses stared toward Wolf, twitching their ears.

Someone appeared to be working in the stable, but Wolf was too far away to get a good look at the man. Or woman, for all he knew.

Striding forward, crossing the shallow arroyo, he continued to look around for the bushwhacker. Ahead lay a clay-colored boulder. Out from one side of the boulder a spidery cane cholla bearing yellow-green fruit grew at an angle.

A stocky, broad-shouldered man wearing a low-crowned black sombrero and a neck-knotted, green silk bandana stepped out from behind the boulder, aiming a Henry repeating rifle straight out from his right shoulder. "Hold it, Stockburn."

Wolf stopped. He had both Colts aimed out before him, at the hard-faced, almost pretty, black-hatted deputy whose five-pointed star glinted high on his gaudily embroidered shirt. The young firebrand's thick, dark-brown hair blew in the dry breeze. His light-brown eyes were cold and hard.

"Funny," Wolf said, glancing at the silver spurs on the young man's black boots. "I didn't fancy you for a bushwhacker, Rafael." He squeezed both Colts tightly, thumbs on the hammers.

Rafael held his rifle steady on Stockburn's head. Wolf could feel the burn of the sights just beneath the brim of his black sombrero.

"What? You think I took that shot at you?" Rafael grinned tightly. "No, no. Not me, amigo. That'd be too easy. You'd be lying dead right now."

"What're you doing out here, then?"

"I was just up the street." Rafael flared a nostril, and both eyes turned a shade darker. "Returning to the courthouse from the undertaker's place. I heard the shot, saw the rifleman on the roof. Saw you run out of Mama Isabella's Café. I tried to cut the shooter off but he slipped past me." He jerked his head slightly, indicating behind him. "A minute ago, I heard a horse ride out at a hard gallop. He's gone."

"Did you get a look at him?"

"Not a good one. You?"

"Nope."

"You gonna lower those pistols, Stockburn?"

"Not until you lower that Henry."

Rafael grinned his chilly grin again. "I guess we got us a Mexican standoff, then."

"Wolf!"

Hank's yell had come from behind him. Running footsteps sounded.

Keeping his eyes as well as his Colt on Rafael, he said, "On the count of three."

"All right."

"One . . . two . . . three . . ."

Neither man lowered his weapons. Rafael smiled, cheeks dimpling, that diamond-shaped cleft cutting deeper into his chin.

Stockburn returned the smile with a mirthless one of his own.

He lowered his Colts. A half second later, Rafael lowered the Henry.

Wolf glanced over his left shoulder as Hank came jogging up behind him, a pearl-gripped, short-barreled Merwin & Hulbert pocket revolver in her hand. Her red hair danced in the breeze and flashed in the sunshine.

"Hold up, Hank," Wolf said. "All's well." He narrowed one eye at Rafael. "I think."

Rafael looked at Hank and snarled, "Ah . . . the rifle-wielding gringa *roja*. Your woman, Stockburn? Does she always have to watch your back?"

"I'm my own woman," Hank said, snootily, glowering at Rafael. "But, yes, I always have to watch his back." She stopped beside Wolf, cocked one foot out, snaked one arm across her belly, and held the Merwin & Hulbert barrel up before her. "Were you the cowardly devil who threw that chunk of lead through the café window?"

"If I was, chiquita," said Rafael with heavy-lidded eyes, "the big gringo wouldn't be standing here right now. They'd be hauling him feet first to the undertaker's"—he slid his acrimonious gaze back to the railroad detective—"where my kid brother is just now being fitted for his own wooden overcoat." He shook his head slowly. "But an ambush? That's not how I work. I don't shoot a man until I can see the fear in his eyes."

Stockburn holstered both Colts then strode forward, his own eyes hard, his expression grave.

He stopped three feet from Rafael and glared down at the shorter man. "I've apologized for Tomacito though I didn't have to. I did it to be polite. That boy tried to feed me a pill I couldn't digest, and he died for his foolishness. You chew that up and swallow it, Rafael, or stay the hell out of my sight. I have train robbers to track, and I can't be looking over my shoulder to see if one cork-headed deputy sheriff is about to shoot me in the back."

Rafael bunched his lips as he stared up at Stockburn. A sheen of emotion veiled his eyes for about two seconds before he fought it off, and a cold, predatorial fury returned to his gaze. "I believe what you said about Tomacito. That doesn't mean I have to like it, Stockburn. It was your gun that killed my brother . . . my blood . . . all I have left of my family. Forgive me if that's a tough pill to swallow. That said, I am not now nor ever have been a back-shooter. If we get down to it, Stockburn—you big arrogant gringo!— we'll be going head-to-head. *Mano y mano!* Until then, I want to know why my brother was on that train. I want to know who he was running with. Who he was robbing that train with . . . when he should have been working honestly over in Bottleneck. It doesn't make any sense—do you understand? I turned him around. Got him a good job!"

The young man gritted his teeth. A wavering sheen of tears closed over his eyes once more. Rafael sucked in a deep breath and gave what sounded like a brief, snarling wail of uncompromising grief, then quickly brushed his shirtsleeve across his face, wiping it of all emotion.

Again, he glared. Eyes dark as two lumps of coal, he looked up at the taller Stockburn and said, "If you find out before I do, let me know. You do that, big arrogant gringo—Mr. Wells Fargo with your two fancy pistols and your pretty gringa roja with her pearl-gripped *pistola*, who watches your back—I'll consider your debt to me . . . for Tomacito . . . more or less paid." He lowered his voice. "In the meantime, I'll be looking into it myself. Until you have any answers for me, stay out of my way. When I see you, I see the blue face and dull eyes of my dead *hermano!*"

With that, Rafael shouldered his rifle, wheeled, and walked back through the brush in the direction of town.

Stockburn and Hank watched him go.

She said, "He's *seems* pretty broken up."

"He does."

"Was it him who fired through the window?"

"No."

"Are you sure?"

"Until a minute ago, I wasn't."

Hank squinted up at Stockburn. "What changed your mind?"

"Rafael wants answers. He thinks I can provide them. Until I can, he won't come hunting for me."

"And afterwards?"

"I don't know," Stockburn said with a sigh. "I reckon it depends on how much pure chili pepper he has in his veins. Around the border, there's a mix, and you just never know."

CHAPTER 15

As Stockburn trotted Smoke up a low hill, he glanced at the sky, wary of another monsoon gully-washer. A few, slate-gray clouds hovered, and the wind was still blowing, but so far he and Hank had run into only one light shower after leaving Lac Cruces. The rain had splattered the dirt of the old stagecoach trail they'd followed east of town, then through a pass in the Organ Range and along a dogleg in Dripping Springs Canyon. They'd spotted a few settlements and old mines, but it was pretty much empty country. What little gold there'd been had already been mined. The stage still ran from Alamogordo but only once or twice a week. A spur rail line had stolen away most of the stage business.

About the only thing that drew people out that way was Wooly Carson's Buzzard's Bench relay station, which doubled as a saloon and as a dance hall on weekends or whenever enough folks congregated to make a party. Most of the folks congregating at Wooly's place were of the long-coulee riding variety, which made the place, as some would say, more *interesting* than others.

More dangerous than others, too.

Most lawmen wouldn't go near the place unless they

were backed by a posse, but it was hard to form posses willing to ride there, given the place's tough-nut reputation. It was said that Buzzard's Bench had its own graveyard, and every few days, Wooly or one of his hired hands added a grave or two, sometimes three or four, judging by how wild and wooly the previous weekend had been. Stockburn knew it was true. He'd seen the bone orchard spread out in a little side canyon east of the main lodge.

Only a fiery, leathery old catamount like Wooly and his whang-tough Apache wife, Gerta, could run a place like Buzzard's Bench for as long as they had without falling prey to one of the human wolves that prowled here. A short, thin, bow-legged gent with a gray beard that dropped to nearly his belt buckle, and blue eyes that always shimmered humorously, though could storm into violent anger at the drop of a hat, Wooly had been tough as rock salt even back when Stockburn had first known him, when they'd been riding for the Pony Express together. Wooly was a little guy with a great capacity for humor and self-deprecation, but almost immediately upon meeting him, even the largest, toughest men seemed instinctively to know not to cross him.

Wooly was a good source of information, but as far as Wolf knew, he didn't give out such information to anyone but his good friend Stockburn and maybe one or two other favored and trusted lawmen. He also gave out information only on the nastiest wolves who prowled his territory, knowing that the pack had to be culled from time to time, winnowed of its most savage members, especially the most vicious members who had caused, or who Wooly anticipated would eventually cause, trouble at Buzzard's Bench.

Even Sodom and Gomorrah needed to be swept out from time to time.

It was a precarious rope Wooly walked.

And he worked it with his husky, Apache wife, Gert, who could wield a hide-wrapped bung starter as handily as any Dodge City bouncer. The woman didn't say much—in fact, Wolf couldn't remember her ever saying anything at all to him—but she didn't have to. Those Indian-dark eyes and the bungstarter as well as the big gal's heft did all the communicating necessary.

Wolf reined Smoke to a stop at the top of the rise and stared down into the hollow beyond. The Buzzard's Bench station yard was surrounded by a dinosaur's mouth of copper and tan, jagged-edged rocks piled sometimes as high as two hundred feet.

Hank checked down the zebra dun she'd stabled with Frisco Alvarez, and gazed into the hollow at the Buzzard's Bench station, as well. She and Stockburn blinked against their own dust being blown up from behind them then swirling ahead on the wind, pelting the rocks lining both sides of the trail.

"Humble place," Hank said.

"What'd you expect—the Larimore Hotel?"

Hank fluttered her copper-lashed eyes at him. "No champagne and feather mattresses, I bet."

"Just Wooly's rotgut, and you have to empty your own slop bucket."

Stockburn chuckled and booted Smoke on down the slope. Hank put her own mount into a trot, flanking him. As he neared the hollow and slid his gaze around the main building—a two-and-a-half-story mud-brick, wood-frame affair with a front gallery balanced on stone pilings—a cool apprehension hopscotched along his spine. He glanced toward the several outbuildings including the long, low former bunkhouse Wooly and Gerta used as a dance hall on weekends and holidays, and frowned.

No people appeared in the yard. No horses stood in the

corral off the main stable, which was where the customers of Wooly's and Gerta's usually put up their horses, and fed and watered them from the windmill creaking and banging in the wind in the yard's center. Aside from the wind's rushing and moaning, there was an eerie stillness about the place made even more haunting by the clattering of the windmill's blades and the squawking of the chains of the shingle hanging over the veranda announcing BUZZARD'S BENCH STATION in blocky, hand-painted letters. WOOLY CARSON, PROP.

Stockburn brushed his thumb across the pocket of his coat in which that ominous note resided. *The Buzzards dine well at Buzzard's Bench.*

It was then he heard the squawking and barking being shifted this way and that by the wind.

Hank must have heard it, too. As they put their horses up to one of the two long hitchrails fronting the main station house, she said, "What's that sound?"

Stockburn cocked his ears, listening. Apprehension reached deep into his belly as he half consciously identified the sounds. Without saying anything, but his heart quickening, he reined Smoke to the left and rode around the lodge's east front corner. Hank followed him as he trotted the gray stallion down the side of the deep building and around patches of prickly pear and bouncing tumbleweeds, the horse shying at greasewood branches slithering across the ground, imitating snakes.

Stockburn's eyes watered at the cloying, sweet smell of death at the same time his gaze found the buzzards.

He sucked a sharp breath and cursed. Puckering his nose against the stench, he shucked his Yellowboy from its scabbard and blasted three bullets into the ground near where the black, ragged, bald-headed carrion eaters were feeding and quarreling and fighting over whatever dead thing they were feeding on. He did not shoot any of the birds; watching them chortle madly and bounce and leap into the air, spreading their large, grizzled, fanlike wings as they took flight was adequate. Even buzzards, as ugly and obnoxious as they were, had a place and couldn't be blamed for merely doing what they'd been placed there to do.

When the last of the dozen or so birds had reluctantly taken flight, flinging what Stockburn took for buzzard curses back behind them, he swung down from his saddle. Closing his arm over his nose, trying to squelch the putrid stench, he glanced up at Hank. She did the same thing. Still, her eyes watered as she regarded him incredulously, horror in her eyes.

"Best wait here," Stockburn said into his arm.

Hank nodded. She was a tough gal, but she saw no reason to endure such a stench—and likely such a grisly sight—when she didn't have to. She'd proven her ruggedness to Stockburn a year ago in Dakota.

Holding his rifle low in one hand, he walked over to where he could see several bodies lying facedown in the sand and prickly pear of a shallow wash staging the stage station's main building. The cadavers had been fed on for a couple of days and nights, making it hard to identify, or to even count them.

He saw enough to know Wooly Carson and Gerta lay among them. He identified Wooly by his long, blood-caked beard, and Gerta by her size and her traditional calico skirt. The others would be the bartender and the stage line's hostlers and the girls who worked upstairs. It was hard to tell anything about them since obviously more than the buzzards had been working on them. Probably coyotes, maybe even a mountain lion.

Stockburn didn't linger over the carnage. He looked

quickly around the ground and toed a murky print. Then the repugnance of the scene and the stench drove him back over to where Hank stood holding the reins of the zebra dun and a powder-blue kerchief over her mouth and nose. Stockburn raised his arm atop his saddle and pressed his nose against it. His eyes were watering from revulsion and heart-searing fury.

Hank studied him with a grave expression. "Is it—?"

Stockburn nodded. "Wooly, Gert, the men who worked for them. The girls. They must have been ambushed. Took them by surprise. Probably hid up in the rocks and fired into the yard." Wolf punched his saddle and cursed loudly.

"How long ago?"

"Two, maybe three days. There's not much left of them. Not enough to bury. The carrion-eaters might as well finish what they started."

"I'm sorry, Wolf."

"For what?"

"I know what you're thinking."

"What?" Stockburn lowered his arm and looked at her in bitter fury. "That I got another friend killed? His wife and those who worked for him? You're damn right, I did."

Stockburn cursed again, grabbed Smoke's reins, and led the horse back around to the front of the station house. He dropped Smoke's reins and walked out into the yard, stopped, spread his boots a little more than shoulder-width apart, and planted his fists on his hips. His heart burned, thudding. He scoured the yard with his eyes, his detective's keen, probing gaze scrutinizing everything for a clue the killer or killers might have left.

Had to be more than one. Three at the very least. They'd probably surrounded the place, shot several outside and the rest inside then dragged them out into the wash. They'd probably dragged them, wounded, taunting them, maybe, then finished them in the wash.

Stockburn scrubbed an angry hand down his face, raked a thumbnail through the thickening stubble on his cheek. "These were revenge killings, that's for damn sure. Someone figured Wooly must have spilled the beans to me. They were exacting revenge on Wooly, and on me. They wanted to make sure I knew what they'd done. They wanted to rub my face in it. Well, they've rubbed my face in it."

He spat distastefully.

Leading the zebra dun, Hank walked up behind him, dropped the reins, and stopped to Wolf's right. Looking up at him over his shoulder, she said, "What do you mean, you got *another* friend killed?"

"Never mind."

"What did you mean, Wolf? What other friend do you think you got killed?"

"Never mind." Stockburn kicked a rock and strode deeper into the yard, looking around. "Walk around. Take a good hard look at every nook and cranny. I want to know who did this."

"What're we looking for?" Hank asked behind him, holding her hat down so the wind wouldn't take it.

"Anything."

"The rains and the wind likely covered any sign the killers left behind, Wolf. This looks to have happened at least a couple of days ago. Right after the train robbery, most likely."

"I know, but look, anyway!" Stockburn headed for the main stable and the corral angling off of it, adding under his breath too quietly for Hank to hear above the wind, "It's the least I can do for Wooly." He cursed again in burning frustration.

The day was late. Shadows were long. The wind seemed to be abating.

As he looked around inside the barn—scouring the deepening shadows for what, exactly, he had no idea—he pondered the possibility he'd jumped to the conclusion that the information Wooly had passed to him was the reason he'd been killed. Wolf didn't know that for sure. Wooly ran a snake den. Sooner or later, he was bound to get bit.

Still, the note Frisco Alvarez had passed to Hank, intended for Stockburn, was too important a clue to overlook. At least someone else thought it had been the information Wooly had passed to Stockburn that had gotten him and the others killed. Not that whoever had written the note was necessarily correct unless he had firsthand, possibly eyewitness knowledge, but there was a chance he was.

Also, there was a good chance the note-writer was the killer.

Wolf froze suddenly. What if the killer had lured him there for more than just to rub his nose in the killings? What if he and Hank had been lured into a trap?

He turned quickly and strode back out through the open double doors and stopped.

Hank was walking around to the right of the windmill, head down, one hand raised to hold her hair back behind her cheek. She used the other hand to hold her hat on her head. She wore a long, dark wool skirt, black ankle boots, and a white blouse. The long ends of a red, neck-knotted bandanna blew in the wind, tangling with her windblown red hair. The Merwin and Hulbert was holstered high on her right hip. The pearl grips shone brightly against the yard's deepening shadows.

She stopped suddenly, looked up, and cast her gaze toward Stockburn standing in front of the barn.

His heart quickened again as he looked around, probing the shadows. He returned his gaze to Hank and said calmly, "Hank, go into the cabin."

Hank cupped a hand to her ear. "What's that, Wolf?" She jerked suddenly and stumbled forward.

A wink later, the whip-crack of a wind-torn rifle report reached Stockburn's ears.

CHAPTER 16

Stockburn shouted, "Hank!" as the young woman took another stumbling step forward and dropped to her knees. As she lowered her head, the wind blew her hat off. Wolf shuttled his gaze to the cabin's east flank where a man knelt on one knee.

Partly hidden by a wagon-sized boulder, he lifted the barrel of the rifle in his hands, pumped another cartridge into the action, and leveled the barrel at Stockburn.

As Wolf snapped his own rifle to his shoulder and cocked it, he took hasty aim and sent three quick screeching rounds caroming toward the bushwhacker. The bullets chunked into the ground to the man's left and into the boulder. He jerked back with a start, pulling the rifle down. The boulder hid him for a moment and then he reappeared on a steel dust horse, galloping out from behind the boulder and angling back toward the wall of mounded rocks.

Casting a quick, concerned glance toward Hank, Stockburn ran forward, then raised the Winchester again and fired another round toward the fleeing ambusher. The bullet hammered the stony ridge wall just as the rider disappeared into it, apparently climbing a trail up the ridge, the boulders comprising the ridge hiding him from view.

Wolf ejected the spent, smoking cartridge from the

Yellowboy's breech and ran toward where Hank remained on both knees, clutching her right shoulder with her left hand. "Hank, dammit," Wolf cried as he ran, "are you all right?"

Hank tossed her chin in the direction of the fleeing bushwhacker. "Get after him, Wolf!"

Stockburn hesitated. "Are you all right?"

Again, Hank tossed her chin, her red hair blowing in the wind, glinting in the last rays of sunlight angling into the canyon from over the sawtooth western ridge. "Get that bushwhacker!"

Wolf considered the girl, considered the rifleman, then, fury rekindling inside him, he ran over to where Smoke stood with Hank's zebra dun, shifting his feet nervously and whickering. Neither horse had enjoyed the gunfire. But then, Stockburn hadn't enjoyed it, either. He never did—especially when he . . . or a close friend like Hank . . . was the target.

He grabbed the reins, hauled himself into the saddle, and touched boots to Smoke's ribs. The horse knew the score. He had gone after enough other bushwhackers to know he was going after another one.

Smoke knew his rider and he didn't balk. He swung onto the trail angling up the ridge through a corridor of sharp-edged rocks, put his ears back, and stretched his stride in a heart-pumping climb, reaching the top of the ridge in less than a minute.

Wolf drew back on the reins and pulled his hat off his head, for the wind was blowing with more vigor atop Buzzard's Bench. Looking around, he watched the darkening rocks turn the deep red of old velvet drapes. In the corridors between them, darkness pooled like black ink. All around Stockburn were only the rocks, sparse, wind-tussled brush, blowing sand and grit, and sliding shadows.

The ambusher had taken one of those several corridors through the rocks, and was gone. The coming night had swallowed him even as the detective sat the blowing horse, looking around in burning frustration.

As the rage built to a head inside him, he threw his head back and shouted, *"Whoever the hell you are, we'll meet again!"*

As the day's final defeat, the wind ripped the words from his mouth muffling them, tossing them straight down like dropped candy from a kid's torn pocket. Innocuous. Benign.

Wolf looked at the ground around him.

His gaze came to rest on one small spot. Frowning curiously, he dropped from the saddle and then to a knee. His gloved fingers traced a fresh horse print, obviously the print of one of the hooves of the fleeing bushwhacker's horse. Even as Wolf studied it, the wind blew in bits of red sand. But before the wind obliterated it completely, he pressed his right index finger to the small star scoring the sand on the right side of the shoe's impression.

He mounted up and rode back down to the canyon.

As Smoke walked out of the trail's corridor and onto the canyon floor, Stockburn's scrutinizing gaze held on something in the rocks to his left. He reined Smoke to a stop, swung down, and walked over to the pale object fluttering against a cranny in the ridge wall.

A sheet of paper with writing on it buzzed like an insect as the wind held it nearly flat against the rocks, making its edges flutter and whine. Stockburn picked up the leaf and held it up in both hands. He muttered the words aloud as he read the heading professionally printed across the top of the leaf. MANDRAKE & SONS GUNS AND AMMUNITION. and then the smaller letters below the larger ones. BOTTLE-NECK, WEST TEXAS.

Wolf shoved the paper into his coat pocket, mounted up, and hurried back into the yard where he saw Hank sitting on the top step of the lodge's brush-roofed front gallery. He reined up, dropped to the ground, and hurried over to her. She sat clutching the bloody top of her shoulder, her face taut. Her hat rested down against her right thigh.

"Oh, for Pete's sake," Wolf groused. "Let me take a look."

"It's not bad."

Wolf took a knee on the step beside her. "I'll be the judge." He pried up her hand to expose the ragged wound through the torn blouse. It appeared to be a graze, but it galled him. "Dammit, Hank. You're going back to Las Cruces, and that's final!"

She turned her head up toward his, smiling. Blinking slowly, she rose up off her butt and before he knew what she was doing, she'd planted her lips against his. She kissed him tenderly before pulling slowly away. "We made a deal," she said gently, smiling. "So you can go to hell."

He knew what she was doing. She was punching him back off balance, and she'd done a good job of it. He continued to feel her supple lips against his own, at once amazed and exasperated by how she'd weaponized her feelings for him. He gained his feet a little unsteadily, and drew her up by her right hand. "Come on. Let's get you inside, you stubborn roja," he said, trying to put some steel into his voice but having trouble after the unexpected kiss.

Hank in tow, he crossed the gallery to the front door, which had several bullet pocks in it, and drew it open by its heavy wooden handle. He stepped inside, squinting against the shadows, and pulled Hank in behind him. He looked around the main room laid out with long tables and benches, which had once served as a dining room for the stage passengers and which continued to do for the nightly visitors for which Buzzard's Bench had become a home away from home of sorts.

A long bar, crudely constructed of pine planks laid across beer barrels, stretched across the room's far side. It was flanked by a door beyond which lay the kitchen and Wooly and Gerta's living quarters. To the right of the bar, stone steps climbed to the second story, which served as a hog ranch where the girls plied their trade. Stockburn remembered Wooly'd had three or four girls up there—not of the top shelf variety by any means. So far out in the high and rocky, beggars couldn't be choosers. Wolf also remembered that Wooly charged a pretty penny for those mostly haggard, worn-out, gap-toothed women who'd spent their better days in El Paso or Abilene.

"Anyone here?" Wolf called, looking around.

He'd seen no horses in the barn. Not even Wooly's mule which Wooly or his hired men had used to pull his wagon into Las Cruces on supply runs. Someone had either taken the mule or run it off, possibly because no one was here to feed it. Had the killer or killers been tender-hearted enough to free the mule, or had someone come by after the killings and turned it loose?

Doubtless, Wooly and Gerta had regular customers. Likely gold-digging desert rats not unlike Skinny MacDonald and his daughter Violet. The leavings of a few diners—plates, cups, glasses, and unlabeled bottles—remained on a few of the tables. They could have been left there by the killers or by others who'd passed through since the killings to help themselves to whatever grub they could scrounge in the kitchen.

Hard to tell.

The place stunk of burned beans. Maybe Gerta had been cooking when the killers had come to punch her ticket.

"Anyone here?" Wolf called again as he walked slowly toward the bar.

"Quiet as church mice," Hank said, standing near the window left of the door, peering out. She was still holding her hand over her bullet-burned shoulder.

"For now," Wolf said. "It's early yet."

He walked into the kitchen and came out a few minutes later with a pan of water, an unlabeled bottle, and a cloth. Hank remained at the window, staring out. As Stockburn crossed the room to her, she turned toward him and glanced around, raking her gaze across the low ceiling from which wagon-wheel candle chandeliers hung and to which soot, dust, and cobwebs clung. Gerta hadn't been much of a housekeeper.

The wind continued to blow, making the timbers creek and pelting the walls with sand.

"Kind of eerie," Hank said. "This big old building out here in the middle of nowhere. Its occupants lying dead out back."

Stockburn set the pan of water and the bottle on a table near the door, on the far side of the table from the door and the windows. He wanted to be able to see outside. "Come over here. I'm gonna clean that wound."

"I told you. It's a shallow graze."

He sat down on the bench and tapped the table before him. "Humor me."

Hank scowled then flounced ironically around the table and sat down to Wolf's right.

"Show me that shoulder," Wolf growled at her.

Hank smiled up at him. "Do you want me to disrobe for you, Wolf? Is that what this is all about?"

"Be serious, will you?"

"Grouch." Hank wrinkled her nose at him then set her hat on the table and unbuttoned her blouse far enough that she could peel the collar back to expose her shoulder. Stockburn dampened the cloth then went to work, gently cleaning the shallow gash through the flesh atop the pretty redhead's pale, freckled shoulder.

Hank grimaced as he worked.

"A hair lower, it would have struck the bone," he said.

"A hair higher it would have missed me altogether." She shook her hair back and tipped him a saucy grin.

Stockburn frowned as he worked. "That bullet was meant for me."

"How do you know?"

"I was in the barn. The shooter couldn't see you clearly because of all the shadows. He thought you were me. He was out to get me here, just as someone else tried in town. Likely another gang member, or someone who'd thrown in with those killers and didn't want me sniffing around. Maybe the two who'd tried before. Instead, whoever it was got *you*."

Wolf dribbled whiskey over the clean burn.

Hank sucked a sharp breath through her teeth. "Damn!"

"Don't cuss. It ain't ladylike."

"Go to hell! You could have warned me you were going to douse me with firewater."

"What fun would that have been?" Stockburn smiled and set the bottle on the table. "You'll live. I cleaned you up. I don't even think we'll bandage it. The air will make it heal faster." He took a deep pull from the bottle then set it down and slid it toward her. "Nip?"

Hank winced as she looked at the bottle. "Just to dull the sting. Looks homemade."

"Oh, it is. Wooly's own. Rather famous around here."

Hank took a sip, held it in her mouth for a time, then swallowed it. Her eyes bugged as she made a face, a flush rising in her cheeks. "I see why!" she choked out.

Stockburn chuckled then took another pull. He set the bottle down on the table again and pulled out his makings sack.

"Are we going to spend the night here, Wolf?"

"As good a place as any. It'll be good dark soon. I'll be riding over to Bottleneck first thing in the morning."

"You mean *we* will be riding to Bottleneck," Hank corrected him, taking another tentative sip of the whiskey and making another face as she swallowed the panther juice.

"I reckon *we* will be going to Bottleneck, my stubborn roja." Stockburn pulled the receipt out of his coat pocket, set it on the table before him, and smoothed the wrinkles out. "Because of this."

"What's that?"

"I found it fluttering among the rocks a few minutes ago—near where that bushwhacker fired on us."

Hank lowered her head to peer down at the wrinkled leaf. "A receipt?"

"From a gun shop in Bottleneck, for two boxes of .44 rounds. I'm thinking it might have blown out of the shooter's pocket or maybe his saddlebags when he was scurrying around behind that boulder, or when he broke out from behind it. Maybe a saddlebag pouch blew open."

"That receipt could belong to anyone, Wolf. There's no name on it. It could have been blowing around in this canyon for hours."

"Maybe, but the date on it is three days ago. I think there's a good chance it belonged to our shooter, all right. I wonder what that T.C. stands for—initials scrawled and circled near the bottom of the receipt. Hmm." Staring down at them, Stockburn drew on his quirley. "Leastways, it warrants checking out." He tapped a finger against the table and stared out the window left of the door, pondering.

"Why is someone so determined to have me scoured from their trail?"

"Do you think it's Deputy Sanchez? He might have followed us out from town?"

"I don't know. I can't figure him. He's a tough one to read." Wolf took a sip of the whiskey then another drag off the cigarette. He blew the smoke toward the window beyond which the wind was dying and the yard was filling with cool, velvet shadows against a green and periwinkle sky shot with salmon silhouetting high, mares' tail clouds.

"Could be one of the pair who attacked Violet. They were determined for sure," he added in a soft, ruminative mutter.

"Who's Violet?" Hank said beside him.

"Long story."

"I'll bet," she said.

"Shush."

"Was it the pair who attacked Violet who gave you this?" Hank touched the bandage encircling his forehead.

"Yep." Stockburn reached up and gently pulled the bandage out away from the crusted bullet burn on his left temple. He removed the entire length of felt encircling his head, and tossed it onto the table. The cut was healing. The bandage was a nuisance.

He turned his head to one side, leaned back, and poured some of the whiskey over the cut. Burning only a little meant it was healing well.

Hank grabbed his arm. "Let me see." She leaned forward to scrutinize his temple. "Nice stitch job." She arched a brow at Wolf. "Your Violet's doing?"

Stockburn smiled. "My Violet's doing."

Hank pulled her mouth corners down in reproof and released his arm. "So, let me get this straight. You killed the first batch of train robbers. Five men."

"Six men including young Tomasito. That's right," Stockburn growled.

"You left the train chasing Tomasito, shot Tomasito when he drew a bead on you, and one of the two men who later attacked Violet, looking for you, gave you that nasty burn across your head."

Stockburn had explained it all to Hank on their ride out from Las Cruces. He'd been sketchy about Violet, however, not wanting to enflame Hank's jealous streak.

"Then while you were lying at the bottom of that canyon, another batch of robbers struck the train, shot the two express guards, and absconded with five hundred head of cattle."

"You were keeping up!"

"I'm smarter than I look."

Stockburn pecked her cheek.

Ignoring him, Hank said, "And two from that batch returned to the canyon looking for you."

"To make sure I was dead, I reckon. They were disappointed. Not so disheartened they didn't figure they'd make a little time with Violet, however. I should have killed them both then and there, but I didn't want to risk a bullet hitting Violet. They got clean away." He paused, thoughtful. "They must have sent someone else out here to Buzzard's Bench to exact revenge on Wooly . . . unless"— he scratched his chin with his thumb—"they'd fed the information to Wooly to lure me to the train. They must have known I'd be distracted by the first wave of robbers, and they would have the opportunity to take me down with relative ease. Or so they figured."

"Then why kill Wooly? Since he'd served their purposes."

"They killed him after I survived to send a message to both of us—him and me."

"And that message is?"

"This is what you get for informing on your customers. The message to me was I got my friend killed. They tried to rattle me . . . as well as lure me into another ambush."

"Since the robbery was a success, why not just head out with their cattle?" Hank asked. "Why so determined to scour you from their trail? And to exact revenge on Wooly?"

"Because they want to rob it again, I'm thinking."

"The same train, you mean?"

Wolf nodded. "I figure they're not done with the Rio Grande & Cerro Alto Rail Company. They're gonna keep hitting that train as long as it keeps shipping cattle. They're gonna steal all the beef they can until it stops getting shipped. And they're gonna kill everyone who comes looking for them. Everyone who gives information on them."

Stockburn mashed out his quirley on the table, shaking his head and blowing his last lungful of smoke out through his nose. "They must have one hell of a lucrative market somewhere, because they sure are determined cusses. They don't want me trackin' 'em down and ruining their fun."

"And because you killed Tomasito, you have the added problem of Rafael Sanchez."

"Maybe, maybe not. Like I said, that deputy's hard to read. Could be he wants to find the robbers as bad as I do . . . *and* find out why Tomasito was riding with them. He likely won't try to plant me six feet under till that mystery is solved."

"Tomasito's death wasn't your fault, Wolf."

"Like I said, down here it doesn't matter. I dropped the hammer on the b—." Stockburn cut himself off and lifted his chin, frowning.

"What is it?" Hank asked.

Wolf raised his hand to silence her. Pricking his ears, he heard the sounds more and more clearly above the lessening wind.

Hank did, too. She turned to Stockburn, eyes widening. "Riders," she said.

"Yep. A half dozen headed this way."

Stockburn grabbed his hat and his Yellowboy and headed for the door.

CHAPTER 17

Wolf glanced over his shoulder at Hank standing near the table, her hand on the pearl grips of her holstered Merwin & Hulbert. "Stay inside."

To his surprise, she nodded.

He opened the door and stepped out onto the gallery. As he did, the riders galloped toward him from a trail on the northeast side of the canyon. They were shadows jostling against shadows, for nearly all of the light had bled out of the sky. The wind had died entirely, and the hoof thuds sounded inordinately loud in the sudden, almost eerie silence of the canyon at Buzzard's Bench. The carrion eaters behind the roadhouse must have been taking a break, or maybe they were waiting for full dark to reappear.

The riders were laughing and talking as they rode.

Stockburn smelled tobacco smoke on the wind. His horse and the zebra dun tied to the hitch rack whickered uneasily and stretched looks toward where the half-dozen men drew rein twenty feet from the gallery, horses snorting, tack squawking.

They'd fallen silent. Their eyes had found the tall, black-clad man on the gallery holding the Yellowboy on his shoulder. Wolf didn't sense immediate trouble from them. Their voices had owned the casual, happy air of men chinning after a hard day of work. Likely saddle work. All five wore the gear of range riders—ranch hands heading to Buzzard's Bench for a drink and maybe a plate of food after a hard day punching cows on the desert.

One sitting his sweat-lathered, blowing mount turned his head slightly to one side and said, "What's goin' on, big fella? What's with the rifle?"

"Been trouble here," Stockburn said. "Buzzard's Bench is closed. Permanently."

The riders shared dubious glances. Because of the darkness that had settled heavily over the canyon, Stockburn could see only shadowy outlines of their faces beneath their hat brims. One of the horses stomped and blew, rippling a wither.

Another of the riders turned to Stockburn and said, "Pshaw! What kind of trouble? We're thirsty, dammit. It's been a long damn day."

"And a long ride out here!" added another man, sitting at the rear of the small pack.

"Wooly's dead. Same with Gerta and their hired hands. The girls, too. Murdered."

"Murdered?" asked the first man who'd spoken who seemed the smallest and oldest of the bunch.

"That's right."

"Who murdered 'em?" asked one of the other, younger riders, canting his head suspiciously to one side. "You, maybe?"

"I'm Wolf Stockburn, Railroad Detective for Wells Fargo. Wooly was a friend of mine. I found him dead. I'm closing the place down. Sorry for the trouble, fellas, but I reckon it was a whole lot more trouble for Wooly and Gerta."

The tallest of the five spat angrily to one side, whipped chaw from his lips with the back of one gloved hand, and turned his head sharply toward Stockburn. "There's gonna be trouble for you, Mister Wells Fargo—less'n you let us in there to get after that liquor."

"Ain't your place to close up Buzzard's Bench," said the first man. "I don't care if you are Wells Fargo."

"Well, I'm closin' it."

"He says he's closin' it, J.C.," said one of the men behind the smaller, older man. There was challenge and friendly jeering in his voice. "He don't seem to care about your opinion on the matter."

The speaker and another man laughed. Stockburn could see the white lines of their teeth in the darkness.

J.C. drew a deep breath. His thin, stooped shoulders rose and broadened. "All right then, boys. I don't see any point in causin' trouble. We'll mosey back to the Agua Verde. I'm sure old Mordecai has a bottle hidden away somewhere in the cookshack. That'll have to do us."

The tallest man said, "That ain't like you, J.C.. Turnin' tail like this."

"Yeah, well," J.C. said, brushing a gloved fist across his nose, vaguely sheepish, "this is what happens when you put on a few years. You learn to pick your battles. I've heard the name Stockburn." Giving Wolf the wooly eyeball, he neck-reined his rangy American horse around, the horse pitching a little, and said, "Come on, boys. Pull your horns in. Let's go!"

He'd just touched spurs to his horse's flanks. As he headed out at a trot, the other four reined their own horses around to follow him. Only two followed. The other two— the tall man and one of the others—jerked back toward Stockburn. The guns in their fists winked in the last, fading light.

Wolf had seen it coming. He'd seen the tension in both men's shoulders a full minute ago, a stiffening in their right arms. That was the tell-tale sign they were not going to listen to J.C. and head peacefully back to the ranch. They were young, thirsty, brash, and stubborn. They weren't going to take no for an answer.

Both left their saddles amidst the screeching of Stockburn's Yellowboy.

The tall man threw a bullet past Wolf. It struck the front of the adobe stationhouse with a spanging wail. A half-second later, the big man was dead, even before he hit the ground. His suddenly pitching horse wheeled and kicked him with a soft, crunching thud of a shod hoof against fragile human bone and flesh.

The other, shorter man whimpered where he'd fallen, his own mount sidling away from him. He tensed, arching his back on the ground, then gave a liquid sigh and expired, his body relaxing against the ground.

J.C. and the other two men swung their horses back around, looking toward their two fallen brethren in silent shock. They lifted their chins. Stockburn knew they were gazing back at him through the thickening darkness.

He waited, smoking Yellowboy still extended from his right hip. He'd already pumped a fresh round into the action. His right thumb held steady on the hammer.

J.C. raised both hands to his shoulders, palms out. "Jim, Palmer—throw 'em over your horses."

"Oh, Christ!" Palmer said.

"Just do it, Jim!"

As Jim and Palmer dismounted and walked over to the two dead men, J.C. rode toward Stockburn, tan wisps of dust licking up around him. He drew rein so close to Wolf the detective could see the man's long, craggy, large-nosed face in the darkness, beneath the brim of his gray, badly weathered, Texas-creased Stetson.

"You got trouble now, Stockburn."

"They drew on me."

"I don't doubt it a bit. Still, you got trouble. Those men ride for a man who looks after his own so they keep lookin' out for him. That's the way it works."

"Please relay my condolences to the head honcho. And you might inform him how it works for me. You draw on me and you're slower than me, you die. If he doesn't like it, tell him he can kiss my—you know what."

J.C. chuckled at the detective's gall. It was a dark laugh. "All right. I'll tell him just that. In those words, exactly."

"Now, kindly get the hell out of here. If I see any of you raggedy-assed cow nurses again tonight, your boss is going to have more empty saddles to fill."

J.C. gazed back at Stockburn, the craggy-faced man's eyes wide and unblinking.

Finally, he reined his horse around. The other two riders finished tying the two dead men belly down across their saddles and remounted their own horses.

"Come on. Dammit!" J.C. said with quiet intensity. He spurred his big American into a lope.

The other two followed, leading the pack horses and casting owly looks back over their shoulders at Stockburn. Wolf kept the Yellowboy leveled on them.

Behind him, the door squawked. Hank stepped out to stand beside him. "You sure know how to make friends, Wolf."

Stockburn depressed the Yellowboy's hammer and set the rifle on his shoulder. He sighed. "Don't I?"

"You could've let them come in for a drink."

"The place is closed, and I got no time for drunk cowhands." Stockburn set his rifle on his shoulder and turned to Hank. "I'll buy you one, though."

* * *

Stockburn had another few tugs on the bottle while Hank whipped up a quick meal in the kitchen. After they'd eaten their beans seasoned with jerked venison and drank several cups of Hank's awful coffee—it tasted more like scorched, weak tea than coffee—Stockburn went out and sat on the porch and listened to the predators go back to work on the carrion remaining behind the old station house.

Hank came out later, sat in a hide-bottom chair beside him, and took a couple of dainty sips from his bottle while they stared out over the dark canyon under an arched ceiling of glittering starlight. They listened to the predators fighting behind the place, making scuffing sounds in the sand and scrub.

Hank glanced at Wolf and said, "Should we do something?"

"What's the point? They'll get them sooner or later. They always do."

Hank hiked a shoulder, gave a little shudder, trying with minimal success to suppress her revulsion. She turned her chair toward Stockburn, who sat in his own chair, the front legs about six inches off the gallery floor, his boots hiked on the woven mesquite branch rail. He'd removed his hat and coat and rolled his shirtsleeves up his tan, corded forearms. He wore his pistols and his Bowie knife; his Winchester leaned against the chair to his right, always ready.

Hank picked the bottle up from where it sat nearby, took another little sip, and set the bottle back down. Leaning forward, she rested her elbows on her knees, entwined her hands, and said, "Tell me your secret, Wolf."

Pulled up out of a deep reverie about things he'd rather

not think about, he looked at the pretty redhead. "What's that?"

"You know—the one you don't want anyone to know about."

She must have been reading his mind. Women. How can they do that so easily?

His mustached mouth quirked a faint smile. "That's why it's a secret, darlin'."

"But it haunts you so."

"It's that kind of secret."

"Was it someone in your family or a friend?"

"Friend."

"How long ago?"

"A long time."

"Before Wichita or after?" He'd been known as the Wolf of Wichita when he'd worn the town marshal's badge for that less than fare city.

"Before."

"That's a long time."

"Seems like yesterday."

"Won't you ever tell me?"

"You'd see me in a whole different light if I did."

Hank smiled and shook her head. "I couldn't."

"I don't want to risk it."

"You like it that I love you, don't you?"

Stockburn turned to her, giving a sad expression. "I wish you didn't, though. For your sake."

"You can't ever love me back?"

He shook his head. "Not in the way you'd like."

"That's not going to stop me." Hank looked down for a time. She a drew a deep breath then returned her sad gaze to him. "I feel sorry for you, Wolf. A man who can't forget the past, forgive himself for his own sins, is a very lonely man indeed."

She rose from her chair. "I'm going to go find a bed and sack out for a few hours."

"There's plenty to choose from."

"I wish they'd stop making that infernal racket."

"It'll die down soon. I 'spect they're almost finished."

Again, Hank shuddered. She walked around behind Stockburn, placed her hands on his shoulders and pressed her lips to the top of his head. "Good night, Wolf."

"Good night, Henrietta." He patted her hand.

She turned and went inside.

Stockburn took another sip from the bottle and stared out across the dark canyon. He wasn't sure why but the snarls of the carrion eaters had suddenly become music to his ears.

CHAPTER 18

Several sets of riders rode up to the Buzzard's Bench station house during the deep hours of the night—owlhoots on the run from various catch parties, no doubt. They were probably looking to rest their mounts or to exchange them for fresh ones, and for food, drink, and whatever else they had the time and energy for.

Stockburn had barred the front door.

The outlaws had pounded on it and called and then, apparently, hearing and possibly witnessing the grisly work of the carrion eaters behind the place, had given voice to their incredulity if not downright horror, and thudded off into the otherwise quiet desert night.

A couple of what Stockburn supposed were posses rode up to the place, as well. A glance out his window picked up a sheriff's or marshal's badge in the starlight. They, too, soon grew discouraged by the barred door and distressed by the carrion's quarreling, and rode away in the night.

Between interruptions, Stockburn slept deeply despite his being a troubled man. Out on the trail, he'd learned to let go of his nagging concerns, for sound sleep was important for keeping his wits about him and his senses keen.

He was up at dawn's first blush. Hank's own door

opened just as he was heading down the stairs. After a quick breakfast of eggs, bacon, and coffee, they saddled their mounts and rode up the same trail the shooter had taken out of the canyon. The man's trail was easy to follow, given that star tattoo in the impression of his horse's shoes. He'd headed southeast through the chaparral. When he'd reached the rails of the Rio Grande & Cerro Alto Rail Company, he'd ridden along the rails' north side, continuing straight east toward where the Cerro Alto Mountains humped like a giant purple storm cloud, its belly sagging to the tan desert beneath it.

Not long after reaching the rails, the bushwhacker's tracks intersected with those of another horse. The second horse and rider had been milling in one place along the tracks, and then had continued east with the bushwhacker. The two riders had ridden together for around two miles, then the second horse had veered south from the bushwhacker's mount, crossed the rails, and dwindled off down a shallow arroyo sheathed in soapweed and mesquite as it angled through low, rocky hills and sandy dikes stippled with every cactus that grew in that part of the Sonoran Desert.

The sun's molten heat pulsed down from a brassy sky as Wolf stood between the rails, one boot on the southern rail, gazing off down the arroyo.

"Who do you suppose they are, Wolf?" Hank stood behind him, taking some water from her canteen. "Any idea at all?"

Stockburn spat grit from his lips in frustration, removed his hat, and scrubbed a shirtsleeve across his sweaty forehead. "Nope. Can't say as I do. Probably the same pair who came looking for me at Violet's place . . . after notching my temple for me . . . but I can't be sure. All I know is

one of 'em tried to turn me toe-down again last night at
Buzzard's Bench, and hit you instead. He'd headed straight
on east toward Bottleneck in the Cerro Alto. The rider he'd
met up with headed south."

"There's only one way to follow them both."

Stockburn squinted over his shoulder at the redheaded
railroad detective. "We split up."

Hank arched her brows and shrugged. "Why don't you
follow the bushwhacker? I'll follow the second fellow. I
have a feeling we'll be meeting up again . . . maybe where
they're holding the cattle."

"Could be." Stockburn drew a breath then spat to one
side as he shuttled his gaze from the purple hump of the
Cerro Alto to the dark mouth of the arroyo doglegging
south through the rugged hills. Apprehension nagged him
like a shrew. He hated worrying about people—why he
preferred riding alone—but he was worrying about Hank,
and no mistake. "I don't know."

"I'll be fine." Hank slung her canteen over her saddle
horn then led her dun up onto the railbed. "I can take care
of myself."

"Rough country, Hank." Stockburn gave her a dark look.
"And I don't mean just the country's rough. The men in it
are rough, too." He remembered what had happened to
Violet. "Savage."

Hank gave him a reassuring smile. "So am I . . . in a
pinch."

"Don't make any moves alone. You understand me?"

"I won't. The southern rider's trail might lead to where
they're taking those cattle. Possibly, to where the gang
holds up between robberies."

"And if so, you're gonna feel like the lone rabbit at a
rattlesnake convention." Stockburn cast his glance back

east, toward the Cerro Alto. "On the other hand, you might feel the same way in Bottleneck."

"Either direction it's six of one, half dozen of the other." Hank placed a hand on his shoulder and looked up at him, the hot dry breeze ruffling her long red hair. "I'll scout south. When I've gotten the lay of the land, and the men in it, I'll ride up to Bottleneck and find you. By then, you might have a good handle on whose running things in the mountains."

Stockburn nodded. "Makes sense. Since the ambusher is headed that way, someone's pulling the strings up that-away. That's where Tomacito was supposed to be working, too. The train starts from there, where the cattle are loaded. It's hit down here." He waved his hand toward War Lance Pass humping up in the south, then shuttled his gaze back east. "Someone in Bottleneck is orchestrating what goes on down here." He chewed his lip as he stared east for a time, then turned back to Hank. "You be damned careful, young lady."

Hank ticked two fingers to the brim of his sombrero. "If you're not careful, Wolf, I'm gonna start thinking you care more about me than you let on." She swung lithely up onto the dun's back, her legs long and supple beneath her wool riding skirt. She winked at him, clucked to the horse, then rode down the rail bed and into the arroyo.

Quickly, she disappeared from view. Nearly as quickly, the thuds of the dun's shoes faded to silence.

Then the only sounds were the cicadas and the faint ratcheting of the breeze making the branches of the creosote shrubs rub against each other. The sun beat down like a bellows, leaving almost no shadows. The rocks were so bright they were hard to look at. Noon was a nasty time in the desert.

He strode back down the railbed, grabbed Smoke's reins, and swung up into the saddle. Glancing once more in Hank's direction, he couldn't help feeling a fatherly protectiveness toward the girl. No, not a girl, he reminded himself. She was a young woman. A professional young woman who got paid for entangling herself in dangerous situations, same as Stockburn did. She had a good head on her shoulders, would do all right, would *be* all right.

Knowing their paths would cross again soon, he booted Smoke on up the trail.

The star-marked prints of the bushwhacker's horse disappeared from time to time as Stockburn rode east. Sometimes, in rocky terrain, they disappeared for long stretches, but they never failed to reappear again. Just one hoof indentation, or one indentation and part of another, enough that Stockburn was reassured he was shadowing the man to Bottleneck.

After an hour's ride, by turns cantering and walking Smoke so's not to unduly fatigue or overheat the mount, it became apparent horse and rider were gradually climbing into the Cerro Alto Mountains. The chaparral grew thicker along each side of the trail and along the railroad tracks on their freshly-graded bed to his right. Occasionally, the tracks spanned narrow canyons via creosote-soaked trestles. Here and there, oaks lined the trail, and in the shade of the oaks grew desert ferns amongst which apricot-colored hummingbirds fluttered and buzzed.

Several springs bubbled up out of the rocks, usually in an arroyo shaded by more oaks and freshened and cooled by the ferns. Stockburn stopped at each spring he came to and watered himself and his horse, and topped off his canteen.

By around two-thirty in the afternoon, he crested a pass

and stared down into a mile-square, canyon-scored basin in which what could only be the town of Bottleneck. Bathed in the light of the high-desert sun, it sprawled before him at the highest point of the Cerro Alto Mountains. Like most new and hastily erected western towns, Bottleneck appeared to have been constructed without much forethought as there didn't appear to be a main street. The small number of business buildings, mostly constructed of adobe brick, were clustered here and there on the bowl's higher rises. The crests of the rises were bald and dusty while their sides, scored with two-track trails, were stippled with chaparral and occasional cedars, oaks, and junipers.

As Stockburn rode into the town, the railroad tracks curved away on his right, on the far side of a shallow, brush-choked ravine. The tracks jogged along the crest of a stone dike right on through the middle of Bottleneck and ended at a neat, low-slung, red-brick, tin-roofed building on the settlement's far eastern edge as well as on its highest ridge.

A wooden sign hanging beneath the building's front veranda read WEST TEXAS & CERRO ALTO RAILROAD, BOTTLENECK, TEXAS. The depot building was flanked by a maze of cattle pens where dust rose from the cattle milling and lowing inside the pens. Men working in and around the pens, yelling and whistling and waving their hats at the cattle were obscured by the roiling, brightly sunlit dust.

Following a trail into the hilly town, Stockburn was a good hundred yards from the depot and the pens, but the green manure smell of the cattle was strong in his nostrils. The dust was no longer visible, but he could feel it in his eyes.

To the left of the depot and the pens stood a large,

red-brick building with a front gallery boasting white pillars and fronted by a good dozen saddled horses and one small, black, leather seated carriage with red wheels. A black Morgan horse stood in the carriage's traces, head and tail drooping.

Large letters painted across the building's high, wood, false façade proudly hailed SHACKLEFORD COUNTY CATTLEMEN'S ASSOCIATION & STOCKMEN'S HOTEL. Men in the bright neckerchiefs of the Southwestern cow puncher lounged around the building's gallery, some on the gallery's wooden rail, others in wicker chairs. A few brightly clad young women fluttered like gaudily plumed birds amongst the sunburned, mustachioed men. Wolf could hear the men talking and the girls giggling and laughing huskily.

He followed the trail to the top of a low rise and continued on between a blacksmith's shop on his left and a leather goods shop on his right. Beyond the leather goods shop lay a small, ancient-looking, mud-brick building maybe twenty-feet square, its brush roof sagging in the middle. A weathered sign hanging under the roof's overhang announced HOLLIS RENFRO—BEER & TEQUILA. A smaller sign beneath that one offered TOOTH EXTRACTIONS—TWO BITS.

As Stockburn rode almost even with the place, a man's bellowing wail caromed out from inside. The wail rose quickly in volume. The front door burst open and a short, fat man in a striped apron flew out of the place to land with a loud thud and a shriek on the stoop. He rolled wildly across the stoop and into the street directly in Wolf's path. He came to rest on his belly in a roiling dust cloud.

Stockburn drew back on Smoke's reins, stopping the horse six feet away from the short, fat man in the apron.

Wolf rose in his stirrups to peer over Smoke's head and twitching ears at the man who was nearly bald and who sported a thick walrus mustache. He lay belly down in the street, arms thrown out to both sides. In his right hand, he held a wooden-handled dental key. A bloody tooth was held fast in the steel jaws at the end of the key's shaft.

Somehow, the fat man had managed to hold onto the key as well as the tooth in its jaws during his violent leave-taking of the grog and tequila shop which apparently doubled as a dentist's office. The short, mustached man lying before Stockburn had to be the dentist himself.

"Damn you, Hollis," came a bellowing wail from inside the so-called dental parlor. "You musta took out half my jaw!"

With *jaw*, the speaker ducked out through the grog shop/dental parlor's open door. Straightening and cupping one hand to his face, he staggered across the stoop and out into the street, not so much as giving Stockburn a passing glance. He was as tall as Wolf, though considerably younger. He was a big, lean man in his early thirties clad in denims and a sweaty buckskin tunic down the front of which he wore a necklace of animal claws—wolf or wild-cat claws.

The brim of a dusty, black Stetson shaded the upper half of his strong-jawed but fleshy boyish face. A good-looking kid in a hayseed way. At least, he would have been good-looking if an enraged scowl hadn't been twisting it and making hot coals of his amber eyes. Blood had dribbled down one corner of his mouth and down his neck creating a long, dark-red stain down the right breast of the tunic.

The short, fat man rolled onto his back and stared up in terror at the rawboned kid standing over him. "I'm sorry, Vincent, but it had a deep root!"

"Oh, Lord," Vincent said, reaching down and plucking the dental key from the short man's hand. He held the key up in front of him, angry eyes nearly crossing as he regarded the bloody tooth in its jaws. Spitting blood with each word, he yelled, "You sure enough did! Look there. You ripped a chunk the size of a sewing thimble outta my dadblamed jaw, you fat old quack!"

Still gazing down over Smoke's twitching ears, Stockburn saw that while the chunk of jaw clinging to the end of the bloody tooth's root was nowhere near as large as a sewing thimble, it was large enough to see how it would cause the young man great distress. It was the size and shape of a small-caliber bullet head.

"Quack!" Vincent railed, lowering one shoulder to let the leather lanyard of his sawed-off, double-barreled shotgun drop down his arm. "You're nothin' but a damned old snake oil salesman, and you're lowdown, to boot. I'm gonna do Bottleneck a favor and blow your damn head off once and for all!"

"No! Please, Vincent!" the dentist screeched, folding his arms over his face. "Don't kill me! I was only doin' what you paid me to do! You know that tooth was grievin' you for weeks now! You couldn't sleep! You couldn't eat or do *nothin*'! You *begged* me to pull it though I told you last time I wasn't never gonna pull another one o' your teeth ever again!"

"Now I remember why, you old snake charmer!" Vincent lowered the double-bore to within inches of the dentist's head and drew both hammers back with his thumb. "This is it for you. I'm gonna do the citizens of Bottleneck a big favor!"

Stockburn drew the Peacemaker .45 from the holster on

his left hip, aimed it down over Smoke's head, and cocked it. "Hold on, kid. You're not going to do any such thing."

Vincent lifted his head to look up at Stockburn. His eyes widened and grew as dark as late-summer storm clouds.

Because of the blood staining Vincent's shirt, Stockburn hadn't seen the badge pinned to it.

CHAPTER 19

Wolf narrowed his eyes, studying the tin star all but hidden by the blood that had dribbled down from the man called Vincent's jaw. It bore the words *Town Marshal*. He looked at the man's amber eyes, knowing his own peepers must betray his sudden incredulity.

"How dare you draw down on me," Vincent said from deep in his throat with a strange amalgam of fury and astonishment.

The so-called dentist continued to howl and moan while covering his head with his elbows.

"You're about to kill a man in cold blood, there, uh, Marshal Vincent." Wolf smiled with equanimity. "I don't think you really want to do that. Why don't you give yourself a minute to calm down. Then, if you still want to blow the quack's head off"—again, he smiled, this time with irony—"hell, go ahead and do it. I have to admit, that's a good bit of jaw he pulled out of your head."

Vincent continued to stare darkly up at Stockburn.

Finally, the marshal's eyes softened a little. His lips stretched a slow, reluctant smile. He looked down at Hollis Renfro, at whose head his double-bore was still aimed. He eased both hammers down in their cradles and said,

"Looks like you just got yourself a new lease on life, Hollis. I reckon the man's right." He glanced around at the half dozen or so folks staring at him from stoops and shop windows. "I'd be settin' a bad example, I reckon, blowing the town dentist's head off right here on First Avenue . . . without benefit of trial."

Vincent turned his head and spat a wad of blood into the dirt beside the cowering dentist. "Go on. Git up." He slung the shotgun back behind his shoulder. "Git off the street before I change my mind."

The dentist lowered his arms and looked warily up at Vincent, whose dark shadow angled across him. Looking at Stockburn sitting the big smoky-gray stallion, Hollis heaved himself to his feet, grunting and whimpering. Casting Vincent another frightened glance, he brushed off his broadcloth trousers then hurried back into his grog and tequila parlor doubling as a dentist's office.

Stockburn silently opined that after the man's close brush with the smoking gates, he would likely think long and hard about taking down that second shingle hanging over his door despite the likely hit it would mean to his monthly income.

Turning a sheepish look up at Stockburn, who had returned his Colt to its holster on his left hip, Vincent brushed his fist across his bloody jaw and said as though around a mouthful of rocks, "Who're you? I'd think you was Hollis's guardian angel but I don't see any wings." He smiled with one side of his face, more blood oozing from between his lips.

"Stockburn. Wells Fargo."

"Railroad detective?"

"That's right. I'm here about the train robberies."

"You don't say?" Vincent narrowed a vaguely skeptical,

vaguely jeering eye as he gazed up at the mounted detective. "So . . . Wells Fargo finally got around to sendin' someone."

"The company was waiting for me to finish up my last assignment, which found me in Mexico. Took me a while to get back. When I did, I found a telegram from the home office waiting for me at Western Union in Las Cruces."

"No rest for the wicked, eh?" Vincent grinned, then his face crumpled into a sour expression.

"You can say that again. You the only law here?"

"That's right. Vincent DePaul." He cupped his jaw with his hand, bent forward as though with a pain spasm, and cast another angry glare at the building hunched behind him. Glancing up at Stockburn again, he said, "I'm the only law needed in Bottleneck. I keep the place buttoned down. When the cow punchers and the Mescins get a little wild on the weekends, I bust heads. Most of 'em know that an' toe the line. Except some o' the Mescins. They like to see how far they can push me." He smiled devilishly. "That's all right. Nothin' I like more than bustin' Mescin heads."

"I see." Stockburn drew a breath, realizing the big lawman in Bottleneck might not be playing with a full deck. He'd have to work around the man's diminished capacity as well as his obvious temper. That was all right. Stockburn had experience working with local law. They weren't always the best of men but the only men the town could get to pin tin stars on their shirts. "Say, Marshal DePaul—"

"Call me Vincent. Everybody does. I don't mind. I like bein' sociable." Again, he smiled though it was a crooked smile, involving only half of his mouth.

"All right, then. Vincent it is. Say, Vincent, I followed a horse here. I should say I followed a horse and rider here."

"To where?"

"To Bottleneck."

"Oh." Vincent frowned. "From where?"

"Buzzard's Bench."

"Oh." Again, Vincent frowned, narrowing his eyes which betrayed the slow machinations of his thinker box. "What was you doin' there?"

"Stopped to see an old friend. He's dead."

"Who is?"

"Wooly Carson. Gerta, too. And the rest of their crew, including the girls."

"The girls too, huh? Damn! Injuns?"

Feeling a little too much like a target, Stockburn swung down from his saddle and stood holding Smoke's reins. If the ambusher was still in Bottleneck, he could take another shot at Stockburn at any time. Wolf looked around, probing the shadows on both sides of the street with his slow-roaming gaze. "I don't think so."

"Well, who then?"

"I don't know. But while I was there, someone tried to core me with a rifle. He got away, but I tracked him here."

"Hmmm." Vincent turned his head to slowly peruse the street around him and Stockburn.

"Whoever the ambusher is, he would have ridden into town yesterday. All I know about him is he's riding a horse whose left rear hoof has a star stamped into it."

Vincent spat another gob of blood into the dust. "A star?"

Stockburn nodded. "Any blacksmiths or farriers around here who stamp stars in their shoes?"

Again, Vincent looked around the street as though the farrier of topic might leap out from a break between buildings, revealing himself. He rubbed his jaw, deep in thought. "None that I know about." He looked at Stockburn, his eyes brightening with speculation. "Say, you think that rider with the star, the one who bushwhacked you, had somethin' to do with the train robberies?"

Stockburn silently opined that maybe he'd judged Vincent's thinker box workings too harshly. Or maybe the man was smarter than he looked. You just never knew about people. "Could be. How did you—"

"I don't know. I figured you wouldn't take the time to track him if you didn't think he had somethin' to do with the train robberies." Vincent scowled. "Would you?"

"Probably not." Stockburn scrutinized the man carefully, a little suspiciously. He couldn't help it.

Suddenly there seemed something a little suspicious about Vincent DePaul. Like maybe he was a whole lot smarter than he wanted Wolf to know. Or maybe he knew more about the train robberies than he wanted *anyone* to know. Wearing that badge certainly didn't exclude him from a list of possible suspects—one that had yet to be formulated beyond Vincent DePaul himself.

Stockburn canted his head to one side and narrowed one eye. "Vincent, do you have any suspicions about who the train robbers might be?"

Instantly offended, Vincent said, "Hell, no!" Just as quickly, he moderated his tone. "I mean . . . I wish I did. Wouldn't that be a feather in my hat? Even though my jurisdiction ends where the town ends, I'd love nothin' better than to run them rannies to ground. They're wreakin' havoc on the ranchers in the Cerro Alto. Without the ranchers raisin' cattle to feed all them new Injun reservations to the west, Bottleneck wouldn't be. *I* wouldn't be. I mean, I wouldn't be wearin' this star. Hell, the stock pens over yonder by the train station is filled with beef ready to be hauled down to Las Cruces but the ranchers are too afraid to make another run till them bandits is turned toe down. Another big loss could ruin half of 'em!"

He looked down at the badge on his shirt, winced, and ran a big thumb across it, smearing the blood. "But, hell, I'm just local."

"I understand three federals went missing."

"Yep, they sure did. Nice fellas, too. They bought me a steak dinner the night before we rode out."

"You all rode out together?"

"Just a coupla miles southwest. See, I know a shortcut trail around the Comanche Buttes. They wanted to get southwest of the buttes, cause that's where they figured the cattle from the train were likely hazed, on account of there's fair grass out that way, not far from Injun ruins near the Rio Grande."

"Beyond the Comanche Buttes, eh?"

"Yep. Fair grass out that way."

"And they just disappeared?"

"Leastways, so far," Vincent said, quickly. "I mean, they haven't shown up . . . as far as I know. I reckon they woulda checked in with me. Ain't seen hide nor hair of 'em in three weeks. I hear the federals are sendin' some more, but, hell, we're a long way off the map out here and I reckon most of their men are too tied up elsewhere. I'm sure they'll get around to it sooner or later . . . especially since that beef was meant for the reservations."

"Hmm." Stockburn glanced around again, making sure no one was training a rifle on him. He looked back at Vincent and asked, "What'd you do before you pinned the star to your shirt, Vincent?"

"Ran a few cattle on a shotgun ranch up north of here. Just me an' my ma. After I fought the 'Paches in Arizona with General Crook, that was. I was in the army for four years. Then went back to ranchin'. When Ma died, I was all alone. I saw a notice in the Las Vegas newspaper about how this new town called Bottleneck in the Cerro Alto was needin' a capable lawman. Sick to death of chasin' cows outta mud wallows and flooded arroyos, I came here an' talked to Mister Darlington, an'—"

"Who's Mr. Darlington?" The name was familiar, but Stockburn couldn't pin a face to it.

"He's the owner of the Rio Grande and Cerro Alto Railroad Company. He followed the ranchers here and built most of the town. Him and Mr. Ramsay did with some eastern mucky-mucks, I hear. In fact, Mr. Darlington an' Mr. Ramsay are just now powwowin' over to the Stockmen's Hotel."

"Darlington and Ramsay, right," Wolf said nodding, his memory clarifying. They had been mentioned in the telegram his home office had sent to him in Las Cruces.

Darlington owned the railroad that was shipping the cattle, and Gordon Ramsay, owner of the Agua Verde Ranch in the Cerro Alto, was also the president of the local Shackleford County Cattlemen's Association. The two parties were in business together. The Cattlemen's Association organized the ranchers who raised the beef they then arranged with Darlington to ship to Las Cruces, to Tucson, and Las Vegas from where the beeves on the hoof were offloaded and herded to the reservations in northern Arizona and northern New Mexico territories.

Hungry Injuns up that way.

"They're both over at the hotel, you say?" Wolf asked Vincent.

"Sure enough. Come on. I'll walk with ya over there." Vincent spat more blood then swung around and started walking south along the rutted street. Leading Smoke, Stockburn kept pace beside the man.

As they walked, Vincent said, "They're powwowin' about the holdups. I heard they was gonna call in gunslicks to hunt the robbers down and take back their cattle—if they ain't already been sold in Mexico, that is. I was gonna go over an' listen in but my tooth got to hurtin' me so bad—I ain't slept through a full night for over a week—I decided to bite the bullet and go over an' let that quack take it out. Big mistake!" He cast another acrimonious glare over his holder. "Didn't know he was gonna break my jaw!" Turning forward, he kicked a rock in anger before regaining stride. "I reckon I shoulda known. That's what he done to me before! Take it from me, Stockburn—I wasn't the first one who almost blew that man's head offen his shoulders."

Stockburn gave a wry laugh as they descended a rise.

Climbing another low one, they deadheaded toward the imposing Stockmen's Hotel before which a good dozen horses stood tied and the fancy leather-seated carriage sat with the sleek Morgan hitched to it. The hotel's front door opened, and a pretty young woman stepped out in a print, wasp-waisted day dress, white gloves, and matching bonnet. Hooked over her arm was a wicker basket.

She stepped out into the sunlight, smiling almost giddily, dreamily, a high red flush in her cheeks. Curly blond hair spilled across her shoulders.

As the young woman started walking west, Vincent slowed his pace until stopping altogether. His thick, dark-brown eyebrows swelled and stitched as he stood glaring at the pretty blonde, as though he couldn't quite believe what . . . or who . . . he was seeing.

Hardening his jaws, he started forward again, back taut with renewed anger.

"Belle? *Belle!*"

The young woman stopped with a gasp and swung toward the lawman. "Vincent!" Fear and guilt shone in those eyes before an automatic smile, long practiced and not entirely genuine, returned the blush to her cheeks. "Oh, hi, honey! Fancy seein' you here!"

"Fancy seein' you here, Belle!" He stopped before the young woman, who was more than a head shorter than he, and towered over her, fists on his hips. "What are you doing here, Belle? I told you I didn't want you clickin' your heels around the Cattlemen's anymore!"

She looked up at the tall lawman, widened her corn-flower blue eyes in deep concern, and in a pouty little girl's voice said, "Vincent, you're bleeding." She pointed a gloved finger at the blood resembling a red bib on the tall lawman's chest.

"I had a tooth pulled."

"How am I ever going to get that blood out of that shirt, Vincent?"

He brushed her hand away like he was slapping at a fly and continued to glare down at her. "Belle, I told you I don't want you hangin' around down here no more. You don't *work* down here no more!"

"Of course, I don't Vincent! I gave up that kind of work when I married you!" Belle, who Stockburn thought was around twenty-four going on seventy-six, flushed again as she beamed and flounced on her supple hips. "But you know how Mr. Darlington loves my fried chicken. He sent a man over to the house this morning to ask me if I'd serve him and Mr. Ramsay my very own fried chicken—you know, from my momma's recipe?—for lunch today. He and Mr. Ramsay are in a meeting about the train holdups. Mr. Darlington usually has the hotel cook serve his lunch, but he says the cook just doesn't have my touch when it comes to fried chicken. Oh, Vincent, I couldn't turn him down! Why, he paid me two gold eagles for a basket of fried chicken, fried potatoes, and baked beans! Twenty dollars for a single morning's work, Vincent!"

"I told you I don't want you servin' him fried chicken no more! You an' I both know it's more than your fried chicken he's after!"

"Oh!" Belle laughed and covered her red, bee-stung mouth with one plump, gloved hand. "Vincent, he's an old man!" She flounced again on those nicely molded hips. Those weren't the only things nicely molded on the lovely blond. That simple day frock was so tight she seemed about to leap out of it in several places. She made the dress appear so alive that it threatened to leave her body altogether and go waltzing off down the street on its own.

With that same fake pout as before, Belle reached up to caress the big, rawboned lawman's cheek and said in her petal-soft but highly exaggerated Southern accent, "Really, Vincent. He was just after my chicken, honey. No need to be jealous. Belle's your girl and your girl alone. I just want to help out when I can, because I know you have so much trou—I mean, I know you work so hard for the peanuts the skinflints in this town pay you. It's not fair for them to treat you the way they do, to look down on you for your lowly upbringing . . . and, well, when I see an opportunity to bring in a little something extra . . . well, I just can't say no. Oh, Vincent, my love—please say you understand!"

"Oh, all right, honey," Vincent said, glancing a little self-consciously at Stockburn who stood about ten feet off the tall lawman's left flank. He smiled and pecked his wife's cheek. "I'm sorry I got disagreeable. You know the way the other men in this town look at you . . . and talk to you when they get the chance . . . just drives me plumb out of my mind!"

Stockburn glanced at the cow punchers lounging around on the hotel's front gallery. All eyes had been riveted on the comely blond since she'd stepped out of the hotel, and they still were. The waddies had likely heard every word between Belle and her jealous husband, and more than a couple were grinning and elbowing each other though Vincent didn't seem to notice.

Having witnessed the dynamite keg of the man's temper, Stockburn hoped he would not.

"You run along home, now, honey," Vincent said. "We're gonna go in and palaver with Mr. Darlington and Mr. Ramsay."

Belle tilted her head to see around her husband. She raked Stockburn up and down, blinked once, slowly, and said, "Who's your friend, Vincent? I don't believe I've seen him around before. I'm sure I'd remember." She fluttered her long, blond lashes.

"Oh, this here is Mr. Wolf Stockburn, honey." Vincent placed one hand on Belle's arm as he turned to face the railroad detective. "Mr. Stockburn, this is my dear lovely wife, Belle. Ain't she purty as a picture?" Smiling proudly, the town marshal crouched down, puckered up, and pressed his lips to Belle's cheek. Seeing the blood he'd left on her fair skin, he quickly brushed it off with his thumb.

"She certainly is a rare beauty." Wolf removed his hat and held it over his chest. "Mrs. DePaul, the pleasure is all mine."

"Mr. Stockburn is a railroad detective for Wells Fargo, honey."

"You don't say!" Belle squealed. "I've surely heard of such men but I've never met one before. Never thought I'd live to see one in the flesh. Really? You're a Wells Fargo man, Mr. Stockburn?"

Flushing and giving the young woman a gentle push, Vincent said, "Well, uh, Belle, you'll have to excuse me and Mr. Stockburn. Like I said, we gotta go in an' visit with Mr. Darlington and Mr. Ramsay."

"Oh. Oh . . . all right," Belle said, sidling away, her blue

eyes riveted on the tall, gray-headed, black-clad railroad
detective.

"Good day, Mrs. DePaul," Wolf said, following Vincent
toward the broad wooden steps of the hotel's front gallery.

"Pleasure, Mr. Stockburn," the young woman sang out,
smiling brightly over her shoulder as she flounced away.

"No, no," Wolf said, setting his hat back on his head.
"The pleasure was all mine!"

As he and Vincent crossed the galley to the hotel's front
door, Stockburn ignored the chuckling of several cow
punchers around him.

CHAPTER 20

Stockburn was glad Vincent had ignored the snickers on the gallery, as well. Or maybe he didn't notice? The town marshal of Bottleneck seemed to notice a lot of things about his pretty wife, and he worried about plenty of those things. But maybe he had a few blind spots.

On the other hand, maybe when you married a gal as pretty and obviously as coquettish as Belle, you acquired blind spots out of necessity. If you didn't, at one time or another you'd likely find yourself having to pistol whip every man in town.

"What do you think of Belle?" Vincent asked as he led Stockburn up the hotel's broad, carpeted staircase. He cast a proud smile over his right shoulder, showing some dried blood at the left corner of his lower lip.

"She seems . . . uh . . . very nice."

"Purty, too, ain't she?"

"Very."

"Sometimes I think she's too purty," Vincent said, plodding heavily up the steps and grinning back at Stockburn again. "Leastways, too purty for me to sleep nights, thinkin' about all the trouble she could get into while I'm at work. The men around here—well, they *knew her*, if you get my drift, back before Belle and I married a little over a year ago."

"Oh, I see."

Vincent stopped as they gained the second-floor hall. "Tell me, Mr. Stockburn, would you have done it? I mean—would you have married an upstairs girl?"

"I suppose if I loved her I would have."

"Even one so purty?"

"Especially one so purty."

"Even that all the men know . . . and remember . . . and ogle all the damn time so it about makes you grind your molars down to a fine powder?"

"Uh . . . Vincent . . . shouldn't we catch Mr. Darlington and Mr. Ramsay while they're still in their meeting?"

"Oh, sure. Of course! I'm sorry, Mr. Stockburn!"

"Not at all, not at all," Wolf said, relieved to have been released from the uncomfortable conversation. Obviously, Vincent had his hands full with the woman he'd married. On the other hand, many a man would not mind having their hands nearly as full.

Following Vincent down the hall, Wolf cleared his throat to quash a wry, involuntary chuckle.

Vincent stopped at a door about halfway down the hall, and knocked. On the other side of the door, boots thudded and spurs chinged. Beneath it all, Stockburn heard two men talking. The door knob turned with a soft screech, the latch clicked, and the door opened about two feet. The face appearing in the two-foot gap was vaguely familiar, long and craggy with an inordinately large nose with a bulbous, pitted tip. The man, however, wasn't very tall.

Yes, the gent was familiar, indeed. But for the life of Stockburn, he couldn't place it.

"What do you want?" asked the long-faced man, glaring coldly up at Vincent.

"Hello, Mr. Ford," Vincent said, doffing his hat and kneading the brim with his fingers. He'd suddenly become an over-friendly dog. A truckling one, at that. "I got a Wells Fargo detective here, Mr. Wolf Stockburn, to see Mr. Darlington and Mr. Ramsay."

The short, ugly man's washed-out eyes switched to Stockburn, and that big nose flared its nostrils. The craggy face pinched up like the man had just taken a bite of a sour apple. "You."

Wolf remembered where he'd seen the man before. On horseback out front of the Buzzard's Bench station the previous night. "We meet again, J.C.."

"Who is it, J.C.?" asked a man behind J.C. "Who's there?"

"Just the man who killed two of your riders last night, Mr. Ramsay." J.C. drew the door wide and turned to half face the two men in tailored business suits sitting at a table behind him.

The leavings from a recent meal, two half-filled brandy goblets and two smoldering cigars, sat on the table between the two men. Amidst the smell of the cigars, Stockburn smelled Belle's fried chicken.

"What're you talking about?" said the slighter of the two men at the table. He was just under average height but whipcord thin with a neat cap of gray hair on his square head, and a neatly trimmed gray mustache. He had a brooding look.

"The man who shot Waco Pierce and Randall Nolan, Mr. Ramsay," J.C. said, glaring at Stockburn. "At the Buzzard's Bench Station." He smiled with only his teeth, not his eyes. "And said you could kiss his—"

"You did?" Vincent asked Stockburn, eyes wide in surprise.

Stockburn stepped into the room and hooked his

thumbs behind his cartridge belt. "Wolf Stockburn, Wells Fargo. I have a nasty habit of defending myself." He parried the small, gray-haired man's gaze with a direct one of his own. "You're Ramsay, I take it?"

Ramsay slid his chair back awkwardly, for the legs caught on the deep carpet. The napkin draped over his right leg sailed to the floor. "I am Gordon Ramsay. I'd like to know what you were doing out at Buzzard's Bench, Mr. Stockburn. More to the point, I'd like to know why you were out there gunning down my men when you should have been investigating the train robberies. Do you know how many beeves we've had stolen over the past couple of months, since we started shipping cattle to the Indian reservations?"

Stockburn lifted his chin and scratched his neck. "I'd say around three thousand."

The second suited man rose from the table. He was taller and darker than Ramsay. He was about Ramsay's age, early sixties, but he carried a considerable paunch behind his floral vest framed by the lapels of his red velvet Prince Albert coat. The lapels boasted some kind of sleek fur, possibly mink. The red velvet was adorned with gold stitching, which matched that of the man's floral waistcoat. His hair was thick and wavy as it flowed straight back from his high, freckled forehead. His round, steel-framed spectacles glinted in the light of two gas lamps bracketed on the walls.

"Mr. Stockburn, I am Graham Darlington. I own the Cerro Alto Railroad." He stepped forward, extending his hand to Stockburn.

"What are you doing, Graham?" Ramsay said. "Don't shake this man's hand. He shot two of my men last night. Do you know how hard it is to get good men to punch cows out here, with kill-crazy banditos and rustlers behind every rock and cactus?"

Ramsay was a fiery little bull-dog. He wore an ivory-gripped .44 high on his right hip, and the flap of his gray wool jacket was pulled back behind it as though he were considering using it.

Darlington smiled behind his glinting spectacles as he shook Stockburn's hand. "Oh, come on, Gordon. Are you really going to shoot a Wells Fargo detective? One who's been sent here to solve our problem? If he can, that is. You do know others have come . . . and they've failed, don't you, Stockburn?" He considered the detective over the tops of his glasses.

"Yes, I heard."

"Wells Fargo can go to hell! They were in charge of those deliveries, and look what happened! They put two old men on the last train. Cannon fodder!" Ramsay turned his little, pale gray eyes on Stockburn and said, "You can leave the same way you came, Stockburn. Before I or one of my men blows you out of your boots. I protect my own, see, so they protect me—and there's plenty to be protected from in these parts!" Ramsay was snarling like a leg-trapped coyote, showing his teeth and jerking his head so violently a lock of his gray hair dropped down over his forehead. He had one small, pale hand on the ivory grips of his holstered .44.

"Gordon, please!" Graham Darlington cajoled the rancher in exasperation. He turned to Stockburn, smiled, and shook his head. "Please, Mr. Stockburn, take a seat. Ramsay will calm down in a minute. Have a drink, Gordon."

"No, I won't calm down in a minute," Ramsay shot back. "I lost two good men last night." He pointed an angry finger at Stockburn. "That will be charged to your account! Besides, Graham and I have made plans to bring in our men. So, like I said, you can—"

"Gordon!" Darlington bellowed, pounding his fist on the table. "Please, sit down and hear the man out."

"He's one man. We'll hire a dozen men. Good trackers and killers. That's what we need. Good trackers and killers!"

Stockburn said calmly, "You have the money to hire a dozen good trackers and killers?" He looked from Ramsay to Darlington and back to Ramsay again. "Do you know how much it would cost to hire that many *good* trackers and killers? Men that you can trust? Who won't take your money and then your cattle, as well? Sure, they'll take your cattle and what in holy hell do you think you'll be able to do about it, Ramsay?"

Stockburn chuckled then stepped forward and hiked a foot onto a chair at the table. He leaned over, resting one elbow on his raised knee. "Who were you thinking? Curly Walters? Maybe Hannibal Lee? Possibly Ed Thorn from over in Arizona? Maybe Rake Hanford?" He cast his shrewd smile between the two men. Ramsay flushed and looked at Darlington. Darlington flushed then, too, and looked down at the table—a sheepish schoolboy caught planning to throw a snake into the girls' privy.

"Yes," Stockburn said. "All good trackers and killers. They each have their own gang." He paused for effect then narrowed his eyes shrewdly, adding, "And how much will they cost? And how far can you trust any of them? Just how reliable are any of those men? Besides," he quickly added, "Hannibal Lee was shot by U.S. marshals near Deadwood Gulch last month. He and his top hand, Merle Schraeder, were shot down like dogs. I heard about it just before I left Kansas City. Rake Hanford is in the territorial pen in Colorado. I don't know about the others. They might still be on this side of the sod. If so, they're likely as old as both of you."

The two businessmen turned to each other slowly and shared a dubious stare.

"You're gonna have to settle for me whether you like it or not," Stockburn said. "At least until the feds get around to sending more deputy marshals. Being way out here, I have a feeling you're not very high on their priority list. And neither is your beef meant to feed Indians they've recently been at war with. I'd apologize for your two dead men, Ramsay, but I don't make phony apologies. They had it coming." He reached forward, took an uneaten chicken leg off one of the two plates on the table, and bit into the crisp meat. Chewing, he groaned, nodded, and glanced at Vincent DePaul, who stood staring at him in wide-eyed shock, a trace of a beleaguered smile stretching his mouth. "Your wife does cook good chicken. I'll give her that, Vincent."

Ramsay's jaw dropped and his face turned red then pale. His eyes blazed as he leaned forward against the table. "Who in the hell do you think you are?"

"A professional," Stockburn said, chewing. "Here to do professional work. If I can't do it, nobody can."

"You alone?" asked Darlington. "Don't you think you're going to need some help?"

"I usually don't. I am working with another detective, though. We'll hook up again soon, most like." Stockburn didn't mention that the second detective was female. That would likely go down about as well as his having shot two of Ramsay's Agua Verde riders out of their saddles last night.

"All right," said Darlington, nodding slowly, his lips pursed. "Where do you start?"

"I already have." Stockburn glanced at Vincent then

took another bite from the chicken leg, turned around, and walked to the door.

The bulbous-nosed J.C. Ford stood near the door, scowling angrily at the big man walking toward him. "You've got some nerve, Stockburn," he said tightly, clenching his fists at his sides.

"That's what it takes." Stockburn stopped and shoved what remained of the chicken leg into the breast pocket of the man's collarless shirt. "Nerve."

J.C. looked down at the chicken leg in his shirt pocket and then glared, teeth clenched, up at the big Wells Fargo detective. Wolf smiled, then walked out of the room, turned left, and strode down the hall.

Vincent hurried to catch up to him, casting nervous looks back over his shoulder. Keeping his voice down, he said, "Do you know that them two whose horns you just filed are two of the most important men in this whole town? No, in this whole *county!*"

"Yeah," Stockburn said as he and Vincent started down the stairs. "That's why they needed their horns filed. They only respect men who can stand them down. Besides, they're behind the times. The kind of men they were going to hire are dinosaurs. I'm what they get now. A Wells Fargo detective. A professional. But they can't go around thinking I'm some tinhorn squarehead who sits down to pee. They have to see that while a fella like me is what comes with the modern age . . . and the iron horse . . . I can still hold my own against two old mossyhorns like themselves."

"They prob'ly got the hint when you shot two of Ramsay's men last night! I didn't know you done that!"

"You didn't ask," Stockburn said as they reached the hotel's first-floor lobby.

As they strode toward the big oak desk toward the front door, Vincent chuckled and glanced behind him and up the stairs. He ran a sleeve across his mouth and cackled a devilish laugh. "When you swiped that chicken leg off of Ramsay's plate, I thought he was gonna drop a calf right then an' there!" He wheezed out another laugh.

Stockburn pushed through the door. As he stepped out onto the hotel's front gallery, one of the men, whom Stockburn assumed was an Agua Verde rider, stepped in front of him, blocking his way.

"Hold on." The man was a little shorter than Stockburn, but wider. He wore a pistol and two bowie knives. He had a big, suety, freckled, red-bearded face, and his small eyes were flat with contempt. "What'd you say your name was again?"

CHAPTER 21

"Wolf Stockburn."

The big man blocking Wolf's way turned to one of the several other men spread out across the gallery fronting the Stockmen's Hotel.

That man rose slowly from his chair, making the whicker creak. "Yep, that's who J.C. said shot Waco and Nolan, all right."

Men rose from their chairs. The girls who'd been sitting with them stumbled away, casting wary glances from the Agua Verde riders to Stockburn. Those riders who'd been lounging against the porch rail, smoking and drinking beer, set their beers and cigarettes down on the porch rail and moved in with the others, squaring their hips and shoulders at Stockburn.

Wolf glanced at Vincent standing to his left. "Best step wide, Marshal. No need for you to get caught in this little, uh . . . misunderstanding."

Vincent looked at the Aqua Verde riders, opened his mouth to speak, but apparently found no words. He raised his hands, palms out, then sidled to the left, glancing guiltily at the railroad detective, who had returned his attention to the big man in front of him.

"Little foofaraw, huh?" the big, bearded man said. "Mister, you mess with Agua Verde riders, you're messin' with a *whole heap* of trouble. We take care of our own."

"Back up, Jasper. Back up," said one of the men flanking the big man.

Jasper took three strides straight back on his heavy legs and held his hands over his two holstered Russian revolvers. He'd already unsnapped the keeper thongs from over the hammers.

The eyes of the Agua Verde riders bored into Stockburn.

He stared back at them blandly, his back straight, hands ready to make their move.

"Jasper, what on earth is going on over here?" a young woman's voice cut through the silence that had been stretched tight as Glidden wire. "Everybody looks so serious!"

Boots thudded softly on the gallery steps and then the head of a pretty, dark-skinned, chocolate-haired, young lady rose up from behind Jasper's beefy left shoulder. The girl was flushed and a little out of breath. She smiled as she glanced up at Jasper then made a face of mock anger as she leaned a shoulder into Jasper's, and pushed him to one side.

"Miss Lana!" Jasper complained, glancing at the young woman and then quickly shutting his strained gaze back to Stockburn. He grabbed the girl's arm. "You stay out of this!"

Miss Lana pulled her arm free, glowering up at the bearded man. "Stay out of what? What in blazes is going on, Jas—oh, hello!" She'd turned her head toward Stockburn and stood gazing up at him, smiling.

She was a small girl, maybe five-feet-two and a hundred and ten pounds or so. But well built. Pretty in an earthy way though there was nothing at all earthy about her velvet gown—orange-colored with a brown corset over a cream silk blouse with puffy sleeves. The corset and sleeveless blouse were cut low enough to reveal a good bit of light-copper cleavage. If she didn't have some Indian blood, with those high cheekbones and dark skin, then she certainly had some Mexican in her. Maybe both. She spoke with not a trace of an accent, however.

Her slender arms were full of orange skirt, which she'd lifted high to avoid tripping over while climbing the gallery steps. Releasing all the pleats and folds made swishing sounds as they tumbled to hang straight down her legs to the floor. A little self-consciously she straightened her delicate feather and lace hat, which sat pinned atop her pinned-up hair, which looked a little damp from a recent bath.

Stockburn had a feeling she knew how ridiculous and superfluous the hat was. Unhandy decoration—and why she'd pinned it so carelessly to her head. But she didn't seem self-conscious about its garishness at all. Maybe she liked how it contrasted her earthy, dusky-skinned, dark-eyed beauty.

Stockburn certainly did.

Judging by the humor dancing in her eyes and pulling at her lips—fairly radiating off of her, in fact—she was having one hell of a jumping good time being exactly who she was, silly hat and all.

"Hello," Wolf said, his throat a little tight. In three seconds, he'd forgotten all about the imminent showdown with the Agua Verde riders. They seemed to have forgotten about it, too. All eyes were on the girl. As flinty hard as the cow punchers' eyes had been only a few seconds ago, they were now as downy soft as those of twelve-year-old boys in love with their pretty schoolteacher.

The girl shifted her weight to one hip, gazed with cool coquettishness up at Stockburn, and said, "And who, may I ask, are you?"

Jasper stepped forward and placed a hand on the girl's shoulder. "Now, Miss Lana, you gotta—"

"Lana!" The stentorian voice thundered from inside the hotel, behind Stockburn. It was accompanied by two sets of quickly striding feet. "There you are!"

Lana leaned to one side to see around Stockburn and said, "Hello, Papa. Sorry I'm late. I reckon I slept in. It was a long stagecoach ride yesterday."

"Well, I'm glad you're here, young lady. I don't know why you don't stay at the Stockmen's. It's so much nicer than the Lone Star's humble digs."

"Yes, but the Lone Star's food is so much better"— the girl smiled as she playfully reached up and flicked Ramsay's nose—"if you prefer huevos rancheros to gruel and poached eggs for breakfast."

"Yes, well . . ." Stepping past Stockburn, the rancher glanced up at the detective with an incredulous expression, then took the girl's hand. "Come along, dear." He glanced at the men standing on the gallery, still facing Stockburn, and said, "Come on, gentlemen. My daughter is here at last. Time to saddle up. Much work to be done at the Agua Verde!"

"Mr. Ramsay," Jasper said as Ramsay and the pretty girl who was improbably his daughter, started down the gallery steps, "we were just having a conversation with Mr. Stockburn about our two dead pards, sir."

"Oh, you were, were you?" Ramsay stopped near the hitch rack to which the Morgan was tied. He cast a cold, dark glance at Stockburn then slid his gaze to J.C. Ford, who had just stepped out of the hotel with Graham Darlington. The rancher switched his gaze back to the big bearded Jasper. "Not here. Not now." He looked at Stockburn again, curling part of his upper lip. "There's a time and a place for everything, gentlemen. Not in the broad daylight in the heart of town, for the love of Mike!" His tone was as threatening as his eyes.

Young Lana, standing beside her father, looked up at Stockburn again, this time with renewed interest, one brow arched. She turned to her father with a curious expression, but before she could ask the question that started moving her lips, Ramsay led her to the side of the carriage and helped her climb up into the rear seat.

J.C. Ford brushed past Stockburn, rudely nudging the detective's elbow, and descended the gallery steps. With a dark look at Stockburn, he picked up the two trunks the girl must have deposited there, and set them in the carriage beside her. He untied the reins from the hitch rack and climbed into the front seat of the carriage beside Ramsay.

As the other men mounted their horses, Ramsay turned to Stockburn once more. "You have one week to find out where those cattle are going, Stockburn. One week. Then I fire Wells Fargo, sue them for the losses incurred, and take my men off their normal ranching duties. I hire the toughest nuts in the business. I'd rather not use them for that, since it's your problem, but I will if I have to."

He glanced at his men, some of whom were still mounting. "Make no mistake. Times might be changing, but there are still some tough nuts in this country. I know, because they ride for me. First, we give you a chance to clean up the mess your company caused by letting those trains get robbed. Good day, sir," he said with a stiff, two-fingered

salute as J.C. Ford flicked the reins over the Morgan's back
and the chaise lurched out into the street.

The mounted riders cast threatening looks at Stockburn
as they turned their horses and booted them after the
carriage. The girl, Lana, glanced back over her shoulder at
Stockburn. The dust was rising and the riders further
obscured Stockburn's view of the beguiling temptress, but
he thought she smiled just before turning her head back
forward.

How many temptresses are out this way, anyway? he
silently opined, remembering Violet.

Stockburn walked to the top of the gallery steps and
stood gazing out over the street at the quickly disappearing
carriage and the Agua Verde riders. Absently, he dug into
his shirt pocket for his makings pouch.

Vincent stepped up to stand beside him again, chuckling and patting him on the back with a sheepish air.
"Sorry about that, Stockburn," the beefy young marshal
said. "But Mr. Ramsay done pulled strings with the town
council to give me this job. I don't know. I reckon he saw
somethin' in me that looked promising. Probably my size.
He's a little man, and littler fellas respect a man's size, I
figure. I ain't much good with a six-shooter. That's why
I carry the twelve-gauge here. Don't worry, it gets the job
done." He patted the shotgun hanging off his shoulder.
"Like I was sayin', I don't see no sense in bitin' the hand
that feeds me. That's why I stepped away. Not cause I was
afraid, ya understand."

Wolf said, "I'd have done the same if I'd been in your
place."

Vincent looked at him askance. "You don't think I'm
yaller, do you?"

Stockburn smiled and shook his head. He was staring

at the street. In fact, what he was staring at had him more than a little distracted.

"All right, then," Vincent said, cupping his tender jaw in his hand. "I think I'm gonna wander on home, have a coupla shots of whiskey to kill the pain in my busted jaw, and keep an eye on that crazy wife of mine." He glanced over his shoulder at Darlington.

Stockburn glanced at the railroad owner, as well, and saw the flush rise in the man's pale, sun-starved face. Chuckling, Vincent dropped lazily down the gallery steps and angled across the street to Stockburn's left, heading generally southwest, occasionally spitting more blood.

Darlington remained behind Stockburn for a time, then stepped up to take Vincent's place beside the railroad detective. "Sorry about Ramsay, Stockburn. Gordon's a tough hombre. But it takes tough hombres to settle this country."

"I'm sure it does." Stockburn continued to scrutinize the street about ten feet in front of the gallery steps as he slowly, mechanically dribbled tobacco into the wheat paper troughed between his fingers. "It's a tough country anywhere in the west, but especially this far off the beaten path."

"It certainly is," Darlington said.

Slowly rolling the wheat paper closed around the tobacco, making soft crinkling sounds, bits of tobacco leaking from both ends of the cylinder, Stockburn cast the railroad owner a sidelong glance. "Does Ramsay have any enemies?"

"Any man who's gotten as far as Gordon has is sure to have enemies. I can't think of anyone specific, however. He didn't take his land from anyone. Except for the Indians, of course. A band of Comanches had called these mountains home, but they were no match for Ramsay's men and the army out of Fort McCallister he had backing him. There's only a few left. A raggedy-heeled lot living out in the Wet Rocks country. Why do you ask?"

Wolf scratched a match to life on his shell belt. "Just wondering if it could be a personal matter—the thievery. Or just money."

"Just money, I would think. Personal matters are usually settled in other ways, aren't they, Mr. Stockburn?"

"You'd be surprised by the way some personal matters are settled, Mr. Darlington."

"Yes, I suppose I would." The railroad owner drew a deep breath. "Well, I'd better get back to work." He canted his head toward the Cerro Alto line's depot station, which apparently doubled as a main office. It sat maybe two hundred feet to the west of the Stockmen's Hotel. "I have more than a few letters to write to creditors and clients after that latest holdup as well as prepare for a meeting of the Cattlemen's Association later tomorrow evening. I hope I can avoid a hanging. Those ranchers are rather worked up and out for mine and Gordon's heads!"

"Good luck."

"I certainly hope you find the culprits soon, Mr. Stockburn. As well as the cattle."

"I'll do my best." Stockburn stepped down to the street.

"Good grief," Darlington said, scowling down at Stockburn from atop the gallery steps. "What are you looking at down there?"

Holding his cigarette in his left hand, he traced the outline of a horseshoe print with the index finger of his right hand. He was pretty sure it was a print left by a hoof of Ramsay's Morgan. The shoe by itself wasn't puzzling.

What had Stockburn's interest piqued was the star adorning the shoe between the toe caulk and the shank.

It was the same star that had decorated the shoe of the bushwhacker's horse. On the same foot, as well. The left rear one.

CHAPTER 22

"This shoe mark," Stockburn said, indicating the star in the shoe print on the street before him. "Do you recognize it?"

Darlington walked down the gallery steps and his shadow passed over Stockburn's hand indicating the shoe print. The railroad owner crouched and frowned behind his glinting spectacles. "Hmm . . . no . . . no. Can't say that I do." He straightened, frowning down at Stockburn. "Significant?"

"Maybe. Or . . . maybe not." Wolf straightened and stood looking around, puffing his cigarette.

"Well, as I said, I'd best get to work." Darlington headed to his office.

Stockburn merely grunted as he cast his gaze past the depot station that doubled as the railroad line's main office to a small cluster of buildings on the next rise beyond it to the south. Over there lay a barber shop, a saloon, a feed store, and a gun and ammunition shop. More specifically, Mandrake & Sons Guns & Ammunition shop.

Absently, Stockburn brushed his hand across that pocket of his coat in which nestled the receipt he'd found among the rocks at Buzzard's Bench Station. He was about to walk over to Smoke and mount up, but stopped when he realized he'd been feeling a chill between his shoulder blades, despite the near one-hundred-degree heat.

He had a lot on his mind so he hadn't given the feeling the attention he normally did. When something was wrong or when someone was watching or following him, he usually felt a physical sensation of angst that usually came in the form of a cold witch's hand pressed flat, fingers splayed, between his shoulders.

He turned to see a man standing in the break between two low, unmarked adobe brick buildings that had probably been there before Bottleneck had become a town. Both structures were flanked by a small barn and a stock pen sheathed in tumbleweeds and chaparral. The man just stood there, tall and dark, with long, dark hair. Still as a statue. He held a cigarette down low in his right hand. His big face, a brown splotch from where Stockburn stood, was indistinct.

A sudden wind gust obscured the man. Stockburn blinked against the blowing dust as he placed his hand over the grips of one of his .45s. He relaxed the hand when the man suddenly flicked his cigarette out into the street. The wind took the stub and blew it away, bouncing it along the ground. Orange cinders glinted before they died. Stockburn watched the man turn and walk deeper into the break between the two adobe brick hovels.

Gone.

His only feature Stockburn had been able to make out was his long black hair, which the wind blew wildly despite the red bandana tied around his head. The man was gone but that cold hand remained between Stockburn's shoulders.

Feeling like walking over to the gunsmith's shop, Wolf glanced at his horse standing at the hitch rack fronting the hotel. He decided to leave Smoke where he was. Slower that way. More time to look around, ponder. To figure out why that cold witch was keeping her chill hand on his back.

He walked toward the depot station and the newly laid rails, which dead-ended at the story-and-a-half station building, ghostly quiet, there being no train on the siding. Likely there wouldn't be another train in Bottleneck—at least not one leaving Bottleneck—until the robbers had been run to ground, the cattle returned to Gordon Ramsay and the rest of the ranchers who belonged to the Cattlemen's Association.

Stockburn mounted the cobblestone platform that ran along the near side of the rails and fronted the depot building. As he crossed the platform as well as the rails, he shuttled his gaze to Mandrake & Sons Guns & Ammunition shop. Again, his brows furled a curious frown. A short, thin, bald man stood in the shop's open doorway. He'd been staring toward Stockburn, but as soon as Wolf turned his head toward the shop, the little man lurched with a start and, feigning a casual air, ran a feather duster far too busily along the frame of the doorway he was standing in.

He cast a furtive glance toward Stockburn. Seeing Wolf still staring at him, he jerked his head back straight then, again trying very hard to appear casual, turned slowly and ambled away from the doorway, the small shop's deep shadows consuming him.

Stockburn cast a befuddled scowl toward the gun shop and scratched his head. The town was getting curiouser and curiouser.

Not having forgotten the man with the long black hair who'd been giving him the wooly eyeball from between the two old hovels, Stockburn glanced behind him again. No sign of that man. Still, that cold hand remained pressed to his upper back. A needling sensation at best.

He closed on the gun shop. A wood frame building

calling itself Lyin' Lyle's Whiskey Emporium sat about thirty feet to the right of it. A half dozen saddled horses stood in the shade of the brush arbor fronting the humble little place slouched under a rusted corrugated tin roof. A clay olla with a gourd dipper hung from the gallery ceiling near the front door from which the slow patters of a piano being played leisurely mingled with the occasional gusts of the wind and the ticking sounds of the wind-blown sand and grit. A moldering gray box on the front rail was adorned with three wine-red roses fluttering in the dusty breeze.

The saloon was the sight of the most activity Wolf had seen so far in Bottleneck.

Stockburn climbed the two steps to the small stoop fronting the gun shop. He crossed to the door and peered inside. Shelves of ammunition lined the wall to his right. A glass display counter ran along the wall to his left. Several new-model rifles with glistening, freshly varnished stocks were displayed in wall racks behind the counter. The little man—bald on top with a horseshoe of long, silver-gray hair hanging to his shoulders—had gray goat whiskers to go with his goatlike face, and was running his feather duster along the pistols displayed in baize-lined wooden boxes atop the counter. More pistols were displayed inside the counter along with boxes of ammunition coinciding with the pistols' calibers.

He slid his washed-out blue eyes toward Stockburn standing in the doorway. "Well, hello there, stranger. Didn't see ya there!"

Wolf smiled affably. "Hidy."

The bald little man extended his small, pale hand, the nails rimed with gun oil. "Jeff Mandrake at your service."

"Wolf Stockburn."

"Pleased to meet you, Mr. Stockburn."

"The pleasure's mine, Mr. Mandrake." He looked around. "Where are your sons?"

"Oh, there ain't none." Mandrake gave a devilish grin. "I just put that on the sign to make it sound like a family business. You know—a business of long-standin'. I did the same thing in Benson and again in Silver City an' now here. I'll be damned if it don't help. I think it makes me seem more honest to have a family—a prideful owner with impeachable integrity and thus the desire to have his sons continue the business long after he's nothin' more than a few shovelfuls of dust in a box."

Stockburn chuckled. "If you say so, Mr. Mandrake."

Mandrake slapped the counter. "What can I do you for? Need fresh pills fer them purty forty-fives, do ya?" He whistled as he looked over the counter at Stockburn's holstered hardware. "I'll say, them's sure some fine-lookin' shootin' irons!"

"Thank you, but I'm here for another reason." Stockburn pulled the ammo receipt out of his coat pocket. "I'm wondering if you'd remember who purchased these forty-four cartridges a few days back. There's no signature, just the initials T.C. circled at the bottom." He smoothed the receipt on the glass counter and turned it so Mandrake could read it.

The shop owner made a face as he scowled down at the leaf. He picked it up and held it down and at nearly arm's length away from him, then dropped it back down on the counter. "Nah, must've been a cash transaction. No name on it."

"You don't remember who you sold two boxes of forty-four cartridges to? I realize it's a common caliber but don't those initials mean anything to you? You must have written them."

Mandrake scowled down at the leaf on the counter again, stretching his lips back from his teeth, slowly shaking his head. Suddenly he stopped shaking his head. His face slackened a little, and his cheeks lost their color. Slowly, he raised his gaze to Stockburn. His face was suddenly flat and unreadable though there was something in his eyes.

What?

Apprehension?

Slowly, he shook his head again. "Nah, nah. Sorry, Mr. Stockburn. I can't help you." He slid his gaze to the door flanking the railroad detective. The washed-out blue orbs suddenly glinted fearfully, and he said, "Now, if you don't mind, I put a pot of coffee on the range in the back room an' I best get to it before it scorches."

Stockburn turned toward the door that opened off the shack's rear wall, behind the counter. "Funny, I don't smell fresh mud."

"I'm sorry, Mr. Stockburn." Mandrake leaned forward, splaying his hands out on the countertop, his goatlike features owning a testy, demanding air. "I can't help you. Good day, sir!"

"You're an observant man, Mandrake," Wolf said, returning the man's testy gaze with a hard, suspicious one of his own. "You were watching me for a long time before I headed this way. Looks like you have a lot of time on your hands, too. Are you sure you don't remember?"

The man shoved his face up close to Stockburn's, and jutted his jaw. "Good-day, sir!"

"All right," Wolf said, holding his hands up in supplication, palms out. He turned toward the door. "You let me know if—" He stopped when he saw a tall, dark man with long black hair blowing in the wind, raise a rifle to his shoulder.

Clad in a calico shirt, buckskin trousers, moccasins, and with a red bandanna knotted around his forehead, he was the man who'd been giving Wolf the wooly eyeball between the two adobe hovels a few minutes ago. An uncorked bottle stood on the ground near the Indian's right boot. In his late-fifties, early sixties, with a long, leathery face and deep-set black eyes, he cocked the Spencer repeater in his hands and pressed his cheek to the stock. "Time to die, Wells Fargo man!" he bellowed tonelessly.

CHAPTER 23

Instinctively, Stockburn ducked a quarter eye blink before flames lapped from the Spencer's barrel. The bullet screeched through the air where Stockburn's head had been a moment before and made a dull smacking noise. The thunder of the Spencer reached Stockburn's ears and then his Colts were in his hands and he was straightening, raising both pistols, firing. He put two pills into the sinewy Indian's brisket before he even knew what he was doing. It was all instinct.

The man grunted and stumbled backward, kicking over the whiskey bottle. He dropped the rifle and toppled like a windmill in a thunderstorm, throwing his muscular arms nearly straight out to both sides. He quivered a little as he died, grinding the heels of his moccasins into the dusty street.

The overturned bottle made a dark wet stain in the dirt near his feet.

Remembering the odd sound the Indian's bullet had made, Stockburn glanced behind him. Mandrake was not standing where he'd been standing a moment before. Wolf discovered why a moment later, when he stepped up to the counter and leaned forward. The reason Mandrake was not standing behind the counter was because he lay behind it just like the Indian lay out on the street—flat on his back, arms stretched out to both sides.

The only difference was that Mandrake was sporting a bullet wound in nearly the dead center of his forehead. His pale blue eyes had rolled up in their sockets as though to get a better look at the pill that had just killed him.

"Damn," Stockburn said, wincing guiltily. "Sorry about that, fella." He turned around, walked out into the street, and stood over the Indian who lay staring up at him, both rheumy eyes wide open. His thick-lipped mouth was half open, forming a nearly perfect O.

His black hair was long and grizzled, with only a few strands of silver. His face, however, looked like a relief map of New Mexico Territory—all pits, seams, shallow arroyos, and deep fissures in which a good bit of stubborn western dust and grit had collected over the years. His skin was copper red with darker undertones.

Full-blood Comanche.

An Indian feather tattoo adorned the left side of his neck, just beneath his left ear, which was missing its lobe.

"Well, I'll be damned," Stockburn said, mostly to himself, his voice pitched with surprised recognition. "If it ain't ole Comanche Joe."

"Comanche Joe, all right." The voice had come from near the Cerro Alto rails behind Stockburn.

He turned to see Vincent DePaul stepping across the rails. The big lawman held his shotgun down low along his right leg and his hat on his head against the wind with his other hand.

"You know this man, I take it," Stockburn said as Vincent stopped to gaze down grimly at the dead Indian.

"Yep," Vincent said, nodding. "Sure do. Everyone around here knows Comanche Joe. Lives back in the mountains apiece with a bunch of Comanche misfits. Tame misfits, mostly. They keep to themselves, but Joe comes to town now an' then to tie one on." He glanced at Stockburn. "How do you know him?"

"Hell, I arrested him damn near fifteen years ago. In the Indian Nations. He was one of the first train robbers I took down as a Wells Fargo agent. He and a few other disgruntled men from various tribes were preying on the Atchison, Topeka and Santa Fe Railway. I and a couple of deputy U.S. marshals out of Judge Parker's court ran Joe and his gang to ground near the Canadian River. Parker gave him twenty years in the Arkansas Pen. He busted out after six. Never to be seen again . . . till now."

"Oh, Joe's been seen aplenty. Like I said, he lives just a little over that way. Or *lived*, I reckon. With a brood of Comanches, mostly his own women an' children. They gave the army the slip, refused to be hazed onto the reservation in Oklahoma."

"You've had this old train robber living out here and you never told anybody?"

"Ah, hell. I just learned who he was only a few months ago. He might've been a wild hoorawer at one time, but he's just a harmless old Injun drunk now. *Was*, I mean. I mean, aside from tryin' to clean your clock. He recognized you, I guess. Maybe in his addlepated way, he thought you was here to arrest him again, an' he wasn't gonna have it. He was just a crazy old drunk, Stockburn." Vincent threw out an arm to indicate Lyin' Lyle's Whiskey Emporium, outside of which six or seven men, including a fat man wearing a soiled green apron, milled. All were bearded, sun-seared desert types, and almost all had soapy beer mugs in their hands. "He liked Lyle's place in partic'lar."

"This ain't gonna go down well with his people," said the apron, who stood atop Lyin' Lyle's front steps, fists on his hips. The man who Stockburn assumed was Lyin' Lyle had thick blond hair combed to one side, a thick mustache of the same color, and two pink jowls that served as shelving platform for his rosy-cheeked head. "They look after him." He glanced to the southwest and said, "Someone'll likely be comin' for him. When he's been gone too long, two or three of the bunch usually come to town, sniffin' around for him, to take him back. They're right protective of that old man." He shifted his warning gaze to Stockburn. "And they are, well, Comanche."

"Tame, mostly," Vincent told the railroad detective. "Still, I'd, uh . . . I'd—"

"Yeah, I'll watch my back," Stockburn said, gazing down at the dead old Comanche train robber, still trying to wrap his mind around having found . . . and killed . . . the notorious Comanche Joe way out there. "I'm right used to it."

Vincent chuckled. "Rough country out here, ain't it?"

"Rough country." Stockburn nodded. "Curious country, too. I don't know what to make of it. I'm trying to track train robbers but the only train robber I've so far run down . . . and by accident . . . is this one here. And only because he tried to shoot me."

"He *was* a train robber," Vincent corrected.

Stockburn squinted at the rawboned young lawman. "You sure about that?"

"What? You think Comanche Joe's been the one stealing the cattle off Darlington's railroad?" Vincent chuckled, shook his head, and spat saliva flecked with blood into the street. "Nah. No. Maybe a few years back. But not anymore. Not Comanche Joe."

"What about his people?"

"Queer, silent folks. Dress like Comanches, but never been a threat. Never stay in town too long. Just come in to buy supplies. They're mostly self-sufficient up there around them springs near Wet Rocks. Never get drunk an' cause trouble. Like I said—"queer, silent folks". Harmless. They live together in peace, an' that's all I care about." He glanced at one of the men standing on the stoop near Lyin' Lyle. "Ed, run over an' tell Charlie Black to bring his wagon over here and load up Comanche Joe, will you? He can hold him there until his people come for him."

"You got one more in the gun shop," Stockburn said, though his mind was still on Comanche Joe and the other "queer, silent folks" living together around the springs near Wet Rocks.

As the man called Ed strode off to fetch the undertaker, Stockburn stretched his gaze to the southwest, where those Wet Rocks apparently were. He'd find out where exactly and maybe ride into that country and pay a visit to Comanche's Joe's people.

Maybe they were more than just queer and silent. Maybe Comanche Joe had tried to drill Stockburn a third eye for another reason besides revenge. Maybe he didn't want him sniffing around and possibly getting too close to him and his queer silent brood up in the Wet Rocks country.

Had Joe been the man who'd tried to bushwhack him at Buzzard's Bench?

Had Joe's queer, silent folks killed Wooly and Gerta Carson?

Stockburn looked at the young lawman. "Say, Vincent, did Joe come to town on a horse?"

"Yessir. A fine one at that. His folks trap and gentle the wild ones up there, don't ya know?"

"Can I see it?"

Vincent's thick brows stitched in a frown. "What would you want to see his horse for?"

"Let's just say I'm curious."

"Well, hell If you want to look at his horse, look at his horse." Vincent canted his head to indicate the adobe brick and wood-frame livery and feed barn not fifty yards away to the west. A sign over the big double front doors read simply LIVERY & FEED. Below it, in smaller, sloppily painted letters ONLY ONE IN TOWN.

A bent old buzzard of a man, stooped over as though he had a fifty-pound feed bag on his back, and chewing tobacco like a cow chews its cud, stood near the open doors, regarding Stockburn and Vincent dubiously. He had little buzzard's eyes and wore a striped serape and ragged straw sombrero.

"All right," Stockburn said, heading toward the barn. "I'll take a look."

Vincent followed, hanging back a little, scowling curiously. Stockburn pinched his hat brim to the bent-up old buzzard he assumed was the barn's owner. The old buzzard did not acknowledge the greeting but only turned stiffly, looking like he would fall facedown on the ground at any second.

Vincent followed Stockburn into the barn.

"Which one?" Wolf asked, gazing down the main alley. He could see only three or four horses in the stables on each side of the alley.

"That one right there," Vincent said, pointing to the first horse on the left side of the alley. "The big appy."

Stockburn walked down the alley. He cooed to the fine appaloosa watching him suspiciously, twitching its ears. He opened the door and stood calming the horse for a time, patting its left wither. When he'd gained the horse's trust, he walked around it slowly and calmly checked the left rear hoof. He dropped the hoof then checked the others.

He stepped back out of the stall and into the alley, and sighed.

"No star?"

Stockburn closed the stable door and latched it. "No."

"I didn't figure. The old man's been drunk for two days. He didn't have time, nor was in any condition, to ride out to Buzzard's Bench and pot shoot you."

"I reckon you're right, Vincent." Wolf lifted his chin and scratched his neck. "He sure had a chip on his shoulder, though. And even drunk he recognized me as soon as he saw me. It was almost like . . . well . . ."

"Like what?"

"Like he'd been expecting me."

"Expecting you? To come here? Comanche Joe?"

Stockburn nodded, his own dark suspicions growing but not taking any resolute form. They were like the shadows of birds winging around in front of his face. He couldn't make out colors or species.

He did, however, suspect that he'd come to the right place to look for answers to his questions. He just wished he could form better answers so he could arrive at firmer conclusions.

Who were the train robbers? Where did they come from? Where were they now? Why were they preying on the Cerro Alto line to the exclusion of all other lines in the area? Not that there were that many railroads out there. But the only thing this spur line carried was cattle from the Shackleford County Cattlemen's Association.

And they were carrying the beef to Indian reservations.

That fact pretty much excluded Joe. Comanche Joe wouldn't try to keep the government from feeding Indians. He'd been raiding railroads in the Nations because he'd been fighting against the incursion of the White Man.

"Are any more shipments planned?" Wolf asked Vincent. "I mean, soon. Looks like those cattle pens are a might full."

"Not that I know of, but them herds was trailed a long way from the outlying ranches, and the cattlemen don't want to haze 'em back and run a bunch of tallow offen 'em. They're gonna run out of feed soon, so—"

"I know. Soon, they won't have a choice." Stockburn glanced at Vincent. "Is the train still in Las Cruces?"

"Far as I know."

Stockburn walked down the alley and out the barn's open doors and into the street. He stopped and looked around, pondering. "No point in making a run, though, until we have more men to guard those cattle. They'd be shipping them right into the robbers' hands."

"We could maybe hire a few boys from these parts. Maybe the cattlemen would put their own men on those trains."

Stockburn looked at the several saloons—dumps mostly—sitting up the street on his right. But the cowboys who'd hazed the cattle into the pens flanking the depot were out there on the front stoops, milling, talking, cavorting with fallen women, drinking beer and shuttling their curious gazes from Stockburn and Vincent to Comanche Joe still lying dead in the street to Wolf's left.

The ranch hands looked like capable enough cow punchers. But very few looked older than twenty. They were not seasoned gun hands. No telling what they'd do when they found themselves trapped on a train with guns blasting away at them from fast-moving horses.

"Those men are needed on the range," Stockburn said, "Let me keep snooping around for a bit. Maybe I can figure out who the robbers are. For some crazy reason, I have a feeling I'm close."

"Really?" Vincent seemed surprised.

"Yeah. Nothing adds up yet, but I have a feeling it will soon. Don't ask me why, but I do." Stockburn turned to the old buzzard of a liveryman. "Señor," he said in his rudimentary Spanish, "is there a farrier around here who marks his shoes with a star?"

The old man's wiry gray brows lumped over his eyes, and he grunted, "*Estrella*?"

"Si. *Estrella*." Stockburn toed the design in the dirt. "Like that."

The old man looked down at the star. He seemed to study it closely. His posture hid the expression on his face but his ears appeared to turn dark beneath his natural dusky color.

"Ah, hell," Vincent said. "Roberto don't know of nobody who hammers stars in his shoes. Not around here." He raised his voice a little that Stockburn noted as a faint, cajoling edge. "Ain't that right, Roberto?"

Slowly, Roberto lifted his gaze to Stockburn, bunched his lips, and shook his head. Stockburn looked at Vincent.

Vincent smiled his unctuous smile that did not match the coldness of the young lawman's eyes. "See, I told ya."

CHAPTER 24

Wolf splashed whiskey into his water glass then set the bottle back down on the small table beside his bed in the Lone Star Inn, which Lana Ramsay had recommended so highly—at least for its Huevos Rancheros. He sat in a ladder-back chair by the bed and the table, long legs extended, the heels of his boots propped on the windowsill.

The window was open. It was around nine o'clock. A storm had blown through, kicking up a fuss and dropping maybe a half inch of rain, but it had passed quickly. He was enjoying the cool, fresh air feathering the curtains back from the window, rife with the smell of creosote and sage as he considered rolling a cigarette. Nothing like a smoke to help him ponder.

He had much to ponder but he postponed the cigarette. He'd just sit and enjoy the fresh smell of the desert mountains for a while. Breathing in and out, arms crossed on his chest, leaning back in the chair, the front legs about six inches off the floor, he pondered.

He'd stabled Smoke in the hunched-up old buzzard's livery barn, which was just east of the hotel. He'd eaten a steak with beans and drank two beers in one of the saloons, which was half filled with the restless cowboys who'd herded the cattle to Bottleneck from the surrounding ranches. Those cowboys, most obscenely young, had nothing to do but wait for orders from the ranch managers, get stupid drunk, and have their ashes hauled by Bottleneck's "ladies of the evening," who'd appeared soon after sundown like wildflowers after a spring rain. The red lanterns had been lit in the whorehouse windows, and the foot traffic between the saloons and those humble and garishly painted shacks picked up significantly.

Still, it was fairly quiet. Nearly all twelve rooms of the Lone Star Inn were occupied, but most of the young punchers were still on the prowl and likely would be till after midnight. Only a few were in their rooms. Through his room's west wall, Stockburn could hear the tones of desultory conversation punctuated by occasional laughter.

At least two of the young punchers were meritorious enough to have turned in early. Stockburn thought he could hear the occasional sputters of a shuffled card deck, which meant the two hands were playing poker. Sometimes he could faintly detect their cigarette smoke on the breeze through his window.

He didn't think about the train robberies too long. He'd already thought about them a great deal, and there was no point in letting his mind become a spinning top. He'd already digested what little he knew. The thing pressing on his mind was the man who'd tried to ambush him and Hank at Buzzard's Bench.

Was he still in town?

Of course, it had been impossible to track after he'd entered Bottleneck. His prints had been erased by the day's traffic. Roughly twenty-four hours ahead of Wolf, the bushwhacker might still be in Bottleneck or he might have passed on through. Impossible to know.

Just in case he was still on the lurk and intent on drilling Stockburn a third eye, Wolf kept close watch on the street below and on the rooftops on the street's opposite side. It was dark, but the darkness was relieved by the crisply kindling stars and by the wan illumination of several distant oil pots. Also, the street was relatively quiet except for the distant pattering of a piano and the low hum of a crowd in one of the nearby saloons or parlor houses.

If someone was out there, approaching and bearing down on Stockburn with a rifle, he'd see him or hear him. He'd kept his room dark. Enough light came from the street that he could move around without stumbling, but not enough to making him a target in the window.

Finally, in his ponderings he came to Hank.

He hoped she was having better luck tracking her quarry than he was tracking his. She must be, or he'd probably have met up with her already. She must be planning on staying overnight out in the desert. He shrugged. Or maybe she didn't have a choice?

What did that mean?

You know damn well what it means, you fool. She might be dead. That morbid thought brought him to a morbid memory—Mike.

Before he started indulging his own self-torment with the memory of that night in San Francisco so many years ago—nearly half of his life ago though it often seemed like yesterday—he reconfirmed his decision to take Comanche Joe back to his people in the morning.

Comanche Joe was a train robber. At least, he *had been* a train robber. Stockburn considered the coincidence that a man he'd put away years ago for robbing trains happened to be in Bottleneck, the very place from which the robbed trains had originated. And that he'd tried to shoot

Stockburn so soon after Wolf's arrival, as though he'd been expecting him.

Were Joe's "queer, silent folks" the bank robbers?

Stockburn was going to find out.

Deciding to have one smoke and one more belt before turning in, Stockburn reached for the bottle but forestalled the movement when footsteps sounded in the street beneath his window. A single walker moved quietly, spurs chiming faintly.

Stockburn dropped his feet to the floor, slowly rose from his chair, and stepped to the window. Sliding the curtain to one side with the back of his hand, he peered into the street.

The footsteps accompanied by the faint spur chings grew louder. Coming along the street's near side, the walker was trying to walk quietly but without much success. The footsteps stopped nearly directly below Stockburn's open window. Looking down along the front of the adobe building, he didn't see anything. Then a man's hatted head leaned out away from the hotel's front wall and it turned until his face peered up toward Wolf's window.

Tensing, Stockburn released the curtain and stepped back quickly, one hand on the grips of his cross-draw Peacemaker. He could feel his pulse in the palm of that hand.

Maybe five seconds passed before the footsteps sounded again, complete with faint spur chimes. Stockburn stepped up to the window and peered out again.

A man was walking away from the hotel and into the street, heading toward the livery barn to Stockburn's left and on the opposite side of the street. Wolf could see only the man's silhouette, but he identified him right away. Roughly Stockburn's own height, but rawboned and loose-jointed, the man slouched as he walked. He wore a dark Stetson, a denim jacket, and a pistol holstered on his right hip.

Vincent hadn't been wearing the jacket earlier, but it was the Bottleneck town marshal, all right. He walked with exaggerated concentration on the balls of his feet, trying to be as silent as possible and still not having much success. He was too large and heavy-footed for the grace he was trying to perform. Stockburn imagined the man's lips stretched back from his teeth in concentration. The spurs rang softly.

When his big, shadowy figure merged with that of the barn, the young lawman stopped and turned his head to peer back toward the hotel, lifting his chin so that Wolf knew he was gazing at his own window. Again, Stockburn stepped back.

Vincent had obviously learned what room he was in.

Why was he skulking around out there?

The lawman swung around suddenly, opened the barn doors clumsily, making even more noise when hinges squawked and the doors shuttered, then disappeared inside. He reappeared a few minutes later, pushing both doors open and cursing under his breath when both squawked on their hinges again and one raked loudly along the ground, bouncing and kicking up dirt.

In the side paddock, a horse whinnied, causing an echo, and several horses stomped around, wandering toward the front of the barn to check out what all the commotion was about.

Quickly, Vincent swung up onto the back of the horse he'd led into the street. Not bothering to close the doors behind him, he cast one more furtive look toward Stockburn's window then swung his horse to the east and booted it into a trot. After a few strides, he batted his heels against the mount's flanks again. The horse gave a loud chuff and lunged into a ground-consuming gallop.

Stockburn stared down at the dust settling like gray fog in the street's purple murk. "Where you off to, sonny boy?"

He remembered how Vincent had not so subtly discouraged the livery barn owner from talking about the farrier who'd marked his shoes with stars. Again, suspicion grew in the railroad detective, making his heart quicken. The man's odd behavior, riding out of town so late at night, and so furtively, quickly doubled and tripled that suspicion.

Stockburn grabbed his hat, his coat, and his Yellowboy repeater, and hurried out the door. Less than a minute later he leaped down the steps of the hotel's front gallery and crossed the street toward the livery barn. In front of the barn's open double doors, he stopped and fished a lucifer out of his shirt pocket, snapped it to life on his thumbnail, then crouched, lowering the light from the flickering flame to the finely churned dust, manure, and straw in the street.

The prints of Vincent's horse were plain. Stockburn held the match down close to one of them and clucked his tongue. Sure enough, that star was stamped into the left rear shoe of Vincent's horse. "I'll be damned," Wolf said under his breath, waving out the match and dropping it.

He rose, hurried into the barn, and could hear the livery barn owner snoring in a back room. Leading Smoke out of his stall, he quickly saddled and bridled him, snugged the Yellowboy into the scabbard, and mounted up. Intermittent stretches of light from oil pots and saloon windows as well as from starlight, made it easy to follow Vincent's fresh horse trail out of town to the south. The shaggy two-track trail followed a slender canyon with a sandy creek bed winding along on its right side.

Once out of town and on a strait stretch of trail lit by

the stars and a rising sickle moon, Stockburn booted Smoke into a hard gallop, trying to keep pace with Vincent. He didn't want to catch up to him, just get him in sight and follow him, though something told the detective he knew where the Bottleneck lawman was headed.

The night was cool and clear. In the chaparral off both sides of the trail, owls hooted. Coyotes yammered in the rocky hills. Rising in all directions, they resembled giant sawblades silhouetted against the desert clear sky liberally flour-dusted with twinkling stars. At one point, the shadows of several low, scampering creatures crossed the trail in front of Stockburn, at which Smoke lifted his head and whinnied shrilly.

Stockburn winced, hoping the horse hadn't alerted his quarry to his presence. He leaned forward and patted Smoke's left wither, warm and sweat-damp from the fast pace he'd set and as sure-footed and deep-bottomed a mount Stockburn had ever ridden for the Pony Express.

"Just coyotes, Smoke," he said into the horse's ear. "Nothing to be afraid of. Now that rabbit we're trailing, he'd best be afraid."

The last word had no sooner slipped through his lips than a high-pitched scream rose from behind a hillock off the trail's left side. Snarls and the sound of several small, quickly scuffling feet followed.

"Yep, sure enough," Wolf mused aloud. "Didn't I tell you?" He wagged his head. Even though he'd witnessed it more times than he could count, nature's cold savagery always amazed him. One life had just been sacrificed so others could live.

He and Smoke bounded up a low pass between two stone spires that blotted out the sky for a time. On the pass's other side, the trail curved to the southwest then dropped into a canyon choked with brush and oaks.

He came to a fork in the trail and reined Smoke to a grinding halt, curvetting the blowing horse, then leaned forward to read the two wooden signs leaning to either side of the trail dappled with the shadows of large oaks and starlight. The sign pointing along the fork's right tine read O'BRIEN MILL CREEK RANCH. The sign pointing along the fork's left tine read RAMSAY AGUA VERDE.

Stockburn dismounted and, holding Smoke's reins, walked to the left. Crouching to scrutinize the ground, he'd just spotted Vincent's tracks on the trail when, above man and horse's breathing, the rataplan of a galloping horse rose along the trail heading for the Agua Verde. Faint but unmistakable in the silent desert night. Stockburn cast his gaze up the trail, which appeared to curve around the far side of a steep, blocky formation maybe fifty yards ahead. The hoof thuds dwindled swiftly to silence.

Vincent was just then following the trail around the formation's far side. Stockburn had nearly caught up to him.

Heart beating anxiously, Wolf swung up into the leather and booted Smoke ahead along the trail angling toward the Agua Verde. Hope rose in him. Finally, he had something. He didn't know what, but he sensed it was significant.

Vincent had lied about not recognizing that star in the bushwhacker's horseshoe. The star was in his very own mount's shoe! He had to know about it. The question was what did his knowing about it mean?

Was he the bushwhacker? Was he in league with the train robbers?

If so, what was his connection to the Agua Verde? Certainly, Gordon Ramsay wouldn't be sending men out to steal his own cattle off the train. Would he? If so, why?

Stockburn wagged his head. He had some answers but as was always the case, those answers only led to more questions. Maybe soon he'd have more answers than questions, which would mean he was close to solving the case.

He followed the trail that in turn followed the twists and turns of an arroyo on the trail's right side. Large oaks and sycamores spread their spidery boughs toward the stars, and cedars hunched in the rocks lining the arroyo, which appeared mostly dry save for the faint sheen of a rivulet likely leftover from the previous rain.

He'd just started slowing Smoke down to a canter when a sound rose on the trail's right side.

Stockburn's heart quickened and, halting Smoke by drawing back on the reins with his left hand, he reached across his belly for the Peacemaker holstered on his left hip. As the horse skidded to a halt, Wolf saw several rocks tumbling down the side of a bluff maybe a hundred feet off the trail. Bounding and rolling and clacking against each other they kicked up dust. A couple caromed through the brush, making snapping and crackling sounds, and rolled onto the trail twenty feet ahead of Wolf and Smoke, where they stopped, dust rising around them.

Heart beating quickly, Stockburn stretched his gaze up the side of the bluff in time to see the silhouette of a horse and rider lunge up toward the crest. The horse gave a low whinny, hooves thudded, and more rocks rolled down the bluff in the wake.

Vincent's silhouetted figure leaned forward in the saddle, whipping his rein ends against the mount's right wither. The tired horse blew and shook its head, rattling the bit in its teeth, then lunged forward. In two seconds, horse and rider were out of sight, their dust sifting like fog against the stars.

"Where in hell are you off to, son?" Stockburn grumbled, staring up the butte.

Only one way to find out . . . as long as Vincent hadn't heard or seen him behind him and wasn't fixing to shoot him out of his saddle.

For keeps, this time.

CHAPTER 25

Expecting the flash of a rifle at any moment, Stockburn kept his gaze on the top of the bluff humping up in the darkness and pulled the Yellowboy out of its scabbard. He cocked it one-handed, eased the hammer to off-cock, and rested the barrel on his saddle pommel.

He clucked Smoke off the trail and into the brush and rocks , pausing at the bottom of the bluff. After a moment, Stockburn started the horse up slowly, ready to raise the Winchester and shoot at any movement. Smoke put his head down and dug his front hooves into the loose shale and gravel, climbing, lunging, and springing off his rear hooves.

Stockburn held the reins and gripped the horn with his left hand, leaning forward, keeping his gaze on the lip of the bluff where he expected to see the silhouette of a head and a rifle barrel. He kept his right thumb on the Winchester's hammer, his right finger taut against the trigger.

Making the final lunge up onto the crest of the bluff, Smoke stopped and blew.

Wolf raised the Yellowboy to his shoulder, clicking the hammer back to full cock, aiming down the barrel and

sliding it from left to right. He saw nothing but a few
fringes of Mormon tea, rocks, and Spanish bayonet.

The clang of a shod hoof off a rock sounded somewhere
ahead.

He peered into the darkness beyond him. Movement
there—the shadowy bounce and sway of a horse and rider
moving off along the chaparral brushed with starlight,
quartering to the southwest. Beyond the moving figure, on
a low rise overlooking the web of intersecting canyons,
stood several large cream buildings with red tile roofs. The
one on the highest piece of ground appeared a house,
others barns and stables, most likely. The long, low one to
the left was probably a bunkhouse. In the foreground stood
several corrals, a windmill, and several smaller outbuildings
of pale adobe.

The Agua Verde headquarters.

He saw the wooden portal with the obligatory cross-
beam likely bearing the Ramsay name and brand lower
down in his field of vision, where the tan line of the trail
entered the yard.

Stockburn switched his gaze toward the movement in
the chaparral. Vincent was heading toward the headquarters, taking a roundabout way. He didn't want to enter
via the main trail, which meant he was visiting on the sly.

Whom did he intend to see?

Stockburn gigged Smoke forward, glad several tall oaks
and cottonwoods as well as boulders rose between him and
the ranch headquarters, obscuring him from view. Most
ranchers posted night pickets in rough country, but he
could see no lights burning anywhere on the headquarters.
Most folks were likely in bed asleep. Except perhaps a
possible picket or two.

He rode along the top of the rise, which slanted gradually
downward until he found himself following the meandering

course of a wash, heading around the headquarters' south side. It was too dark in the wash to see any prints on the ground, but he was relatively sure Vincent had taken that route as the detective saw no other way to get to the headquarters from the main trail. Around him was thick brush and rocks and cactus. The wash was the only clear route.

At one point he reined his horse to a stop then lifted his chin and listened. After a few seconds of heavy silence save only his and his horse's breathing, he heard brush snapping and the occasional thud of a horse's hoof somewhere ahead.

He smiled. He was on the right track, all right. Vincent was maybe a hundred yards up the wash. Stockburn put Smoke ahead at a slightly faster pace, not wanting to lose Vincent once he gained the headquarters.

After another ten-minute ride along the sandy-bottomed arroyo, he abruptly reined Smoke to a halt. Ahead along the arroyo stood the silhouette of a horse, the mount's rump touched with starlight. A faint jingle of a bridle chain sounded as the horse turned its head toward him and Smoke. One ear twitched. Then the other.

"No, no," Wolf whispered, his heart quickening anxiously. "Don't do it!"

The horse whinnied, tossing its head.

Stockburn reached quickly forward and wrapped his gloved hand over Smoke's snout before he could answer the inquiring neigh. Gritting his teeth, the detective quickly turned the horse and walked him back around a bend in the arroyo, all the while wondering if Vincent had seen him.

When no rifle belched and no one called out, he dismounted, led Smoke up the southern bank and maybe a hundred feet away from the arroyo. Tying him to the branch of a large mesquite, he whispered, "Stay boy."

Holding the Yellowboy low so the starlight wouldn't

reflect off the brass breech, he made his way back to the arroyo and stopped near the bank he'd just left. He dropped to a knee, and stared up the draw toward where Vincent's horse stood, its head turned to stare back at the mysterious human. The horse gave an incredulous switch of its tail then, apparently not overly worried, drew its head farther back to chew a bug or a weed seed from its left hip.

Stockburn rose and moved forward into the arroyo. Stepping up to Vincent's horse, he placed a calming hand on its hip then walked on ahead of it. The horse rammed its snout against him, sniffing, whickering faintly.

"Shhh."

Quietly, Stockburn stepped up onto the bank and the narrow trail through the brush and cactus clumps leading away from the arroyo. After he'd walked maybe fifty yards along the trail, a building humped up ahead of him, on the fire side of a wash lined with trees. He dropped to a knee and studied the building from behind a large, dead, sun-bleached sycamore.

He was facing the yard of the Agua Verde headquarters. More specifically, he thought he was facing the rear of the main house. He swept his gaze beyond the wash, past a privy and some small adobe sheds, including what appeared a wood shed and a stable with an adjoining corral. The stable and corral were a good distance off to Stockburn's right. He could see the inky blots of several horses standing inside the corral. None were moving but staring toward the back of what Wolf opined was the main ranch house—a rambling, white-washed, tile-roofed adobe affair built in the Spanish style. It was large and sprawling—as imposing as a small fortress.

After a few seconds' scrutiny of the place, he saw what the horses were staring at. A shadowy figure was moving from Stockburn's left to his right along the house's rear wall. Keeping close to the house's wall where the shadows were deepest, it moved along the wall until it came to the right rear corner. The figure that could only be Vincent DePaul, if not a night guard, paused then slipped quickly around the corner and out of Stockburn's sight.

Wolf ran across the wash, crouching, avoiding rocks and other debris, trying to move silently, wincing at every thud and crunch of his boots. He prayed that none of the horses whinnied and gave him away to the skulking Vincent. When he gained the rear wall, he paused to catch his breath for a second then moved along the wall before slipping around the corner.

He moved down the side of the house and around an outward jutting section that boasted several dark, deeply recessed windows and a flagstone patio trimmed with several bright, potted plants and stone statues limned with watery starlight. Stockburn ducked under the windows, moved quietly across the patio on the balls of his feet, and continued walking until he saw Vincent's thick silhouette ahead of him, maybe forty feet away.

The lawman had stopped and was crouched against the wall. A soft scraping sounded—a window opening. He was trying to gain entrance to the house!

Who was he visiting at that hour of the night?

Vincent lifted one leg through the window, lifted the other leg, and his silhouette disappeared. The window scraped closed.

Stockburn hurried along the building's rear wall, shouldered up beside the window, doffed his hat, and turned his head to see inside.

Through a three or four-inch gap in the middle of heavy drapes, he peered into the room beyond the window. A match flared to life, then Stockburn saw that Vincent had lit a lamp on a large, ornate dresser. Under a large, oval-shaped painting of a sleek black horse in a green meadow, it abutted the room's opposite wall. Vincent's figure appeared large and menacing in the shadows beside the lamp, limned by the dull amber glow.

Vincent raised the match to his face, blew it out, and stood there by the lamp burning on the dresser. He seemed to be gazing at something to Stockburn's right, but Wolf couldn't quite see what the man was looking at. He held his head back away from the window, so Vincent wouldn't see him.

Vincent suddenly swept his hat off his head, dropped it on the dresser beside the lamp then walked toward Stockburn before angling past the window toward what he'd been staring at on Wolf's right.

The marshal stopped then threw his large body forward and down. He bounced. There was a muffled groan.

Wolf adjusted the angle of his view until he could see Vincent lying belly down on a canopied, four-posted bed, apparently struggling with a person who'd been lying there asleep.

Stockburn stepped a little farther to his left, so he could see more clearly into the room on his right, where the bed was. Although there were more shadows than light he could see Vincent struggling with the person on the bed. He lay belly down atop the struggling person, holding his right hand over the person's mouth.

A feeble ray of light angling over the man's right shoulder told Stockburn he was grinning. He thought he could hear the lawman chuckling through the glass.

Wolf's heart thudded. Vincent was suffocating someone before Wolf's eyes, and having a whale of a good time doing it!

Stockburn began to raise the Yellowboy and reach for the window, intending to open it, but stopped suddenly when he heard a sharp crack of a hand against flesh. He peered closer. The person in the bed was sitting up and facing Vincent, who had closed his hand over his mouth, shoulders jerking as he laughed.

"Damn fool!" Stockburn heard a girl's voice remonstrate the man. Her long, dark hair hung past her bare shoulders, obscuring her face.

"*Shhh!*" Vincent said, still snickering and holding a finger to his lips. He glanced over his left shoulder at the room's door to the right of the dresser on which the lamp burned.

Holding the bedcovers against her chest with one hand, the girl punched his chest, angrily jutting her chin and hard jaws at him. She punched him again, cussing him quietly but angrily, her sleep-tangled hair flying around her head.

"You scared holy hell out of me, you fool!" she castigated the big man just loudly enough for Wolf to hear through the window.

She punched Vincent yet again, and again, as though trying desperately to do some damage to that big, unmoving body. Vincent laughed. He grabbed her arms and pushed her down on the bed and again covered her body with his own. He held her down, kissing her.

Again, Stockburn almost opened the window and shoved his Yellowboy's barrel through it before he saw the girl slowly snake her arms around Vincent's neck as she returned his kisses and moved her body alluringly beneath his own.

If he hadn't thought he'd be heard through the window, Stockburn would have whistled his surprise.

Lana Ramsay. And Vincent DePaul. Well, now. I'll be a monkey's uncle.

CHAPTER 26

Wolf pressed his back against the adobe wall of the house, to the left of the window, and cast his gaze into the inky darkness beyond the horse stable and the Agua Verde yard. He raked a thumbnail down his unshaven jaw, pondering.

Why was a rich gal like Lana Ramsay making time with a big, temperamental fool like Bottleneck's town marshal? Vincent already had a gal—the saucy, delectable Belle. From what Stockburn had seen, she was all any mortal man could handle.

Maybe she was too much to handle?

The biggest question, of course, was what did Lana Ramsay see in the lumbering, soft-in-his-thinker-box Vincent DePaul?

Stockburn turned his befuddled mind to the star hammered into the shoe of Vincent's horse. It was in the shoe of the horse that had carried Lana and her father out here to the Agua Verde headquarters, and it had been in the shoe of the horse the bushwhacker at Buzzard's Bench had been riding, as well.

"Damn curious," Wolf couldn't help mutter aloud, scowling unseeing into the night, his mind a tangled web of clues that did nothing to disentangle themselves.

Suddenly, his mind returned to the moment at hand, and he realized he was hearing quiet sobs issuing from behind the window just off his left shoulder. He turned to his left and cast his gaze back through the window and over to the big bed on his right.

Lana was sitting up on her knees, sobbing in Vincent's arms. Her head hung down, her face again obscured by her hair. The covers had tumbled down around her knees, and a strap of the sheer, skimpy silk nightgown hung off one long, slender arm.

A nicely put-together gal, Stockburn couldn't help reflecting while wondering what she was crying about.

He had his answer a second later when she lifted her head sharply, casting her tear-streaked face at Vincent, and narrowed her eyes in fury as she said, *"Stockburn?"*

Hearing his own name spoken with such animosity and at such an unexpected time literally rocked Wolf back on his heels. He stumbled back against the house, nearly nudging his hat off his head, catching it before it could tumble off his shoulder.

Resetting it, wincing against the banging of his heart against his ribs, he returned his attention to the window in time to see Vincent nod and purse his lips as he ran a soothing hand down Lana's back. Stockburn held his breath but he still couldn't hear what Vincent said next. He only saw the man's lips move. However, he did hear Lana say, *"Drunk?"*

Again, Vincent nodded.

Lana said, "Who let him go to town? They were told not to let him go to town!"

Vincent shrugged. "You know Joe. I reckon he grabbed a hoss and lit a shuck before anyone could stop him. Needed a drink."

Lana said something Stockburn couldn't hear.

"In town," Vincent said. "At the undertaker's."

Lana hung her head again, sobbing. "*Dead?* Noo!" she wailed against Vincent's chest.

"I'm so sorry, honey," Vincent said, holding her tight and patting her back. He used the first two fingers of his right hand to lift her chin, angling her face up toward his.

In the light of the lamp, Stockburn saw the shimmer of the tears streaking her cheeks.

"Let me comfort you, honey," Vincent said and lowered his head to kiss her.

She scrunched up her face in anger again and slapped him. She didn't seem to care who heard the sharp crack of her hand against Vincent's cheek. "Stop it! My father's dead! Leave me alone and go back to your woman in town, Vincent!"

"Oh, Lana . . . honey!"

She swabbed tears from her cheeks with her hands, sniffed, and looked at him. "Really?" she said in a little girl's voice almost too softly for Stockburn to hear, but the night was quiet enough, and they were speaking just loudly enough that he could make out pretty much everything they said. Or he thought he could, anyway, by straining his ears.

"Of course. Haven't I told you a thousand times? Hell, Belle's carryin' on with Darlington, thinkin' he's gonna take her away from here. Damn fool. Hell, I don't even care. I hope he does! That leaves you an' me, Lana." Vincent had been about to draw her to him again.

But she pushed him away with both hands. "Hold on, hold on. First things first, cowboy. Stockburn first, then it's time to move the herd. We'll hit the bank in Bottleneck and burn the town to the ground. That will finish Ramsay and the other ranchers once and for all!" She dropped her feet to the floor and rose from the bed.

"When? You don't mean—?"

"Right now! We'll pick up Jess and Snake-Eye at the line shack." Naked, Lana moved to the dresser.

Still sitting on the bed, Vincent stared at her skeptically. "Can't we wait till—?"

"No!" She opened a drawer and rummaged inside. "If it hadn't been so dark at Buzzard's Bench, I'd have killed him right then and there. We've had plenty of chances, dammit, and we didn't make good on any of them. Snake-Eye and Jess should have killed him *days* ago!"

"Stockburn. He's slippery."

Pulling undergarments onto her lithe, spectacular body, Lana scowled through the dancing curtain of her hair at the Bottleneck town marshal. "That murdering louse doesn't suspect you, does he?"

"Oh, hell, no. Why would he? When he rode into town I was havin' a tooth pulled." Vincent cupped his jaw and made a face, as though the jaw still grieved him. He followed Lana with his eyes, his gaze again concerned. "He followed you to Bottleneck. I mean—you're what . . . or *who* . . . brought him to town."

She frowned. "I am? He did?"

"He tracked that star in your horse's shoe."

"What star in my—?"

"The one Henry Starr taps into his shoes," Vincent said. "You know—like a signature?"

Lana was pulling a tight pair of black denim trousers up her long, filly-like legs. "Damn. I never thought of that. Damn Henry! That star marks our trail!"

"It sure does."

"Are you riding that grullo Ramsay gave you?"

"Of course. A damn good hoss. Why wouldn't I . . ." Vincent let his voice trail off, his eyes widening with the shock of realization. Thinking, he brought his right index finger to his bottom lip.

"Yeah," Lana said, buttoning her blue denim shirt over the thin cambric chemise she'd pulled on. "Henry shoed it. Which means it's wearing that star, too. Just like all of the broncs in Ramsay's own personal remuda."

Vincent cursed.

"He didn't trail you out here, did he?" Lana asked him pointedly.

"Oh, hell no. I ain't some tinhorn, Lana. I'd never let myself get followed."

"You better not have." She pulled on black leather gloves, shrugged into a black leather jacket trimmed down the front with silver conchas. She grabbed her hat and a pistol, which she wedged behind the large silver buckle of her black leather belt, then moved to the window.

Suddenly, she was only inches from Wolf's face.

"Come on, you big galoot," Lana said to Vincent as she lifted the window. "We got work to do!"

Stockburn had been so riveted, not to mention surprised by the wealth of information he'd just gleaned from the pair's conversation, he hadn't anticipated their sudden leave-taking through the window. He quickly stumbled backward, nearly tripping over his own feet.

Only seven feet away, Lana dropped a black-clad leg over the windowsill. Knowing he had no time to flee without being seen or heard, Wolf dropped straight down to his butt and pressed his back taut against the house. He drew his knees up against his chest, and, while not a praying man, prayed they wouldn't see him. He might know a good bit of their story, but he did not know why they were robbing the trains or where the stolen beef was being held. Not to mention where the other gang members were. He needed to follow them to the beef and the other killers and thieves.

The information that she was Comanche Joe's daughter

was almost too much for him to wrap his mind around. If that was true—Stockburn *could* see a familial resemblance though Lana was a whole lot prettier than Joe had been— what was she doing at the Agua Verde with Ramsay?

Although Stockburn had a good many answers, there were still plenty of questions he needed answers for before he could take them down.

Sitting back against the base of the adobe house, he hugged his knees and lowered his head, trying to make himself as small as possible—not an easy task for a man his size. He turned his head slightly to watch Lana set both feet onto the ground to his left. Behind her, Vincent grunted and wheezed as he wrestled his own big frame through the window.

When he'd set both feet on the ground, he closed the window, and Lana said, "I'm gonna fetch a horse."

"I'll come with you. Where's Star?"

"In the bunkhouse," she said softly as they tramped off along a well-worn path in the direction of the stable flanking the house to the east, roughly sixty yards away. The path was sparsely sheathed in mesquites and cedars.

Stockburn watched them go, their silhouettes dwindling and merging with the stable beyond them. Vincent's spurs rang faintly. Apparently, they weren't worried about pickets. Everyone in the headquarters must be snug as bugs in rugs. Vincent followed Lana, towering over the pretty girl dressed almost entirely in black, to the stable doors and then inside. Stockburn remained where he was, confident the shadows of the large house adequately concealed him.

A few minutes later, Lana led a rangy horse out of the stable by its bridle reins. Vincent strode along beside her. A shaggy dog followed them out, happily wagging its tail. The stealthy pair paused in front of the stable, looking around cautiously. As far as Stockburn could tell, no one else was out and about. The yard was as silent and dark as a cemetery, the stars offering the only illumination.

Lana shooed the dog into the stable. "Stay, Rex. Stay, boy" And closed the doors.

Vincent turned to the girl, crouching, trying to nuzzle her neck.

Another sharp *crack!* as she slapped him.

"Ouch!"

"Shut up!" Lana cajoled him. "Lead on, you hulking idiot!"

Sullenly rubbing his cheek, Vincent tramped toward the game path he'd taken into the yard.

Stockburn still sat back against the house, watching the pair and the rangy chestnut gelding cross the yard from left to right on the other side of a shallow wash, maybe fifty yards away. Mesquites and a few large rocks along the wash partly concealed them. The horse shook its head, rattling the bit in its teeth, and Wolf heard Lana hiss at it, shushing it.

Finally, they disappeared into the brush southwest of the yard.

Stockburn doubted they'd see Smoke. He'd picketed the horse well away from Vincent's mount. The gray was smart enough to know he and his rider weren't out there for kicks and giggles; he wouldn't do anything to give away his presence, and thus Stockburn's.

At least, Wolf hoped he wouldn't. Even the best horse was notional.

When the pair had been out of sight for a minute or two, Stockburn rose, quietly brushed off the seat of his pants, looked around, then strode nearly straight out away from the house. He crossed the wash then took the trail back in the direction of the horses.

Walking slowly, not wanting to stumble onto his quarry,

he took his time along the trail, giving the duo plenty of time to reach Vincent's horse and ride away. He quickened his pace only when the hoof thuds of two horses came to his ears on the otherwise quiet night.

One of the horses snorted. Tack squawked. More thuds sounded as the riders put the mounts into trots along the wash.

Stockburn tensed, reflecting they were likely passing Smoke's position.

No whinny.

Thanks, Smoke. He hurried into the arroyo, noting the two sets of fresh tracks scoring the scalloped sand and gravel. He quickened his pace up the arroyo then up the southern bank and over to where he'd left Smoke tied in the trees. Seeing his rider, the horse shook its head and pawed the ground. It had been a long ride out there, but he was rested and still game. Excitement was in the air.

Stockburn shoved the Yellowboy down in its boot then swung up into the leather. "Let's go, boy." He headed Smoke back toward the arroyo. "We're damn close to bustin' this whole scheme wide open." He eagerly patted the mount's right wither. "Just got me a feelin'!"

Boy, did he have questions, though. He'd get those answers soon. But first, he'd let Lana and Vincent lead him to the cattle, to the two men who'd killed Skinny Macdonald, and to the whole rest of their gang. Then he'd find out why Lana, Comanche Joe's blood daughter, wanted to ruin her foster father, Gordon Ramsay, and all the other ranchers in the Cerro Alto Mountains.

Why she intended to rob the bank and burn the town of Bottleneck to the ground.

He followed the pair along the main trail back toward Bottleneck.

They didn't head straight back to town, however. They'd

swerved off the trail and took a barely discernible horse trail nearly straight south. He followed the trail through a flat stretch of scrub and cactus-stippled desert and into a narrow canyon. He followed them across the canyon and onto a plateau ringed with bald, stone spires. Almost indiscernible among the large rocks and cabin-sized boulders sat a small stone shack with a curl of smoke issuing from its chimney pipe and unfurling against the stars.

Stockburn reined Smoke up well short of the cabin and watched the silhouettes of Lana and Vincent ride up to the humble place, calling out, identifying themselves. After a brief palaver with what sounded like two men in the cabin, the two men came out, grumbling sleepily, walked behind the shack to a stable, and saddled two horses. Wolf watched them exchanging words with Lana and Vincent, though he was too far away to hear what they were saying. They grunted and spat. Leather squawked and spurs rang.

One of the horses neighed indignantly, as nonplussed as the men in the cabin at being disturbed at such an ungodly hour.

Who those men were, Stockburn wasn't sure. He had a damn good feeling, however, that they were the two men who'd sent him rolling into the canyon in which Violet had found him with that bullet crease in his forehead. The two men who'd gone to Violet and Skinny's cabin looking for Stockburn and, not finding him, had decided to while away some time savaging Violet.

He couldn't see them clearly in the darkness, only minimally relieved by a growing pale blush in the east, but they were of similar sizes to the two men Stockburn had scared off Violet. Tall and lean. Both wore dusters and high-crowned Stetsons. He frowned. What had Lana called them?

Snake-Eye and Jess? Wolf nodded. Yeah, that sounded about right. Violet had called them that, too. He ground his molars in anger.

The four rode out away from the cabin, heading nearly directly west, likely toward Bottleneck. Stockburn followed, staying about fifty yards behind them, wary of riding up on them and getting shot out of his saddle.

He didn't ride up on them, but he still got shot out of his saddle.

Fifteen minutes after he'd followed the four owlhoots out from the cabin a bullet suddenly spanged off a rock to his right. Smoke had been hot-footing it around what appeared a pair of exploratory mine shafts chiseled out of the rocky ground to each side. The horse spooked, rearing suddenly.

Stockburn tried to tighten his hands around the reins too late. They'd already been ripped out of his hands and he was sailing backward off Smoke's left hip in a blur of sudden motion. He struck the ground between the two shafts and rolled down a declivity toward one of the shafts gaping at him darkly.

No, he thought, desperately trying to claw at the ground for purchase. *No, no, no.*

The fates said *yes, yes, yes.*

His flailing hands raked along the steeply sloping ground, unable to find a hold on the hard surface lightly covered with sand and pebbles. His hat bounced off his shoulder. The black mouth of the shaft swallowed him whole, and he went tumbling into that cold well of darkness like a cork in a maelstrom sucked into the ocean's deepest morass.

Bouncing, bouncing, bouncing as he fell, rolling . . . rolling . . . forever rolling . . .

Oh, how he rolled!

CHAPTER 27

On her hands and knees, Henrietta "Hank" Holloway lowered her head and blew very softly on the small flames licking up around the dry grass and shredded pine bark she'd mounded in the center of her stone fire ring. She'd chosen her camping spot in a low area at the very edge of the very wide, sandy wash she'd been following for nearly the past twenty-four hours, ever since she and Stockburn had forked trails along the Cerro Alto rails.

The rider she was shadowing had followed the wash several hours ahead of her.

A storm had passed a couple of hours earlier, making the rider's tracks harder to follow, becoming impossible to follow after dark had settled over the vast and lonely desert she'd found herself in. Hank had chosen to bivouac for the night before heading out after the rider first thing in the morning. At the moment, she was having a devil of a time getting the tinder to start, for the storm had soaked most of the fuel.

The sputtering flames were her third attempt—her fourth precious match wasted. She'd taken the current fuel from beneath a cut bank's overhang, where it seemed to have remained relatively dry. She pooched out her lips and blew again causing the flames to lengthen and the tinder to crackle and smoke. Very carefully she added a small strip of dry pine she'd shaved from a larger branch with her Barlow knife. The flames nibbled the edge of the pine strip, growing briefly then dwindling. White smoke rose along the edges of the fuel.

"No, no, no," Hank chewed out in frustration. "Don't do that!"

Quickly, she again blew on the flames. As they grew, she slid more of the strip over them until the flame clung to the strip, spreading, burning, growing.

"Good!" Very slowly, Hank added more dry fuel, graduating finally to a couple of small branches, which she criss-crossed over the fist-sized pyre, then rose to gather more dry wood quickly, before the flames consumed all of the fuel and died.

She was dying for a cup of coffee.

Quickly, she gathered more wood from under a large sycamore that had fallen over the wash from the northern bank, pulling a large ball of dirt and roots with it. She lay two extra, dry branches beside the fire then strode off to gather more wood—enough to have a fire long enough to cook coffee and beans, after which she'd let the flames die. She thought she was pretty well concealed at the edge of the wash, with a couple of boulders and some screening chaparral, but she didn't want to take any chances.

As Wolf had warned her, it was savage country teeming with savage men. Like the man she was following. If he was one of the train robbers, that is. If he'd had a hand in killing the people at Buzzard's Bench, Hank had herself seen the evidence of his savagery, and he was a cold-blooded savage, indeed.

Coming back from the fallen sycamore with an armload of relatively dry wood, what felt like a hand reached up to grab her right ankle, tripping her. She stumbled forward, dropping several branches as she fell to her knees, cursing. Glancing behind her, she expected to see a rock or maybe a tree root humping out of the ground, but frowned, staring at an oddly-shaped object at the very edge of the firelight. She couldn't quite make it out.

She pushed herself to her feet and walked back to the object in question, crouching to get a better took at it. Her eyes widening in shock, she gasped and stumbled backward, tripped over her own feet, and struck the ground on her butt.

Propped on her elbows, she stared at the hand forming a claw as it poked up out of the ground. That's what had grabbed her ankle. A hand.

Well, it hadn't really *grabbed* her ankle though that's what it had felt like. It was so stiff and solid she had merely tripped over it. *A hand?*

Yes, a hand.

Hank shivered though the day had lost only a little of its heat. She glanced around, suddenly feeling as though she were being watched from the brush. A hand was there . . . in the wash. A man's hand. *Who did it belong to? How had it gotten here?*

Of course, if there was a hand, there was probably something the hand was attached to. She had to get a closer look.

Steeling herself, she climbed to her feet, and looked at the hand again. She brushed herself off then bracing herself yet again, walked slowly over to the appendage pushing up out of the sandy ground. She dropped to her knees beside the hand, and lowered her head for a better look.

It was a man's hand, all right, the fingers curled inward toward the palm, forming a nice trap for her ankle. The hand was badly swollen. A swollen, pasty blue. A turquoise ring adorned the small finger though the finger had swollen up to the size of a small sausage, and the gold band was buried in the flesh. Even the stone was half concealed by the flesh. The nails were thick and a little yellow. At the base of the hand lay part of a wrist, also swollen. On the wrist, Hank could see about two inches of a blue cotton shirt cuff.

Was the rest of the man buried under the sand and gravel, which, Hank could see in the light of her dancing flames, appeared to have been disturbed not all that long ago? Beside it, the cut bank appeared to have been caved in on the floor of the wash.

Was the rest of the man's body buried under that caved-in dirt and gravel?

Hank drew a breath. She had to find out.

She leaped with a start when a coyote's yammering wail rose behind her, nearly causing her to leap out of her skin. She turned her head sharply to see a lone, gray coyote sitting on a flat rock in the middle of the wash, some feet away from her. Facing her, its eyes glowing an eerie yellow in the light from her fire, the beast lifted its long, pointed snout and cast another series of yodeling wails toward the sky in which pointed silver stars arched brightly across the firmament.

"Oh, go away!" Hank hissed at the coyote, facing it and bending slightly forward at the waist. "Go away, damn you! I don't need you out here, scaring me, too!"

The coyote mewled deep in its throat, whimpered a little, then turned, leaped off the rock, and loped across the arroyo. Its gray blur merged with the brush on the other side, causing a fleeting rustling sound and then silence.

Hank drew a breath to quell her heart's fluttering.

She looked at her fire and cursed. It was nearly out. By adding more kindling and then some larger branches, she got it going again and built it up enough to get a pot of badly needed coffee going. If she was going to dig up that body to see who was sharing her bivouac she needed a strong cup of coffee.

Meanwhile, until it boiled, she'd start on her grisly task.

She dug a cup and a bowl out of her warbag, then walked over to the disrupted sand and soil between the hand and the caved-in cut bank. Drawing another breath, she fought off a wave of revulsion then dropped to her knees and started digging.

Pausing only once . . . when her coffee boiled . . . she filled a cup and sat back and sipped it, staring out across the arroyo. The only sounds were the distant yammering of coyotes, the occasional screech of a nighthawk, and her zebra dun idly munching grass on the bank where she'd tied him to a picket pin with an eight-foot length of rope.

The horse was her only company. Isaac was his name. Wells Fargo had bought him for her when she'd started traveling as a detective, though they'd let her pick him out. She'd chosen well. Isaac, a stalwart American gelding, or quarter horse, was a good friend on lonely nights—just her and Isaac and a campfire and the stars.

She didn't usually camp with a dead man, but then, Wolf had warned her about the savage country, hadn't he? *She hadn't had to venture out alone* south of the Cerro Alto, after the rider who was likely one of the train robbers, but that's what she'd done.

So, there she was . . . camping with a dead man.

Sipping her coffee, Hank continued thinking in the same vein. She could have remained an express agent. If so, she'd likely be sleeping on a nice feather mattress in a town, maybe resting up for another train ride in the morning. But, no, she'd been infected with the detecting bug when she'd ventured out with Stockburn after the Devil's

Horde the previous summer. Truthfully as infected by the man himself but unable to separate one from the other.

So . . . she was trying to prove herself to him. But prove what exactly? That she was woman enough for him? Even though she wouldn't have married him if he'd tumbled for her? She fully realized they were far too much alike.

Loners.

She chuckled to herself. "Don't be a silly girl, Henrietta. Back to the task at hand." She finished her coffee, built up the fire a little, and set the pot on a rock near the flames to keep it warm.

A minute later she was back on her hands and knees near the hand, digging with her cup and bowl and sometimes even with her bare fingers.

She stopped for another cup of coffee and to cook some beans and jerky, which she ate quickly with a third cup of coffee. Her hunger sated, she went back to work.

An hour later she sat back on the heels of her riding boots, staring in wide-eyed shock and horror at the three dead men she'd uncovered, who lay in the excavated hole around which the dirt and sand Hank had dug up was piled.

The bodies lay sort of entangled. Two lay faceup. The other lay on his side, one arm draped across the belly of another. Two were middle-aged. One was slightly younger, maybe in his early thirties. He wore a thick black mustache and long sideburns. His eyes were partway open. All were dirty and bloated and crusted with dried blood. Rigid in death. Deeply befuddled, crestfallen expressions on their faces.

The stench was terrible. Hank had tied a bandana around her nose and mouth so she could work without suffocating.

A deputy U.S. marshal's badge, glistening in the starlight

and flickering umber light cast by Hank's fire, was pinned to the shirt of each man. Her heart thudded heavily.

Leaving the bodies downwind of a slight breeze that had mercifully risen about an hour after sunset, she rose and walked slowly back to the fire where the stench wasn't so bad. Sinking back against her saddle, she drew her blanket over her, for a chill had settled over the desert. She sat there for a long time, staring out across the dry wash toward the bodies she could barely make out in the one a.m. murk and which gradually faded from her view as her fire died. The last she saw of them was the umber firelight reflected dimly off their badges until those three pinpoints of light faded to darkness.

Then there was only herself. And the stars and the distantly howling coyotes, and the quiet scratching of burrowing creatures in the chaparral surrounding the wash. And the dark, winged, snaggle-toothed phantoms that assailed her.

She'd never felt so alone.

Nor frightened.

She fought off the urge to cry, forced herself to be strong, to act as though he were there, watching her.

Stockburn.

She didn't realize she'd slept until she woke suddenly when her horse whinnied. Jerking her head up, Hank opened her eyes. Buttery morning sunlight flooded the arroyo. Shadows stretched out from the brush on the far side. She listened to the raucous rattle of morning birds . . . and the slow thuds of an approaching rider.

Lifting her head, she saw him riding slowly toward her from the south, from just beyond where she'd excavated the three dead lawmen. Quickly, she grabbed her Winchester carbine from where she'd leaned it against a rock to her right, flung the blanket aside, rose, and jacked a round into the Winchester's action.

"Stop right there," she ordered, slowly sidestepping out into the wash and leveling the Winchester on the man and the speckle-gray horse riding toward her.

He was stocky, dark-haired, and he wore a red cotton shirt with gaudy green piping. A shiny silver badge was pinned high and proud over his left breast. A green silk bandanna was knotted around his neck. His low-crowned, black felt sombrero did little to shade his fine-featured, red-tan face, since he was facing the low morning sun. The Henry rifle in his hands glinted little bayonets of sharp sunlight as he cocked it one handed. Curveting his horse, he aimed the rifle out from his right hip at Hank.

Rafael Sanchez curled a sneering grin, and said, "El Roja . . . we meet again."

CHAPTER 28

He wasn't sure how in hell he wasn't knocked out, but he wasn't. Unless he was dead. And in Hell . . . if Hell was as black as the inside of a glove and smelled like rotten eggs, was all sand and rock, which you couldn't see because of the darkness, and once you got there you felt like you'd been beaten by three angry bruins wielding clubs.

Stockburn lay on his back, staring up at nothing but darkness, taking inventory of himself. He was sure he must have broken some bones. They sure felt broken. He wasn't sure how far he'd fallen down the hard, steep wall, but it must have been a good two hundred feet. He'd thought he was going to continue rolling into the next century.

Nah, couldn't have been that far. If he'd fallen that far, he'd be dead. Which brought him back to that possibility as well as the possibility that he was in Hell. But it wasn't very hot. In fact, it was cool. And water was running somewhere. In fact, he thought he could feel a dampness through his clothes.

Voices came to him from far away. They wavered tinnily, echoing off the sides of the shaft at whose bottom he lay, wondering that if he sat up, would several broken ribs impale his lungs?

Only one way to find out. Grinding his back teeth, he drove his elbows into the ground, feeling sharp pebbles and gravel grinding into his skin, and heaved himself up to a sitting position. At least, he sat up as far as he could. He had to duck his head a little because the stone wall angled down close over his left shoulder.

Again, he took stock.

His ribs didn't hurt any worse than they had a second ago. That meant no broken ribs. What about his hips, arms, legs?

He wriggled around a little, flexed his legs.

Nothing seemed broken, but everything hurt. Especially his bullet-notched temple. He swiped a finger over the stitches and it came away slick with blood. A couple of stitches had pulled loose. At least he hadn't broken anything. He didn't feel the kind of stabbing pain you felt when something was broken. And everything seemed workable. As long as working them didn't cause him to pass out from the pain.

Again, voices. Echoing. Men's voices and then a woman's voice and then a man's voice and then the thud of a bullet smashing into the ground close enough it threw sand and gravel at Stockburn. The thud was followed by the wail of a rifle, slightly muffled by distance but echoing around the hole, just the same.

"Hey, Stockburn, you alive down there?"

The rifle screeched two more times, loudly echoing, the bullets kicking more sand at him.

"Did you get him?" a voice said from somewhere above, sounding thin and faraway yet echoing. He thought it was a girl's voice but he couldn't be sure. He felt as though he were hearing someone speak under water.

"Hell, I can't even see him!"

Wolf's eyes had adjusted enough to the darkness that he

could see a little better around him. At least, he could see
the walls of the shaft rising in a ragged circle around him.
He could also see the reason the bullets fired from above
weren't ripping his flesh. At the bottom of the shaft was a
trough, or a depression, deeper than the rest of the shaft's
floor. He'd come to rest in the trough. A thumb of rock
bulged out over the depression, offering cover from the
bullets fired from above. At least, pretty good cover. It
didn't quite cover him completely, but so far it had pre-
vented any of the bullets from tearing into him.

His stalkers would have to have a very good angle from
above to hit him down in the trough.

He canted his head to his right, peering up around the
side of the bulge. The top of the shaft was an irregularly
shaped circle of starlight. Four people stood around the
hole, almost at equal distances apart. They stared down at
him, all holding rifles.

One of the figures rammed a round into the action of
his rifle and aimed down into the shaft.

Stockburn pulled his head back behind the thumb of
rock, and winced, closing his eyes, preparing himself for
the blast. The bullet slammed into the floor maybe a foot
to his right, just beyond the bulge. The hammering wail of
the rifle pounded around the shaft, making his ears ache.

Cursing under his breath, Stockburn reached for the
.45 on his left hip . . . and cursed again. The Peacemaker
wasn't in its holster. He'd lost it rolling down the shaft.

He brushed his hand across the holster thonged on his
right thigh and sighed in relief as his hand wrapped around
the smooth, ivory grips. With his index finger, he unsnapped the keeper thong from over the hammer then
pulled the piece from the leather.

From above came the metallic rasp of a cartridge being
ejected from a breech. It was followed by the clinking of

the cartridge bouncing down the side of the shaft. Clink, clink, clink, clink, clink, clink . . . *clink!*

Starlight winked off the brass casing as the shell rolled to a stop on the shaft floor, maybe four feet away from Stockburn.

Wolf canted his head to his right. He slid the Colt out around the side of the bulge, and clicked the hammer back.

"Hey, Stockburn!" yelled one of the four standing at the top of the shaft, peering down at him. The shooter raised the rifle to his shoulder again and angled the barrel down toward the bottom of the shaft. "You dead ye—"

The roar of Stockburn's Colt cut him off.

The shooter screamed and flew straight back, triggering his rifle shot skyward. He made a resolute plunk as he fell. Just like that, he'd been standing over the shaft, and then he was gone

The girl—Lana Ramsay—cursed shrilly.

Stockburn stared up toward the top of the shaft seeing only the faintly glittering stars, and grinned. The circle was empty.

Three of his four assailants reappeared at the top, angling Winchesters down toward the bottom of the shaft again.

Stockburn pulled his head back behind the bulge in the shaft wall and raised his hands to his ears just as the violently belching reports rocketed around the shaft and bullets ricocheted angrily off the walls. One slammed into the thumb of rock angling down only inches above Wolf's head.

Sand sprayed his eyes and peppered his chest.

Realizing he had cover, they were slamming the bullets off the walls, hoping a ricochet would find him. Good thinking. Several came close, thudding wickedly into the shaft floor inches from where he lay, shielded by the bulge.

If they bounced a round off the side of the shaft near the floor, the shaft would be his final resting place.

He pressed his hands against his ears, squeezed his eyes closed, and gritted his teeth against the onslaught.

The bullets hammered the shaft around him, several more coming devilishly close. Many slammed into the lump of rock shielding him from the shooters, peppering him with more sand.

Finally, the shooting tapered off before stopping altogether, but the echoes continued to chase each other around the shaft for several seconds.

Lana Ramsay yelled, "Hey, Stockburn—how you feeling now?"

Wolf didn't say anything. Let them think he was dead. Let them get curious enough they either went down to check on him or assumed he was dead and rode away.

The girl yelled, screaming shrilly and with unbridled anger, "Stockburn! Hey, Stockburn, are you still alive you murdering—" Her voice broke and she sobbed. Then there was the metallic rasp of a rifle being cocked and she flung another round down the shaft, screaming profanity.

The bullet thudded into the floor several feet from Wolf, who squeezed the Peacemaker in his hands, chewing his lower lip, waiting.

"He's dead," Lana said. "No way anybody could have survived all the lead we threw down there. Come on, boys. Let's ride. We have cattle to move!"

A few rocks and sand dribbled down the shaft as the three surviving stalkers apparently wheeled and moved away from it.

Heading for their horses?

At least, that's what Lana wanted Stockburn to believe.

Continuing to squeeze the neck of the Colt in his hands, he slid his head out from under the bulge of rock and cast his gaze toward the top of the shaft. The ragged circle of sky had grown paler, the stars weaker. Nothing moved up there.

A horse whickered then hooves thudded. The thuds faded quickly and once more silence descended the shaft.

Had they all left?

Stockburn waited, staring toward the mouth of the shaft, pondering what he would do in their situation?

If his quarry had slipped through his fingers several times before, Stockburn figured he'd try to trick the quarry into believing he'd ridden away, but he'd leave at least one rider behind to watch the shaft and shoot anything that moved down there.

But perhaps they didn't think there was any way he could climb out.

He stuck his head a little farther out from behind his covering bulge and tipped his head back, scrutinizing the shaft walls being revealed more and more by the intensifying dawn light. The shaft had been cut at an angle, but whoever had cut it—or blasted it with dynamite—must have used a rope ladder to get down. The walls were nearly as smooth as a baby's bottom. He saw some pits and gouges he could probably use to help him to climb out, however.

A faint relief touched him. But only a faint one. If he tried climbing now, there was a good chance he'd get shot off the wall. He had to figure out if anyone was up top.

He cleared his throat, moistened his lips with his tongue and called, "Hello?"

No response except for the piping of the morning birds.

"Hello? Hello-Hello, up there? Anybody here?"

Nothing.

Stockburn's heart quickened. Had they left him alone? Only one way to find out.

He pushed himself from behind the bulge of rock and onto the main floor of the shaft, keeping a close eye on the lightening mouth of the shaft above him, expecting to see a head and rifle slide into view at any time. Holding the Peacemaker barrel up in front of him, he took a step forward, kicking something that clattered along the shaft floor.

He glanced down. Pale light from above shone on the ivory grips of his other Peacemaker. He dropped to a knee to pick it up, he dusted it off with his hands and inspected it closely. A bullet might have clipped the barrel slightly, but it was otherwise, miraculously, in fine shape. He holstered it and looked up.

The mouth of the shaft was still clear. More and more gray light washed over it, almost hiding the stars.

He stepped to the shaft wall and looked for a way up. Finding what he believed to be one, he considered the Colt in his hand and looked up at the mouth of the shaft again. He chewed his lip, weighing his options.

Then again, he had none.

He couldn't climb up out of the shaft holding the gun. He'd need both hands, which would leave him defenseless against anyone who might show themselves at the top. His only other choice was to remain down there and starve.

Reluctantly, staring at the mouth of the shaft, he holstered the Colt.

Unease rippled up his back as he reached for a handhold and then a foot hold and started climbing. It was tricky going. The wall was at nearly a forty-five-degree angle. Not too severe a slope, but it was slick from water seepage, and the hand and footholds were few and far between. A thin cover of sand—*damp* sand—and water made it even more perilous.

Still, going slowly and controlling his breathing as well

as a threatening panic, knowing he could be shot off the wall at any second, he kept inching his way upward, shifting his position from left to right and back again, setting his course by the pits and fissures and small chips and knobs in the rock that offered even a modicum of support.

He climbed, breathing in and out, in and out, not looking down but only at the wall and then up. Occasionally, a hand or foot slipped from a hold, but he compensated with the opposite hand or foot, and continued climbing.

He paused to look up and to rest.

So gradually as to be almost unnoticeable, the ragged circle of light had grown lighter as well as larger.

He was fifteen feet from the top. And continued climbing until he was ten feet from the top.

Wolf placed his right boot on a knob of rock. It broke off. He grunted, heart thudding as that foot dropped, slamming him flat against the slope. Resting only a moment, he rammed his left boot toe more firmly into the pit he'd found for it.

He gripped a thumb of rock just above his left shoulder with his left hand. Not an easy maneuver since his fingers were bloody and slick from having the skin scraped from their tips, as were all five fingers of his other hand. Desperately, he felt for another prop for his right foot. Finding one, gritting his teeth and grunting with the effort, he eased his weight onto it, unsure it would hold him.

It did. At least, for the moment.

He glanced down at the shaft floor the size of a washtub. A shadow that could have come only from above slid through the light on the floor.

Stockburn's heart thudded. Stiff with dread, he looked up.

A tall man in a long, black duster stood smiling at him from beneath a broad-brimmed black Stetson. Pearl morning light flashed off the barrel of the Henry rifle angled downward over the mouth of the shaft at him. The toes of the man's brown boots extended an inch over the lip of the shaft, causing sand to dribble down into the shaft.

"Mornin', Wells Fargo," the grinning man said, narrowing his pale blue eyes. He had a thin, blond beard and handlebar mustache. His pale eyes glinted devilishly. The morning breeze made his duster ruffle a little.

Stockburn swallowed a dry knot in his throat and glanced at the barrel of the rifle ready to bore a hole through his forehead. He returned his gaze to the evil-eyed man squinting down the barrel. He'd seen those pale-blue, devilish eyes before. They'd been behind the flour sack mask of the man who'd shot him into the canyon where Skinny McDonald's mine lay.

Wolf said, "Let me guess. Snake-Eye?"

Snake-Eye winked slowly in the affirmative.

Stockburn saw the man's gloved right finger draw back against the Henry's trigger. He closed his eyes. The rifle barked. He damn near loosened his grip on the wall but something made him maintain his hold.

He opened his eyes, blinked. He was amazed to find he was still able to open his eyes and to blink. He was still alive. No bullet had hammered into his skull.

The echo of the Henry's bark caromed skyward, but . . . it hadn't been loud enough to be the Henry's bark.

Wolf looked up in time to see Snake-Eye stumble forward, kicking sand and gravel into the shaft. The man's face was crumpled in misery. Blood oozed from a wound in his chest. He dropped the rifle, which caromed down past Stockburn, the rear stock coming within two inches of braining him. Snake-Eye followed the rifle, winging toward Stockburn, who pressed himself taut against the wall but was nearly ripped off it when Snake-Eye clawed at his right sleeve in passing.

Then the man slammed onto the wall of the shaft six feet below Wolf, and rolled . . . and rolled . . . and rolled . . . until piling up at the bottom with a heavy thud that made Stockburn wince with remembered agony.

He looked up at the mouth of the shaft.

A slender, high-busted female figure clad in men's denims and a calico blouse stood over him. Long, straight blond hair blew in the breeze.

Stockburn blinked, scowled. *"Violet?"*

The girl from the desert smiled down at him. She dropped to her knees and stretched a hand down into the shaft.

CHAPTER 29

"Drop the Winchester, *El Roja*," Sanchez ordered.

Hank shook her head and cast the deputy a frigid smile. "Not a chance."

"Come on," he said. "Do it."

"Drop yours or I'll blow you out of that saddle."

Sanchez grinned. "You shoot me. I shoot you. *¿Cual es el punto?*" What's the point?

"You're the one I've been following."

"I know. Why?"

Hank felt an incredulous flush rise in her cheeks, knowing he'd known she was on his trail. She'd thought she was being more careful than that. Keeping the Winchester angled upward from her right hip, the barrel aimed at the deputy's chest, she said, "You met the bushwhacker at the railroad tracks. You two rode north together before you broke away to the south and the bushwhacker continued north."

Sanchez frowned. "What bushwhacker are you talking about, El Roja?"

"You know which one." Hank glanced at her shoulder. "The one who tore my blouse at Buzzard's Bench. Probably believing I was Stockburn. It was almost dark in that canyon." She'd repaired the rip with thread from the small sewing kit she carried, but she wasn't much of a seamstress. The blouse had obviously been torn and crudely repaired. Also, the blouse around the tear was still blood-stained, for, try as she might, she hadn't been able to get the stain out of it.

"I don't know anything about any ambush at Buzzard's . . ." Sanchez let his voice trail off. His dark brown brows beetled over his eyes. He looked away, still frowning, thoughtful.

"Yeah," Hank said, curling her upper lip in a shrewd smile. "Maybe you do, after all, eh?"

Sanchez looked back at her. "Tracks can be deceiving, El Roja."

"What're you talking about, Deputy?"

"They don't always tell you what you think they're telling you. I was scouting the country south of the tracks when I spied a rider coming from the direction of Buzzard's Bench. She looked worried. Kept looking back over her shoulder."

"*She* looked worried?"

"Si. This country has more than one beautiful woman in it, El Roja." He narrowed his eyes a little, and for a second or two he let them roam indiscreetly down Hank's shoulders over which her thick red hair hung, and down to the cleavage of her blouse, between the flaps of her black leather vest.

Hank scowled at him, flaring one nostril with bald disdain. "I'm up here, Deputy."

"Si." Again, he smiled. "You certainly are."

"Who was she?"

"Lana Ramsay."

"Who's Lana Ramsay."

"Daughter of Gordon Ramsay. Big rancher from up by

Bottleneck. Head of the Shackleford County Cattlemen's Association." Sanchez tossed his chin toward the low, foggy blue mountains rising in the far eastern distance, almost out of sight from this vantage.

"You're saying she was the one who took a shot at me at Buzzard's Bench? She was the one gunning for Wolf?"

Sanchez studied her, his expression again gravely thoughtful. "I don't know," he said. "Was she?"

Hank watched him closely. He appeared genuinely befuddled as well as curious. Deeply curious. But then again, he could be a very good actor. He certainly had a bone to pick with Stockburn, given that Wolf had shot his younger brother.

On the other hand, Rafael Sanchez didn't seem like the sort of fellow who would do his dirty work from hiding.

"What're you thinking about?" Hank asked him.

Sanchez probed a tooth with his tongue, making a face. "I'm thinking about the rider who rode past me in Las Cruces. The one who took a shot at you and Stockburn in Mama Isabell's Café. I only caught a glimpse, but now as I remember, that rider was riding a horse very similar to the chestnut that Lana Ramsay was riding yesterday along the railroad tracks."

He looked off again, thoughtful.

Turning back to Hank, he said, "I rode over to see if she was all right. She looked troubled, bothered, kept looking over her shoulder. I thought maybe someone was following her. She assured me she was fine, just found herself riding later than she usually did and had been a little spooked by a coyote." He shrugged. "So, since she wasn't all that far from her ranch headquarters, I left her and headed south, looking for sign of the train robbers."

"What about Buzzard's Bench?"

"What about it?"

Hank narrowed a skeptical eye. "You don't know what happened there?"

"No." The deputy frowned even more severely, suspiciously. "What happened there?"

"Carson and his wife and their hired help were all gunned down and tossed into an arroyo behind the station building."

"When did this happen?"

"A few days ago, judging by the condition of the bodies. Probably right after the train robbery."

"Do you know why they were killed?"

"Wolf . . . er, Detective Stockburn thinks it's because that's how he learned the train was going to be robbed . . . from Wooly Carson. Whether or not the killers intended or did not intend for Carson to share the information with Detective Stockburn, Wolf believes they had been expecting him to try to foil the last robbery. The killers returned to Buzzard's Bench and cleaned house, so to speak."

Absently, Hank wondered if this Lana Ramsay had left the strange note regarding Buzzard's Bench with the liveryman in Las Cruces. If she'd tried the bushwhack there, she probably did.

"Si," Sanchez said, nodding slowly. "Loose lips have caused many a man to lose his tongue in this country."

"Even if those lips had been expected to be loose?"

Sanchez smiled. "Loose lips can't be trusted. This is tough country. It's a sa—"

"I know. It's a savage country."

"Where is Wolf . . . er, *Detective* Stockburn?" Sanchez revised the question with a faintly jeering smile.

"He followed the bushwhacker to Bottleneck."

"Hmm. Do you think he's safe all by himself?" Sanchez said, no little jeering in his voice and oily grin this time.

Hank felt a warm flush of pride rise in her cheeks, remembering how she'd filed the deputy's horns in Las

Cruces, which is obviously what he was remembering, as well. He didn't seem to harbor a grudge about it, though most Mexicans would have a hard time living down being bested by a woman. Her lips cracked a smile. "No telling what kind of trouble he'll get into up there, but he's too big to hogtie."

She'd been only vaguely aware that they had both gradually lowered their rifles. She held hers straight down along her right leg, the barrel aimed at the ground. Sanchez had rested his atop his right shoulder, his gloved hand on the rear stock, well away from the trigger.

"Want some coffee?" Hank asked him. "I was about to build up my fire. I don't normally sleep this late, but I was up late last night, digging up those three federals over there."

Sanchez followed her gaze to the dead men and jerked with a start. "*Mierde!*"

He apparently hadn't seen the bodies yet. They'd been partly hidden by the turned-up earth and the dead sycamore extending into the arroyo. He made a face. "I thought I smelled something nasty!"

"It was even worse last night."

Sanchez swung down from his horse. He ground-tied the reins and walked toward where the dead men lay, stiff and blue and obscenely exposed to the morning light. Hank shouldered her own rifle and walked over to the open grave. She stood beside the deputy, again covering her mouth and nose with her bandana. Sanchez covered his mouth with his arm as he studied the three dead deputy U.S. marshals. He walked slowly around the makeshift grave, crouching over the bodies for a closer look.

When he'd walked back over to stand beside Hank, his eyes were watering.

"Two were shot in the back," he said, his voice muffled by his arm.

"The other took one bullet in the side," Hank said into the bandanna, her own eyes watering against the sickly-sweet stench. "Probably as he was turning around to return fire. He's the only one without a holstered revolver. The other two each have a holstered .38 double-action Smith & Wesson and a Colt Lightning .44, respectively."

Sanchez looked at her, scowling. "Meaning what?"

"They were ambushed. Backshot. From about fifteen, maybe twenty feet away. The killer killed two from behind before either one could turn toward him and return fire. The third man—the youngest one there, without a pistol anywhere on his person—was probably turning to return fire. That's why he took one bullet to the side, while he was turning. When he got turned full around, he took the second bullet to his chest. He probably had his pistol in his hand, and dropped it after he was shot. That's why he wasn't buried with it."

Sanchez stared at her, incredulous, deep lines cutting across his otherwise smooth, deeply tanned forehead. "You got all that just by looking at those men?"

Hank nodded. "They were probably mounted when they were shot."

"Now, how in hell would you know that?"

"One of the older two men has a dislocated shoulder. The youngest one took a hoof to his head. His horse probably kicked him as he fell. You can see the shoe mark just above his ear. The last one has a torn shirt sleeve, scuffed and streaked with sand. Yep, they were mounted, all right. I figure the shooter had been riding with them. Likely someone they knew. He turned to ride away but then turned back and shot them, instead. Took them totally by surprise. It probably happened right here in the arroyo, maybe only a few feet away but intervening storms likely washed all sign away."

"I'll be damned." Sanchez smiled admiringly. "El Roja, you know your business."

"Yes, I do." She turned and lowered the bandana as she walked back over to her camp. "I'll have coffee going in a few minutes."

Sanchez walked over to his horse. "In the meantime, I'll rebury them. I have a shovel on my horse. I'll mark the grave and scribble out a map if the federal boys want to send a wagon out here to retrieve them."

"Good thinking."

Sanchez canted a smile at her. "I know my business, too, El Roja." He stopped and turned toward her. "Hey, what's your real name again?"

Hank glanced over at him from where she was mounding tinder and kindling in preparation for a fire. "Henrietta Holloway. Hank for short." She added with a smile, "But I like the sound of El Roja just fine."

Chuckling, the young deputy retrieved his shovel from his horse and started covering the dead men.

Hank sank back against her saddle and studied the young deputy sitting on the other side of the small fire from her, knees raised, elbows resting on them, a fresh cup of coffee in his hands. He was staring across the wash toward the dead men he'd recovered with his shovel and was still sweating from the effort, for the day was heating up again.

He was scowling, looking perplexed.

"What's on your mind, Deputy?" Hank asked him, then took a sip of her coffee.

He glanced at her then turned his head back forward

and sipped from his own cup. "I can't figure it. My brother, Tomacito. He was no train robber. He was full of stable green sure, but—" He ground the heel of his left boot into the sand in frustration. "He was a little wild. Our parents have been dead for years. He got in with the wrong bunch so I sent him up to Bottleneck to be clear of those fake cutthroats and border banditos. I didn't think he'd find trouble up there so easily. Apparently, he did." He winced, cursed under his breath in Spanish, then took another sip of his coffee.

"I'm sorry for your loss. I've had a few of them myself. Stockburn has, too. He didn't want to kill your brother."

The young deputy glanced at her, and there was fire in his dark eyes. "No, but he did."

"He had just cause."

Sanchez curled a nostril and ground his heel into the sand again. "Just cause! My brother's dead. If I hadn't been wearing this badge the other day . . ."

"You'd shoot a man for killing your brother when Tomacito gave him no other choice?"

The deputy tossed another fiery look at her. "It's the way it works down here. In my world."

"You're not that man anymore. You might have been at one time, but you made a different choice. You went a different route. You pinned that badge to your shirt."

"It comes off, you know."

"Only if you decide to take it off forever and go back to your old ways, Rafael."

"Oh, hell. What do you know about it, anyway?" He rose, kicked a rock, and walked several feet out into the arroyo. He took another slug of the coffee, swallowed, cursed again under his breath, and stared southwest along the broad wash's winding course through the lime green chaparral.

Hank gained her feet and walked over to stand beside him. "I know how you feel. You want someone to blame. Right now, you only have Wolf . . . er, Detective Stockburn."

Sanchez gave a caustic snort and turned his face toward hers. "Why do you try so hard to pretend your relationship is only professional? Do you think I don't see you're in love with the big gringo, even though he's old enough to be your father?"

Hank studied him, suppressing the warmth she felt rising in her cheeks. She pursed her lips, nodded slowly. "Fair enough. Then you're smart enough to know that he is not responsible for your brother's death. Only Tomacito himself is responsible . . . as well as those who convinced him to help them rob that train."

Sanchez studied her, his expression inscrutable.

"What I'm saying is that your anger is misplaced, Deputy. It's time to direct it at the real person or persons responsible for your brother's death. On them you can exact your revenge."

He appeared to think about that as he held her gaze with a frank one of his own. He stretched a smile then reached out to run two fingers through the long hair curving back over her left shoulder. "*Dios, que mujer tan hermosa.*" God, you're a beautiful woman.

Again, a warmth rose in her cheeks. She found herself blushing again, and lowered her gaze before lifting her eyes again to his and shaking her hair back from her cheeks. "Gracias, Senor."

"Are your feelings for him reciprocated?"

She shook her head. "No."

"He's a fool. For that alone, he deserves a bullet."

Time to change the subject. "Where do you think they're gathering the cattle? There must be a place south of here, maybe along the river. They're either holding them all for one big sale, or they're selling each batch as they steal them."

Sanchez peered south again. "Si. They must have such a place. They're probably gathering them and holding them for one big sale. Probably to one buyer on the other side of the border. Where they gather them and hold them needs to have water. Especially this time of the year, in the high summer. It needs to have grass for at least two-thousand head."

She studied his handsome profile as he stared south. When he nodded slowly, narrowing his eyes, hope grew in her, lightening her heart.

"What is it?" she asked him.

He turned to her, wrinkling the skin between his brows. "I know a place like that. The people from the Wet Rocks used to gather wild horses there before herding them north to their rancho. I stumbled on it long ago when I was hunting with my father. It's a secret, hidden place. Many markings by ancient peoples. It's supposed to be a forbidden place, a place of ancient sacrifice. We were frightened out of there by the Wet Rocks people, but . . . I remember where it was. Where it is."

He stared south again, nodding slowly. "Si, si. That has to be where they're gathering the cattle!"

He turned to Hank, smiling. "Are up for it, El Roja? It's a good day's ride. Maybe a day and a half since we're getting a late start."

Hank smiled. She threw back the last of her coffee and tossed away the dregs. "I'm up for it."

CHAPTER 30

Stockburn climbed a little higher then reached out and grabbed Violet's extended hand with his left one. She wrapped both her hands around his and, grinding her knees into the dirt beside the shaft, grunted and groaned as she pulled him up and he grabbed the edge of the shaft with his right hand and hoisted his head and shoulders free of the shaft.

Finally, he lay on his side beside the flaxen-haired girl, who lay panting beside him, exhausted from the struggle of hauling his big carcass out of the earth.

"Good Lord," she exclaimed, breathless. "How did you end up down there, Wolf?"

He, too, was breathless. "Oh, I don't know. I just saw that hole in the ground and decided to go down and say hidy to any Chinamen who might be skulkin' around down there."

She rolled toward him and punched his back.

Stockburn rolled onto his back. He was as tired and sore as he'd ever been in his life. "I was trailin' Lana Ramsay and some friends of hers, including Vincent DePaul." He scowled up at the girl gazing down at him, her tan cheeks flushed from exertion. He reached up and nudged her chin with affection. "What in blue blazes are you doing this far off your home range, young lady?"

"We're not that far off my home range, you big handsome lug." Smiling, she leaned down and brushed her lips across his. "That fella down there?" She lifted her chin to indicate the man lying dead at the bottom of the shaft.

"Snake-Eye?"

"Him and his friend—"

"Jess." Stockburn looked at the man lying dead on his back six feet away from the shaft, one of Wolf's own .45 rounds having carved a puckered hole in the middle of his forehead.

"That's the other one," Violet said, glancing at the dead man, too. "They came callin' on me again. Only, I hid in a secret cellar Skinny dug to store all the gold he intended on extractin' from this desert . . . though of course he never got around to it . . ." She brushed a tear from her face.

Stockburn caressed her cheek with his thumb. "I'm sorry, honey."

"Oh, hell!" Violet sniffed, then returned to the topic at hand. "They came stalkin' me again, lookin' for you, and when they didn't find me they ransacked the cabin."

"Damn them!"

"They pulled foot and I saddled up my mule and followed 'em to their cabin. I hid in the rocks, keepin' an eye on 'em, intending to follow 'em when they moved again. I was there nearly a whole day and they didn't move . . . until a couple hours ago."

"That's when Lana and Vincent rousted them."

"I stole up close and heard them talking." Violet frowned. "Something about you killin' Comanche Joe . . . and moving cattle. Getting the whole thing tied up fast. She seemed right bent out of shape about you killin' Comanche Joe." The girl looked deeply befuddled. "Ain't he just that old drunk Indian who lives with some other raggedy-heeled Comanches up near the Wet Rocks?"

"I got a feelin' there was more to Comanche Joe than met the eye. I drilled him because he was about to drill me, and Lana's mighty piss-burned about it. Joe was her father. Her *blood* father."

"*What?*"

"You heard right."

Violet gazed up at him in shock. She shook her head, then asked, "Do you always have this many folks gunnin' for you, Wolf?"

Stockburn muttered incoherently, flushing sheepishly, and looked off.

Violet continued. "When those four left the shack back yonder, I realized someone was tailing them. You rode right past me but I didn't call out, fearful they'd overhear."

"Good thinkin'."

"I trailed all five of you, curious about where you all were headed."

"I was, too. Unfortunately"—Stockburn glanced down at the malignant looking dark hole in the ground beside him—"I got waylaid."

"I heard the shot and then saw Lana and the others standing around the hole, firing into it and callin' your name, but I couldn't figure out how you ended up down there."

"Now she and Vincent are a good ways ahead of me, dammit!" Stockburn picked up a small rock and threw it in frustration, then groaned at the pain the sudden movement evoked in his shoulder and battered ribs.

"I'm sorry I couldn't help you out sooner, Wolf. I heard them shooting into the shaft, but I couldn't get close enough to help. Not without 'em seein' me anyway, and I'm not all that great at shooting people in the dark with this old Spencer. In fact, he's the first one I ever shot, and boy, he sure had it comin'!"

"He sure did, honey. Thank you."

"After Lana and Vincent rode out, he laid back in the rocks. It was too dark for me to pinpoint him. When it got lighter, I seen him skulk out of the rocks, and I circled around behind him. When he aimed down into the shaft, I shot him." She hardened her jaws as she gazed down at the dead man, and spat on him. She was no doubt remembering how he and Shake-Eye had nearly savaged her near Skinny's body.

She turned back to Stockburn. "Are you all right, Wolf?" She ran a hand absently down his arm and touched his knee with her other hand, as though feeling for blood. "Are you shot? They flung so many bullets down there, I thought for sure—"

"No, no. I didn't catch a single graze. The Good Lord or whoever looks out for idiot railroad detectives, did his job. There was a little trough down there I hid in."

Violet rose up to inspect his forehead. "Looks like you opened up a couple of my sutures."

"Sorry, honey. I'll be all right."

She wrapped her arms around him, hugging him tightly. "I thought for sure you were dead down there. Especially after Lana and Vincent rode away."

Stockburn hugged her in return. "Just a little bruised is all. I don't have time to complain about it, though. I have to get after those two."

With Violet's help, he heaved himself to his feet with a loud grunt and a raking groan against all the little knife stabs of agony piercing what felt like every inch of him. He'd swear all the injuries he'd incurred in his previous tumble had been aggravated two- or three-fold.

"I don't understand, Wolf," Violet said, looking up at

from where she stood taut against his side, his arm draped over her shoulders. "Why would Lana Ramsay . . . and the marshal of Bottleneck—"

"I'm not at all sure"—Stockburn looked around for his horse in the buttery sunlight bathing the rocky terrain around him—"but I aim to find out." He turned his head in nearly a complete circle, glowering. "Where in tarnation is Smo—oh, there he is." He'd spotted the smoky gray on a low knoll maybe a hundred yards to the west, calmly grazing the sparse grass growing up along the base of a pale stone outcropping. "Damn cayuse pitched me into that hole, an' look at him over there calmly dining like the Prince of Wales."

His words belied his relief at seeing the mount nearby. He'd been afraid Lana and Vincent might have led him off. That's what he would have done. They'd apparently had more important matters on their minds, and hadn't thought about taking the stallion to make sure that if Stockburn was not dead he was at least on foot.

Wolf poked two bloody fingers into his mouth, and whistled.

While Smoke trotted toward him, Violet said, "I'll fetch my mule." She started walking away then turned back to look up at the big, rumpled detective again. "Are you gonna be all right, Wolf?"

Stockburn rubbed his sore jaw as he shot the girl a reassuring smile. "I'm gonna be fine. I'm gonna be even better once I run those two polecats to ground."

"Good." Violet walked back up to him and gave a coquettish tug on his ear, and rose onto her tiptoes to plant a tender kiss on his cheek. "I missed you after you left, Wolf. I got so lonely I almost cried a time or two. I think I might love you."

"Oh, now . . . now, Violet, listen—"

"Yep, I think so." She winked, then strode away.

You don't want to do that, Wolf silently warned the pretty girl. *You don't know this old fool by half.*

As the crow flies, ten miles west of Stockburn and Violet, Lana Ramsay reined her high-strung chestnut to a dusty halt and turned to Vincent DePaul, just then checking down his grullo off her mount's right hip.

"Time to fork trails," she said crisply.

Vincent frowned. "What're you talkin' about? I thought we was gonna ride into Bottleneck and pick up Comanche Joe, take him out to the Wet Rocks."

Lana shook her head. Her dark hair glistened in the brassy, unrelenting sunshine that reflected off the ochre rocks around them. The chestnut shifted its feet, shook its head so hard it nearly slipped its bit, and gave a deep snort, wanting to keep moving.

Lana's own people had caught and broke the horse before selling it to her foster father, Gordon Ramsay, one of their biggest and most frequent buyers. One of Ramsay's rare good qualities was his admiration of the wild broncs that roamed freely through the mountains and the desert surrounding it—mounts that had been the pride of the Comanche people for many generations. Maybe that's why he'd loved the half-wild, twelve-year-old Comanche girl he'd taken in after murdering her mother and extended family—the people who'd raised her on a small rancho in the Wet Rocks country.

The damn fool.

Comanche Joe had been her father. But Joe had many children, and various wives and their families raised the children while Joe had been off robbing banks with a cutthroat bunch of Comanche guerillas determined to wrestle their country back from the white eyes.

Vincent liked how the girl sat the horse. A wild girl on a wild horse. They were each other's equal in spirit. Lana, formerly Oni-Shay—which roughly translated from Comanche meant "careless or carefree rider," or so Lana had informed him—was born to ride such a horse. Just as Vincent had been born to tame such a wild filly as Lana Ramsay. He'd thought he'd tame Belle, but there was no sport in taming a prostitute. Besides, Belle wasn't nearly as wild as Vincent had thought. He'd realized that after he'd met Lana. Belle was only disloyal. An opportunist and a con artist were what she was.

There was a big difference between being wild and being a con artist. Vincent would have shot her already, knowing she was making him a laughing stock by spending time with Graham Darlington but like Lana had said, that would only throw a wrench into their plans to leave southern Texas together after they'd ruined the town and all the ranchers around it.

Belle and Darlington would get what's coming to them in due time.

Oh, and what a time it would be, too!

"Change of plans, my love." Lana rode her horse up closer to Vincent's mount, leaned over and kissed him. She nibbled his lower lip just before pulling away, then swept a gloved hand through her wildly blowing hair, and laughed. "Don't worry. We'll be together soon. I was thinking it through while we rode, and we can't be seen in town together. I don't want anyone to suspect us. Not yet. Especially after those three deputy U.S. marshals were last seen with you before they disappeared."

"Oh, that. Yeah, but—"

"No buts about it, Vincent. You know it's true. Besides,

we took care of Stockburn. There's no point in me riding into Bottleneck. Soon, someone's going to start wondering what happened to Mr. Wells Fargo, just like they're wondering what happened to the marshals. They might tie him to you, too. Especially if someone saw him ride out of Bottleneck after you did."

Vincent winced at the sting of that. Lana had been the one who'd realized someone had been following them last night. Her canny horse had sniffed their shadower on the breeze, and they and her father's former hands, Jess and Snake-Eye—whom Ramsay had fired, and thus they had chips on their shoulders—had stopped and holed up to scour the vermin from their trail.

Yep, it had been Stockburn, all right. Vincent had let himself get hound-dogged by Mr. Wells Fargo. He'd been too intent on seeing Lana again, he supposed. Vincent was surprised the wild girl hadn't cut him loose for that piece of tinhorn stupidity. She really must love him as much as she said she did.

Go figure.

"Yeah, but how 'bout, Joe?" Vincent asked. "Your uncle, Lana. I mean, your *blood father*."

"You're gonna fetch Comanche Joe up to the Wet Rocks by yourself. You're gonna take him home to my family. Then we're gonna move those cattle over to Ortonville and get 'em sold. We'll ride back to Bottleneck and finish the town . . . starting with the bank. That will finish the ranchers off once and for all."

"Oh. Well . . . all right, I reckon."

Lana canted her head to one side and narrowed an admonishing eye at the big man. "I need to know I can count on you, Vincent. You're not getting cold feet, are you?"

"Me? Hell, no!"

"All right, then." She pressed close to him again, kissed

him, let him feel the pertness of her breasts against his chest. "We'll be together again soon. We're going to start a new life together, raising horses on our own sprawling ranch."

"Just you an' me and a whole passel of kids!"

"Exactly!" She pulled her head away from him and twitched his lower lip with her finger. "You be careful in Bottleneck. Understand?" She was glad when he smiled in that unguarded, guileless way of his.

"Sure, honey. Don't worry. I ain't gonna do nothin' to spoil your plans."

Lana smiled then, too. "Bring Joe to the Wet Rocks tomorrow." She paused then added with a warm smile: "I'm counting on you, my love."

"Don't worry. You can count on me if you can count on anybody, honey."

Lana winked. "I know I can." She reined her frisky bronc around, then booted him into a high-stepping trot nearly straight south, toward a serrated edge of bald, red peaks amidst which lay the remote and forbidding Wet Rocks.

Vincent watched her in open admiration until she was nearly gone from sight, wild horse and equally wild rider consumed by the craggy desert around them.

Could such a beautiful, wild thing really be his?

Chuckling to himself, he reined his own horse west and booted him into a hard lope toward Bottleneck.

CHAPTER 31

Vincent rode into Bottleneck an hour after leaving Lana. It was ten o'clock in the morning and quite a few folks were on the street—on the intermittent boardwalks lining each side, coming and going between shops, and criss-crossing the street itself. Why did they all—or most of them, anyway—seem to be looking at Bottleneck's town marshal so strangely?

Did they know that Stockburn had shadowed him out of town last night? Since his jurisdiction as town marshal stopped at the edge of town, were they wondering where Vincent had ridden, so late at night? Were they wondering why Stockburn had followed him?

Of course, they were wondering. He was wondering the same thing himself!

Did Stockburn suspect the town marshal had played— in fact, *was playing*—a key role in the stock robberies? Did Stockburn . . . and everyone else casting him vaguely suspicious looks as his grullo clomped along the street . . . suspect Vincent had led the three federals out of town and made good and sure they'd never return?

To Bottleneck or anywhere else?

As he approached Hollis Renfro's crude, brush-roofed

adobe hut that served as a beer and tequila parlor as well as a "*dental office*," he saw Hollis eyeing him suspiciously just before turning his head away and quickly raising a short brown bottle to his lips.

Vincent checked the grullo abruptly down in front of the place and cast a malevolent glare at the man who'd left a very large hole in the town lawman's jaw. "What the hell are you lookin' at?"

Hollis pulled the bottle down, scrubbed beer froth from his mouth with a grimy sleeve, and frowned. "What?"

"You heard me. What're you lookin' at?"

Hollis knit his brows and drew his head back. "I wasn't lookin' at nothin', Vincent. I was drinkin' my damn beer!"

"I know what you was lookin' at." Vincent hipped around in his saddle and cast his gaze this way and that across the street. More people were looking at him than ever. He turned back to Hollis and hardened his glare. "You was lookin' at *me*!" He thumbed himself in the chest. "I wanna know why!"

Hollis opened his mouth to speak then, apparently reconsidering, closed it without saying a word. With a decidedly apprehensive expression tightening and bleaching his ugly features, he looked this way and that and then heaved himself to his feet. He turned to his left and walked stiffly through the open door of his shack, casting one more guarded look over his shoulder. He slammed his rickety door so hard it almost fell off its hinges.

"Yeah," Vincent growled, glowering at the closed door. "You better turn tail, you cowardly devil!"

He looked once more around the street, feeling as paranoid as ever. Cursing under his breath, he booted the grullo on down the street and down a hill between buttes. An acidic anger burned in him. It burned and burned, growing like a wildfire.

Why?

Wasn't he about to hitch his star to the girl of his dreams? He and Lana were going to drive everyone else out of these mountains. Then they . . . and her people, too, of course, because they rightfully belong there . . . will have the Cerro Alto all to themselves. They'd build a big ranch and raise horses to sell and trade to the Indians who'd be in need of horses once they'd busted free of those government prisons and returned to their homelands and driven out the white eyes.

At least, all the bad ones. Those who didn't see fit to share the land with the Indians.

They'd need horses for that—to wage war against the whites.

Lana assured Vincent that was true, because Comanche Joe had assured Lana it was true.

Deep down, he knew the real source of his anger stemmed from his unease about how well he'd buried the three deputy marshals. The possibility that he had not buried them deeply or thoroughly enough was a vexing, half-conscious thought that needled and chewed at him like a mouse in a locked trunk.

Too many people knew Vincent had ridden out with the three federals. If they were ever found dead, with bullets in them, fingers would begin pointing toward him.

He kept trying to suppress those half-formed worries as he stowed the grullo away in the stable, then quickly tended the horse, rubbing him down and feeding and watering him. He'd let him rest for a while. They'd be pulling out again soon, just as soon as he had packed a grub sack, eaten a bite, and had a cup of coffee with a little whiskey to ease his nerves.

He walked over to the old shack he'd bought with a note from the bank and which he shared with Belle, and went inside. He closed the door behind him and stood looking around, shifting his gaze from the little living room with its shabby, faded wallpaper before him to the kitchen on his left.

No sign of Belle.

He cocked his head, listening. All was quiet. Surely, she was up. Right after they'd been married he'd told her she had to start crawling out of bed before noon. Sleeping till noon was a former habit, and she was no longer that kind of woman.

He looked at the stairs rising before him, between the kitchen and the living room, to the left of the small charcoal brazier, and called her name. From upstairs came the sound of a glass breaking. It broke hard and shattered loudly, as though something had been thrown against a wall.

Vincent crossed the room to the foot of the stairs, standing on a small, flowered rug Belle crocheted to pass the time. Again, he called her name.

No response. All was silent up there now.

"Belle. Dammit, why don't you answer me?" Vincent barked as, one hand on the rail, he started up the stairs, taking the steps two at a time.

Three small rooms were on the second floor—one to each side of the dim, narrow hall and their room, slightly larger than the others, lay at the far end. The door was closed but unlatched. Vincent could see a long sliver of light between the door and the frame.

"Belle?" he called again, striding down the hall, his boots thumping loudly and making the floorboards squawk. His spurs chinged with every heavy, angry step. Drawing up to the door, he removed his hat and shoved the door open, then ducked through the low doorway as he stepped into the room. "Belle?"

He stopped just inside the door. Something crunched beneath his boots—broken glass lying amidst a pool of liquid. He lifted his gaze to peer into the room.

The rumpled bed lay straight ahead of him, the headboard abutting the far wall. A small table stood beside the bed and an old brocade armchair. A couple of glasses, a coffee cup, and a bottle sat on the table. Belle sat on the chair sideways, her bare feet up. She wore a thin cotton nightgown and a frilly pink wrap with puffy sleeves.

She didn't look at him. She sat pouting, resting a cheek against one of her upraised knees. She'd been crying. Her eyes were puffy and red, and tears streaked her cheeks. Her golden curls were a tangled mess.

"Belle, what in God's name is going on?"

She turned her head a little, glaring at him through a sheen of tears. "Where've you been, Vincent?" she asked, flaring her nostrils. Each word had been coated in dark bitterness.

"What?"

"Where've you *been,* Vincent?" she fairly screamed at him.

Vincent scowled at her, incredulous. "Wha—why? I been workin', honey."

"So late at night?"

Vincent walked forward, trying to avoid the glass and what was obviously whiskey on the floor in front of the door. "Well, yeah. I . . . I . . ."

"I watched you sneak out of here last night. *Late* last night."

He stopped about four feet away from her, staring down at her. It was the only place in the room he could stand to his full height, for the walls to either side of him, clad in more shabby, gaudy wallpaper—the house had been a parlor house before Vincent had bought it when the madame had gone belly up, no pun intended—slanted sharply toward the center of the room. "Yeah, well . . . I had my midnight rounds to make, Belle. You know I always have my rounds to make, after the saloons have done closed their doors for the night."

"And those rounds took you all night, Vincent? Rattling door knobs took you all *night*?" Her voice was low and brittle, her jaws hard, eyes sparking. Vincent knew from past experience she was on the verge of one of her screaming spells.

"I ran into some trouble is all. So what? I'm the only damn lawman this town has, Belle. You know the town council is too cheap to hire me a deputy, so I have to do it all myself."

"What kind of trouble?"

"Huh?"

"What kind of trouble did you run into, Vincent?"

Again, he spread his arms. "Just . . . just trouble, Belle. Why in the hell are you givin' me such grief? I work my ass off for you, Belle. I try to give you all the comforts, don't I? Don't I try to make you comfortable, Belle?" He spread his arms a little wider and raised his hands as though to indicate the lumpy bed and the dresser propped on a catalogue because one of the legs was missing, and the bureau that was missing a drawer. "If it wasn't for me, Miss Belle, you'd still be—"

"Did this trouble take you out of town, Vincent?" she spat up at him, her eyes nearly crossed with fury.

"What? No."

"Huh. Well, that's certainly funny. Why did you ride out of town on your horse, then? Why did you ride out of town on your horse like a bat out of hell around one in the morning last night?"

Vincent just stared down at her, tongue tied. His face was growing warm, his chest heavy and hot. He silently scrambled for a response, his brain chugging along in desperation though the unoiled gears were raking against each other.

"Why, I never . . . I never left town, Belle. Is that what someone said? Well . . . they had it wrong. That wasn't me."

"Hah!" she laughed loudly and without a sliver of mirth. "You're a terrible liar, Vincent. Stupid men make the worst liars, so you might as well stop tryin' right now, Vincent, because you're a stupid man, Vincent! Tell me what in the hell you were doing, riding out of town like a bat out of hell at one in the morning last night. Who were you going to see, *Vincent*?" She jutted her chin at him like a club.

He stared down at her, his face growing hotter and hotter, his chest heavier. His voice was very quiet. It sounded like the voice of a much calmer man than he. "Who . . . who . . . ? I mean, who *thinks* they saw me leave town? Was it your friend Darlington, Belle? If so, he's lyin' to you."

"Hah! *Darlington?*" She glared up at him, her brows furled with incredulity, as though he'd spoken the words in a foreign tongue. Again, she leaned forward in the chair and jutted her chin and hard jaws at him. "*I* saw you, Vincent. *I* followed you to the livery barn. *I* was right outside . . . in the shadows beside the barn. You rode right past me."

Vincent had no response. He just stood staring down at her, tongue-tied, hearing a very high-pitched ringing in his ears.

"You know what else I saw, Vincent?" She smiled mockingly up at him. "I saw that big railroad detective saddle his own horse and follow you out of town."

CHAPTER 32

Vincent stared down at his barely clothed wife. His chest rose and fell heavily as he breathed.

Belle narrowed her eyes as she stared up at him with bald accusing. "What have you gotten yourself mixed up in, Vincent?" She said the words slowly and very deeply, raking each word across her vocal cords like an angry hand swept across piano keys. "What is it? What?"

"I don't know what you're talkin' about."

"Did the detective catch up to you, Vincent?"

"What?"

"You heard me!"

"No! I mean, well, uh—" Unable to meet her cold, knowing gaze for another second, and also afraid of what he might do if he remained close to Belle, Vincent turned and walked halfway back to the door and stopped. "Hell, he wasn't followin' me. Leastways, I never seen him." He ground his left fist into the palm of his right hand. "All right, all right, Belle. I did leave town. I didn't wanna tell you cause I didn't want to worry you. I had to leave cause I seen somethin' suspicious over at the lumberyard. Someone rode away, see. They rode away real fast, so I decided I'd better—"

He swung back around to face her and, when he saw the expression on her face, he stopped talking. She had her face scrunched up till she looked like a devil. Her eyes were like slits and on her mouth was a nasty, devilish smile. She shook her head very slowly.

"You think I'm stupid, Vincent, but I'm not. You think that because I was a prostitute , I don't deserve your respect, and you don't owe me the truth. But I know somethin' is goin' on. You've been actin' funny. You've been gone longer than you usually are at night. Sometimes you disappear during the day for hours at a time. I know, because folks came to the house, lookin' for you. Shop owners with problems needin' the law's attention. I had to tell them I hadn't seen you an' I didn't know where you were."

"Oh, hell, they stretch me too thin in this town, Belle! If it ain't one thing, it's another. If it isn't old Evan Lewis needlin' me about his disappearin' goats, its Norman Fletcher complainin' about someone breakin' into his warehouse and stealin' dry goods. I don't got time to run down—" Again, he stopped.

Belle was still slowly shaking her head with that bedeviling expression on her head. An expression of exasperation and suspicion and full knowledge of his own wicked deeds. He'd suddenly realized she wasn't going to believe anything he could say to her.

"Mr. Darlington said you were—"

"Mr. Darlington again!"

"He said you were the last man in town to see those three deputy U.S. marshals alive. He said you four rode out of town and a few hours later you came back—alone."

Halfheartedly, Vincent said, "They wanted me to show 'em that shortcut trail around the Comanche Buttes. So I led 'em out and showed 'em an' when they had a good handle on it—"

"Mr. Darlington asked me if you've been acting different lately, Vincent." She'd said this with a saucy, mocking air.

Rage exploding inside him, Vincent lowered his head and pummeled his temples with his fists. "Oh, god. *Darlington* again! Why don't you just go to Darlington, if you want him so bad! Why do you stay here, torturing me about him? Go to the man! He's got money, an' I know that's all you really want, anyways!"

Belle's upper lip quivered. A tear dribbled out from her right eye and rolled very slowly down her cheek. "I would, Vincent. I would go to him. You know why I won't?"

"*Why?*"

Again, her upper lip quivered. A second tear, this one from her left eye, rolled down her cheek. "Because he won't have me. I ain't good enough for him. I'm a used woman. I'm *soiled goods!*" She smiled, if you could call it a smile, and added in a quaking little-girl's voice, "He just wants us to be *friends!*"

Vincent just stared at her, sort of heartbroken for her at the same time he felt such rage he thought his heart would explode.

She wiped each cheek in turn, sniffed, and looked up at him again. "He suspects you, Vincent. He thinks you might've had something to do with those lawmen disappearing out in the desert. He says Ramsay suspects you, too."

Vincent whipped around to face her once more. "What'd you tell him? Your precious *Darlington*. What'd you tell him?"

She scrunched up her eyes again with burning suspicion and said in a raspy, accusing wheeze: "What-have-you-done?"

"Nothing! I'm just tryin' to do my job! I'm just tryin' to support you, Belle!"

"Someone has led you down the primrose path, Vincent. The primrose path to *destruction!*"

"Oh, go to hell, Belle! You don't know what you're talkin' about! You never have! Darlington's right. You're just a stupid, used-up woman!"

That didn't seem to faze her. Smiling again weirdly, with sinister menace, she dropped each bare foot to the floor in turn and rose. Walking slowly toward him, she placed one foot directly in front of the other, swung her hips saucily, then stopped only inches in front of Vincent. She reeked of whiskey.

He frowned at her curiously as she rose up onto her toes. For a second, he thought she was going to kiss him but then she slid her face to one side, shoved her nose up close to his shirt collar, and sniffed.

She pulled her head back and hardened her jaws and her eyes again. "Who is *she*?"

Vincent's heart thudded. He felt his mouth open as his lower jaw sagged.

She knew.

If Belle knew, who else knew?

"Who is she, Vincent?" Belle said again in a raspy wheeze, her lips only two inches from his. "Whoever she is, she's sold you a bill of goods, Vincent. This won't end well for you. Being involved in the holdups of those trains and the stealin' of the ranchers' stock—oh, my lord, Vincent— it will not go well for you! No, no, no. It will not go— *achh . . . oaf . . . Vin . . . no! Achhhuhoofff . . . Vinc . . . !*"

Slowly, his right hand around her neck, he backed her up against the wall.

Both of her hands pressed against his, trying desperately to peel his single hand off her neck. Her eyes bugged and her mouth opened, issuing strangling sounds, spittle flecking her lips. Already she was turning blue.

His fingers pressed deep into her throat . . . deeper . . .

She clawed at him desperately, raking her nails across his knuckles, tearing his flesh, drawing blood.

He lifted his right hand. Her body rose, her heels lifting from the floor, and then her toes. She fought him desperately, her eyes turning red as blood vessels burst. She kicked the wall and clawed his hands, her eyes growing larger and larger and more and more terrified . . . more and more red. When her feet were a foot off the floor, he stretched his lips back from his teeth and jerked his hand sharply to one side.

He felt her neck snap. It made a popping sound, like the report of a small-caliber pistol.

Instantly, her eyes glazed over, her hands dropped from his, and her head tilted forward. She hung as limp as a rag-doll in his hand, sagging against the wall with her bare feet twitching.

Vincent pulled his hand away and stepped back.

She dropped straight down the wall to pile up on the floor like so much blond-headed trash. Which was exactly what she was. Still, though, as he stared down at her, he couldn't help feeling sorry for her.

In fact, he felt a sob boil up out of his chest and explode from between his lips. "Oh, Belle!" he cried, lowering his head and pressing his forearm against his face, muffling his wails. He stood there sobbing for maybe five minutes.

Then he lowered his arm, looked down at Belle lying in a lifeless heap, gave one more strangled sob, turned, and staggered drunkenly out of the room and down the stairs. He shoved some possibles into a burlap sack, filled a canteen from the handpump, and grabbed his sawed-off shotgun from where it hung from a peg by the door.

He left the house muttering, "Ain't good enough for you, that it?" over and over again.

Returning to the stable, he saddled and bridled his horse.

With his rifle in the leather scabbard strapped to the saddle, and his shotgun hanging down his back by its leather lanyard, he rode over to the livery barn to fetch Joe's fine bronco stallion, which he led to the undertaking parlor. Fifteen minutes later, Vincent left with Joe's blanket-wrapped body hanging belly down across Comanche Joe's saddle, secured with ropes so he wouldn't fall off during the long ride out to the Wet Rocks.

Vincent kept his head down and didn't look at anybody as he rode over to the train station at the eastern edge of Bottleneck. That is, he didn't look directly at anybody, but in the corners of his eyes, he could see folks staring at him curiously, wondering what in hell the Bottleneck town marshal was up to.

What . . . or who did he have tied over that stallion's saddle?

Ignoring them, Vincent set his jaws so hard they felt as though they would shatter, and reined his grullo up in front of the train station. He swung down, and very slowly and with a calmness belying the storm raging inside him, he looped his reins and Comanche Joe's reins over the tie rail.

He stepped up onto the brick platform, walked to the door, opened it, and stepped inside. He stopped about three feet in front of the door and stood there with his boots spread a little more than shoulder width apart, his left hand hanging straight down along his side, his right hand on the rear stock of the shotgun hanging down behind his right shoulder.

He looked around the small waiting room with its tick-tocking clock on the wall, and then at the ticket and telegrapher's cage on his right. The place was empty. At least, the waiting area and the ticket cage were empty save for a few buzzing flies. He looked at the closed door in the shadows at the back of the room. A brass plate commanding

PRIVATE in ornate lettering identified the door as Darlington's office.

A drawer opened and closed behind the door. Papers rattled. A man cleared his throat. Sniffing the stale air, Vincent detected the odor of cigar smoke. Grinding his back teeth, he strode forward, bringing his boots down heavily.

As he approached the office door, Darlington's voice called from behind it in a desultory, vaguely impatient sing-song. "We're closed. No train will be leaving until further notice. Vacate the premises, please. *Thank* yooo!"

Vincent strode straight up to the door and with a fierce grunt, he kicked it in.

As the door exploded inward and slammed against the wall, Vincent stepped into Darlington's office.

"Good God, man!" the moneyed man exclaimed, leaping up out of the chair behind his large desk, a half-smoked cigar in his hand. His spectacles glinted in the light from the Tiffany lamp on the desk, and his regal face was mottled red. "Have you gone insane? How dare you bust your way in—"

"She ain't good enough for you?" Vincent shouted from the doorway, cutting the man off.

"*What?*"

"My wife ain't good enough for you?"

Darlington's lower jaw dropped, his eyes widened, and he shook his head in shock. "I have no idea what in hell you're talking about!"

As Vincent strode toward the desk, he swung the shot-gun around in front of him and wrapped his right hand around the grips. "You think you're too good for my wife? That it, Mister High an' Mighty?"

"I . . . *what* . . . ?"

The man's eyes grew even wider when he saw Vincent take the sawed-off twelve-gauge in both hands and extend it straight out in front of him. He threw up his hands and stumbled back against the wood and glass bookcase flanking his desk. "Wait. My God . . . what are you— ?"

The twelve-gauge's deafening blast cut him off. The single wad of twelve gauge buck slammed him back against the shelf, knocking the small steel locomotive and tender car labeled West Texas & Cerro Alto Railroad off the top of it and to the floor.

Darlington screamed and looked from Vincent to the many small, bloody buckshot holes in his belly. He looked at Vincent again and was about to scream once more when Vincent, smiling, tripped the shotgun's second trigger, blowing the railroad owner back into the bookcase again with such violence it dislodged his glasses, and shattered the bookcase's glass doors.

The man staggered forward, his glasses hanging from one ear, his eyes rolling back in his head. He gave a guttural groan and fell facedown atop his desk. With a series of brief, raking whimpers, he slid down the desk before thumping onto the floor.

"There!" Vincent raged. "She too good for ya now?" He swung around, stomped back out of the office and outside. He gave only a passing glance at the small crowd of people slowly, warily gathering around him, looking from him to the railroad office and back again.

Vincent untied his reins as well as the reins of Joe's horse, mounted the grullo, and rode away, whistling.

CHAPTER 33

"I still don't understand it, Wolf," Violet said as she and Stockburn trotted their horses through the rocky desert in the direction of Bottleneck. "I still don't understand it by half."

"Well, that make two of us, honey. All I know is that Comanche Joe seems to be at the center of this whole thing. That part doesn't surprise me much. Joe was a train robber back before I even started with Wells Fargo. It's Lana. She's the mystery I can't figure. How she ended up with Ramsay . . . how she turned against him and started stealing his cattle."

"For Joe, apparently."

Stockburn shook his head. "Yeah, it's a mystery, all right. She's a wild one, though, and make no mistake. I've seen her at work." He remembered her enraged screams while he lay at the bottom of the shaft, her angry shots fired at him.

"Somehow, she entangled Vincent DePaul in her scheme."

"Why?"

"Oh, it makes sense. She needed at least one white man in power on the *inside* on her side. To help her. And to sort of regulate and calibrate the investigation into the holdups the best he could, and to throw off any suspicious parties, including myself. That's probably why she also employed Snake-Eye and Jess, who, it appeared, led the holdup parties. Likely former hands of her father's, since they were holed up in that line shack. They'd know the country. Only problem about Vincent was—"

Violet glanced over at him from where she rode off his right stirrup. "Yes?"

Stockburn tapped his temple. "The man's crazier 'n a tree full of owls. Temperamental, to boot. Highly emotional. He was in such a hurry to get to Lana last night he didn't make sure he wasn't followed out of Bottleneck. High-strung and careless."

"I hope he's still in town when we get there. Sounds like he could answer some important questions."

"Indeed, honey. Indeed."

Stockburn clucked Smoke into a faster pace. Violet did likewise with her own mule. Together, riding side by side, they chewed up the desert until Bottleneck appeared on the ridge, resembling a scattered heap of trash from the distance of a mile or so. As they rode closer, the shacks and shanties and two- and three-story business dwellings arranged themselves on the town's various knolls at the rocky, nearly bald crest of the Cerro Altos.

As they entered town, Stockburn glanced over at Violet and said, "Honey, you ride behind me. Keep some distance between us."

Violet looked at him with a worried expression, then pulled her mouth corners down, nodded, and slowed her mule, falling back to ride just behind where Smoke's dust curled, shining copper in the late-afternoon sunshine.

"Now, he's done it."

Stockburn reined Smoke to a halt and turned to his right. The short, fat, mustached Hollis Renfro sat on the dilapidated gallery of his squalid shop, under the weathered board sign announcing HOLLIS RENFRO—BEER & TEQUILA. He still displayed the smaller sign offering tooth extractions for two bits. The man had *cajones*. Stockburn would give him that.

"What's that?" Wolf asked the sweating, rumpled man who held a brown beer bottle on his fat right thigh.

"Now, he's *really* done it." Renfro smiled. "I mean, in a big way." He looked delighted.

"Would you mind chewing that up a little finer?" Stockburn said, his growing testiness plain in his voice.

"He killed Darlington. Hell, he killed 'em both. Killed *her* first."

"Who first?"

"Belle. Neighbors heard 'em goin' at it like two wildcats findin' themselves in the same henhouse. After Vincent stormed out of the house, a neighbor went in and found her dead. Poor Belle. She was a good gal. Helluva prostitute! Gone now." Hollis shook his head and sipped his beer. "Too bad." He chuckled again, his delight returning. "Yep, he's really done it, now!"

"Where is he?"

Hollis hiked a shoulder. "Beats me. As long as he don't come here." He added fatefully, "Crazy catamount." He gestured toward a wagon coming along the street. The words CHARLES BLACK & SON, UNDERTAKERS had been painted in large black letters along the side panel of the box. "Here they come now, I 'spect."

Violet rode up beside Stockburn, frowning at him curiously. "What's going on, Wolf?"

Stockburn looked around cautiously. "Sounds like Vincent's off his rocker. I mean, he *was* off his rocker, but it sounds like he really came off it. Killed his wife. Murdered the head of the Cerro Alto Railroad."

The detective booted Smoke into the street. The wagon continued toward him. An older man and a younger man, both in ill-fitting suits and wearing dusty bowler hats, sat on the driver's seat. They eyed Stockburn dubiously as he pulled the gray up close to the wagon and glanced over the side panel.

He winced when he saw Darlington and Belle lying sprawled side by side on the floor of the box, bodies flopping against each other with the wagon's pitch and sway. The man's guts were leaking out of his belly, which had obviously been opened up by the twin blasts of a shotgun. No doubt, a double-barreled, twelve-gauge coach gun from relatively close range.

Belle's half-clothed body didn't have any blood on it, but her head lay at an awkward angle. Her staring blue eyes were so badly bloodshot that the whites were totally red.

Strangled. Likely, her neck had been snapped, as well.

They stared up at Stockburn with none-too-vaguely befuddled expressions on their pale, stiff faces, as though they were waiting for the answer to a burning question.

"Yep, he's off his nut, all right," Stockburn said.

"You can say that again," said the older man, who was driving the wagon on past Stockburn.

Stockburn turned his head to follow the man moving away with the wagon. "Where is he? Where's Vincent?"

The driver turned to gaze back over his left shoulder at Stockburn. "The folks up at the train station say he rode out of town like a donkey with its tail on fire." He turned his head back forward.

As the wagon continued to roll away, the younger man, who was probably the older man's son, judging by their similar features, turned his head toward Stockburn. "He's packin' Comanche Joe, don't ya know. Come an' got him before he carved up the railroad fella."

He shrugged, glanced at the two bodies in the box behind him, then turned to the older man driving the wagon. "Together at last." Father and son chuckled briefly. The wagon dwindled off into the distance, pulling its dust cloud along behind it.

Violet turned to Wolf. "What're you gonna do, Wolf?"

"I'm gonna give Smoke some water, a bag of oats, and an hour's rest. I'm gonna have me a steak and some beans and a pot of coffee, and then I'm gonna get after him." Stockburn glanced at the sky. "Looks like the nice weather's gonna hold for a change. I'm gonna follow him as far as I can tonight." He booted Smoke forward, heading for the livery barn.

"I'd like to ride with you," Violet said, riding off Smoke's right hip.

"Not a chance, sweetheart. I've already lost one girl out there in those infernal rocks." He gazed toward the Wet Rocks country—a cluster of jutting blue teeth beyond hills and shelving dikes in the far southwestern distance. "I'm not gonna risk losing another one."

Violet frowned. "Who's the other one?"

"Her name's Hank."

"A girl named Hank?"

Stockburn's chuckle belied his worry about the pretty, redheaded detective's fate. "Yeah," he said, angling toward the barn outside which the old Mexican buzzard sat, smoking a loosely rolled cornhusk cigarette. "A girl named Hank."

Stockburn and Violet sat down to a big meal in the Frenchman's Restaurant in Bottleneck. There was nothing French about the food in the place. At least, not if there was anything French about steak, beans, a side of canned greens, a basket of crusty brown bread served with butter, dried apple pie with a liberal topping of fresh whipped cream, and several large mugs of coal-black coffee.

Wolf devoured his meal in half the time it took Violet to eat hers and drink the bottle of beer she'd ordered. Stockburn rolled and smoked a quirley while she finished, not minding the wait. He needed a short rest to refresh his weary and battered body before hitting the trail again, though the urge to get after Vincent and Lana and to run the stock thieves to ground once and for all was a fine elixir.

After all this was over, he'd probably realize how sore he was. Maybe before heading back to Kansas City he'd loll in one of those soothing hot springs up around Santa Fe. Those warm mineral baths were supposed to have amazing healing properties. After this job, amazing healing properties were going to be needed in no short supply.

No doubt about that.

When Violet had finished her dessert and a second bottle of beer, Stockburn led her over to the Territorial Hotel. He rented a room for the girl and ordered her to stay put until he returned for her. In the event he didn't return, she was to saddle her mule and hightail it back to her claim shack. Even if he wasn't able to run the rest of the stock thieves to ground, she should be safe at her and Skinny's old shack, since she and Wolf had punched the tickets of Snake-Eye and Jess.

"Under no circumstances are you to ride out looking for me, young lady. Do you understand?" He was standing in her rented room's open doorway. Violet stood looking up at him with concern. She moved only her lips but did not speak.

He placed his hands on her shoulders and crouched over

her, narrowing one eye with deep admonishment. "Do you understand?" He hoped she wasn't as stubborn as Hank.

Violet nibbled her lower lip and nodded. "I understand, Wolf." She took one of his hands in her own, kissed it, squeezed it, and gazed up at him imploringly. "You return to me, do *you* understand?"

"Oh, I intend to." Smiling, he brushed his knuckles across her chin. "Can't wait, in fact."

"I'll be here . . . waiting."

"All right, then."

Stockburn straightened and started to turn away.

"Wolf, wait!" Violent flung herself into his arms and kissed him on the lips. It was a long, warm kiss.

He hadn't been ready for it. Nor had he been ready for the passion this young woman stirred in him. He found himself with his hands on her shoulders again, returning her kiss with every bit as much fervor as she put into it. When he finally shoved her away, both were a little flushed and breathless.

He looked down at her, dumbfounded. *No,* he told himself. *No. You remember who you are. What you are. What you did. You can't have her. You doomed yourself for love a long time ago.*

In San Francisco.

Violet slowly lifted a hand toward his cheek and opened her mouth to speak. He turned away abruptly, said, "Goodbye, honey," and hurried out into the hall, down the stairs, and over to the livery barn.

Fifteen minutes later, he'd picked up Vincent's two-horse trail out front of the train station and followed it out of town to the southwest. He had his rifle and his two six-guns, his warbag containing his trail supplies including some old jerky and hardtack, and a fresh canteen of water.

He didn't know where the Wet Rocks were, exactly. It seemed no white men did. At least, no whites beyond Vincent, Snake-Eye, and Jess, that was. Lana must have told Vincent or shown him the way, for, judging by his two sets of horse tracks, his route appeared decisive. He knew where he was going and he was making haste to get there.

Stockburn just hoped he didn't lose the man's trail. The farther he traveled through the desert southwest of Bottleneck, he found himself in as vast a stretch of wild and rugged desert as he'd ever seen—a few small playas, ancient lakes, which were relatively flat but gave brief relief from the bulk of the terrain, which was all towering monoliths of red sandstone; deep, narrow canyons that seemed to circle back on themselves or simply end at stone walls; tabletop mesas, eroded arches, and steep climbs to narrow passages over craggy passes, with only more of the same forbidden terrain beyond.

No wonder few white men had ever visited that country before. It was as good a place to get lost as Stockburn had ever seen. Vincent must be following a map. At least, a map in his head. It was hard to believe such a simple fool could find his way. On the other hand, he had very good motivation. He was on his way to meet the so-called love of his life—the wild and savage Lana.

The girl had Vincent in the palm of her hand. Stockburn wondered when she was going to close that hand, and squeeze. Probably just as soon as Vincent was no longer useful.

The sun sank gradually, changing the light from brass to saffron to salmon to copper and then green. Long shadows stretched out across the chaparral.

Stockburn pushed on. As long as he could follow the shoe prints of Vincent's horses, he would continue.

Then he lost the trail on the stone floor of a stone-walled canyon. He continued through the canyon and found himself facing three more, narrower canyons branching off from the main one. He scoured the ground for tracks but found none. The canyons' stone floors would not accept a shoe print. All he found were some fur-tufted rabbit bones and a pile of day-old puma scat.

Too stubborn to stop and wait for morning to relocate Vincent's trail, Stockburn chose one of the canyon mouths at random, and pushed on. He figured there was a good chance all three canyons opened out onto a main one again.

He was wrong. After another hour of searching for Vincent's sign, he found himself hopelessly lost on a low rise with pockets of bristling cactus and brush and black volcanic rocks humping up all around him. The last bayonets of shimmering copper and green light suddenly bled out of the western horizon, and Wolf found himself in near total darkness.

Darkness save for the light of several bright stars and bushels of dimmer ones.

Coyotes yammered. Distantly, some hunting wildcat gave its screeching cry. Owls hooted.

Cursing, Wolf stopped to tend his horse and make a cold camp. It was going to be a long night.

He sat back against a rock, considered rolling a quirley, and nixed the idea. The smoke might carry to a stalker's nostrils.

Yeah, it's going to be a long damn ni—

The thought was abruptly quashed by something he'd spied out of the corner of his right eye. He turned his head to gaze straight south. At least, he thought it was south. The up and down country he'd ridden through as though blindfolded was good at scrambling a man's sense of direction.

As he stared in whatever direction it was, he started to wonder if he'd fallen asleep without realizing it and had awakened to see the sun begin its slow rise in the east. A strange illumination lay that way. A shimmering umber light that grew steadily until it reflected off several high, toothy peeks jutting up.

Sure enough, it looked like the dawn of a new day.

When Stockburn checked his old railroad turnip, it read 10:47 P.M. The sun wouldn't be up for another five or six hours.

He returned the watch to its pocket and stared at the shimmering light that lit up a good bit of ground over that way, illuminating the fang-like stone walls to each side of it and behind it.

A woman's scream came vaulting from the heart of that ambience to pierce Wolf's heart like a warrior's javelin.

CHAPTER 34

Stockburn's heart thudded as he stared at the shimmering glow in the south. Yeah, it was south, all right. He could tell by the stars and his recollection of where he'd watched the last rays of the sun fade from the western sky.

An icy hand pressed itself against his back, freezing the sweat that lingered there from the long ride.

Again, came the woman's scream. *Hank?* His heart quickened, but when the scream came again, something told him the screams did not come from his redheaded sidekick. Something seemed more primal in the scream that vaulted over him once more. Something wild and dying. A human to be sure. But a wild, dying human.

I'm close, aren't I? he whispered to himself. *The Wet Rocks. They're right over there. That light is coming from them. From the* heart *of them.*

"Oh, I'm damn close," he said, chuckling to himself despite the pressure of that cold hand against his back. The cold hand was reminding him that he was alone, and had no way to know how many Comanches lived over that way. Comanche Joe's and Lana's people. They weren't going to welcome this white eyes with open arms, that was for sure.

He had to tread carefully.

With that thought in mind, he grabbed his rifle and rose, wincing against the stiffness in his joints, which still ached from his tumble down the mine shaft and which the long ride had done nothing to alleviate. Staring at the glow in the south, he stooped to pick up his canteen, and looped the lanyard over his shoulder.

He turned his head to one side, glancing at his horse loose-hobbled twenty feet away. Smoke had his head up, tail arched and was staring toward the ominous glow. It seemed to be radiating up from a canyon amidst those jutting crags, like some jewel radiating light from deep inside itself and casting it far and wide of its setting. The light was reflected in the horse's wide, wary eyes.

"Stay, boy," Wolf said needlessly. Smoke was hobbled, after all. "I'll be back." He started walking away from his cold, dark camp, heading toward the light, adding under his breath, "I hope."

He strode up a slight rise, heading toward a cleft in the low ridge ahead of him. Rocks lay to his left. A deep, stone- and brush-choked gulley was on his right. Between them was a narrow stretch of gravelly ground, which he followed to the crest of the rise. He stopped in the opening in the ridge wall and stared toward the glow.

He couldn't see it much better than he'd been able to from his camp, but it seemed to be coming from a higher elevation and in a cradle at the heart of those thrusting crags. Hard to tell, but he guessed the source of the glow was maybe a mile away.

Resting the Yellowboy on his shoulder, he continued walking. Without the wavering glow dimming and brightening intermittently, which told him it was caused by a fire to which fuel was being added, it would have been almost impossible to traverse the rugged terrain. At least, not without twisting or breaking an ankle or tripping over something and braining himself on the surrounding, sharp-edged rocks that comprised the devil's playground.

But the glow cast enough umber light over the ground that he was able to relatively safely pick his way up over short rises and through narrow corridors, giving passage through natural buttresses of solid rock. As he moved, he was aware that he was climbing, likely following some old Indian trail, for the rocks to each side were marked with colorful pictures of deer, suns, stars, moons, snakes, and several other, more inscrutable images he assumed had their origins in some ancient Indian religion.

The trail he was following grew steeper.

Rock walls rose and fell around him. He passed the black mouths of side canyons and narrow corridors that could lead anywhere or nowhere at all. At one point, his skin crawled when he heard the disgruntled ratcheting of a rattlesnake he'd likely disturbed from its nightly slumber. The alarm had come from several feet away and diminished as the snake wriggled off in a snit for less disturbed environs.

As the glow grew brighter and brighter ahead of him, that cold hand pressed more firmly against his back, between his shoulders. It didn't help any that every few minutes or so he heard that long, raking, agonized primal female wail. And that the screams grew louder just as the amber light intensified in the rocks.

Gradually, a drumming rose, as regular as a metronome.

The soul-rending screams continued. They gave the bone-splintering impression the screamer, a woman, was being slowly tortured to death and she had the strength to scream only every three or four minutes. But when she did, each scream encapsulated every ounce of pain she'd endured between screams.

The drumming continued.

Thum. Thum. Thum . . .

The light grew bigger as Stockburn neared the crest of
the rise he'd been climbing via a narrow corridor between
rocks. A canyon gradually opened before him, roughly the
size and shape of a large volcano. Wolf saw the far wall,
lit as it was by the flickering amber light and shadows cast
by the illumination from below. Firelight. Of course.

As he approached the canyon's edge, he could see more
and more of the opposite wall. His gaze slid down it toward
the canyon floor.

Heart pounding from the steep climb, raking deep
breaths in and out of his lungs, sweating from every pore,
he dropped to his hands and knees. He set the Yellowboy
down beside him, doffed his hat, and set it over the rifle's
brass breech. He licked his lips and steeled himself as he
peered down over the lip of the canyon.

Casting his gaze across the canyon floor below, he
sucked a sharp but silent breath through gritted teeth. He
could see the entire canyon from this ridge of crenulated
rock. It took his breath away.

The fire lay in the canyon's center, in a pit maybe
twenty feet deep and filled with dry wood—a vast blaze
maybe thirty feet in dynameter. The flames licked up out
of the pit to dance and spark, giving off saucer-sized glowing cinders, within a few feet of the crest of the ridge on
the north side where Wolf was stretched out, peering into
the fiery chasm.

The firepit was ringed by five or six young Comanche
men in loin cloths, high-topped moccasins, calico shirts,
and leather bandanas from which white feathers jutted. The
half-dozen youths appeared to be in their early- to mid-
teens. An old man with a willowy body, his bony legs thin
as hickory saplings, gestured to the boys, indicating when
and where more wood should be added to the flames licking

up out of the pit on whose edges they milled, retrieving wood from large piles nearby.

Well back from the pit lay a wooden scaffold maybe five feet high. The agonized screams were issuing from there.

A woman lay stretched across the scaffold, suspended in the air by what appeared lengths of rawhide or maybe animal guts. It was hard to tell as the woman and the scaffold were a good hundred feet below Stockburn's position.

The woman—a young one, it appeared, given the smoothness of her naked flesh—lay writhing, struggling against the sinewy stays, her brown body smudged with blood. Wolf was relieved that she wasn't Hank. As he watched, an old woman stepped out from the crowd of thirty or so older men and women, young children, and teenaged girls, standing on a shelving rise above the scaffold as well as the pit from which the large, conical fire issued.

She had accepted a knife from a younger woman just then turning away from the young woman on the scaffold. Stockburn saw that the blade of the knife flashed blood-red in the firelight.

The old woman held the knife up high above her head as she walked up to the young woman suspended over the scaffold. She stopped before the young woman, lifted her head high and tilted her face to the sky, and yelled something in a foreign tongue before plunging the knife down into the struggling young woman's left breast.

Again, the screeching wail of inexpressible pain rose, for a few seconds nearly obliterating the conflagration's roar.

Stockburn winced, heart hammering.

He stared at the poor girl on the scaffold. Who was she? What had she done to deserve such savage treatment?

Suddenly, he glimpsed movement behind the men and women lined up on the shelf above the scaffold. Stockburn shuttled his gaze toward the canyon's south wall. Near the base of the wall were a dozen stone or adobe brick houses with brush roofs. They were not *jacals* but real houses. What appeared barns, stables, and corrals, lay to the east of the houses.

A full-fledged ranch was down there on the floor of the canyon. A modern ranching operation despite the Comanches apparently clinging to a stone-age religion that included sacrifice as part of a funeral rite. In the next life, Joe would no doubt need a woman. Preferably a young woman to give him many children. But any way you stacked it, what Stockburn was witnessing on that canyon was the bloody murder of an innocent young lady.

The movement Stockburn had glimpsed was centered on the largest of those stone houses, which had a large, brush-roofed, long front gallery.

Focusing his gaze tighter on the house, he saw people issuing down the gallery steps and onto the canyon floor. A half-dozen, at least. Four were carrying something suspended above their heads—a stretcher of sorts. A body lay on the stretcher made of two lodgepoles and hide.

As the group went down into the light of the massive fire, Stockburn arched a brow when he saw Lana Ramsay was at the head of the small pack. Yeah, it was Lana, all right. He recognized her supple figure despite the Indian gear she was wearing—a short buckskin jacket colorfully decorated with beads and porcupine quills. It was buttoned tightly across her breasts, pushing up her bosoms and exposing a strip of her flat, copper-colored belly just above her waistline.

She wore a very short buckskin shirt and moccasins that rose nearly to her knees. On her dark-haired head she wore what appeared a wolf's head cap. A wolfskin cape flowed down her shoulders, mingling with her dark hair dropping down her shoulders and back as she led the procession down the slope toward the fire. Directly behind her were the four braves in buckskins, war paint, and eagle feather headdresses carrying the body of Comanche Joe—who else could it have been?—on the stretcher above their heads.

Two wizened old women in beaded buckskin dresses followed the stretcher, heads down as though praying. Two tall braves in buckskins and beaded headbands brought up the procession's rear. They moved slowly, in time with the metronomic drumbeats, passing a tall, broad man standing back away from the festivities. Remarkable that he was the only one not dressed in buckskins and feathers.

Dressed in white man's casual trail garb, he stood in solemn stillness, head bowed, holding his Stetson over the buckle of his cartridge belt.

Vincent.

While inspecting Lana and the procession moving down the shelving sandstone slope from the house, Stockburn hadn't lost sight of the fact that the knife continued to be passed around to the group gathered in front of the scaffold, and that the knife continued to be plunged—by old women, old men, young women, and young men—into the poor girl's body. Her screams, however, were dwindling considerably in volume, and her writhing was subsiding as her life fluids bled out into the dark-red, glistening pool on the ground beneath the scaffold.

"Lord Almighty," Wolf raked out, running a hand down his face in horror and exasperation. "Why are you killing that poor innocent child?"

Of course, he didn't know that she was all that innocent. She might have been as guilty of murder and train robbery as the rest of them, if these people—Joe's extended clan, it appeared—were responsible for the train holdups, murders, and stock robberies. All indications certainly seemed to point that way.

Lana was obviously one of the higher-ranking members of the clan. Judging by her attire and her position at the head of Joe's funeral procession, Wolf might go as far as to call her a warrior chieftess.

Still, no matter to what degree, if any, the poor girl on the scaffold had played in the Cerro Alto affair, she didn't deserve to be tortured and murdered the way she was. Nobody did.

Stockburn remembered the copper-skinned beauty he'd watched climb the steps of the Stockmen's Hotel the other day—Lana Ramsay in her fetching, flowing, enticingly low-cut gown, with her hair pinned up and that silly fashionable hat on her head. He tried to reconcile that smiling, coy, spirited young woman with the warrior queen he watched now as she led the funeral procession down the slope and around the crowd and the sacrificial girl on the scaffold to stand on the pit above the pyramidal, brightly glowing fire.

The drumbeats stopped abruptly.

The four braves set the stretcher down on the rim of the pit, to Lana's right, and stepped back.

Lana raised her arms and her head as though to follow the fire's highest flames with her gaze, and bellowed words Stockburn couldn't hear above the fire's roar. It wouldn't have done him any good if he had been able to hear the words, spoken as they were in the hard, guttural strains of what was probably some ancient form of Comanche.

Who had taught her the old language?

Joe?

How much time had she spent there, away from the

Agua Verde headquarters? Did Gordon Ramsay have any inkling of whom his adopted daughter *really was*?

On the canyon floor, Lana lowered her arms.

She turned around to face an old man with cascading white locks tumbling across his shoulders. He wore a buckskin robe, adorned with colorful stitching that seemed to form symbols of some kind. The hem of the robe dropped nearly to the ground at his moccasin-clad feet. He wore many necklaces, some beaded, some made from bone, and his wizened face was painted almost entirely white. Except for the lips. His lips had been painted black.

He held the bloody knife out to Lana.

She took the knife. Holding it straight up and down beneath her chin, she stepped around the old man, who must have been a shaman or some such, to the girl lying still now on the low scaffold. Lana bellowed something in that ancient tongue then raised the knife high over the girl's naked, blood-soaked body.

"Ah, hell," Stockburn muttered to himself. "Don't do it, dammit."

He grimaced, fighting off the urge to close his eyes, when Lana plunged the knife straight down into the girl's chest, piercing her heart. Stockburn thought the girl must have been dead, for lately she hadn't been moving or making any sound. He'd been wrong. She convulsed again violently, raising her head once more, and cut loose a scream nearly as shrill and agonized as the first one Stockburn had heard.

While Lana held the knife down, twisting it into the girl's chest, the four braves who'd been carrying the stretcher, crouched over it. They lifted it shoulder-high then tipped it until Comanche Joe's buckskin-clad body slid off and into the firepit.

As it did, the girl on the scaffold gave a final shudder,

lay her head back against the rawhide supporting her, and fell still in death.

Stockburn stared into the canyon in slack-jawed horror.

Something sharp and cold was pressed taught against his neck.

He jerked with a start. He heard the creak of sinew and wood as he turned his head to one side. His eyes widened in shock when he saw the dark, painted face of a Comanche brave staring down at him over the knocked arrow pressed against Wolf's neck.

The brave flared his nostril and curled his upper lip back from his teeth, eyes blazing down at Stockburn while reflecting the light of the funeral pyre before him.

Stockburn's heart thudded. Reacting more than thinking, he jerked his head back and to one side.

The arrow whispered menacingly as it brushed past his left ear to carom into the canyon. Rolling onto his back, Wolf kicked his right leg up, smashing his knee against the brave's backside, drawing the young warrior forward.

The brave screamed and flung his arms out to both sides as he stumbled toward the lip of the canyon, his dark eyes widening in horror. Like a great plumed and colorful bird, he dove straight down into thin air. His body slammed to the canyon floor not ten feet from where Lana stood between the pit consuming Comanche Joe and the sacrificial girl who lay unmoving on the scaffold.

The warrior chieftain stared down at the body then jerked her chin up suddenly. Instantly, her blazing, lunatic eyes locked on Stockburn as though she'd known exactly where he'd be.

CHAPTER 35

"Ah, hell," Stockburn said, backing slowly away from the canyon's rim. "Now, why in blazes did I have to go and do that?" He glanced once more at the dead brave lying near Lana's feet.

Lana whipped her head around, yelling and gesturing. All of the war-painted braves—there must have been a good dozen of them—leaped into action, whooping and hollering as they ran toward the stables and corrals.

"Yep, that tears it," Wolf said under his breath. "My goose is cooked."

He heaved himself to his feet and strode forward, levering a round into the Yellowboy's action. With a fire that size, which could attract unwanted guests, of course the Comanches would have posted pickets around the canyon. One brave meant there were bound to be more. The thought had no sooner swept through his brain than a high *whoosh* sounded on his left, and the arrow cracked into a boulder just ahead and on his right, breaking, the painted shaft glinting in the shimmering light from Joe's funeral pyre.

A gun flashed in the darkness to Wolf's left. The bullet screeched through the air just behind him. Stockburn stopped, wheeled, and flung two quick shots in the direction of the flash, evoking a startled grunt. He hurried forward, trying to retrace his steps. It was hard going, the footing uncertain, rocks everywhere. Still he pushed himself into a jog, knowing a foot could come down wrong at any second and break an ankle. He didn't have much choice. He could sense movement around him, could almost *smell* hot, warpainted bodies closing on him, hurrying toward the cracks and flashes of his rifle. He didn't know how many pickets were along the rim, but sensed at least two were hot on his tracks.

He ran, crouching along the trail, hoping he was on the same trail he'd followed previously. The farther he got from the canyon, the less light illuminated his way. He tripped, fell, cursed, climbed to his feet, and continued jogging.

A rifle cracked behind him, then another from a slightly different position. That was good. Neither shot had come close, which meant he was being followed but neither pursuer knew his exact position. They were just trying to fling lead at him, hoping he'd return fire and give away his location.

He kept going, heart racing, lungs heaving, raking the cooling desert air in and out. Soon, he felt as though he were inhaling sandpaper.

Where was his camp?

He must have gone a mile. It had been a good fifteen minutes since he'd left the canyon. Continuing to move forward, he stumbled over rocks and occasional clumps of dry desert grass or cactus. He glanced over his shoulder. Nothing back there but the fire's diminishing glow. At least, nothing that he could see, but at least two red-skinned devils were after him. Other Comanche braves were likely on their horses and heading out to run him down and kill him slow . . . in grand Comanche fashion.

Once they had their hands on the man who'd killed their head honcho, the big chief himself, Comanche Joe, it would be lights-out for Stockburn. But only after a good two, maybe three days of excruciating, slow-cooked agony, his big Scottish body tucked into a clay pot and suspended over a low fire.

Maybe he should shoot himself and deny them the satisfaction.

Where in blue-bleeping-blazes was his camp?

Breathless, he stopped and kicked a rock in frustration. To his left, a horse gave a quiet whicker. He turned slowly, hope rising in him. *Smoke?*

On the other hand, it could be one of the Comanches' horses.

Crouching low, holding the Winchester up high across his chest, thumb on the hammer, he moved slowly westward, stepping around and over several large rocks. He moved around a gnarled cedar. A pale horse stood with his head turned toward him. Smoke whickered again softly and pawed the stony ground with his left front hoof.

"Smoke!" Stockburn hurried over, resisting the urge to give the horse a big hug. He might be on the verge of a slow, painful death, but there was no point in giving away his dignity before the Comanches won it from him. Besides, Smoke would not respect such a superfluous show of affection.

Still, he was extremely glad to have found his stalwart stallion! Even if it was actually Smoke who'd found him.

Quickly, he gathered his gear and saddled the horse, casting quick looks toward the canyon marked only by the quickly diminishing orange glow of the funeral pyre. An owl hooted. It was answered by another.

No, not owls.

The two Comanches shadowing him were signaling

each other. As he reached up to grab the saddle horn, he paused and cocked an ear to listen. A low thundering rose southeast of his position, maybe a half mile away, beyond a low, dark ridge humping against the stars.

The Comanche warriors were storming up out of the canyon on their sure-footed broncs.

Stockburn cursed and clucked Smoke into a northward trot. With no idea where he was, he had no idea where he was going. But he could keep distance—*good* distance— between himself and the warriors and their lunatic chieftess. He needed to get back to Bottleneck and wire for help from either Wells Fargo or the U.S. marshals, whichever organization could send help fastest. However, the only way their assistance in running the thieving Comanches to ground would do him any good was if he could remember where the canyon lay. That would be a job of work, since he'd been to it and still didn't know where it was. And he still didn't know where the stolen beef was being held.

Anyway, first things first—survive the night. His chances of that didn't look good.

After a half hour of tracing a crazy course through the desert, taking one path of least resistance after another and trying to maintain a generally northerly direction, he heard the low rataplan of fast-moving horses off to his right. He checked Smoke down to a halt and cocked his head to listen.

Five or six sets of horse hooves were clacking on the stone desert floor roughly a hundred yards away. The grunts of Comanches talking among themselves while they searched for him came to his ears clearly on the cool, dry desert air unstirred by any breeze whatsoever.

Were they heading toward him?

He couldn't tell.

While he listened, he heard the clacking and low grunts

of more riders off his left flank. His heart quickened, making his fingers tingle as he gripped the reins. The Comanches had split up—probably into several small groups to scour the night-cloaked terrain for their quarry.

Wolf pushed on, aware that at any second Smoke could misstep and break an ankle, leaving his rider afoot and with the grim task of having to cut his horse's throat. He considered dismounting and walking the horse, but there wasn't enough cover through the stretch of desert he was traversing. The Comanches would likely see him and run him down. At risk of his own life and that of his beloved horse, he had to put as much distance as possible between himself and his pursuers.

That it wasn't working became clear a half hour later. Smoke stopped suddenly and gave a warning snort, tossing his head and looking to his left. Stockburn followed the horse's gaze toward a long, low hump of rock showing roughly fifty yards to the east. The inky silhouettes of maybe a half-dozen riders were just then riding out from behind that low ridge and moving toward him. Their horse-and man-shaped shadows were against the stars twinkling low in the eastern horizon.

Stockburn sucked a sharp breath and swung Smoke closer to another low ridge on his right, hoping they would blend in with the ridge's shadow. He spied the mouth of an opening—a gap maybe twenty feet wide. With haste born of bald-assed terror, he booted the mount into the opening in the side of the ridge. With the length of the horse inside the gap, Wolf swung down from the saddle then turned Smoke back to face him.

He placed a hand firmly on the horse's snout—a command to remain silent. Smoke blinked his understanding. Stockburn dropped to one knee, holding the Yellowboy down low in his right hand, holding Smoke's reins in his left hand. With no way of knowing if the spot would give passage clear to the other side of the ridge, he had to assume it didn't. He didn't want to get trapped between a rock and a hard place—literally. All he could do was hunker there, hoping the alcove concealed him and the Comanches wouldn't investigate it.

Could they track at night? By starlight? Oh, they were good. But were they that good? That patient?

Wolf had a feeling he was about to find out as, kneeling there in his questionable sanctuary with his right shoulder pressed against the gap's north wall, he peered out of the break's mouth, taking shallow, even, quiet breaths.

The Comanches were riding toward him, roughly Indian file, angling so that their current course would put them a little to his left when they reached the ridge he was hiding in like a rat cowering in its hole from stalking coyotes. The clacks of the Comanches' horses lifted a staccato rhythm. Wolf could hear the mounts breathing. Maybe it was his imagination, but beneath the clanging of his own heart against the anvil of his breastbone, he thought he could hear the warriors breathing, too.

One by one they disappeared from his view as they reached the ridge a few yards along his back trail.

Which way would they ride? South away from him, or north *toward* him?

He had his answer a few seconds later when the clacking of the Indian ponies' hooves grew louder. They were heading north. They'd likely reach his position in—oh, say . . . six, five, four, three, two . . . the first rider came into view, leaning forward on his blanket saddle, scouring the ground on the right side of his horse—Stockburn's side of the horse—for sign. He was holding a rifle across his thighs.

The second Indian passed the gap . . . then the third . . .

then a fourth and fifth and, a few seconds later, a sixth. The sixth rider's horse turned its head slightly to glance into the gap, right at Stockburn, just before its head disappeared from view to Wolf's right, the horse's rider following a second later. The last thing Stockburn saw of the horse was its tail giving an owly switch.

Damn. Stockburn stretched his lips back from his teeth, held his breath.

The sixth rider continued riding on past the gap for maybe six or seven clacking strides of his horse before the horse whinnied. The clacking died as the horse stopped.

The horse had seen him.

Damn. Stockburn rose, scuttled forward to the mouth of the gap, and turned his head right, peering north along the ridge wall. The six mounted Indians were turning their horses back toward Stockburn, the ones farthest away putting their mounts several yards out from the wall, so they could see around the other four. The first two grunted something to each other in their own peculiar tongue. They were just batting their moccasin-clad feet against their horses' flanks, heading back to investigate the gap, when Wolf stepped out of the break, squared his shoulders, and thumbed the Yellowboy's hammer back to full cock.

Instantly, the Comanches yelled and jerked weapons to bear.

Spreading his feet a little more than shoulder-width apart, crouching slightly, Stockburn fired straight out from his right hip, kicking up a cacophony of thunder. The rifle spat orange flames into the darkness—six lightninglike lances of crimson that showed the six Comanches in murky silhouette, tumbling out of their saddles, one after the other. Limbs pinwheeling. Long hair flying.

Silence folded over the desert. Silence save for the frenzied clickety-clacks and whinnying and nickering of the Comanches' horses fleeing from the scene of bloody murder. The hoof thuds faded quickly to total silence.

Silence save for the riflelike whipcracks of Wolf's heart in his chest, knowing he'd saved himself for the time being but also knowing he'd given away his position and was likely not long for this world though he was probably doomed to leave it way too slowly indeed.

Over a nicely regulated fire.

He ran into the niche, leaped into the saddle, booted Smoke out of the break, and swung him north.

CHAPTER 36

Stockburn kept a steady pace for the next half hour but finally had to stop when a ridge humped up before him. Starlight shone off a natural stone arch near the crest of the ridge. As far as he could tell in the starlight, another ridge lay beyond that one . . . and possibly another and another.

He was surrounded by such impediments. Well, not entirely surrounded. Behind him lay the relatively flat country he'd just traversed, risking his own life and limb as well as that of his horse. He couldn't go back, of course. The Comanches were back there. They were being very quiet as they followed him, but they were following him, all right.

Comanches never gave up. Especially when they'd lost a half-dozen of their own.

They were patient. They'd take their time. They were on his trail. They'd likely swarm over him just after dawn, when they had some light to see by.

To kill by.

Stockburn slid down from the saddle, took a couple of sips from his canteen, and fed Smoke a couple of hand-fuls of the water, as well. The horse drew it eagerly, the heat from the long ride radiating off his muscular, sweat-lathered body. Stockburn looped the canteen around his saddle horn, took a cautious glance behind him, seeing nothing but night-choked rocks and cactus, then began leading Smoke up the ridge.

He moved slowly, taking his time, wending his way between boulders that should conceal him from the stalking Comanche though it didn't really matter. They knew this country—the position of every rock and cactus, every dike and patch of prickly pear. Every coyote and wolf den. Every wash strewn with the bones of their ancestors.

Finally, he gained the ridge's crest to the right of the large, sandstone arch. He led Smoke down the other side and into a crease between the ridge's northern slope and a granite wall that rose nearly straight up in the air. Looking up toward the top of the giant monolith, Wolf judged it must be at least two hundred feet high. He didn't see a way around it to either side, either. Not without dropping back down the ridge and then heading east or west, but there were more rocks and more ridges that way. At least, as far as he could tell on the dark, eerily quiet, moonless night.

His last night on earth.

He cursed. He'd have to make a final stand. When they came in the morning, he'd take down as many as he could and save the last two pills for himself and his horse. He owed Smoke that much. It had been foolish to ride out alone, he supposed, but with little help, he'd had no choice in the remote country.

Oh, well. His life had always been going to come to that. Every job could have been the last. Somehow, he'd always made it through.

But probably not this time, he silently opined.

Having loosened Smoke's saddle cinch to give the horse some rest and comfort, he crawled back to the crest of the ridge, shouldered up against the arch on his left, doffed his hat, ran his hand through his thick, sweat-damp hair.

Thinking about Hank, wishing he'd found her, he'd wonder about the fate of the pretty redhead throughout eternity, likely as a ghost haunting those silent rocks and deep washes in which the scavengers would scatter his bones. Maybe she was a ghost out there already.

He looked around and wondered then dug his makings out of his shirt pocket.

Taking his time, not worried the smoke might give away his location, for he'd resigned himself to annihilation. Feeling oddly carefree, he rolled the quirley then snapped a match to life on his thumbnail. He touched the flame to the cylinder and waved out the match as he drew the smoke deep into his lungs.

He was glad he'd found Emily, glad he'd found his sister at last, after twenty years of searching. Glad she was alive. Not only alive but thriving as the widow of a wealthy rancher, with a boy of her own. She was Melissa Ann Thornburg now, having changed her name to match the change her long captivity had made in her.

Stockburn mourned all the lost years between losing his sister and finding her again. He mourned his dead parents. He mourned Mike. Vaguely, he wished Mike could have lived so Stockburn could have somehow made it right, what he'd done to his best friend. But there was no way to right the betrayal of a friend. No way to heal the darkness inside you that had caused you to sleep with the woman Mike had been about to marry.

Stockburn looked down at the half-smoked quirley in his hand and nodded. He was ready for the grave, he realized. For the wash in which his bones would be strewn. He was ready to be free of his guilt. It was a heavy thing to carry, and he was tired of carrying it. Not that he didn't deserve to carry it for a few more centuries.

But guilt wasn't going to bring Mike back. It wasn't going to bring Mike and Fannie back together so they could marry and raise a big family together and grow old on their front porch together, with their grandchildren playing at their feet.

Wolf took the final drag from his quirley and mashed the hot coal out against a rock, letting it burn his fingers, welcoming the pain.

Oh, he was ready!

Resigned, he rested his head down against the lip of the ridge and slept.

He slept briefly but upon waking to the warmth of the sun on his cheek didn't think he'd ever slept so well. Listening to the chirping of morning birds beneath the ratcheting cries of a hunting hawk or eagle, there were no moments of confusion. He didn't need time to reorient himself to where he was and what was happening.

He was in the desert somewhere south of Bottleneck in western Texas.

He was going to die today. Likely this morning.

Likely within the hour.

Stockburn lifted his head, scrubbed the sand clinging to his cheek that had been pressed to the ground for the past few hours, and edged a look up and over the ridge crest to peer down the other side. He felt his lips quirk a smile when he saw death waiting for him down there, just like he'd expected it would be.

She would be, rather.

Death in the form of a beautiful, black-haired warrior chieftess, showing as much copper skin as buckskin, squatting atop a low, flat-topped boulder at the base of the slope. She'd replaced the wolf's head cape with a red bandanna tied around the top of her head.

"Good morning, Lana!" Wolf called, lifting his hat and waving it. "How are you this fine desert morning?"

"Better than you, Stockburn!"

A dozen or so braves stood around her and the boulder she was perched on, their horses ground-tied several yards behind them and Lana. All held Winchester carbines, though a few had bow and arrow–bristling quivers hanging down their backs. Young men, war-painted and of all shapes and sizes, they gazed stoically up the slope toward their quarry.

Vincent sat his grullo back with the other horses, beside a fine chestnut Stockburn remembered Lana had taken out of her father's stable at the Agua Verde. Her *foster father's* stable, rather.

Wolf chuckled and yelled, "Vincent, we meet again!"

Wearing his usual slightly baffled expression beneath the brim of his brown Stetson, Vincent shook his head. "How in tarnation did you get out of that hole in the ground?" the Bottleneck marshal yelled up the slope.

"Come on up here, and I'll tell the whole story," Stockburn said, smiling shrewdly. "My voice gets sore, yellin'." He switched his gaze to Lana, who also held a carbine where she squatted atop the boulder. "Before we start the dance, Miss Ramsay, suppose you tell me the why of it. I'll rest easier."

"I don't want you to rest easy, Stockburn," Lana yelled, her voice cold and hard. "You killed my father."

"Why so loyal to old Joe?"

"The same reason we all are," Lana said, glancing around at the war-painted braves. "He was our father. An uncle to some. Even a great uncle to some. But he was our leader. He was going to take back the land the white ranchers stole from us."

"Why did he adopt you out?"

"My mother adopted me out when Joe was up north working against the white man. My mother wasn't worth much. She was a prostitute in Bottleneck. She had too many mouths to feed, so she gave me to Ramsay after he'd come out here. He and his now-dead wife couldn't have kids, so they took me in. I didn't know Joe back then. I just heard his legend around town. He came back from robbing trains in the Indian Territory and saw me out at the Agua Verde one day when he was selling horses to Ramsay.

"He knew right off I was his daughter. He saw himself in me. I saw myself in him. I ran away from the Agua Verde that day and caught up with Joe. Told him I wanted to live with him, wanted to live as a Comanche. He said I'd be a better Comanche if I stayed out at the Agua Verde and bided my time. He wanted me to help him accomplish what he'd decided to do when so many cattlemen moved into his band's ancestral homeland and started killing his sons."

"You gave him valuable information, I take it? About when cattle were being moved . . . and shipped? About Ramsay and the other ranchers?"

"You got it, Stockburn."

"How did you manage to slip away from the ranch so often, without him suspecting you?"

"Most times, he thought I'd arranged to visit a friend in Tucson—the *white* daughter of one of his business partners. I even bought stagecoach tickets. I just never used them." Lana shook her head.

Stockburn could see her smiling even from his distance of seventy yards or so. He could see the white line of her teeth between her dark lips.

"I got my friend to lie for me. Ramsay never questioned his friend about me. He believed me. He always believed me. An arrogant, gullible white man. Instead, I came to the Wet Rocks and learned the ways of my people from Joe. And helped him plan the train robberies."

"Right down to having you and your braves dress as white men . . . to avoid casting suspicion on the Wet Rocks people."

"That's right. They dressed as whites and wore masks, rode shod horses."

Stockburn chewed on that for a time. "It didn't bother you that you were betraying Ramsay?"

Lana shook her head slowly. "Not a bit. He's just another rich white man. Oh, he gave me all the comforts. I suppose I should be more grateful, but he and the other ranchers were crowding my people . . . and hanging my people when they took a cow now and then to sustain themselves. One day, he made me watch him hang a young brave he'd caught on the Agua Verde butchering a cow. He made me watch the hanging of one of my cousins. He wanted me to see the lowly life he'd saved me from, so I'd appreciate the 'white life' he provided me."

Again, she shook her head. Stockburn thought she wore a bitter expression. "I pretended to be grateful. I pretended to love that old jackal. Him and his wife until she died from a milk fever. But after that day, I decided I would kill him one day. I'd help my blood father destroy him and the other white ranchers . . . and return to the Wet Rocks."

"With *Vincent?*" Stockburn called down to her, incredulous.

"Hey!" Vincent said, offended. He rose up in his saddle and pointed up the ridge at Stockburn. "It's different with me. She loves me an' I love her. We work well together— Lana an' me!" He turned to the girl on the rock who kept her steady, dark gaze on Stockburn. "Ain't that right, Lana?"

"Shut up, Vincent," she said without looking at him. "You led him out here, you fool."

"I thought he was dead! So did you!" Vincent insisted.

"You're a damn fool, Vincent," Lana said in a dry, even voice, keeping her gaze on Stockburn.

Vincent switched his pointing finger to Lana. "I helped you, Lana! I made it work! If I hadn't hired that little Mex kid and his friends to jump that train ahead of your bunch—"

"Tomacito Alvarez?" Stockburn called down, angrily flaring his nostrils.

Vincent looked up at him. "Just some Mex kid. A swamper. He wanted to be a bank robber. I caught him stealin' a horse from the livery barn one day, and we worked out a deal for him to rob the train . . . fool you into thinkin' it was his wet-behind-the-ears bunch pullin' the holdups—"

"To distract me," Stockburn finished for him. "And give Jess and Snake-Eye and Lana and her braves plenty of time, so they could hold up the train for real a little higher on the pass," Stockburn finished for him again, everything falling into place in his head.

Vincent laughed. "He thought it was only his bunch holdin' it up, of course. And that I wanted a cut."

Stockburn set his jaws as he glowered down the slope at the brutish town marshal. "You're the reason I killed that boy."

Vincent chuckled and shrugged. "Just some little greaser, Stockburn."

Lana rose to stand atop the boulder, moccasin-clad feet spread wide. She held her carbine straight down along her right side. "Don't worry, Stockburn. He's made me as mad as he's made you. For different reasons, of course. Here's a little gift to you . . . before I kill you."

Casually, she turned, raised the Winchester, and shot Vincent out of his saddle.

Stockburn had seen it coming and took the opportunity of the distraction to leap up onto the lip of the ridge. He raised the Yellowboy to his shoulder, aimed down the slope, and shot Lana off the boulder.

CHAPTER 37

The braves around the front of the boulder jerked instantly to life the second Stockburn's bullet had plowed into the chest of their fearless chieftess. Lana had given a yelp—likely more surprised than anything else—as the bullet had punched her off the backside of the boulder to strike the ground with a thump.

The braves glanced toward where Lana lay then jerked their enraged, warpainted faces back toward Stockburn a half a second before they came bounding up the slope, yowling and yammering like wolves on the blood scent. Stockburn laughed the laughter of the doomed. He was a dead man, but he'd go to those smoky gates—where else would he be headed after what he'd done in this life?—knowing he'd cut off both heads of the two-headed snake he'd come to kill.

Without Lana and Comanche Joe, the tail of the snake would eventually die. The train robberies would cease. The stockmen might not get their cattle back, but at least they'd be able to resume shipping what they still had.

Stockburn ejected the spent, smoking round from his Winchester's breech, levered a live one into the action, and dropped to a knee. Bullets kicked up sand and gravel around him as the Comanches stormed up the long slope, spreading out, triggering their Winchesters, Henrys, and Spencer repeaters.

Calmly lining up his sights on one brave, Stockburn fired. And smiled and blinked slowly in satisfaction as his bullet tore the leg out from beneath the hard-charging red man. The brave rolled a ways back down the slope and lay howling and clutching his knee, glaring wildly up the ridge at his tormentor.

A bullet tore a hot line across Stockburn's cheek as the others closed on him, the nearest thirty feet away. He pumped another round into his own rifle's action, but he was in no big hurry. With only a second or two left, he was not under the delusion he could take down all of the braves scurrying toward him, their black eyes bright with warrior rage.

Wolf triggered a round at the nearest brave howling and sprinting toward him, black hair dancing madly about his bare shoulders. The round missed and grazed the arm of another brave running up the slope slightly behind him.

Twenty feet down the slope from Stockburn, the brave raised his Spencer repeater to his shoulder, and took quick aim at Stockburn. He narrowed a coal-black eye down the barrel, lining up the sights on the big detective's chest. Before the young warrior could squeeze the trigger, his skull opened up like a ripe cantaloupe. Blood and flecks of shredded white brain matter splashed onto the upslope to the brave's right.

Apparently, the bullet that had just killed him had punched into his head just above his left ear. He fell back, struck the slope, and rolled downward, cutting the legs of another brave out from under him, and then both braves rolled together for several dust-billowing feet.

Stockburn had watched the unexpected death of the brave with a strange calm, taking in each detail as though time had slowed to a crawl, considering each thing—the bullet fired from the west and from a higher elevation; the blood, the brains, the two braves rolling together as though wrestling. Wolf quickly but calmly gained the awareness that other braves were dropping, too—one by one, two by two.

Bullets from the east and the west sliced across the slope and plunked into the rawhide clad bodies, evoking startled grunts and sudden groans of unexpected agony. Blood splashed across the sand and gravel. Rifles were thrown wide as the bodies dropped and rolled, hair flying, limbs pinwheeling.

The steady barrage continued. Distant rifles hammered, sometimes in time with each other, sometimes raising a staccato rhythm nearly drowned at times by the screams and wails of the flabbergasted braves. The shooting dwindled when all braves were down. It became sporadic, and then silence descended.

Dust curled up from the slope dropping away before Stockburn.

The braves lay scattered across the belly of the slope, amidst the blood-splashed rocks. One of the young warriors about fifty feet below Wolf's position and to his right, arched his back, gave a strangled cry, then eased his back down and lifted what sounded like his death dirge. His voice was high and thin.

One more rifle shot, fired from the west, punched a bullet through his right ear, snapping his head sharply to one side and painting the slope to his left dark red flecked with the white of brains and bone. The rifle's echo caromed skyward, dwindling.

Stockburn rose and stood holding the Yellowboy straight down along his right leg. He watched two figures slowly approach from both sides of the slope, from where they'd each dropped down from their rocky perch. On Stockburn's right, a green neckerchief fluttered in the wind. The young, dark-haired man wearing it came across the slope with his handsome, brown face canted downward, inspecting his handiwork.

On Stockburn's left, long, copper-red hair beneath the brim of a brown felt hat, fluttered around slender shoulders. High-topped black riding boots kicked rocks as she approached to stand ten feet away from him. Smiling, she held her Winchester in one gloved hand, using her other hand to slide tendrils of windblown hair from her tanned cheeks.

"Hi, Hank."

"Hi, Wolf."

"Nice to see you."

"Nice to see you, Wolf."

"I see you found a friend."

"Stockburn," said Rafael Sanchez, his handsome face expressionless.

Wolf used his Yellowboy's barrel to poke the brim of his sombrero back off his forehead. "About Tomacito . . ."

Rafael sighed and looked down the slope toward where Vincent lay near the unmoving figure of Lana Ramsay, barely seen behind the boulder she'd been squatting on. "I heard."

"We found the cattle, Wolf," Hank said.

Stockburn arched a brow. "Oh?"

"They're in a green canyon just beyond the Wet Rocks."

Rafael used his rifle to point toward the high, pale, toothy peeks shouldering up in the south. "The canyon's fed by several springs near the Rio Grande. They're all there as far as I could tell, grazing contentedly. Those crazy Comanches were likely about to sell them across the river to some Mexican buyer. Drought down that way. They likely would have fetched a good price."

"Probably," Stockburn said. "But it wasn't the money Comanche Joe and Lana wanted. They just wanted to ruin the cattlemen."

"But that beef was headed for reservations," Hank said, scowling her incredulity. "Why would she want to deprive her own people of food?"

"I got a feeling if she was alive, she'd tell us they didn't need the white man's food. That they needed to bust off the reservations, take their own land back from the whites, and fend for themselves."

Hank sighed as she cast her gaze down the slope from which the breeze lifted little curls of dust around the scattered bodies.

"How'd you find me?" Wolf asked.

Hank gave a caustic chuckle. "Oh, you're not hard to find, Wolf." She moved toward him, wrapped her arms around him, and kissed his cheek. "We just had to follow the gunfire." She pulled her head away from his. "We were on our way to Bottleneck. I'd hoped to find you, to tell you about the cattle as well as the canyon we found the Wet Rocks people living in. I should have known you were one step ahead of me . . . as usual."

"Oh, no, darlin'," Stockburn said, playfully flicking her hat brim. "You two were a step ahead of me. Thanks for saving my bacon." He glanced at Rafael. "Both of you."

Am I really all that thankful? he silently pondered.

Mike. Stockburn had been ready to have that anvil relieved from his shoulders.

"Look, Stockburn," Rafael said, flushing, hesitating. "I know that . . . before—"

"Forget it," Wolf interrupted. "I'm sorry about your brother."

Hank and Rafael shared a grim, conferring look. They'd become fast friends, Stockburn could tell. Maybe more than friends.

Rafael turned to Stockburn. "What do you think we should do about those cattle?"

Stockburn jerked his chin toward a billowing dust cloud he'd been watching slowly grow in the southeast. It belonged to a pack of horseback riders just then rounding the southern edge of a north-to-south-lying ridge. Heading Stockburn's way, likely having been lured by the gunfire.

"I have a feeling we won't need to do anything about them." Wolf shouldered his Yellowboy as he gazed at the oncoming riders. Still a long way away, but he could see their stockmen's hats and billowing neckerchiefs. "I'd bet gold nuggets against baking powder biscuits those are Ramsay's men. They followed Lana—and me and Vincent— out from the Agua Verde." He glanced at Rafael. "Let them haze their own cattle back to town. They'll no doubt be shipping again in a few days."

Despite Darlington being dead, Wolf silently opined.

"Me?" Wolf said. "I got a big craving for a steak dinner and a tall glass of whiskey. What do you say we three head to Bottleneck? I'll buy."

Hank and Rafael shared another fleeting—intimate?— glance.

"I'm game," Hank said. "Since Wolf's buying."

"Why not?" Rafael said, shrugging.

They started down the slope together.

Another glance at Hank and Rafael told Stockburn three might be a crowd, but he had an acc up his own sleeve in Bottleneck.

A flaxen-haired desert princess named Violet.

CHAPTER 1

"Help! The railroad dick Wolf Stockburn's gone madder'n a bull buff with a snoot full of cockleburs! Somebody rassle him down before he kills the lot of us and rips the saloon to *smithereens!"*

Stockburn had heard the plea, which an old graybeard had shouted into the street, a half second before a large clenched red fist came arcing toward Wolf from behind a stout shoulder clad in green plaid wool. The clenched fingers were broad and white, pink at the tips, and with dirt showing beneath the thick, shell-like nails.

That fist slammed against Wolf's left cheek. It was a hammering, brain-numbing blow. Having just thrown a punch of his own, this one came before Stockburn could prepare for it. It was obviously delivered by a big man who'd thrown a few punches before. Stockburn flew back onto a table, his six-foot-four-inch frame clad in hard muscle breaking the table right down the middle.

The railroad detective smashed through the table to the floor, both halves of the table dropping toward him at steep slants, spilling onto him several shot glasses and their contents, a whiskey bottle and its contents, a couple of ashtrays, playing cards, coins, and greenbacks.

Wolf sat up, shook his head, then scrambled to his feet, brushing the whiskey and cards and ashes and half-smoked cigarettes off his chest and belly, and looked around for the man who'd thrown the punch. Through a fog of senseless fury, he saw the green plaid shirt before him. The shirt was crowned with a big, square head and a cap of thinning dark red hair behind a bulging forehead, and a thick beard of the same color. The big man, a muleskinner named Whip Larimore, was crouching, waving his fists, smiling at Stockburn in challenge.

His brown eyes glinted with inebriation and open mockery.

"If you liked that one, Stockburn, get up! I got plenty more where that one came from! I'll turn you inside out and beat your head flatter'n a pancake grill!"

Bellowing like a poleaxed bull, Stockburn leaped to his feet then dropped to a crouch in time to avoid another savage blow from Larimore's swollen fist. He heard the whoosh of displaced air over his head. Larimore gave a startled grunt when his punch missed its mark by a good foot. Staying low and still bellowing, Stockburn leaped forward and bulled into the muleskinner's broad, lumpy chest, driving him up off his feet and backward.

Now adding his own yells to Stockburn's as he and Wolf went airborne, flying backward toward a large plate-glass window over which the words THE ATHENAEUM SALOON were written in large green-leaf letters in a broad arc. Those letters separated, shattered, blew outward, and fell along with the rest of the window as the two men, locked together like two rogue grizzlies in a battle-to-the-death over the same sow, flew through it.

They landed together on the boardwalk fronting the saloon, still locked together, raging, lips stretched back from gritted teeth, broken glass peppering them both.

"You four-flushin', double-dealin', fat, ugly poker cheat!" Stockburn raged, rising to his knees, glass tumbling off his head and shoulders. He slammed his right fist across Larimore's heavy jaw.

The man's head was so large and solid it was like punching a side of fresh beef. Larimore shook off the blow, grinning, then rose up sharply to slam his big head against Stockburn's own.

Ears ringing, vision swimming, Wolf sagged backward.

Larimore slammed his meaty fist into Stockburn's left cheek.

That drove Wolf farther backward. Somehow, he managed to lift himself to his feet. He'd seen Larimore gain his own stout legs and knew that if he was low when Larimore was high, that would be the end of him.

Vaguely, beneath the yells of the crowd that had followed him and Larimore out of the saloon and onto the boardwalk, he heard someone shouting his name. The shouts grew louder as the shouter drew closer, but Stockburn gave the shouts no more notice than he would a fly buzzing several feet away.

He was ready when the big bearded muleskinner bolted toward him, bringing a hamlike fist up from his heels. Again, Stockburn ducked. Again, he heard the whoosh and the grunt. He stepped forward, hips and shoulders squared, raised fists clenched, and smashed the right one against Larimore's hard, meaty face.

He followed the right with a left and then another right.

Another left.

Right.

Left.

"Wolf!" a man's pleading voice yelled, closer now than before.

Ignoring the yells, Wolf kept moving forward, crouching, working his feet like a well-trained pugilist, hammering the muleskinner's face with a blur of jabs and uppercuts as Larimore grunted and groaned and staggered backward along the boardwalk fronting the saloon. As the Red Sea parted for Moses, the yelling crowd made way for the two warring bruins.

Smack! Smack!

Smack-Smack-Smack!

Smackkk!

Each blow so dazed and weakened Larimore, his face turning redder and redder with fresh blood oozing from his eyes, nose, and smashed lips, that he was no longer able to raise his hands to defend himself. Each punishing blow so tormented him that he was at the mercy of the big man before him clad in a black three-piece suit with white silk shirt and ribbon tie, broken glass still raining down from his head distinguished by a thick mane of roached, prematurely gray hair that stood out in sharp contrast to the brick red of his broad, chiseled face further singularized by a pair of deep-set, coal-dark eyes.

"Wolf!" came the pleading voice again from behind Stockburn.

Again, Stockburn smashed the muleskinner's face.

"Wolf—stop, galldangit! I ain't gonna say it again!"

Though Stockburn knew the shouter was close behind him, to his enraged mind the man's pleas seemed to come from the bottom of a distant well.

Again, he slammed his left fist against Larimore's jaw. "All right—you asked for it. I'm sorry, old pard!"

Stockburn had started to thrust his left clenched fist forward once more when something hard slammed against the back of his head and everything went as black as night and as quiet as a mountain lake at midnight.

When Wolf opened his eyes again, a poison-tipped Apache arrow of raw misery pierced his pupils to drive deep into his brain. The fiery poison spread like acid, instantly corroding the tender nerves.

"*Ayyy!*" he cried, gritting his teeth.

He lay very still on a cot, a sour wool blanket beneath him. He squeezed his eyes closed, waiting for that arrow to give a little ground. Every muscle in his strapping, forty-year-old body was drawn taut as razor wire.

The arrow slid back a little, giving some ground, the pain abating if only slightly.

Wolf opened his eyes. He wasn't sure where he was. He had no idea how long he'd been out like a blown lamp. It could have been a few minutes, several hours, or, hell, even a few days. His mouth felt stuffed with soiled cotton.

Lying there on the cot, he found himself staring at a small hole at the base of a mud brick wall. Something moved inside the hole. Light glinted off two tiny eyes and then the small, arrow-shaped head took shape as the rat moved closer and stuck its long-whiskered, pink-tipped snout into the room, the sides of the narrow hole pressing the rat's ears back flat against its head.

As the rodent slid its head into the room, the hole slid back to release its ears. The ears sprang straight up in the air. They resembled a mule's ears—albeit those of a rat-sized mule. They were stiff and triangular, a dirty gray color on the outside, pale pink on the inside.

The pointed snout worked, sniffing.

The rat looked around. It looked up at Stockburn.

The pair exchanged stares for stretched seconds. If the rat felt any fear of the man, it gave no indication. It peeped faintly, still working its nose, and pushed its body, roughly the size of a small man's fist, out of the hole and into the stone-floored room. It swung to its right and scuttled along the floor against the wall, head down, sniffing, pausing to nibble what appeared to be tiny bread crumbs, maybe some bits of bacon from a bacon sandwich.

It paused to investigate a very small, shriveled, dried brown apple core, which had to be well over a week old. After giving the core a thorough sniffing, and apparently finding nothing desirable about it, the rat took two steps forward before its vaguely oval-shaped, gray-brown body erupted in blood and torn bits of skin and fur spraying onto the floor and the wall behind it.

The shredded beast lay shivering, little spidery feet quivering, before the mangled carcass lay still.

Blood dribbled down the wall above it.

Stockburn sucked a sharp breath and squeezed his eyes closed as the concussive report of the gun exploded inside his head, threatening to do to his skull what the bullet had just done to the rat.

A man guffawed as the echoes of the blast gradually stopped rocketing off the adobe brick walls surrounding Stockburn. "Sorry to wake ya, Wolf! I been after that rat for a week now!"

More laughter.

Stockburn opened his eyes. The rotten egg odor of gun smoke fouled his nostrils as he turned his head to gaze through the iron straps of a cell door. A tall, skinny man in a worn, sweat-stained white shirt and black leather vest and patch-kneed black denim trousers crouched forward, thin shoulders jerking as he laughed. Waylon Wallace, marshal of Ruidoso, held his smoking Smith & Wesson Russian .44 straight down along his right leg, smoke still curling from the barrel.

That was probably the barrel that had caused the goose egg Stockburn could feel still rising, throbbing, on the back of his head, near the crown. Probing with his fingers, he felt a short cut on the swollen area, crusted with semi-dry blood, which meant he'd been out only an hour or so though it felt like days.

"Thanks a lot, Waylon."

"Don't mention it, Wolf." Still chuckling, his craggy, gray-bearded, sixty-year-old face mottled red with wry humor, the lawman pulled a ladderback chair out from the wall by the door. He dragged it over in front of Stockburn's cell and plopped into it, swinging his arms up and groaning against the creaks in his arthritic hips. "Rats carry rabies, don't you know."

"So do town marshals, apparently. A good dose of rabies must be what made you kiss the back of my head with that old Russian of yours."

"Nope, nope." Waylon crossed his long legs, skinny as broom handles, and wagged his head. "You caused that your ownself. You wouldn't pull your horns in. Not for anything. I gave you fair warning."

"I reckon I didn't hear you," Stockburn lied.

"You would have killed Larimore if I hadn't introduced you to my trusty Smith & Wesson. Not that killing an underhanded varmint like that would have been any real loss, but I'd have had to arrest you for murder. Neither of us would have wanted that, Wolf."

"Small price to pay."

"What caused the foofaraw?"

"He and Fritz Carlson were cheating. They'd been cheating the whole damn game, since six o'clock this morning. I warned 'em twice but I still saw another creased card on the table."

"That's when you went off half-cocked and slammed Carlson's face down on the table? The sawbones is with him now, tryin' to straighten out his nose. Larimore's over there, too, waiting for stitches."

Stockburn looked at him with a question in his eyes.

"Nils Taylor filled me in." Taylor was the barman on duty at the Athenaeum. "Says you exploded like a Napoleon cannon, just reached across the table, grabbed a handful of Carlson's hair, and slammed his face straight down against his shot glass. Then you went for ol' Whip and he went for you, and now you got a forty-six-dollar repair bill due over to the Athenaeum before I can let you out of here."

"They were cheating."

"You started the fight."

"They started the fight when they started cheating."

"You know their cheating ain't what started the fight, Wolf."

Stockburn opened his eyes, squinting against the pain in his head, scowling at his old friend Waylon who'd managed a Pony Express station back when Wolf, only sixteen years old, had been a hell-for-leather pony rider recently orphaned in western Kansas by a pack of rampaging Cheyenne. "What?"

Waylon narrowed his copper-brown eyes at the younger man. "You've played stud poker with both those jaspers before. Everybody knows they cheat but nobody cares because they're so bad they still lose!"

"Oh, go to hell, Waylon!" Wolf rested his head back

against his pillow, which smelled as sour as the blanket. "My head hurts."

"You exploded because of what happencd to Billy."

"Oh, go to hell!" Stockburn fumed again then instantly pressed the heels of his hands to his head, sucking sharp breaths through gritted teeth.

CHAPTER 2

The railroad detective was trying to suppress the raking agony inside his head as well as trying to obliterate the image of the young man, Billy Blythe, lying dead outside the Sierra Blanca Railroad's express car, which robbers had blown off the tracks then peppered with lead before absconding with seventy thousand dollars in payroll money en route to the Pegasus Mining Company in Ruidoso.

"He was so damn young," Stockburn said, grief rolling through him in hot waves.

"Had his whole life ahead of him," Waylon said. "It's not fair."

"I assigned him to that train."

"I know you did, Wolf. But you didn't know Red Miller's bunch was gonna hit it."

"I didn't even know Miller and his kill-crazy bunch of owlhoots was operating in this neck of the woods." Stockburn dropped his feet to the floor, rising, and leaned forward over his knees. "If I had . . ."

"I know—you never would have assigned a kid so green to that payroll shipment."

"Hell, I would have taken it myself!" Stockburn wrung his

hands together, seeing in his mind's eye the freckle-faced
young man he'd pulled out of an outlaw gang around
Las Cruces, befriended, rehabilitated, and recommended
for a messenger job with Wells Fargo, lying dead with his
head resting against a blasted-off iron wheel of the express car.

Blood dribbling down one corner of his mouth, glistening in the sun.

The kid must have come out of the express car, flames
from the explosion wreathing him, Winchester blasting.
There'd been a half-dozen empty casings lying around
Billy's charred, bullet-riddled body.

"He just got married," Wolf said. "I walked Sofia down
the aisle myself on account of her father had passed."

Billy had met Sofia Ortega, the shy young brown-
haired, brown-eyed daughter of a Mexican seamstress, in
the post office one day in Mesilla. He'd stumbled into her,
knocking several parcels out of her arms.

By the time he'd collected them for her, he'd fallen in
love with her. Sofia had returned the sentiment. Before
they'd officially hitched their stars to each other's wagons,
Billy, with Wolf's help, had put a down payment on a little
frame house between Las Cruces and Mesilla.

"Ah, Christ!" Wolf said, raking a big hand down his face,
pressing his fingers deep into his skin as though trying to
plunder his brain of his grief.

"Here—have a cup of this." Stockburn looked to his
left. Waylon was extending a stone mug of steaming black
coffee through the bars while holding a second mug in his
other hand. "Make you feel better."

Stockburn rose with a wince, his head feeling like a
sadistic gnome was inside it, whacking at his brain with a
miniature but very hard hammer.

Stockburn took the mug in his hand then leaned his right shoulder against the cell's right, barred partition. "I'll feel better when I pick up Miller's trail." He blew on the coffee and narrowed his eyes through the steam, angrily. "I can't do that in here."

"You couldn't do it when you were gambling in the Athenaeum, either."

"Yeah, well, I'm waiting for Sofia to ride up here from Las Cruces to claim Billy's body. I can't go anywhere, I can't go after Miller's bunch, till I've seen Sofia." Stockburn winced at the bleak prospect of having to show Billy's bride her young husband's charred, bullet-riddled body. He shook his head and sipped the hot, black brew.

He'd gotten himself entangled in the stud game to distract himself from his misery. He'd drunk too much firewater for the same reason. Waylon was right. He'd started the ruckus with Whip Larimore and Fritz Carlson for the same reason.

He'd had to take out his fury over Billy's brutal murder some damn way. Leave it to him to cut off his nose to spite his face. Someday his Scottish fury was going to get the better of him.

Waylon had been right. He would have killed Larimore if Waylon hadn't intervened. Then where would he be except headed for a gallows?

He was glad he'd been in the area when the Miller gang had struck. In fact, he'd been on the work train one hour behind the express Billy had been on, guarding the payroll money. Wolf had just been finishing up another job investigating illegal whiskey shipments on the Sierra Blanca and was heading back to Kansas City. Instead of heading straight north from Las Cruces to Denver, he'd decided to take the Sierra Blanca to Ruidoso to meet up with Billy for one last meal before they parted. Afterward, he'd take a leisurely horseback ride, astride his smoky gray stallion appropriately if unimaginatively named Smoke, north through the mountains and back to his home base in Kansas City.

As a railroad detective, he spent a lot of time on trains. Sometimes he liked to get away into the wild on his horse—just him and Smoke and the streams and woods, curling up in his bedroll every night after several cups of mud laced with whiskey, stars trimming the sky like Christmas candles, coyotes yammering from distant crags, the heady tang of pine smoke lingering in his nostrils.

He was a loner, Wolf Stockburn was. Always had been, always would be. Whenever he could, he sought the quiet sanctuary of the high and rocky.

He'd be doing that again soon. Only, he wouldn't be seeking sanctuary. He'd be running down the gang that had murdered Billy Blythe and taken the payroll money they'd blown from the Wells Fargo strongbox.

But not until he got out of this cell.

Stockburn frowned at the lawman gazing in at him reprovingly. "Come on, Waylon. Let me out of here!"

"Forget it." The craggy-faced marshal shook his head. "You sit an' stew for a while. If I let you out right away, you won't have learned a damn thing."

"Come on—I'm not an eighteen-year-old firebrand!"

"No, you're a forty-year-old firebrand!" Waylon chuckled without mirth then sipped his coffee. He swallowed, turned, and started walking over to his cluttered desk. "I'll let you out tomorrow. First thing. And then you'll go over to the Athenaeum and pay for the damages."

"I'll pay for them now!"

"No, you'll pay tomo—"

The lawman stopped and turned as the office door latch clicked and the door opened. A matronly, gray-haired lady clad in a green felt hat with a half-veil poked her head into the door. "Waylon, dear, I brought the dinner you asked . . . for . . ."

She let her voice trail off as she turned her gaze toward Stockburn, a surprised, puzzled frown cutting deep lines across the age-wrinkled, Southwestern-sun-seasoned skin of her forehead. She had an oilcloth-covered wicker basket hooked over her left forearm. "I certainly didn't know it was for Wolf !"

Waylon's wife, Ivy, walked into the office, the pleated skirt of her lime-green velvet gown buffeting around her legs and black ankle boots. She clucked in both amusement and curiosity as she strode toward where Stockburn stood just behind his cell door, flushing sheepishly. "Wolf, what on earth are you doing in there?"

"Drunk and disorderly," Waylon said. "Stay away from him, honey. He's as dangerous as a stick-teased rattlesnake!"

"What did you do, Wolf?"

"Ivy, do me a favor, will you?" Wolf said. "Grab those keys over there and unlock this door. Waylon won't stop you. We both know who's been wearin' the pants in the Wallace house for the past—what is it?—thirty, thirty-five years . . . ?"

"Forty-two," said Ivy, shifting her eyes to her husband with mock disdain. "Though it sometimes feels like sixty."

"She might wear the pants at home," Waylon said. "But if my lovely bride touches those keys, I'll lock you two up together."

"Hmmm," Ivy said, flouncing on her stout hips and

arching her brows at Stockburn, playing the coquette. "I might not mind being locked up with such a tall, handsome drink of water as the storied Wolf of the Rails." That was what the newspapers and magazines had dubbed Stockburn several years ago, after his reputation as a dogged rail detective had grown into legend. That was *after* he'd been known as the Wolf of Wichita, having once been town marshal of that fair, hoot cow town.

"I don't know, Ivy," Wolf said, grinning at his lawman friend, "you might not know how to handle a real man after all those years living with that sissy over there."

Waylon had just taken a sip of coffee; with a loud chuff, he blew it into the air before him.

Ivy smiled sidelong at her husband. "He may not look like much, but believe it or not, Wolf, the old boy can still curl this gal's toes from time to time." She flounced over to her husband and rose up on the tips of her shoes to plant a peck on her blushing husband's leathery left cheek. "Can't you, my wild stallion?"

"Wild stallion," Stockburn laughed. "Hah!"

"Oh, hell," Waylon said, his flush deepening as he turned to his desk. "Just feed that damned criminal over there, will ya, honey? I have enough trouble with him alone without you two throwin' in together against me!"

"I have to tell you I'm not exactly hungry, Ivy," Wolf said. "I hurt too bad thanks to that old bruin and the barrel of his Smith & Wesson, not to mention a few lucky licks from Whip Larimore."

"You just wait till you see what I—"

Ivy stopped abruptly as a gun blasted out in the street beyond the office door. "Oh, my gosh!" she said, raising a hand to her mouth.

The first blast was followed by another . . . another . . . and another. Ivy's shoulders jerked with each loud report. Men shouted. A horse neighed shrilly.

"What in the hell . . . ?" Waylon hurried to the door, grabbing his hat off a wall peg and saying, "Ivy, you stay here!"

"Waylon!" Wolf said as more guns blasted in the street. "Let me out of here, dammit!"

But the marshal had already opened the door and run into the street, leaving the door half open behind him. The shooting continued, a veritable fusillade growing more and more heated with every shot. More men shouted, a woman screamed, horses whinnied, hooves pounded.

"Oh, my God!" Ivy said behind the hand over her mouth, staring in shock through the half-open door.

"What's going on, Ivy?" Wolf asked, his heart racing. He walked to the cell's far side and peered through the door but all he could see was dust being kicked up by the running horses, and gun smoke.

Waylon's voice muffled by distance and gunfire, shouted, "Hold it right there, you devils!"

More guns blasted. A man screamed.

"Waylon!" Ivy cried, dropping the wicker basket and hurrying toward the door.

Stockburn shoved his right hand through the door to try to stop her. "Hold on, Ivy! Don't go out there!"

But then she, too, ran through the door and was gone.

Stockburn stared in frustration and horror through the half-open door. The din continued—shooting, shouting, screaming, the thunder of maybe a half-dozen horses.

A horse and rider appeared in the street beyond the half-open door. The pair was galloping from Wolf's left to his right, heading north. As the rider, clad in a cream hat and a black duster, passed the jail office, he cast a glance over his right shoulder and triggered a pistol shot behind him.

He gave a savage, coyote-like howl and then he was gone, galloping off to the north.

"Oh, Waylon!" Ivy Wallace's voice wailed beneath the din. "Wayon! Oh, Waylon!"

Her cries were cut off by an agonized scream.

"Ivy!" Wolf shouted, stretching his right arm helplessly through the strap-iron bands of his cell. "*Ivyyyyy—come back!*"

But something told him she wasn't coming back.

His heart a runaway train inside him, Stockburn grabbed the bars of his cell door and shook them wildly, cursing. He looked at the keys hanging from a peg by Waylon's cluttered desk—from the same peg on which hung Stockburn's cartridge belt and two holstered, ivory-gripped Colt Peacemakers as well as his sheathed bowie knife.

Only ten feet away, but they might as well have been a hundred.

Amidst the din of crackling guns and running horses, thumping sounds rose from the boardwalk fronting the jailhouse. A man appeared, crawling on the boardwalk from Stockburn's left to his right. Waylon stopped just outside the open door and turned a craggy-faced, gray-bearded, agonized look toward Wolf.

"Waylon!"

The man's face was drawn and pale. His hat was gone. He was dusty and sweaty. Blood dribbled onto the boardwalk from his bullet-torn belly as he remained there on his hands and knees, face turned toward Stockburn, the poor man's cheeks sunken, his eyes sharp with pain.

Thumps rose from behind the lawman—the heavy, regular thuds of someone walking toward him. Waylon lifted his right hand from the boardwalk. He was holding his Russian .44. He winced, as though the gun weighed a hundred pounds. Stretching his lips back from his teeth, he tossed the revolver underhanded into the jailhouse. It landed only a few feet away from the lawman then slid up to within three feet of Stockburn's cell.

As the Russian came to a stop, a gun popped in front of the marshal's office. Stockburn stared in horror as a bullet slammed into Waylon's head from behind, pluming his hair then exiting his forehead while blowing out a fist-sized chunk of bone, brains, and blood.

Waylon dropped belly down and lay quivering as he died.

As the foot thuds resounded on the boardwalk, Stockburn dropped to his knees, reached through the bars, stretched his right arm straight out before him, and closed his hand over the Russian .44. Before he could bring the revolver back toward him, a tall, broad-shouldered, long-haired man with a patch over one eye turned through the jailhouse door, kicking it wide.

Wolf pulled the Russian into his cell.

He was too late.

The pistol in the hand of the long-haired, one-eyed man leaped and roared, flames lapping from the barrel. The bullet ricocheted off an iron bar directly in front of Wolf and thudded into Waylon's desk, blowing up papers and toppling an ashtray.

Ears ringing from the ricochet's deafening clang, Stockburn poked the Russian through the bars, thumbed the hammer back, and lined up the sights on the big man before him.

The killer's eyes widened suddenly with the recognition of his own imminent demise. The man's lower jaw sagged in shock.

The Russian spoke.

"Choke on that, you devil!" Stockburn shouted.